UNEARTH

VOL 1

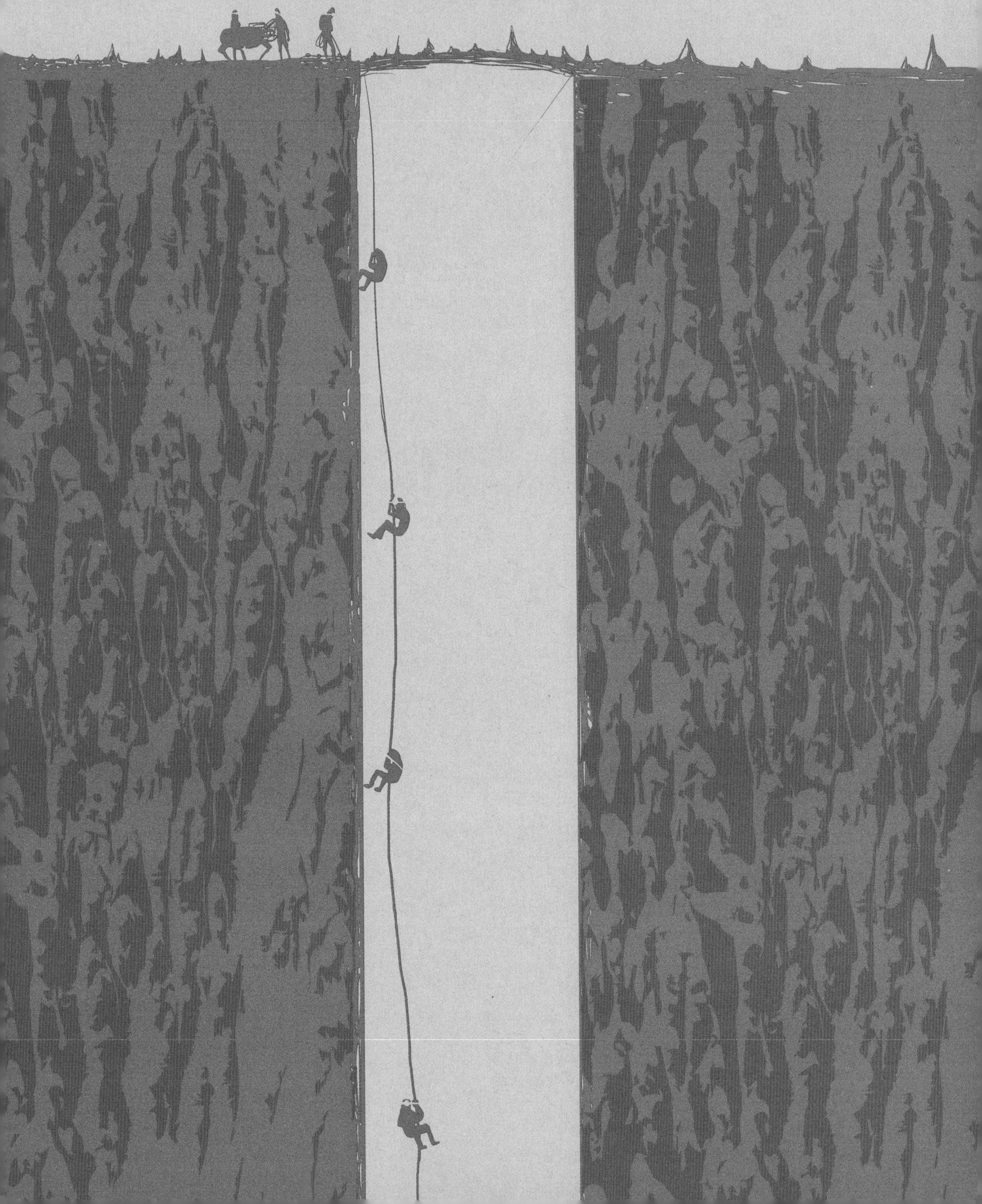

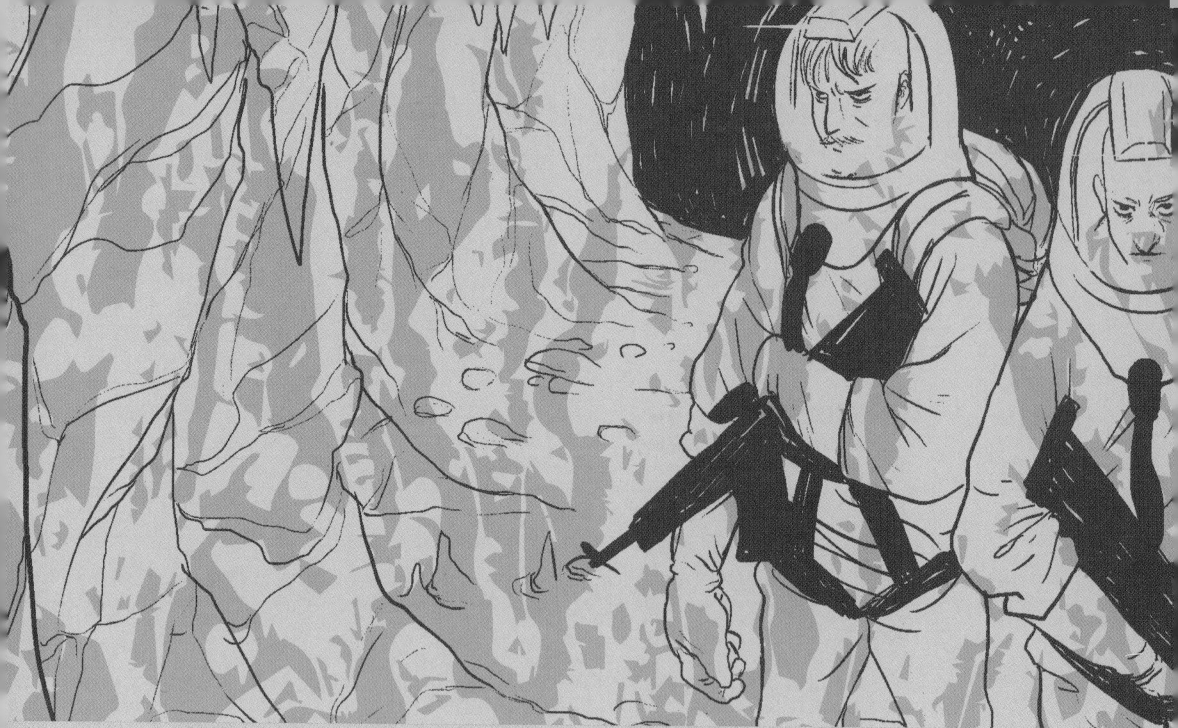

UNEA

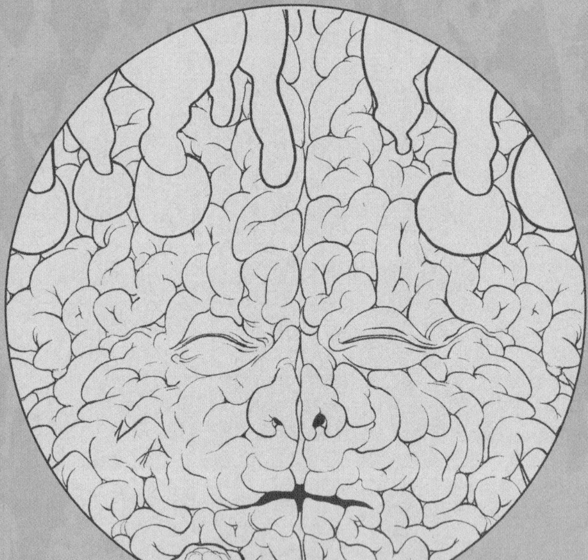

STORY
CULLEN BUNN
& KYLE STRAHM

ART
BALDEMAR RIVAS

LETTERS
CRANK!

EDITOR
JOEL ENOS

ЯRTh

PRODUCTION & DESIGN

RYAN BREWER

EDITORIAL ASSISTANCE ON SUPPLEMENTAL MATERIAL

MATTHEW MITCHELL

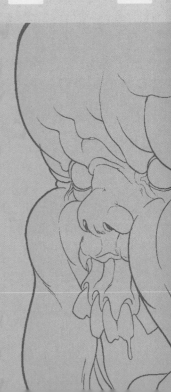

IMAGE COMICS, INC. • Robert Kirkman: Chief Operating Officer • Erik Larsen: Chief Financial Officer • Todd McFarlane: President • Marc Silvestri: Chief Executive Officer • Jim Valentino: Vice President • Eric Stephenson: Publisher / Chief Creative Officer • Jeff Boison: Director of Publishing Planning & Book Trade Sales • Chris Ross: Director of Digital Services • Jeff Stang: Director of Direct Market Sales • Kat Salazar: Director of PR & Marketing • Drew Gill: Art Director • Heather Doornink: Production Director • Nicole Lapalme: Controller • IMAGECOMICS.COM

UNEARTH, VOL. 1. First printing. January 2020. Published by Image Comics, Inc. Office of publication: 2701 NW Vaughn St., Suite 780, Portland, OR 97210. Copyright © 2020 Cullen Bunn, Kyle Strahm, & Baldemar Rivas. All rights reserved. Contains material originally published in single magazine form as UNEARTH #1–5. "Unearth," its logos, and the likenesses of all characters herein are trademarks of Cullen Bunn, Kyle Strahm, & Baldemar Rivas, unless otherwise noted. "Image" and the Image Comics logos are registered trademarks of Image Comics, Inc. No part of this publication may be reproduced or transmitted, in any form or by any means (except for short excerpts for journalistic or review purposes), without the express written permission of Cullen Bunn, Kyle Strahm, & Baldemar Rivas, or Image Comics, Inc. All names, characters, events, and locales in this publication are entirely fictional. Any resemblance to actual persons (living or dead), events, or places, without satirical intent, is coincidental. Printed in the USA. For information regarding the CPSIA on this printed material call: 203-595-3636. For international rights, contact: foreignlicensing@imagecomics.com. ISBN: 978-1-5343-1492-4.

Ch 01

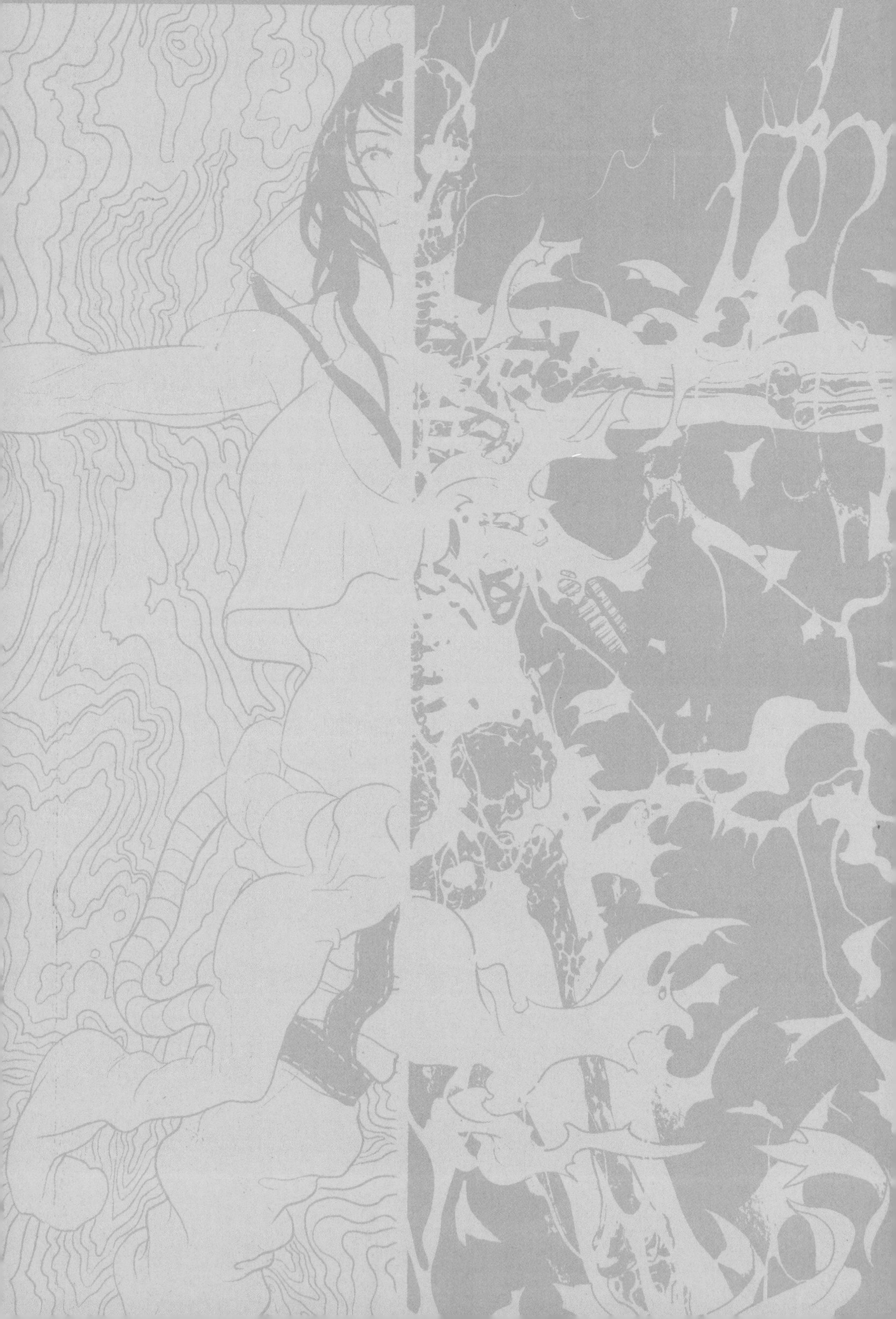

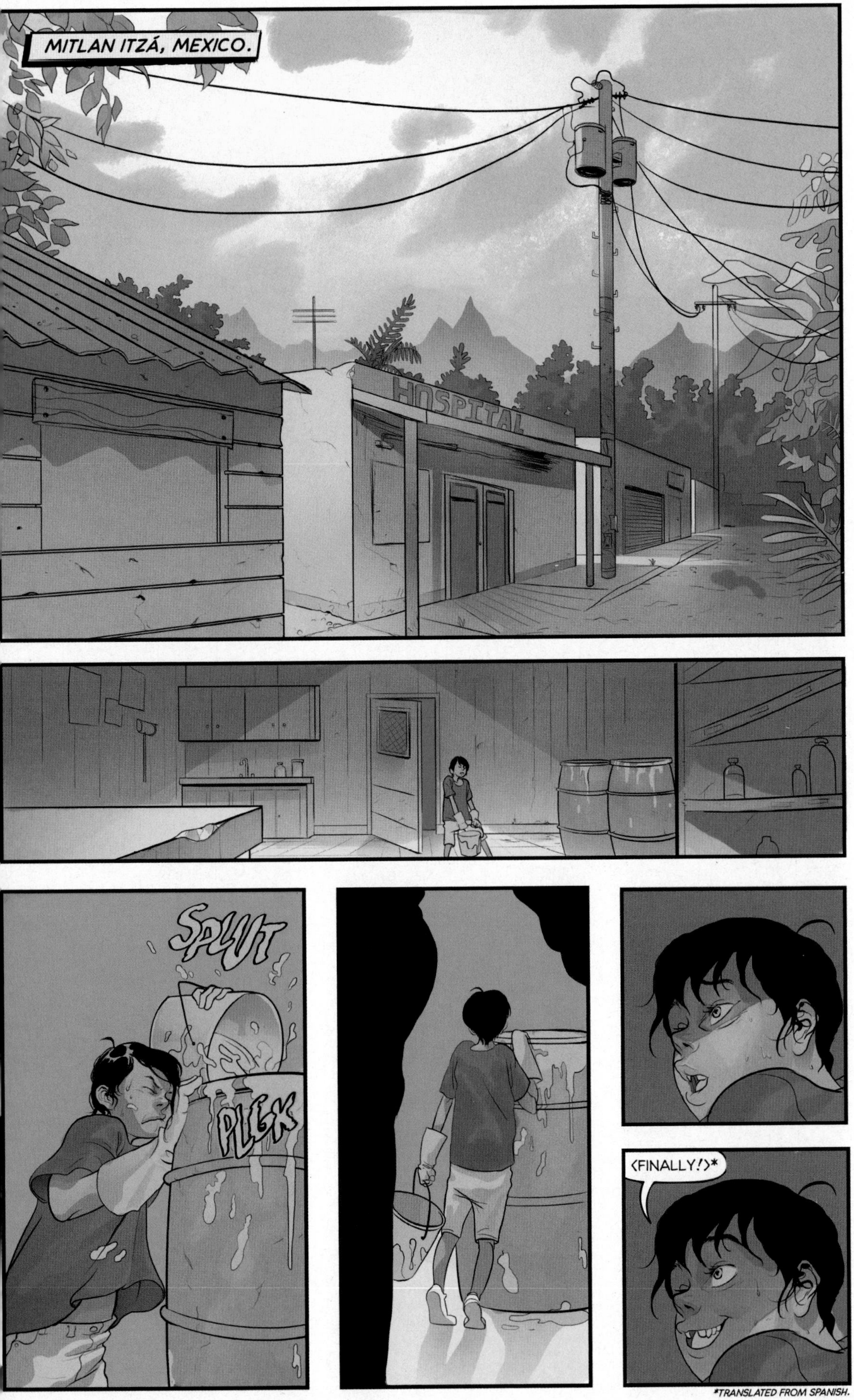
MITLAN ITZÁ, MEXICO.
HOSPITAL
SPLUT
PLUK
<FINALLY!>*

*TRANSLATED FROM SPANISH.

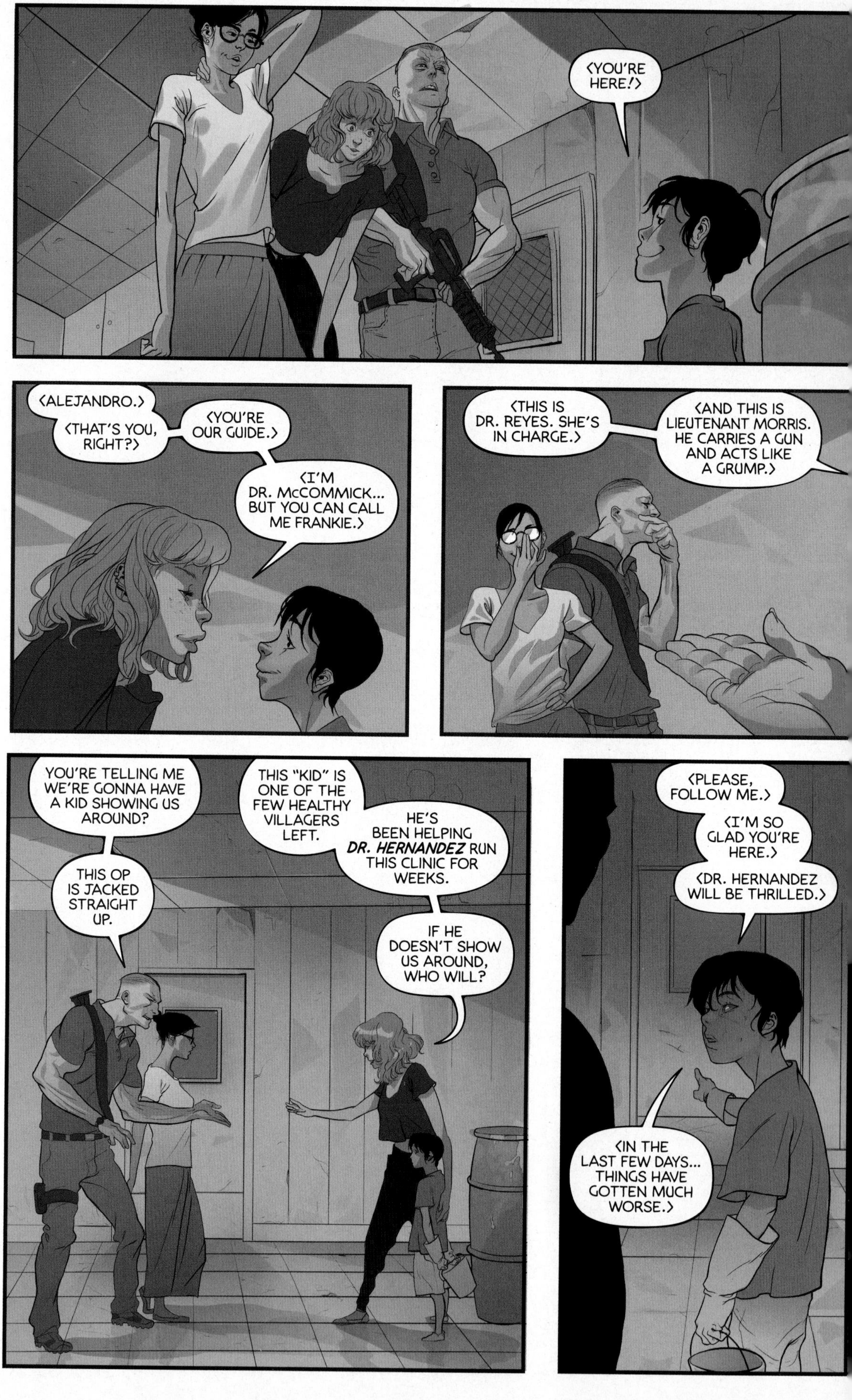

<YOU'RE HERE!>
<ALEJANDRO.>
<THAT'S YOU, RIGHT?>
<YOU'RE OUR GUIDE.>
<I'M DR. McCOMMICK... BUT YOU CAN CALL ME FRANKIE.>
<THIS IS DR. REYES. SHE'S IN CHARGE.>
<AND THIS IS LIEUTENANT MORRIS. HE CARRIES A GUN AND ACTS LIKE A GRUMP.>
YOU'RE TELLING ME WE'RE GONNA HAVE A KID SHOWING US AROUND?
THIS OP IS JACKED STRAIGHT UP.
THIS "KID" IS ONE OF THE FEW HEALTHY VILLAGERS LEFT.
HE'S BEEN HELPING *DR. HERNANDEZ* RUN THIS CLINIC FOR WEEKS.
IF HE DOESN'T SHOW US AROUND, WHO WILL?
<PLEASE, FOLLOW ME.>
<I'M SO GLAD YOU'RE HERE.>
<DR. HERNANDEZ WILL BE THRILLED.>
<IN THE LAST FEW DAYS... THINGS HAVE GOTTEN MUCH WORSE.>

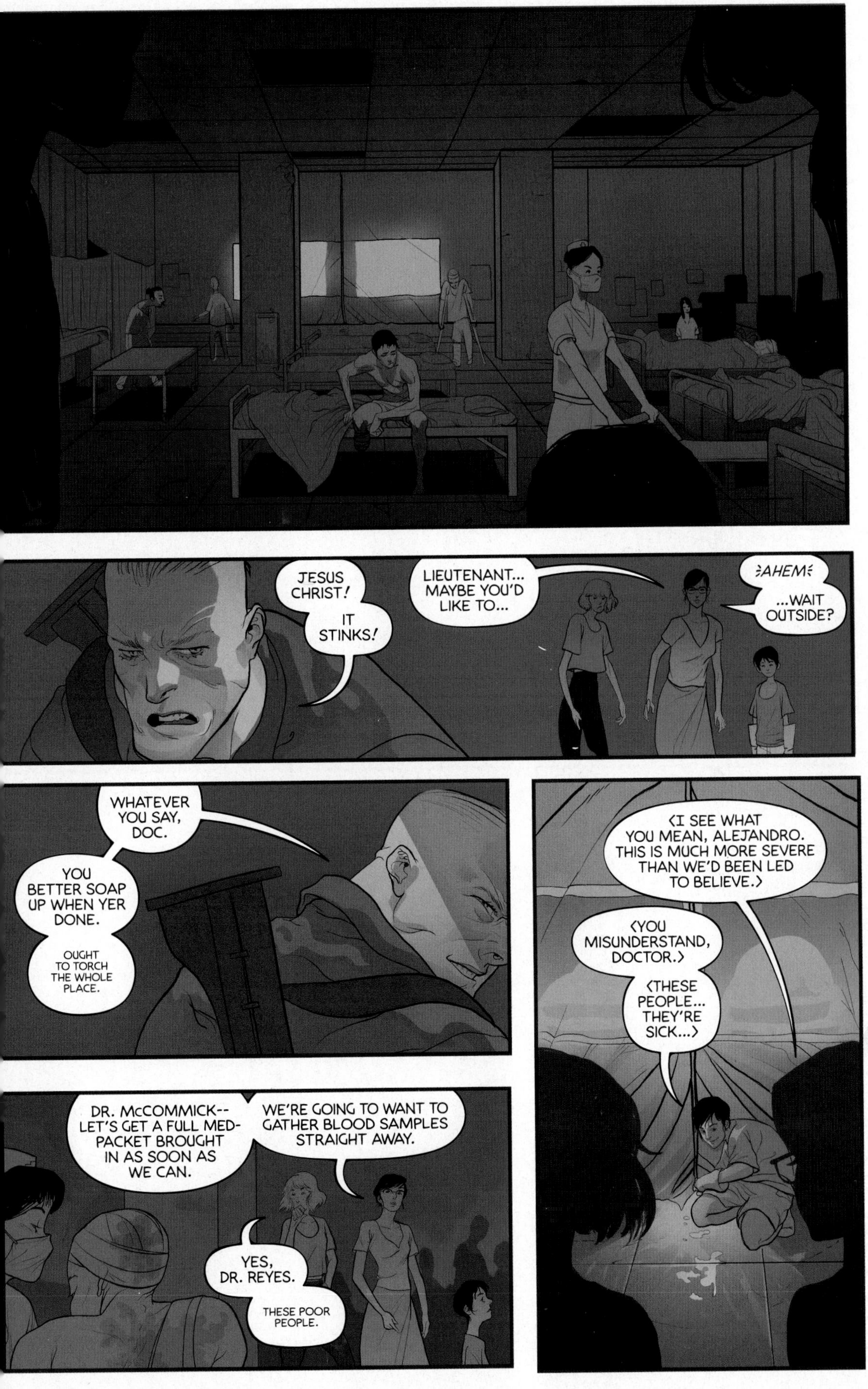
JESUS CHRIST!
IT STINKS!
LIEUTENANT... MAYBE YOU'D LIKE TO...
AHEM
...WAIT OUTSIDE?
WHATEVER YOU SAY, DOC.
YOU BETTER SOAP UP WHEN YER DONE.
OUGHT TO TORCH THE WHOLE PLACE.
<I SEE WHAT YOU MEAN, ALEJANDRO. THIS IS MUCH MORE SEVERE THAN WE'D BEEN LED TO BELIEVE.>
<YOU MISUNDERSTAND, DOCTOR.>
<THESE PEOPLE... THEY'RE SICK...>
DR. McCOMMICK-- LET'S GET A FULL MED-PACKET BROUGHT IN AS SOON AS WE CAN.
WE'RE GOING TO WANT TO GATHER BLOOD SAMPLES STRAIGHT AWAY.
YES, DR. REYES.
THESE POOR PEOPLE.

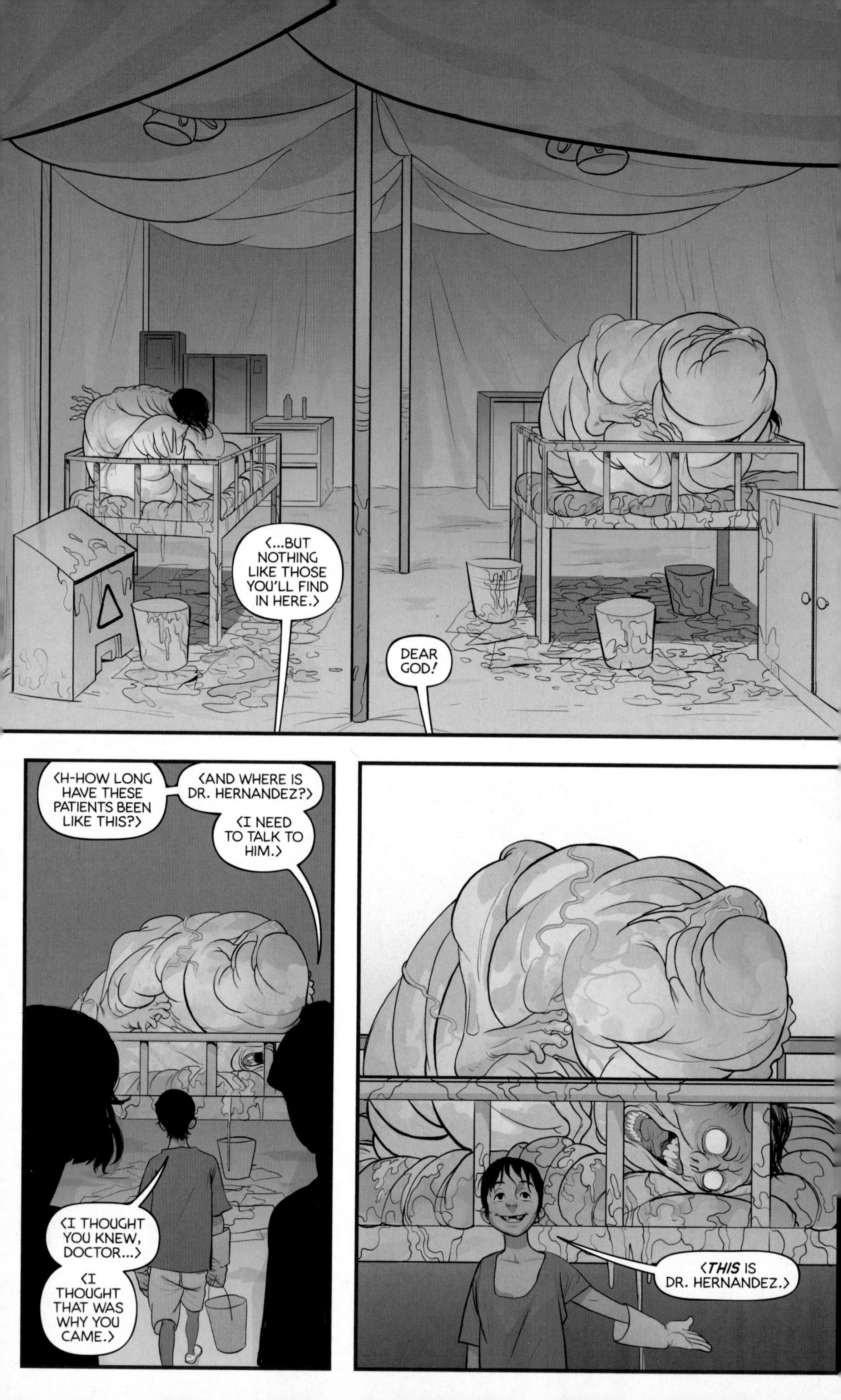
<...BUT NOTHING LIKE THOSE YOU'LL FIND IN HERE.>
DEAR GOD!
<H-HOW LONG HAVE THESE PATIENTS BEEN LIKE THIS?>
<AND WHERE IS DR. HERNANDEZ?>
<I NEED TO TALK TO HIM.>
<I THOUGHT YOU KNEW, DOCTOR...>
<I THOUGHT THAT WAS WHY YOU CAME.>
<THIS IS DR. HERNANDEZ.>

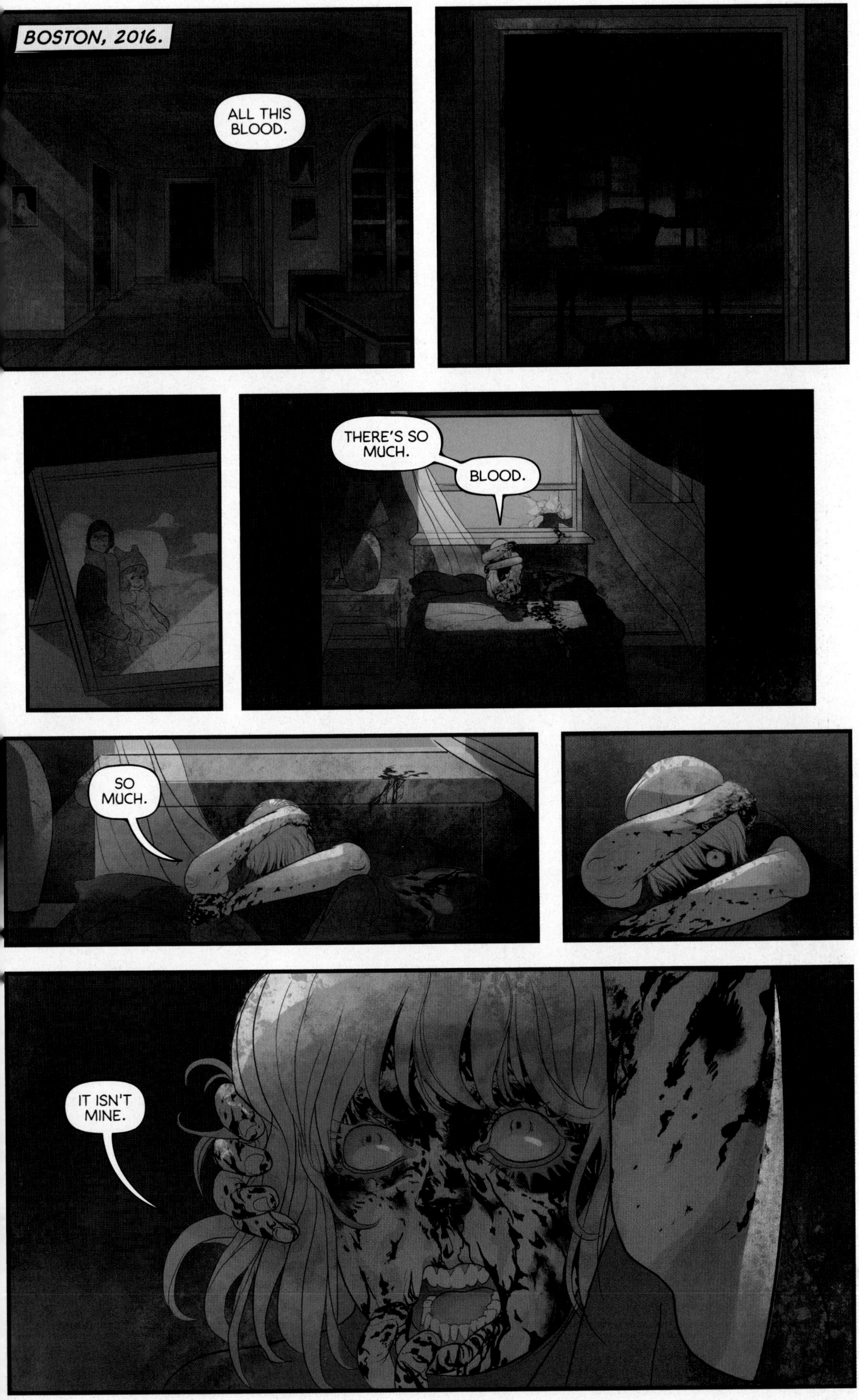
BOSTON, 2016.
ALL THIS BLOOD.
THERE'S SO MUCH.
BLOOD.
SO MUCH.
IT ISN'T MINE.

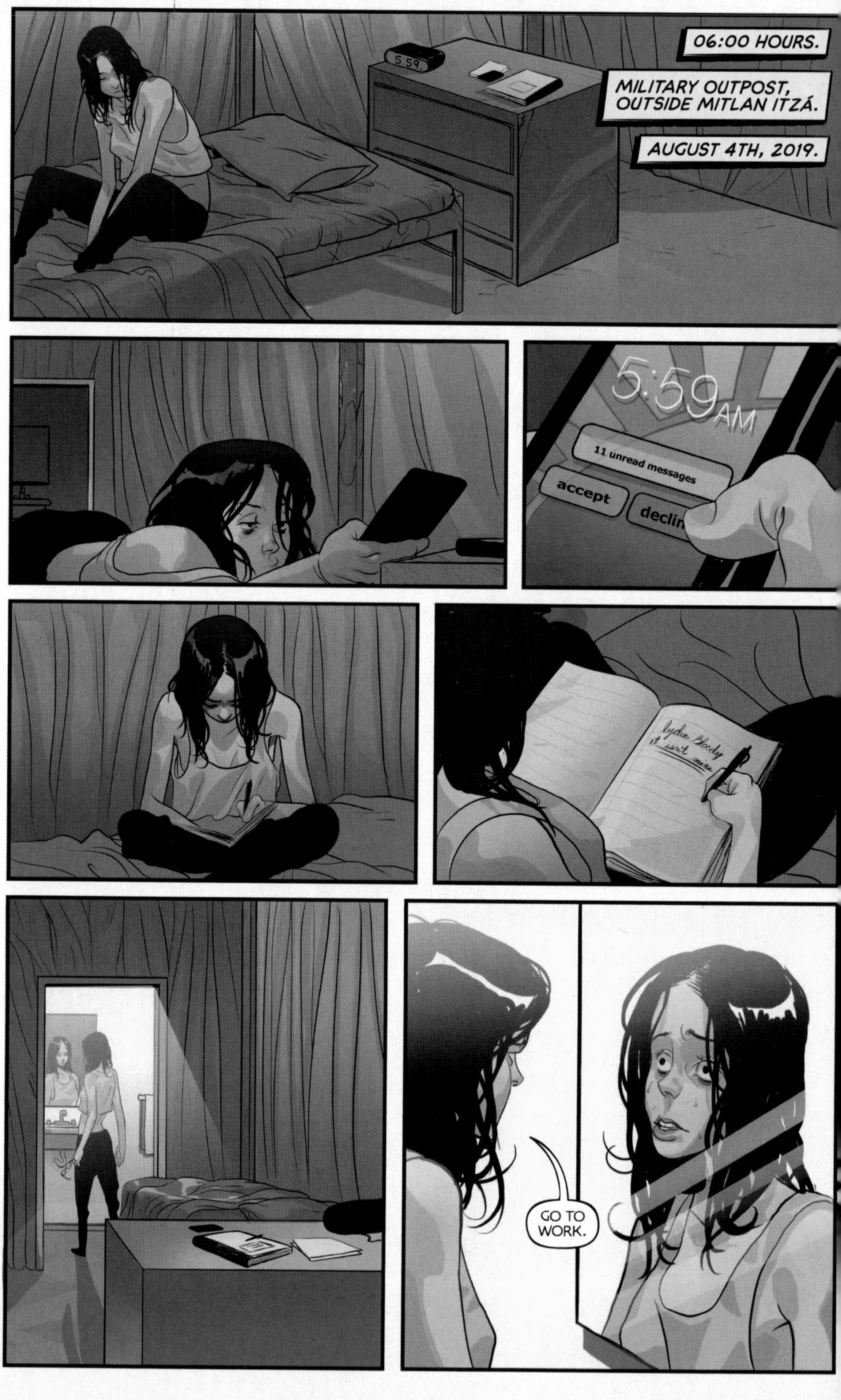
06:00 HOURS.
MILITARY OUTPOST, OUTSIDE MITLAN ITZÁ.
AUGUST 4TH, 2019.
5:59.
5:59AM
11 unread messages
accept
declin
lydia Bloody
it isn't mine
GO TO WORK.

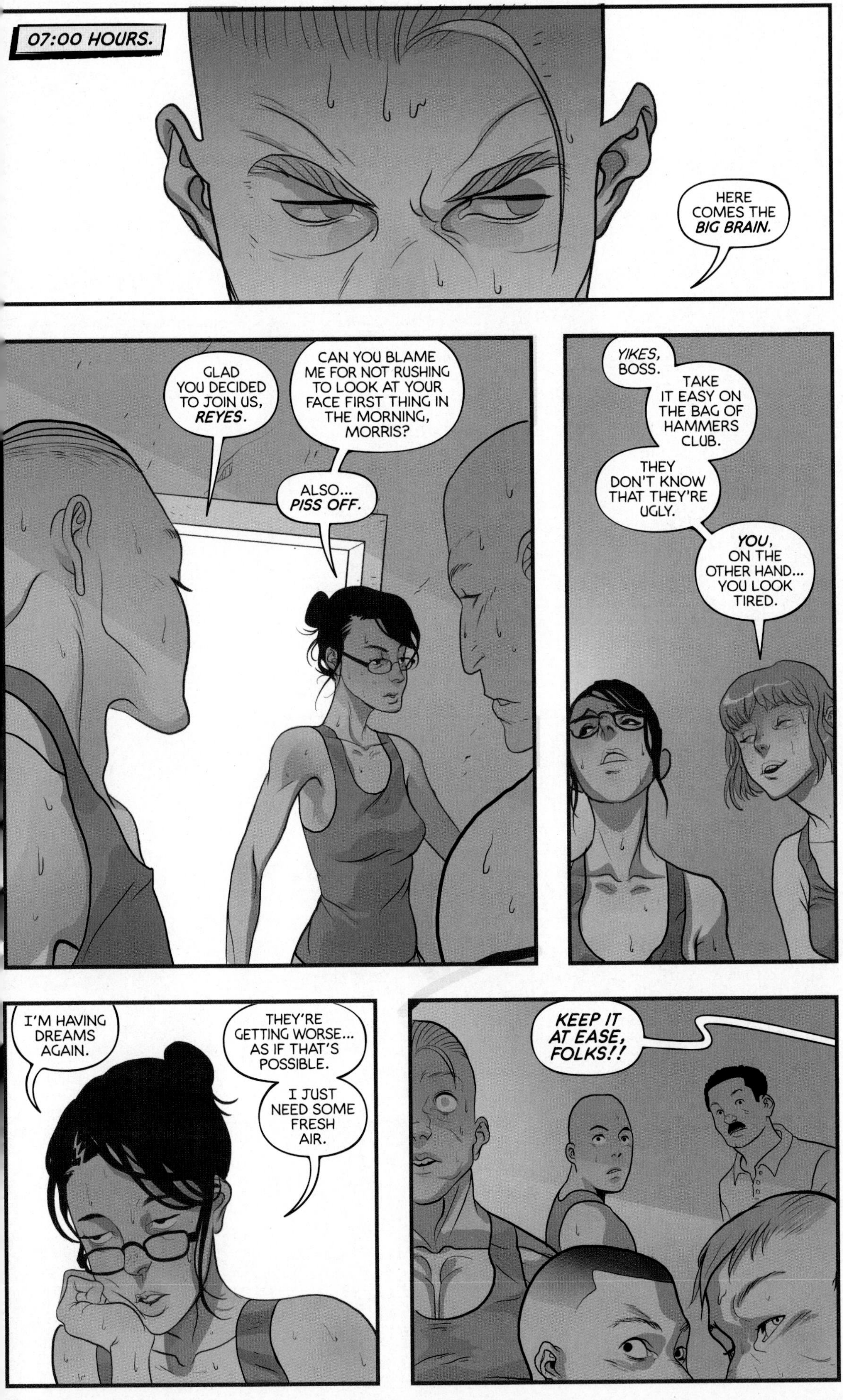
07:00 HOURS.
HERE COMES THE BIG BRAIN.
GLAD YOU DECIDED TO JOIN US, REYES.
CAN YOU BLAME ME FOR NOT RUSHING TO LOOK AT YOUR FACE FIRST THING IN THE MORNING, MORRIS?
ALSO... PISS OFF.
YIKES, BOSS.
TAKE IT EASY ON THE BAG OF HAMMERS CLUB.
THEY DON'T KNOW THAT THEY'RE UGLY.
YOU, ON THE OTHER HAND... YOU LOOK TIRED.
I'M HAVING DREAMS AGAIN.
THEY'RE GETTING WORSE... AS IF THAT'S POSSIBLE.
I JUST NEED SOME FRESH AIR.
KEEP IT AT EASE, FOLKS!!

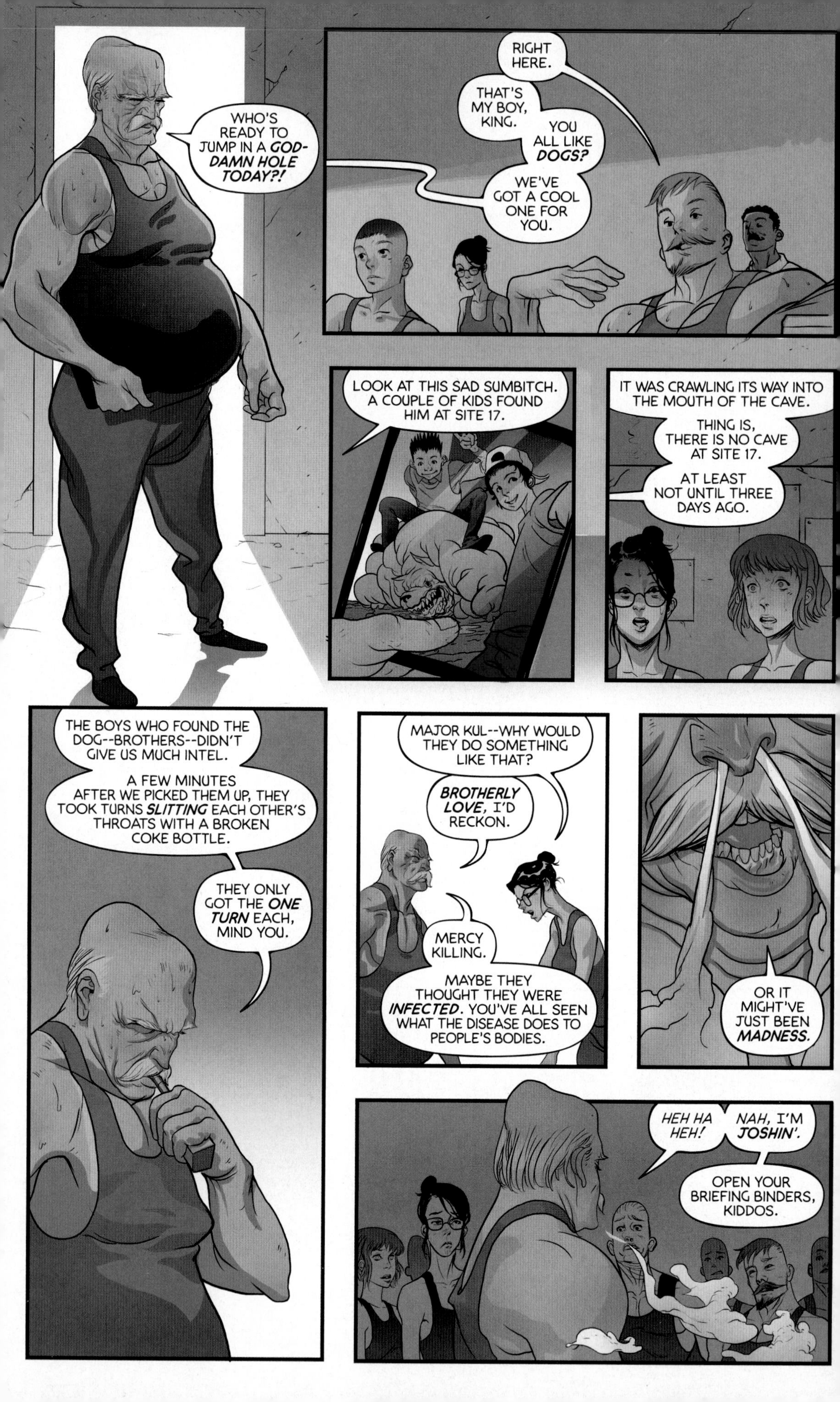

WHO'S READY TO JUMP IN A GOD-DAMN HOLE TODAY?!
RIGHT HERE.
THAT'S MY BOY, KING.
YOU ALL LIKE DOGS?
WE'VE GOT A COOL ONE FOR YOU.
LOOK AT THIS SAD SUMBITCH. A COUPLE OF KIDS FOUND HIM AT SITE 17.
IT WAS CRAWLING ITS WAY INTO THE MOUTH OF THE CAVE.
THING IS, THERE IS NO CAVE AT SITE 17.
AT LEAST NOT UNTIL THREE DAYS AGO.
THE BOYS WHO FOUND THE DOG--BROTHERS--DIDN'T GIVE US MUCH INTEL.
A FEW MINUTES AFTER WE PICKED THEM UP, THEY TOOK TURNS SLITTING EACH OTHER'S THROATS WITH A BROKEN COKE BOTTLE.
THEY ONLY GOT THE ONE TURN EACH, MIND YOU.
MAJOR KUL--WHY WOULD THEY DO SOMETHING LIKE THAT?
BROTHERLY LOVE, I'D RECKON.
MERCY KILLING.
MAYBE THEY THOUGHT THEY WERE INFECTED. YOU'VE ALL SEEN WHAT THE DISEASE DOES TO PEOPLE'S BODIES.
OR IT MIGHT'VE JUST BEEN MADNESS.
HEH HA HEH!
NAH, I'M JOSHIN'.
OPEN YOUR BRIEFING BINDERS, KIDDOS.

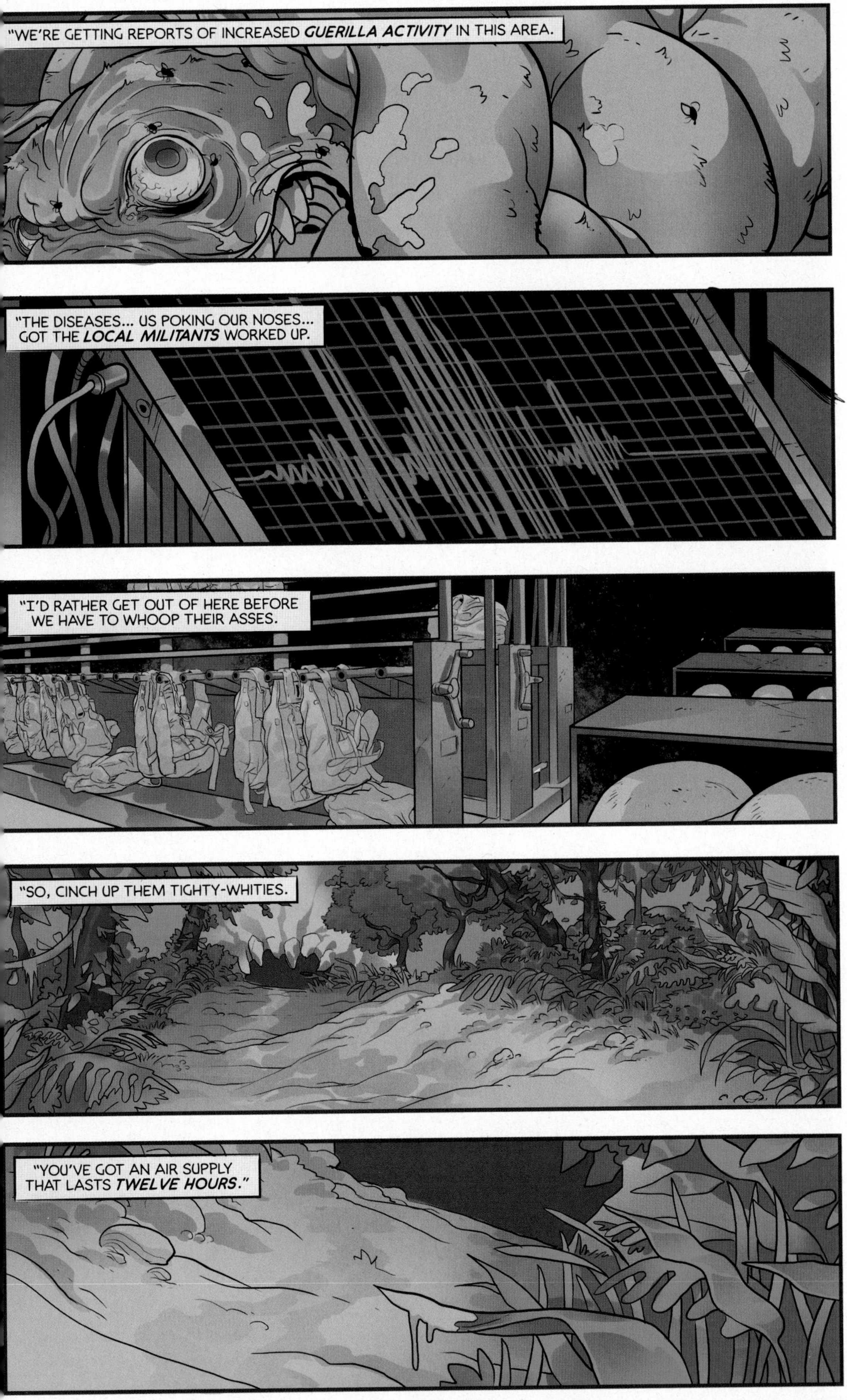
"WE'RE GETTING REPORTS OF INCREASED GUERILLA ACTIVITY IN THIS AREA.
"THE DISEASES... US POKING OUR NOSES... GOT THE LOCAL MILITANTS WORKED UP.
"I'D RATHER GET OUT OF HERE BEFORE WE HAVE TO WHOOP THEIR ASSES.
"SO, CINCH UP THEM TIGHTY-WHITIES.
"YOU'VE GOT AN AIR SUPPLY THAT LASTS TWELVE HOURS."

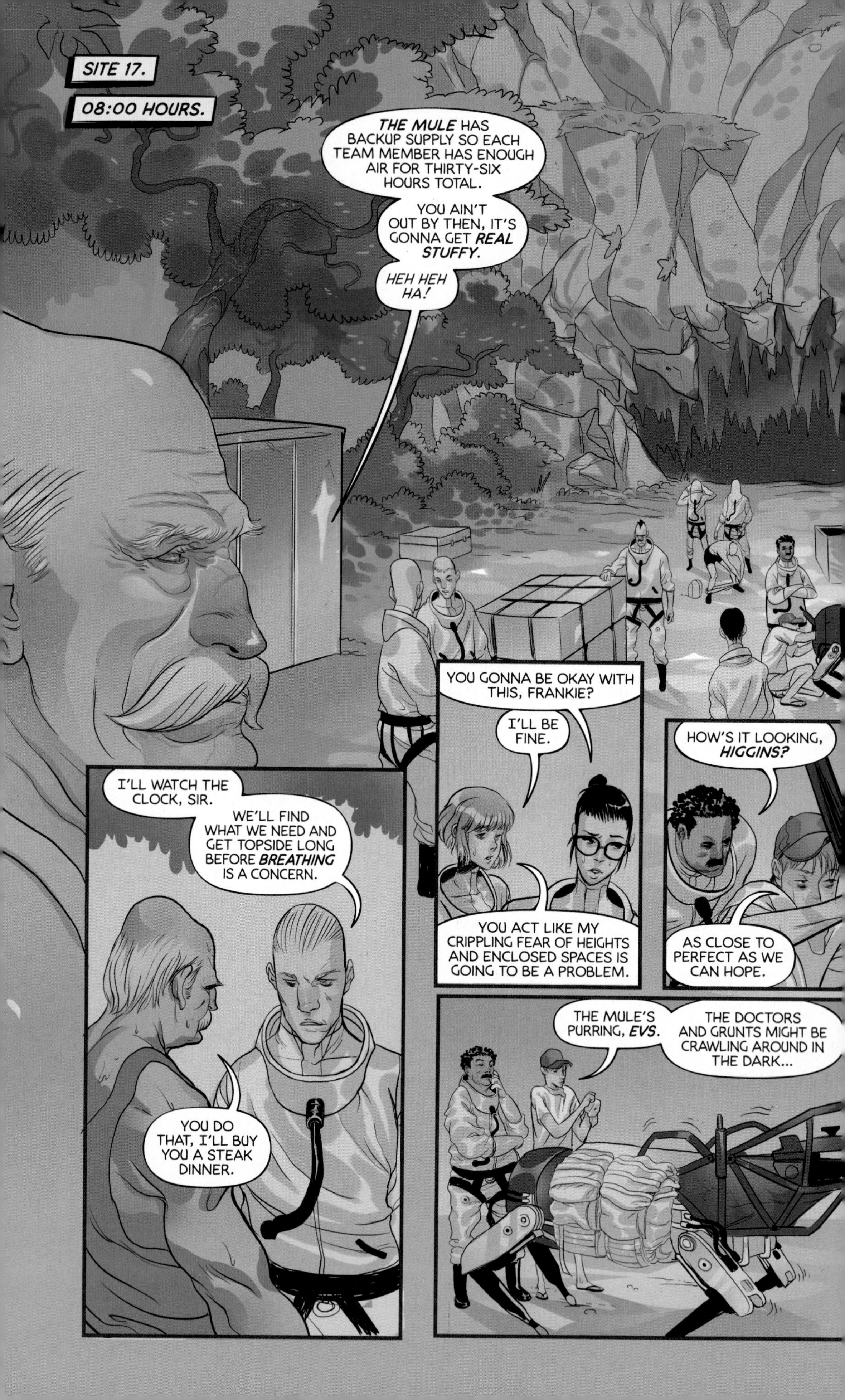

SITE 17.
08:00 HOURS.
THE MULE HAS BACKUP SUPPLY SO EACH TEAM MEMBER HAS ENOUGH AIR FOR THIRTY-SIX HOURS TOTAL.
YOU AIN'T OUT BY THEN, IT'S GONNA GET *REAL STUFFY*.
HEH HEH HA!
I'LL WATCH THE CLOCK, SIR.
WE'LL FIND WHAT WE NEED AND GET TOPSIDE LONG BEFORE *BREATHING* IS A CONCERN.
YOU DO THAT, I'LL BUY YOU A STEAK DINNER.
YOU GONNA BE OKAY WITH THIS, FRANKIE?
I'LL BE FINE.
YOU ACT LIKE MY CRIPPLING FEAR OF HEIGHTS AND ENCLOSED SPACES IS GOING TO BE A PROBLEM.
HOW'S IT LOOKING, *HIGGINS?*
AS CLOSE TO PERFECT AS WE CAN HOPE.
THE MULE'S PURRING, *EVS*.
THE DOCTORS AND GRUNTS MIGHT BE CRAWLING AROUND IN THE DARK...

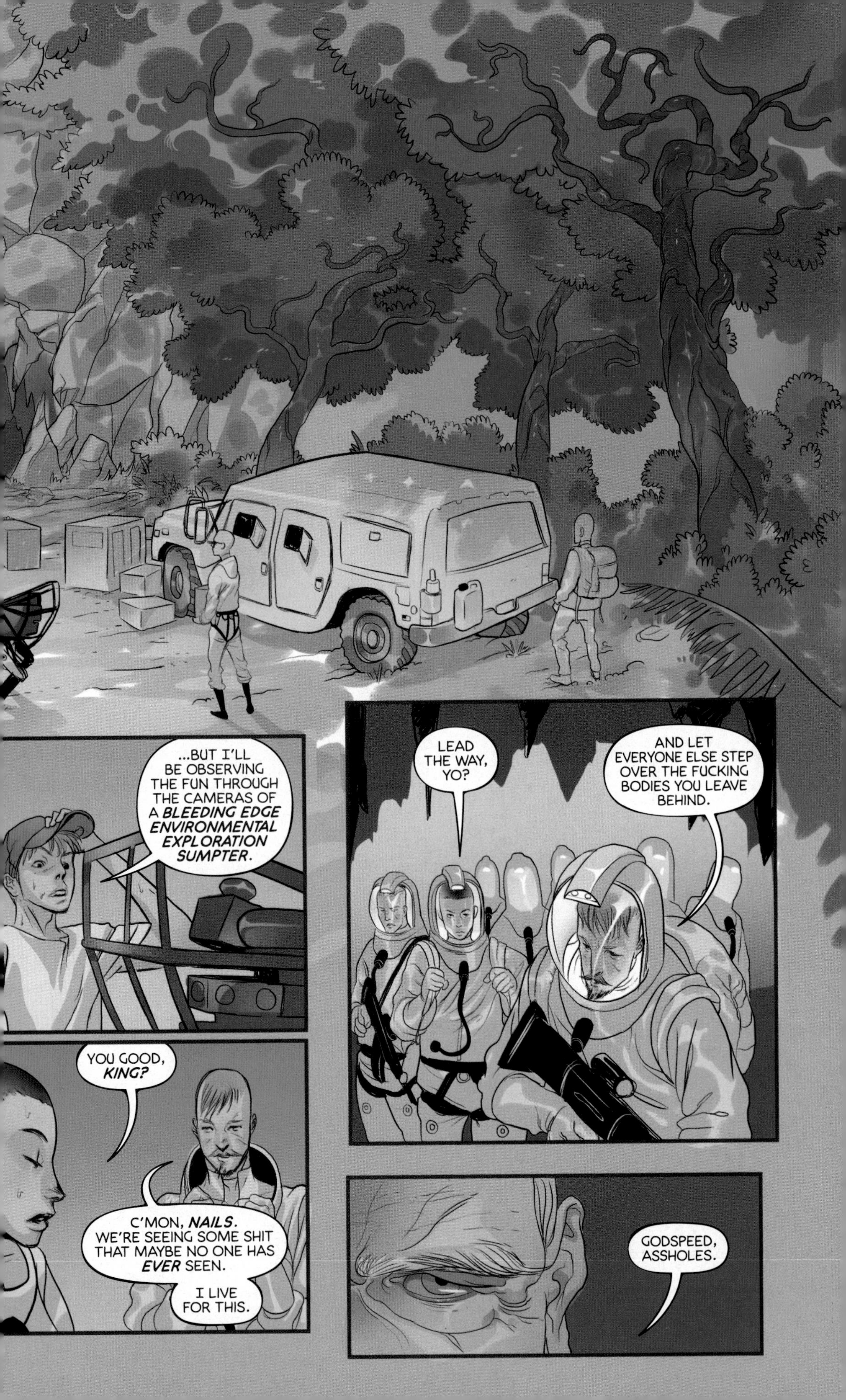
...BUT I'LL BE OBSERVING THE FUN THROUGH THE CAMERAS OF A BLEEDING EDGE ENVIRONMENTAL EXPLORATION SUMPTER.
LEAD THE WAY, YO?
AND LET EVERYONE ELSE STEP OVER THE FUCKING BODIES YOU LEAVE BEHIND.
YOU GOOD, KING?
C'MON, NAILS. WE'RE SEEING SOME SHIT THAT MAYBE NO ONE HAS EVER SEEN.
I LIVE FOR THIS.
GODSPEED, ASSHOLES.

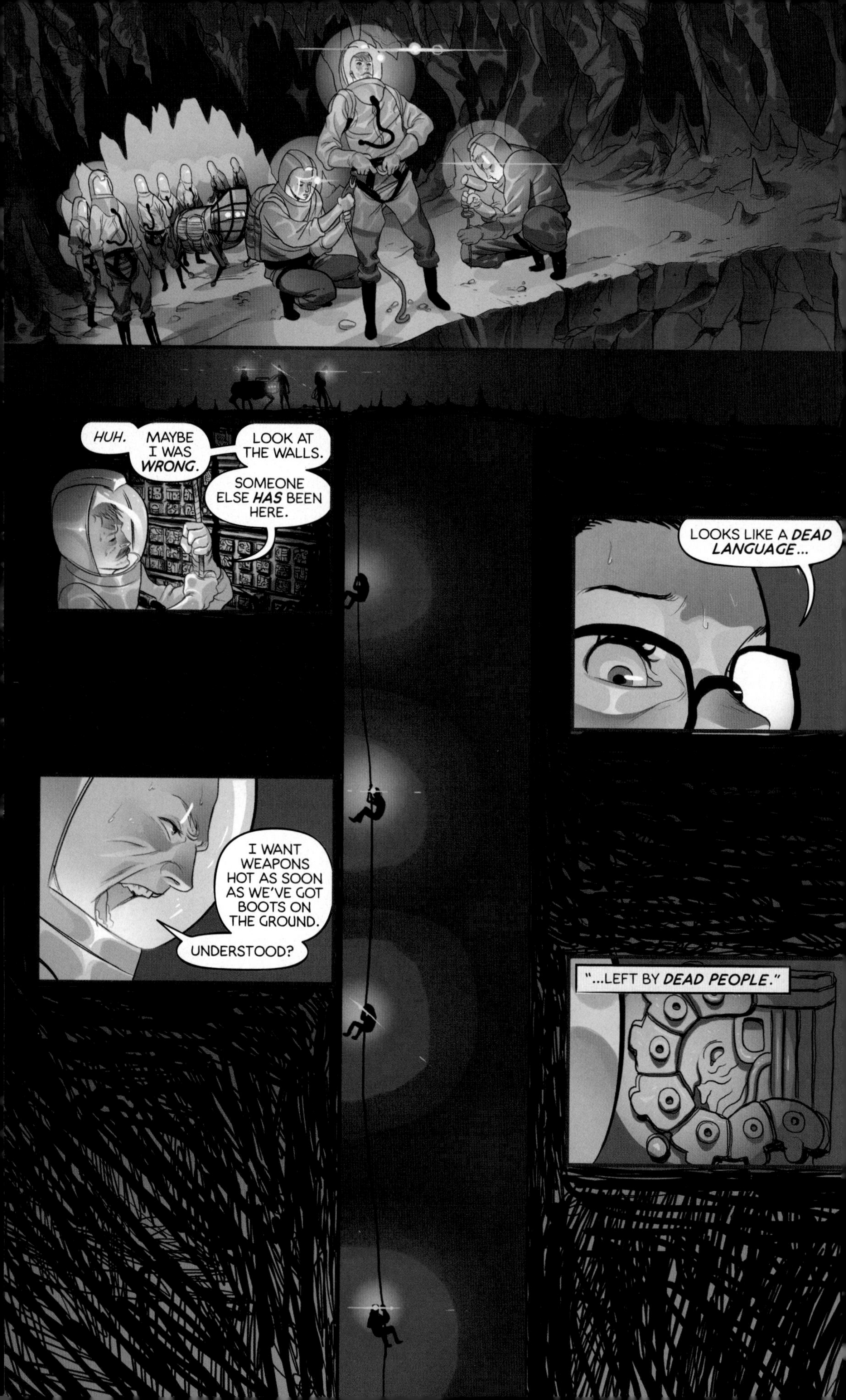

HUH.
MAYBE I WAS WRONG.
LOOK AT THE WALLS.
SOMEONE ELSE HAS BEEN HERE.
LOOKS LIKE A DEAD LANGUAGE...
I WANT WEAPONS HOT AS SOON AS WE'VE GOT BOOTS ON THE GROUND.
UNDERSTOOD?
"...LEFT BY DEAD PEOPLE."

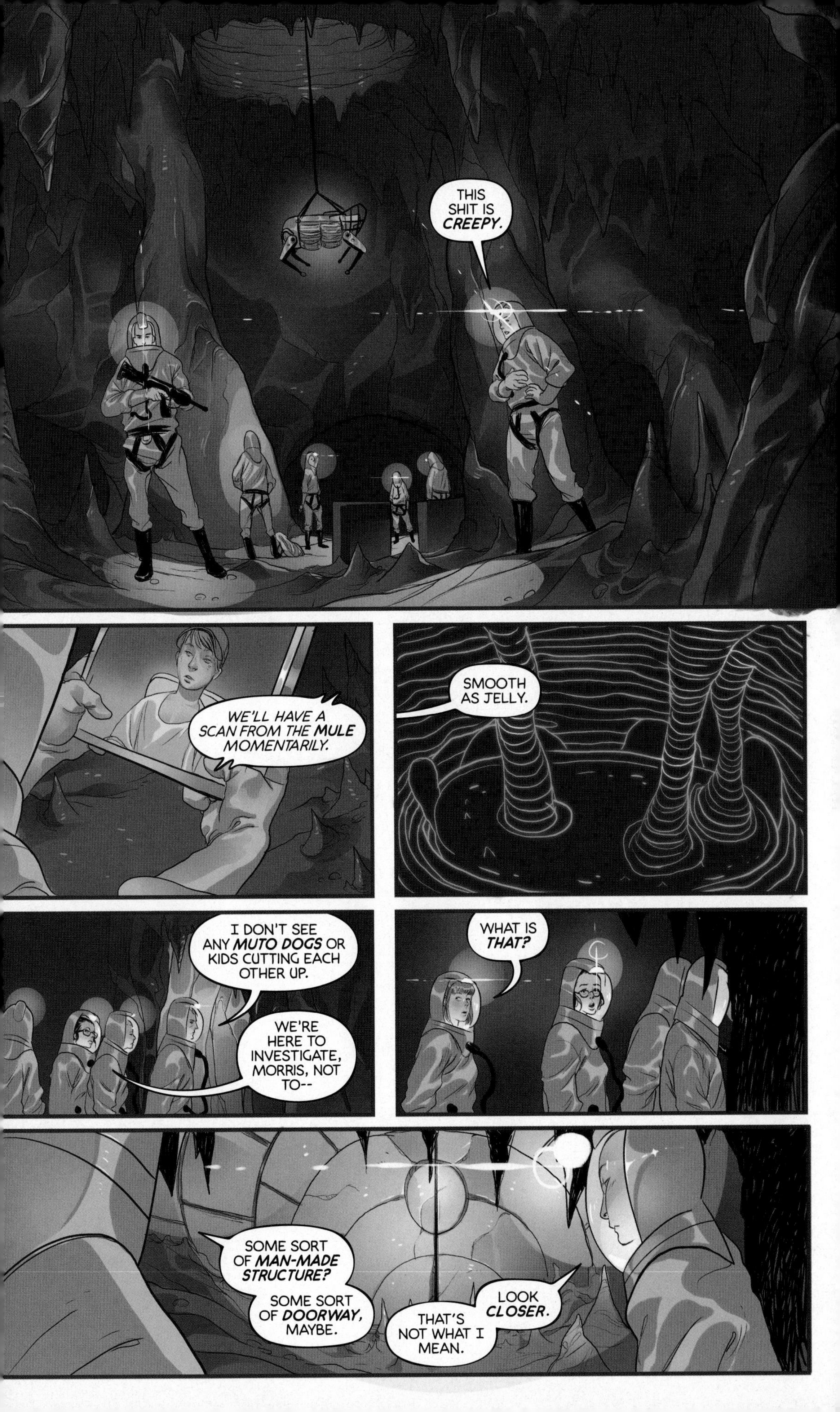
THIS SHIT IS *CREEPY*.
WE'LL HAVE A SCAN FROM THE ***MULE*** *MOMENTARILY.*
SMOOTH AS JELLY.
I DON'T SEE ANY ***MUTO DOGS*** OR KIDS CUTTING EACH OTHER UP.
WE'RE HERE TO INVESTIGATE, MORRIS, NOT TO--
WHAT IS ***THAT?***
SOME SORT OF ***MAN-MADE STRUCTURE?***
SOME SORT OF ***DOORWAY,*** MAYBE.
THAT'S NOT WHAT I MEAN.
LOOK ***CLOSER***.

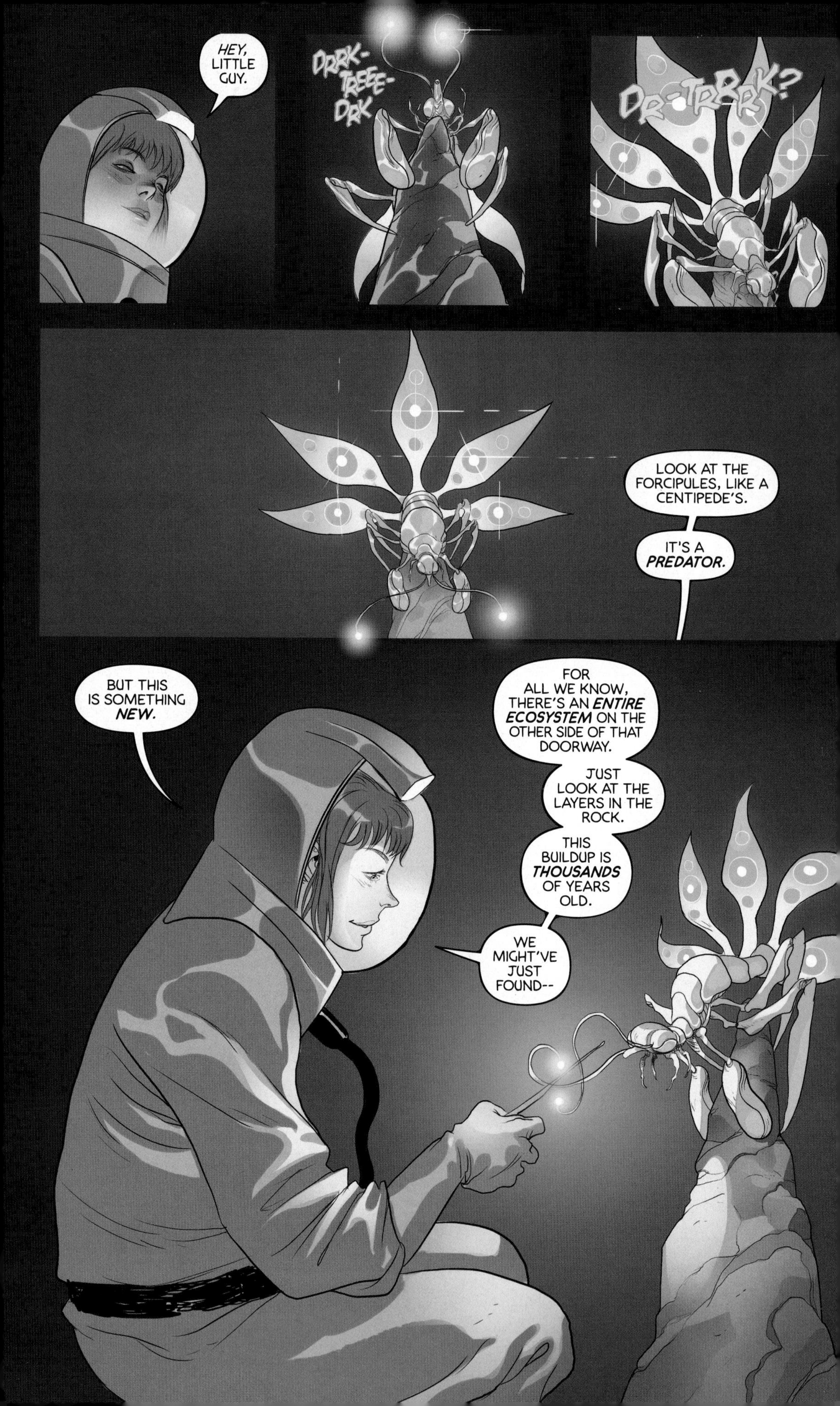
HEY, LITTLE GUY.
DRRK-TREEE-DRK
DR-TRRRK?
LOOK AT THE FORCIPULES, LIKE A CENTIPEDE'S.
IT'S A PREDATOR.
BUT THIS IS SOMETHING NEW.
FOR ALL WE KNOW, THERE'S AN ENTIRE ECOSYSTEM ON THE OTHER SIDE OF THAT DOORWAY.
JUST LOOK AT THE LAYERS IN THE ROCK.
THIS BUILDUP IS THOUSANDS OF YEARS OLD.
WE MIGHT'VE JUST FOUND--

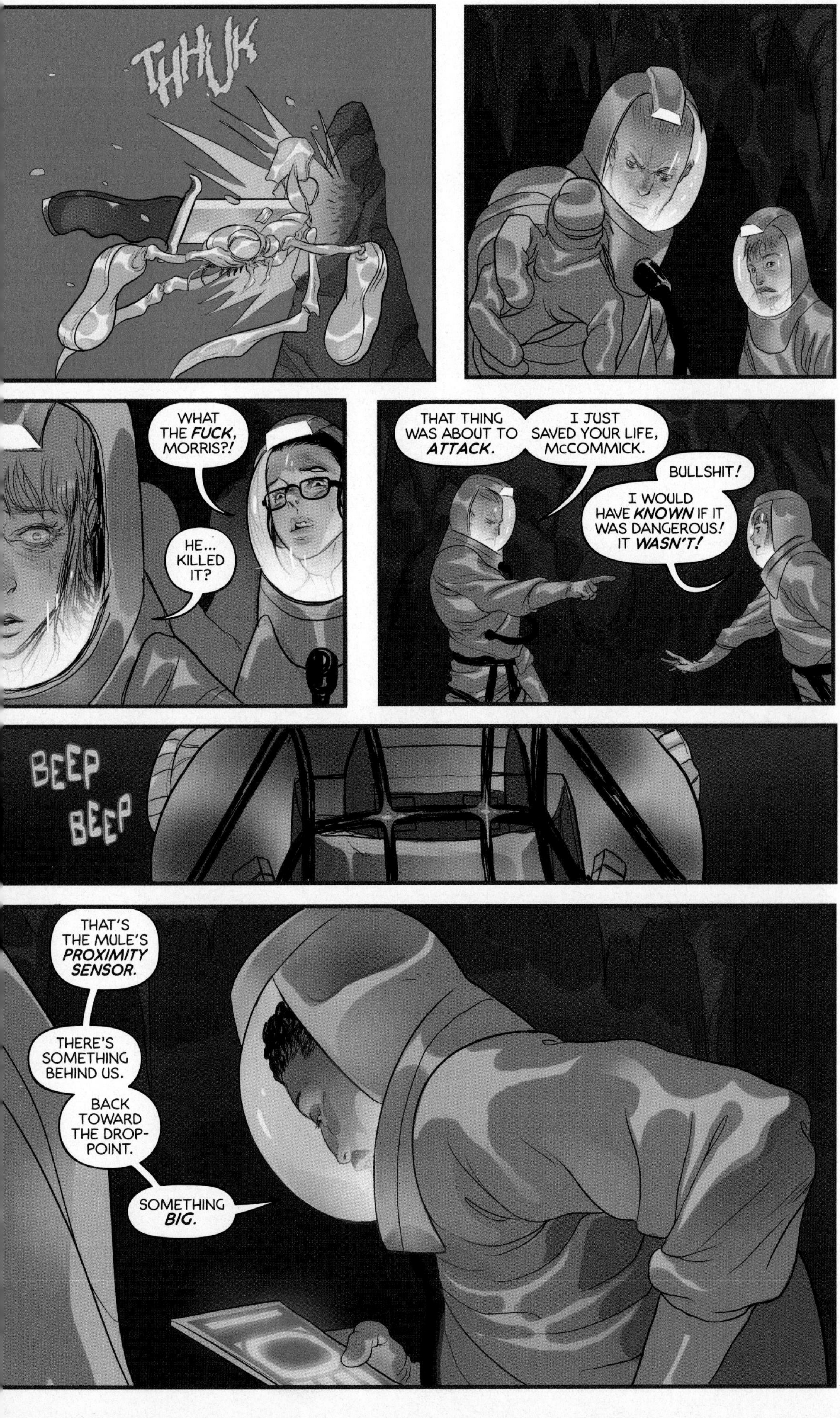
THHUK
WHAT THE FUCK, MORRIS?!
HE... KILLED IT?
THAT THING WAS ABOUT TO ATTACK.
I JUST SAVED YOUR LIFE, McCOMMICK.
BULLSHIT!
I WOULD HAVE KNOWN IF IT WAS DANGEROUS! IT WASN'T!
BEEP
BEEP
THAT'S THE MULE'S PROXIMITY SENSOR.
THERE'S SOMETHING BEHIND US.
BACK TOWARD THE DROP-POINT.
SOMETHING BIG.

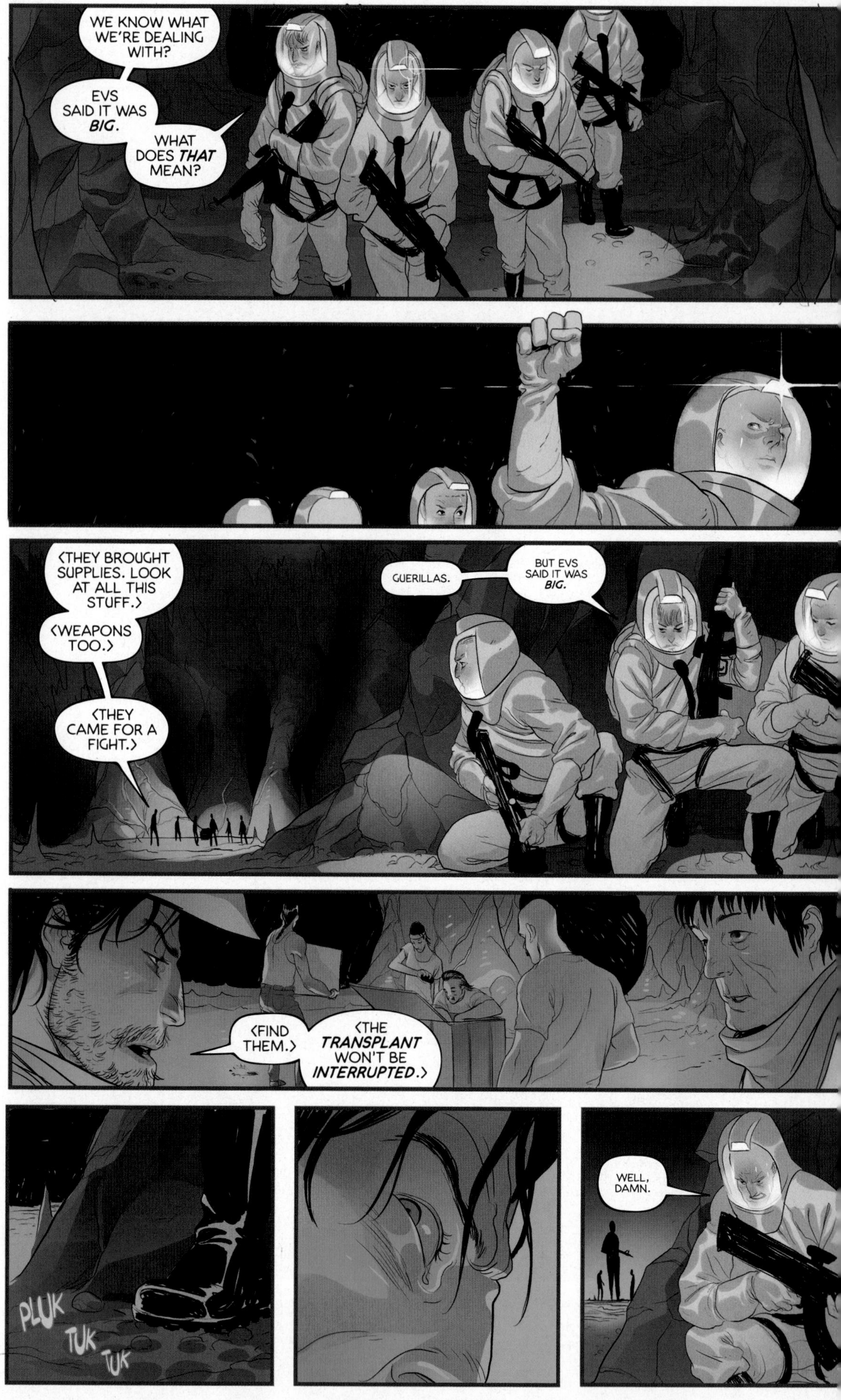
WE KNOW WHAT WE'RE DEALING WITH?
EVS SAID IT WAS *BIG*.
WHAT DOES *THAT* MEAN?
<THEY BROUGHT SUPPLIES. LOOK AT ALL THIS STUFF.>
<WEAPONS TOO.>
<THEY CAME FOR A FIGHT.>
GUERILLAS.
BUT EVS SAID IT WAS *BIG.*
<FIND THEM.>
<THE *TRANSPLANT* WON'T BE *INTERRUPTED*.>
PLUK
TUK
TUK
WELL, DAMN.

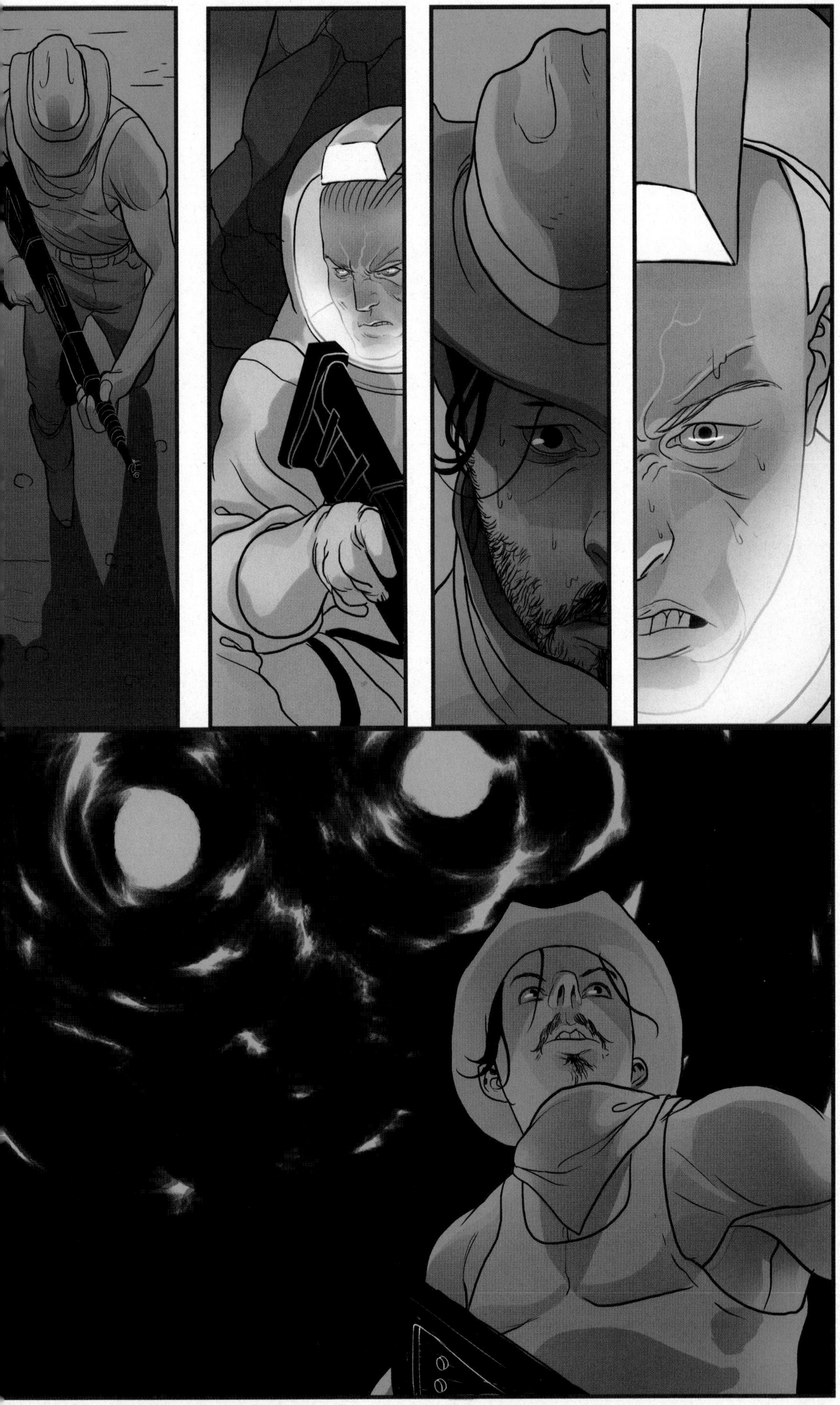

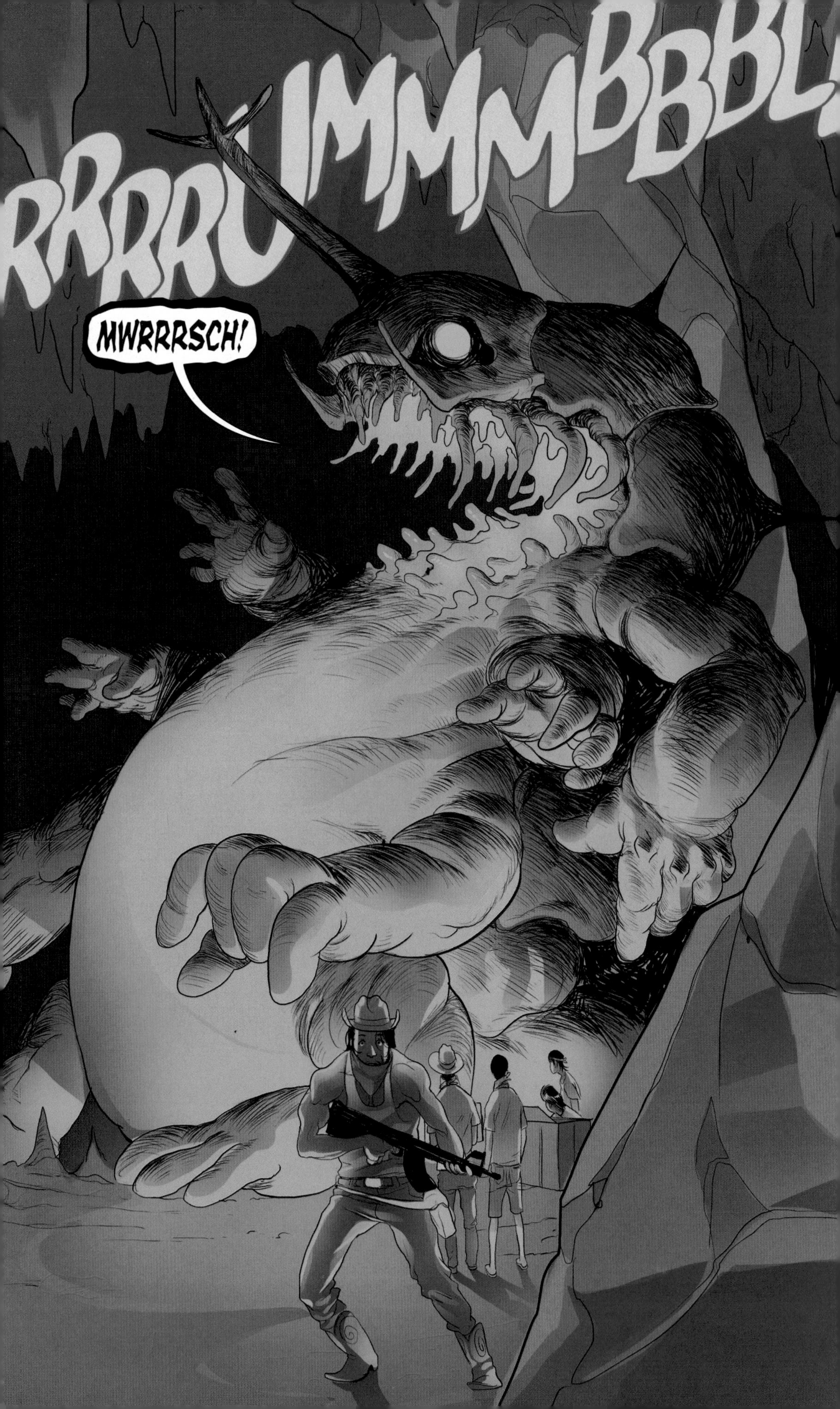
RRRRUMMMBBBL
MWRRRSCH!

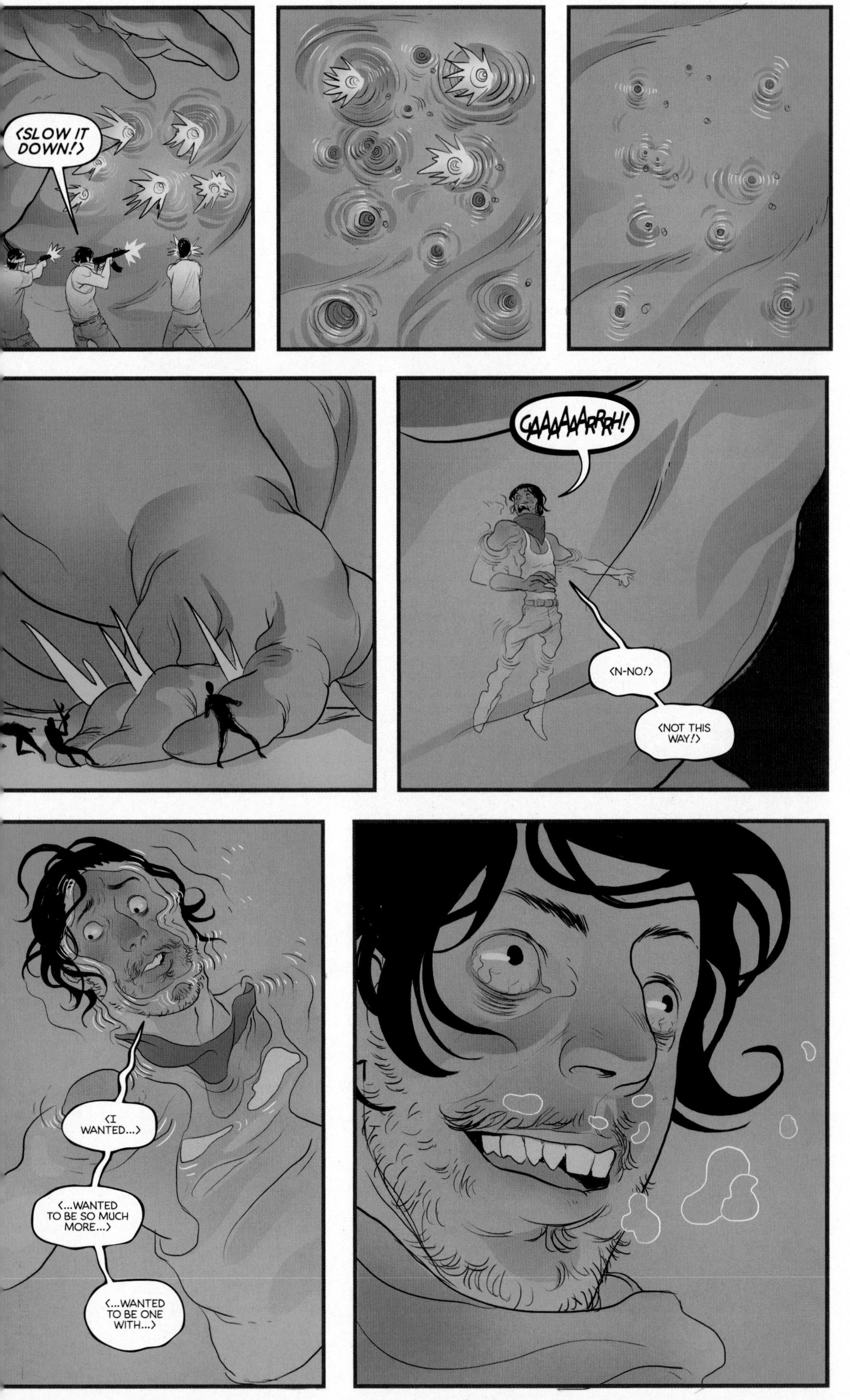

‹SLOW IT DOWN!›
GAAAAAARRRH!
‹N-NO!›
‹NOT THIS WAY!›
‹I WANTED...›
‹...WANTED TO BE SO MUCH MORE...›
‹...WANTED TO BE ONE WITH...›

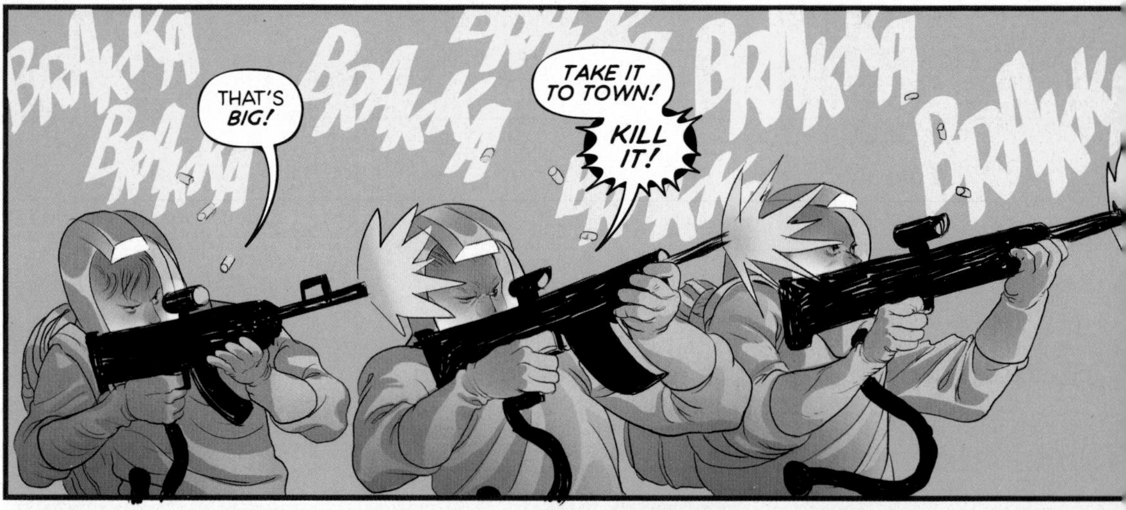
BRAKKA
THAT'S BIG!
TAKE IT TO TOWN!
KILL IT!

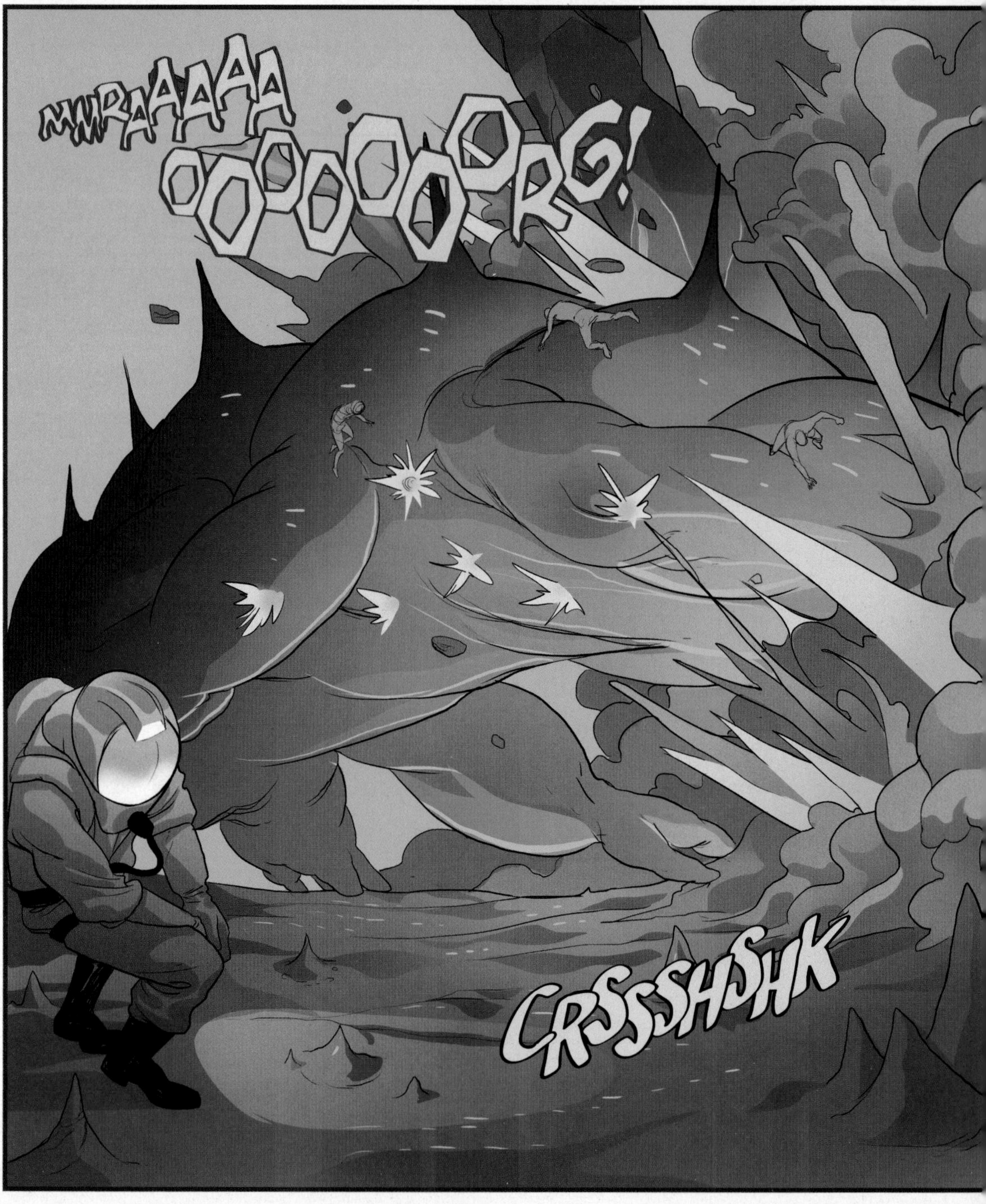
MNRAAAAA
OOOOOOOORG!
CRSSSHSHK

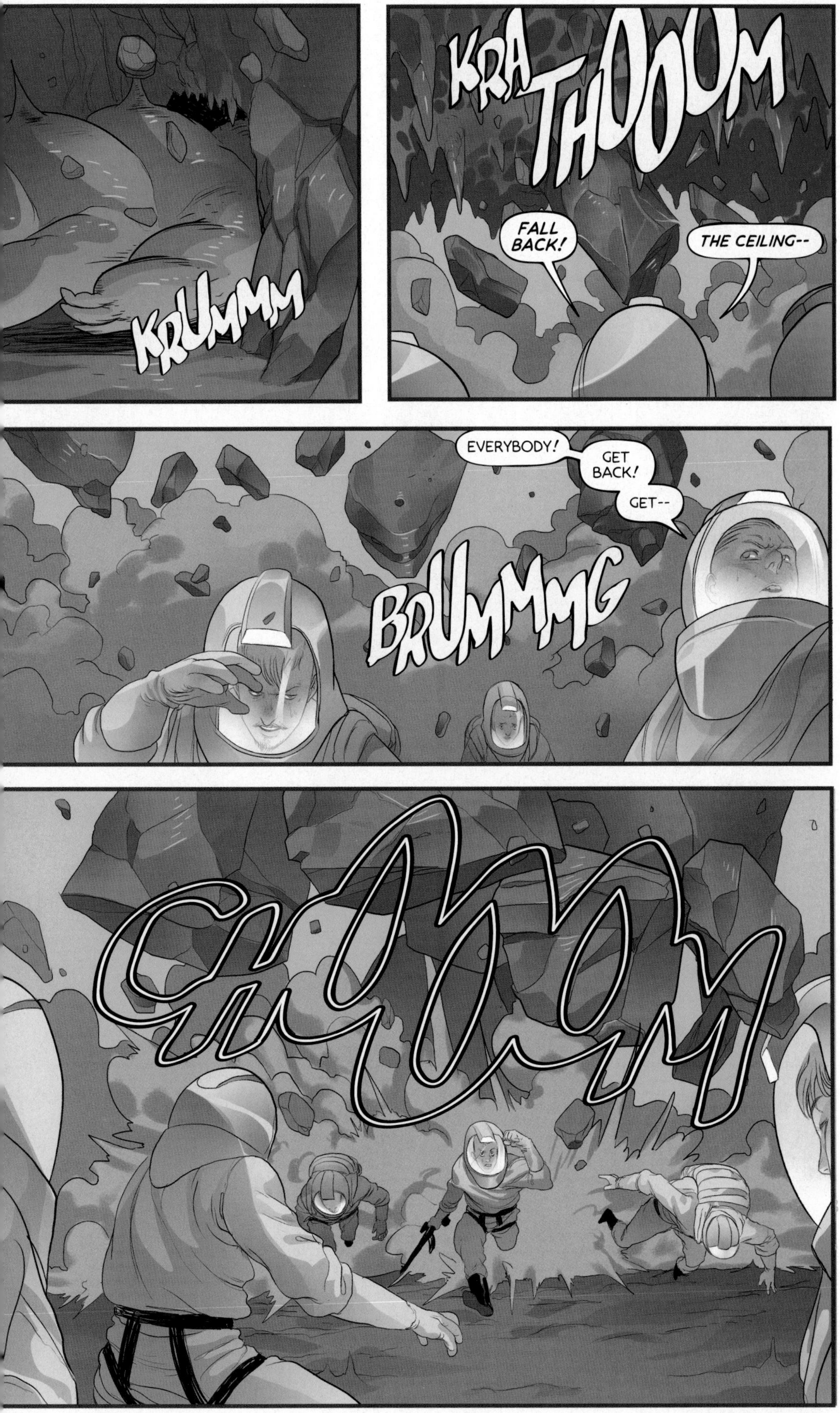
KRUMMM
KRA THOOOUM
FALL BACK!
THE CEILING--
EVERYBODY!
GET BACK!
GET--
BRUMMMG

THE TUNNEL! IT'S **BLOCKED**.

WHAT IN GOD'S NAME **WAS** THAT THING? DID WE KILL IT? OR JUST CHASE IT OFF?

WE'RE **FUBAR!**

NO WAY WE'RE DIGGING OUT OF THIS HOLE NOW.

SCANS INDICATE-- **SSKKKZ**--THE STRUCTURE IS STILL SOUND.

THE MULE CAN--**ZZZK**--MOVE THOSE STONES.

BUT IT'S NOT MADE FOR THAT. IT'LL TAKE A LONG TIME, MAYBE LONGER THAN YOU HAVE CONSIDERING YOUR OXYGEN SUPPLY.

WE CAN HELP, RIGHT? WE CAN MOVE STONES OURSELVES.

BEFORE IT COMES BACK.

THAT'LL CUT--

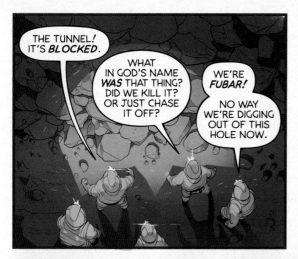

WHO THE HELL--

GET BACK!

GET DOWN!

DOWN!

STAY THE HELL WHERE YOU ARE!

COMING AT ME WITH A KNIFE!

WHO ARE YOU? WHERE'D YOU COME FROM?

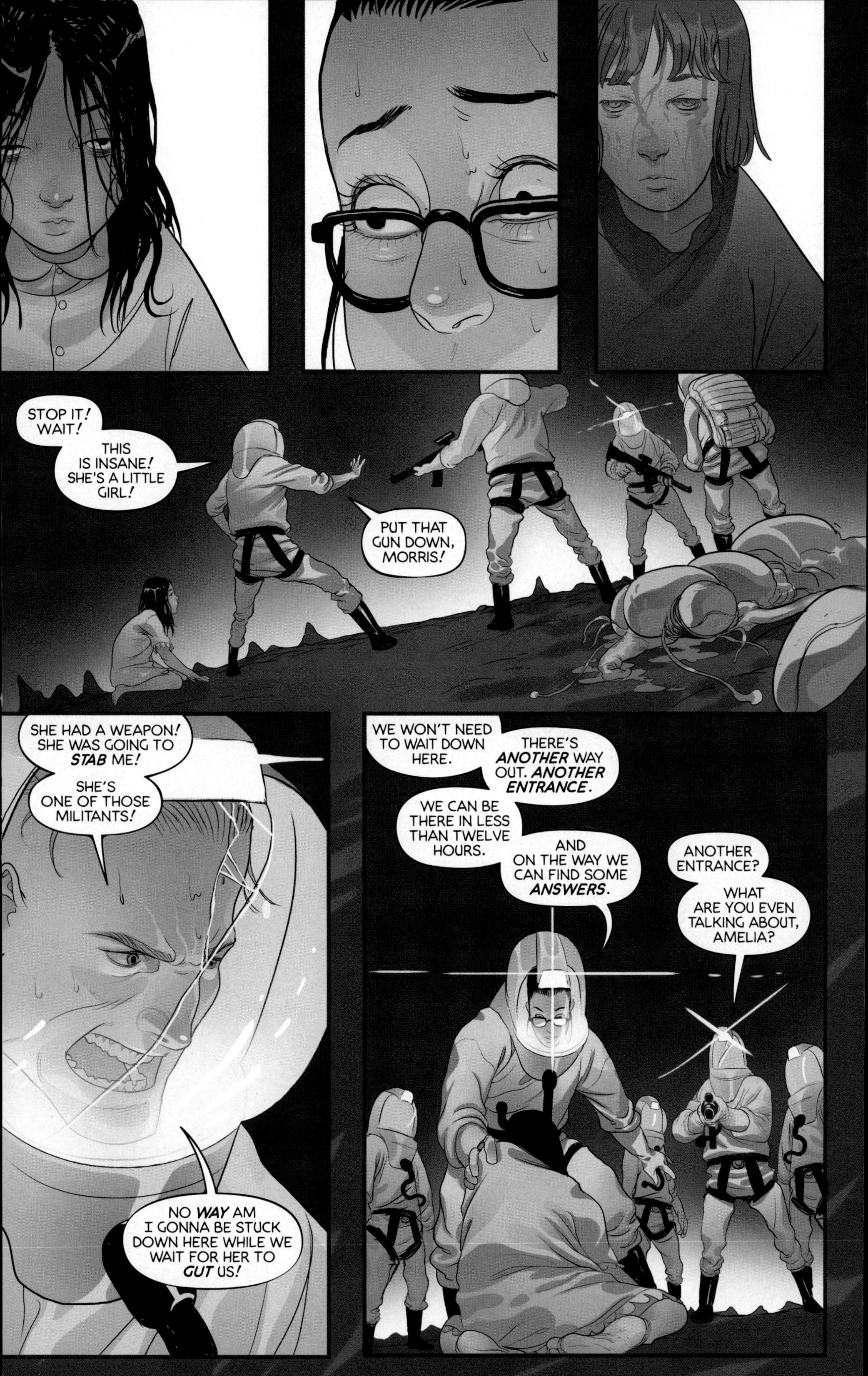
STOP IT! WAIT!
THIS IS INSANE! SHE'S A LITTLE GIRL!
PUT THAT GUN DOWN, MORRIS!
SHE HAD A WEAPON! SHE WAS GOING TO STAB ME!
SHE'S ONE OF THOSE MILITANTS!
NO WAY AM I GONNA BE STUCK DOWN HERE WHILE WE WAIT FOR HER TO GUT US!
WE WON'T NEED TO WAIT DOWN HERE.
THERE'S ANOTHER WAY OUT. ANOTHER ENTRANCE.
WE CAN BE THERE IN LESS THAN TWELVE HOURS.
AND ON THE WAY WE CAN FIND SOME ANSWERS.
ANOTHER ENTRANCE?
WHAT ARE YOU EVEN TALKING ABOUT, AMELIA?

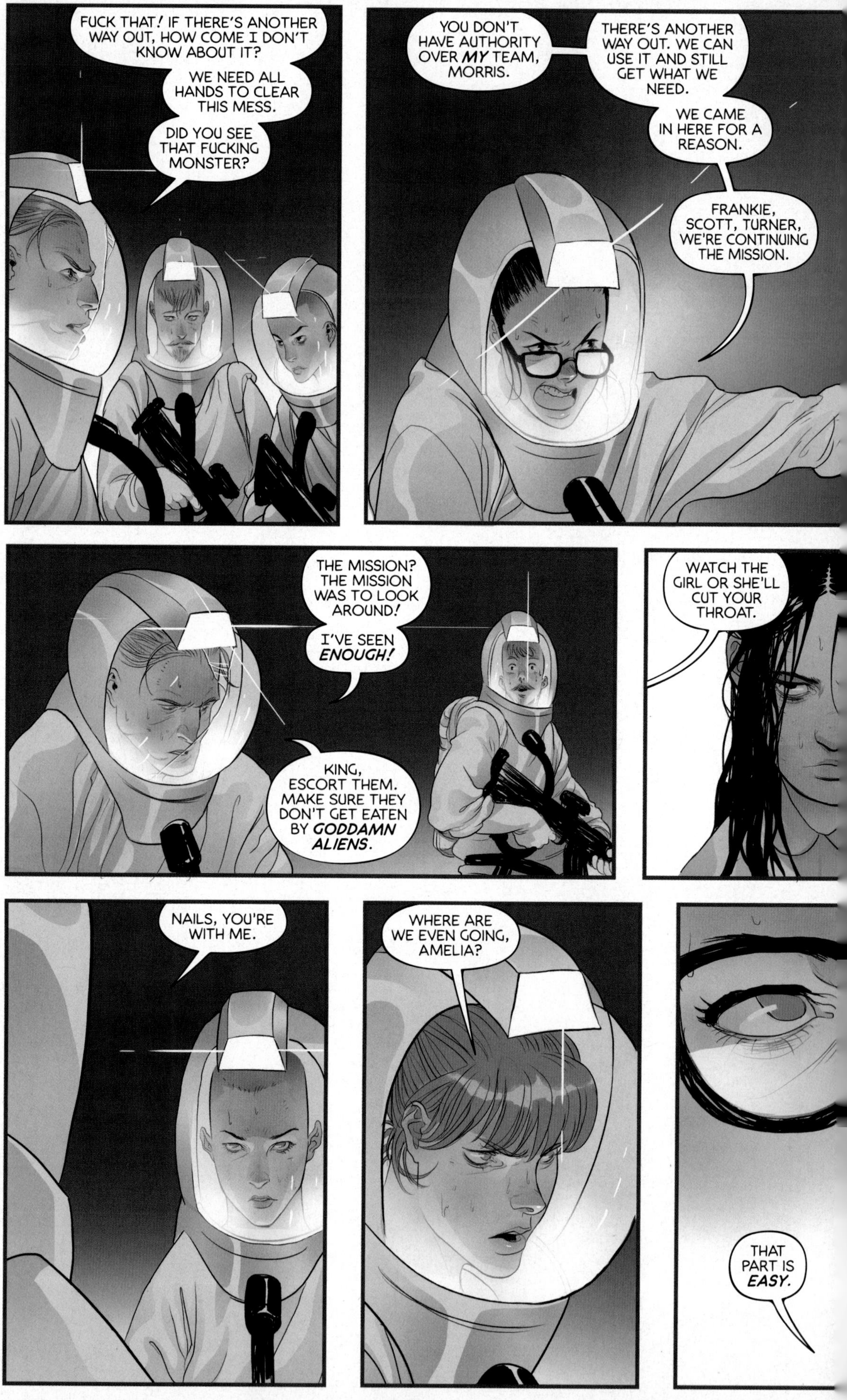
FUCK THAT! IF THERE'S ANOTHER WAY OUT, HOW COME I DON'T KNOW ABOUT IT?
WE NEED ALL HANDS TO CLEAR THIS MESS.
DID YOU SEE THAT FUCKING MONSTER?
YOU DON'T HAVE AUTHORITY OVER *MY* TEAM, MORRIS.
THERE'S ANOTHER WAY OUT. WE CAN USE IT AND STILL GET WHAT WE NEED.
WE CAME IN HERE FOR A REASON.
FRANKIE, SCOTT, TURNER, WE'RE CONTINUING THE MISSION.
THE MISSION? THE MISSION WAS TO LOOK AROUND!
I'VE SEEN *ENOUGH!*
KING, ESCORT THEM. MAKE SURE THEY DON'T GET EATEN BY *GODDAMN ALIENS*.
WATCH THE GIRL OR SHE'LL CUT YOUR THROAT.
NAILS, YOU'RE WITH ME.
WHERE ARE WE EVEN GOING, AMELIA?
THAT PART IS *EASY*.

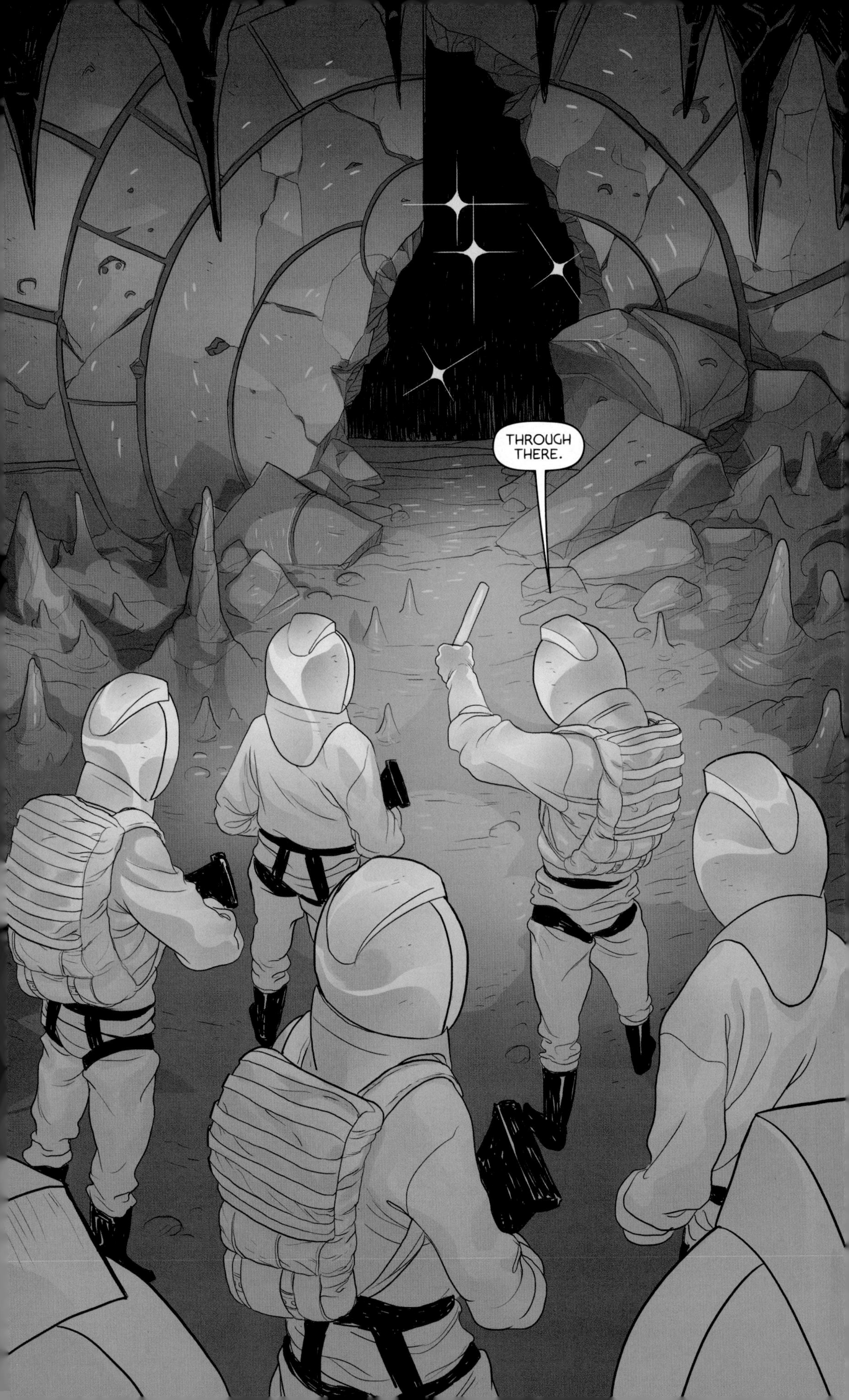
THROUGH THERE.

Ch 02

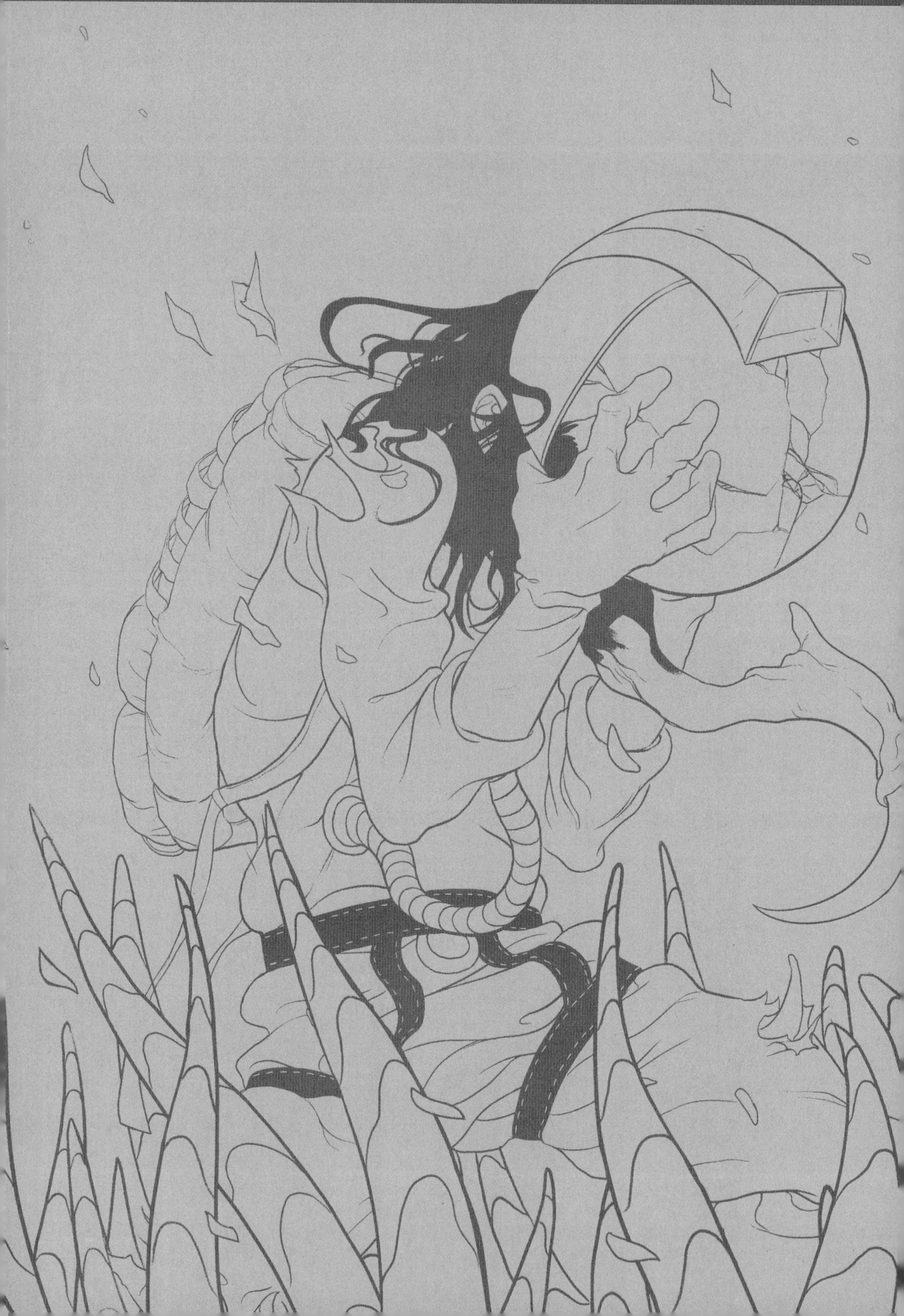

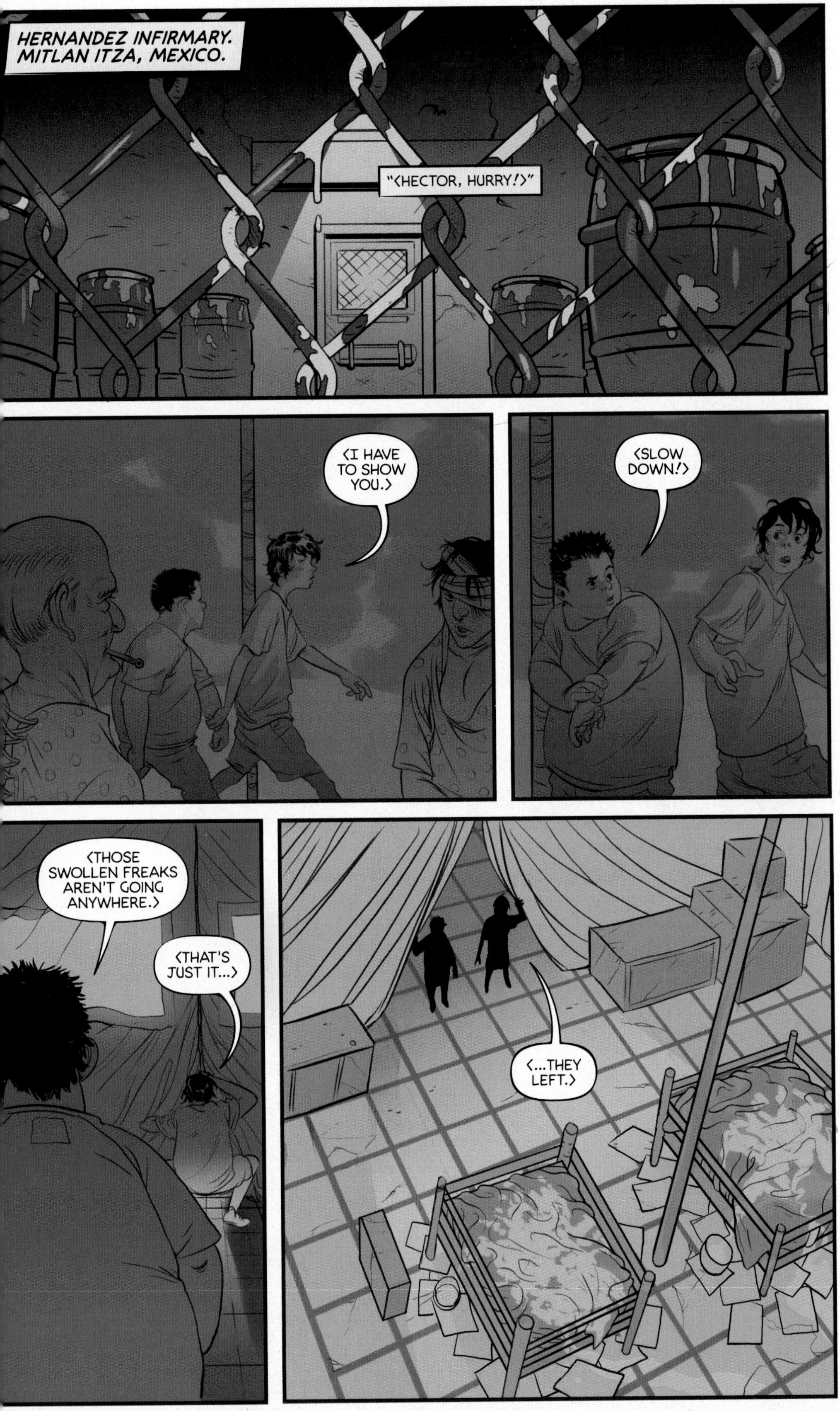
HERNANDEZ INFIRMARY.
MITLAN ITZA, MEXICO.
"<HECTOR, HURRY!>"
<I HAVE TO SHOW YOU.>
<SLOW DOWN!>
<THOSE SWOLLEN FREAKS AREN'T GOING ANYWHERE.>
<THAT'S JUST IT...>
<...THEY LEFT.>

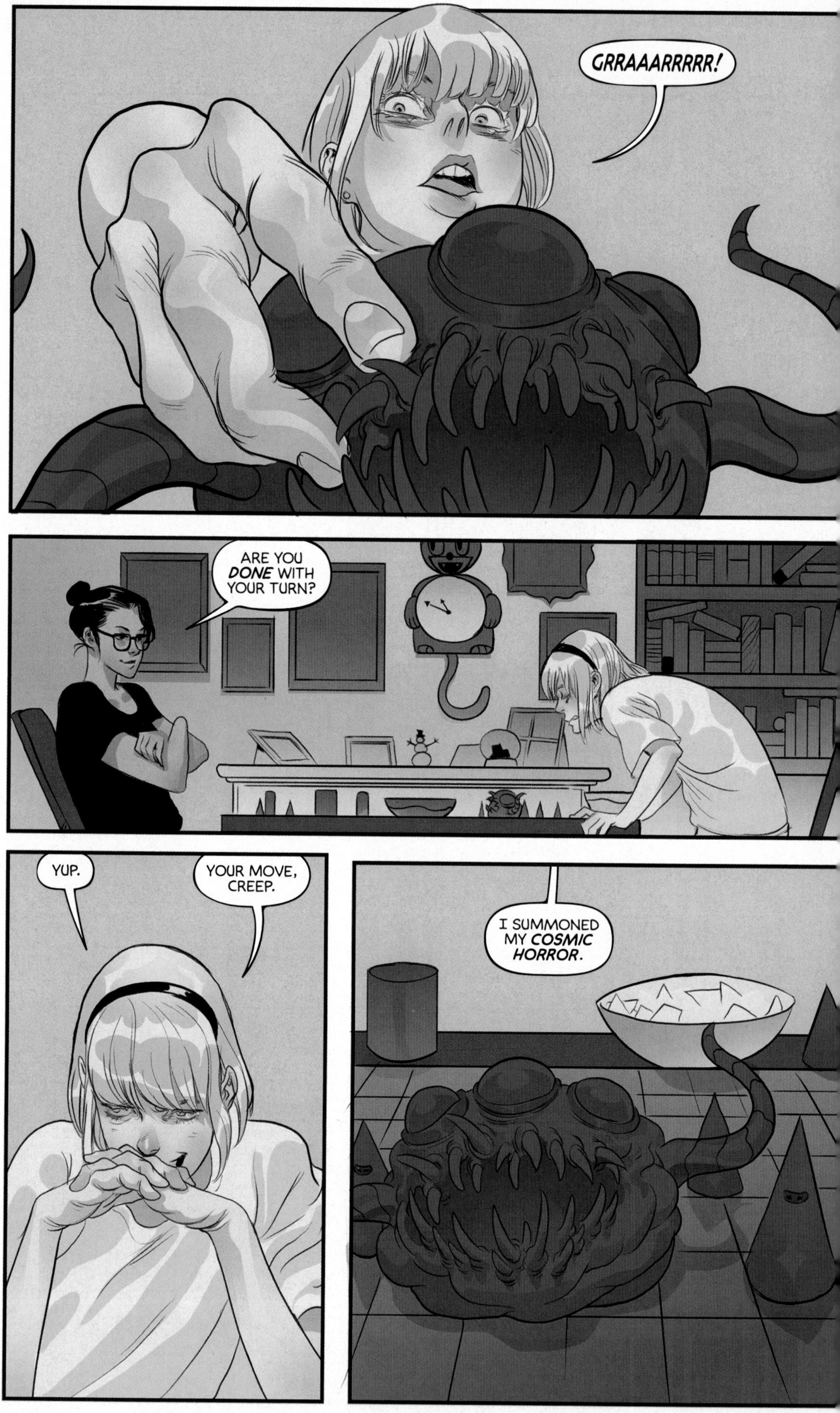
GRRAAARRRRR!
ARE YOU DONE WITH YOUR TURN?
YUP.
YOUR MOVE, CREEP.
I SUMMONED MY COSMIC HORROR.

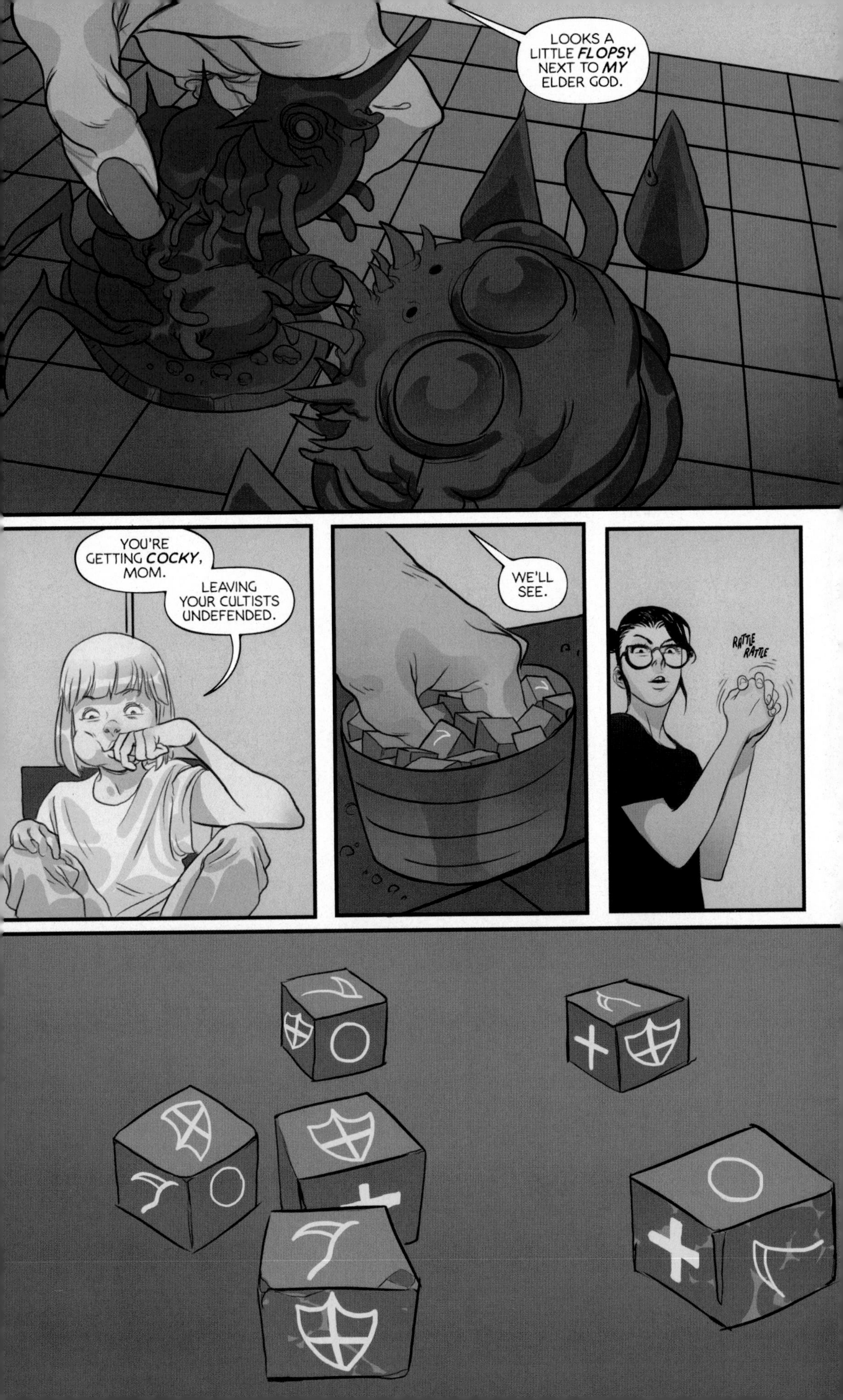
LOOKS A LITTLE FLOPSY NEXT TO MY ELDER GOD.
YOU'RE GETTING COCKY, MOM.
LEAVING YOUR CULTISTS UNDEFENDED.
WE'LL SEE.
RATTLE RATTLE

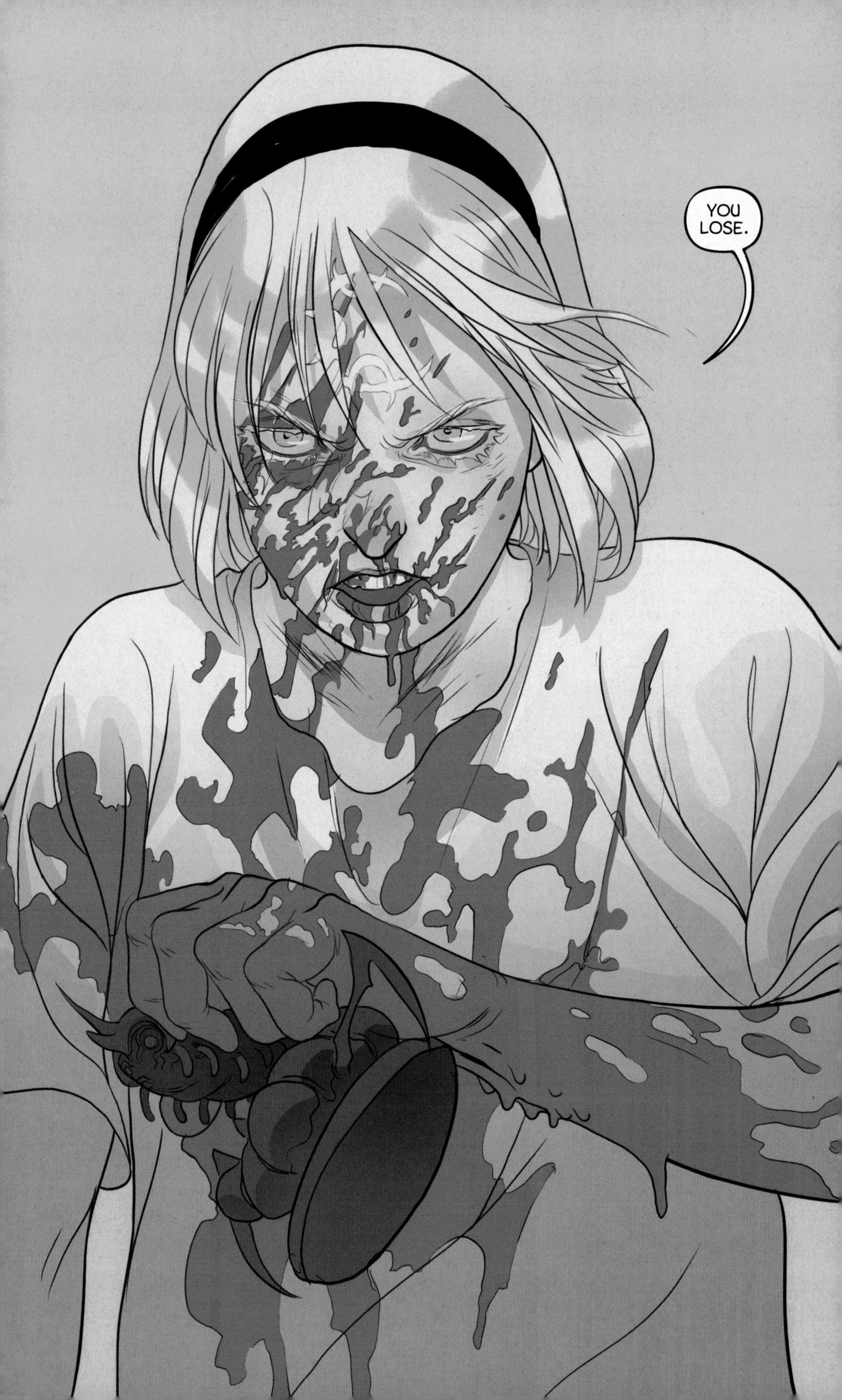
YOU LOSE.

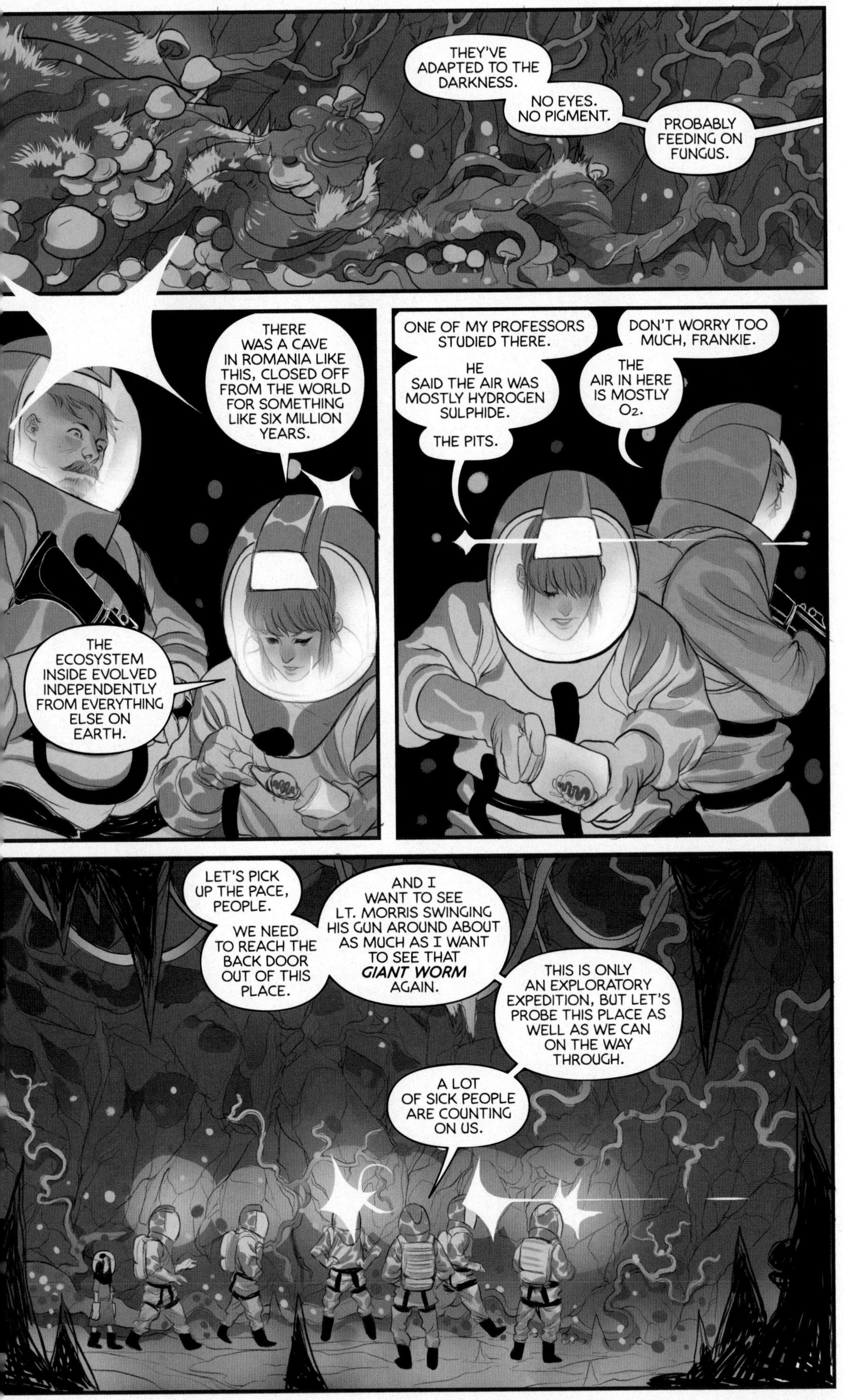
THEY'VE ADAPTED TO THE DARKNESS.
NO EYES. NO PIGMENT.
PROBABLY FEEDING ON FUNGUS.
THERE WAS A CAVE IN ROMANIA LIKE THIS, CLOSED OFF FROM THE WORLD FOR SOMETHING LIKE SIX MILLION YEARS.
THE ECOSYSTEM INSIDE EVOLVED INDEPENDENTLY FROM EVERYTHING ELSE ON EARTH.
ONE OF MY PROFESSORS STUDIED THERE.
HE SAID THE AIR WAS MOSTLY HYDROGEN SULPHIDE.
THE PITS.
DON'T WORRY TOO MUCH, FRANKIE.
THE AIR IN HERE IS MOSTLY O_2.
LET'S PICK UP THE PACE, PEOPLE.
WE NEED TO REACH THE BACK DOOR OUT OF THIS PLACE.
AND I WANT TO SEE LT. MORRIS SWINGING HIS GUN AROUND ABOUT AS MUCH AS I WANT TO SEE THAT ***GIANT WORM*** AGAIN.
THIS IS ONLY AN EXPLORATORY EXPEDITION, BUT LET'S PROBE THIS PLACE AS WELL AS WE CAN ON THE WAY THROUGH.
A LOT OF SICK PEOPLE ARE COUNTING ON US.

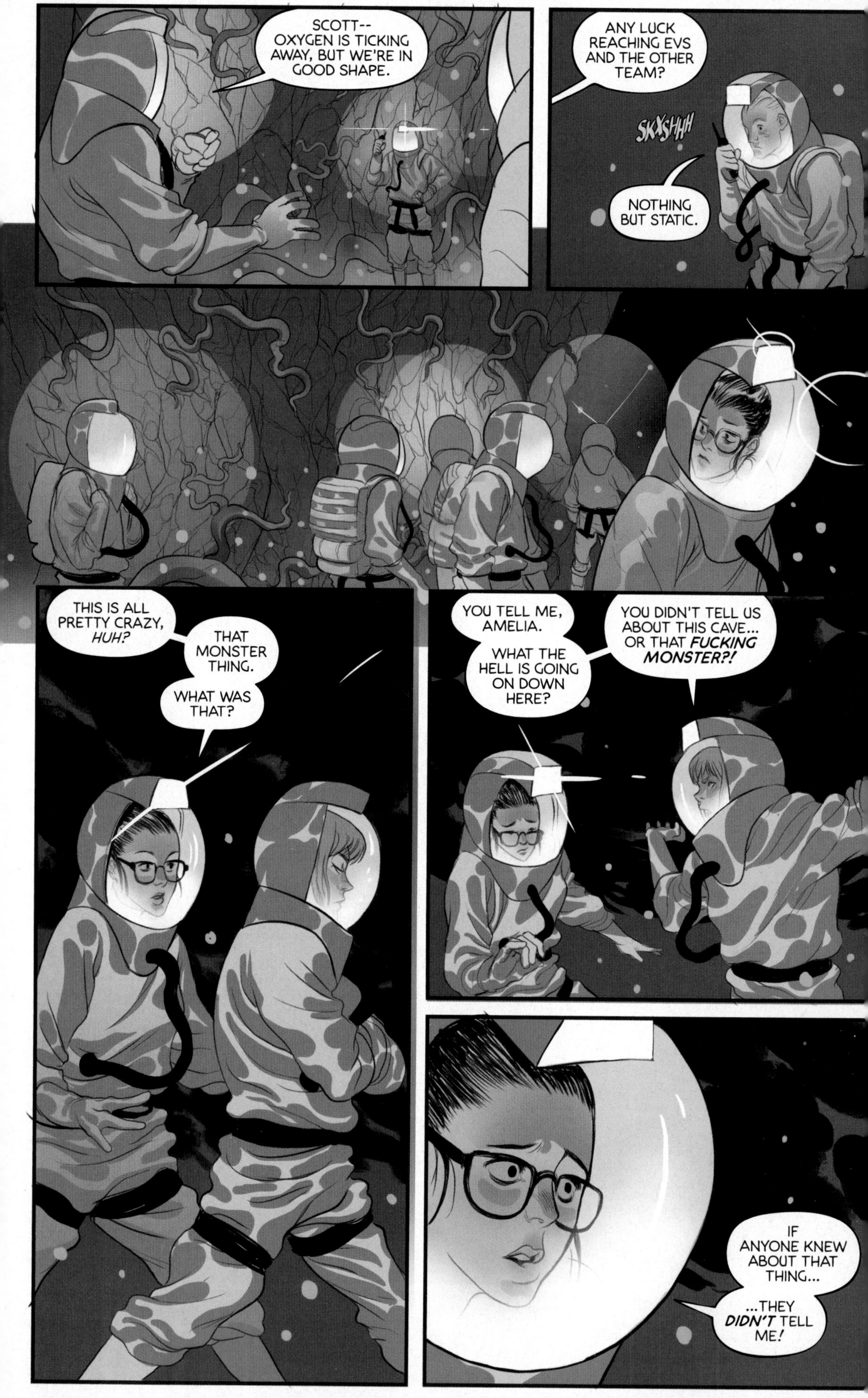
SCOTT-- OXYGEN IS TICKING AWAY, BUT WE'RE IN GOOD SHAPE.
ANY LUCK REACHING EVS AND THE OTHER TEAM?
SKXSHHH
NOTHING BUT STATIC.
THIS IS ALL PRETTY CRAZY, *HUH?*
THAT MONSTER THING.
WHAT WAS THAT?
YOU TELL ME, AMELIA.
WHAT THE HELL IS GOING ON DOWN HERE?
YOU DIDN'T TELL US ABOUT THIS CAVE... OR THAT ***FUCKING MONSTER?!***
IF ANYONE KNEW ABOUT THAT THING...
...THEY ***DIDN'T*** TELL ME*!*

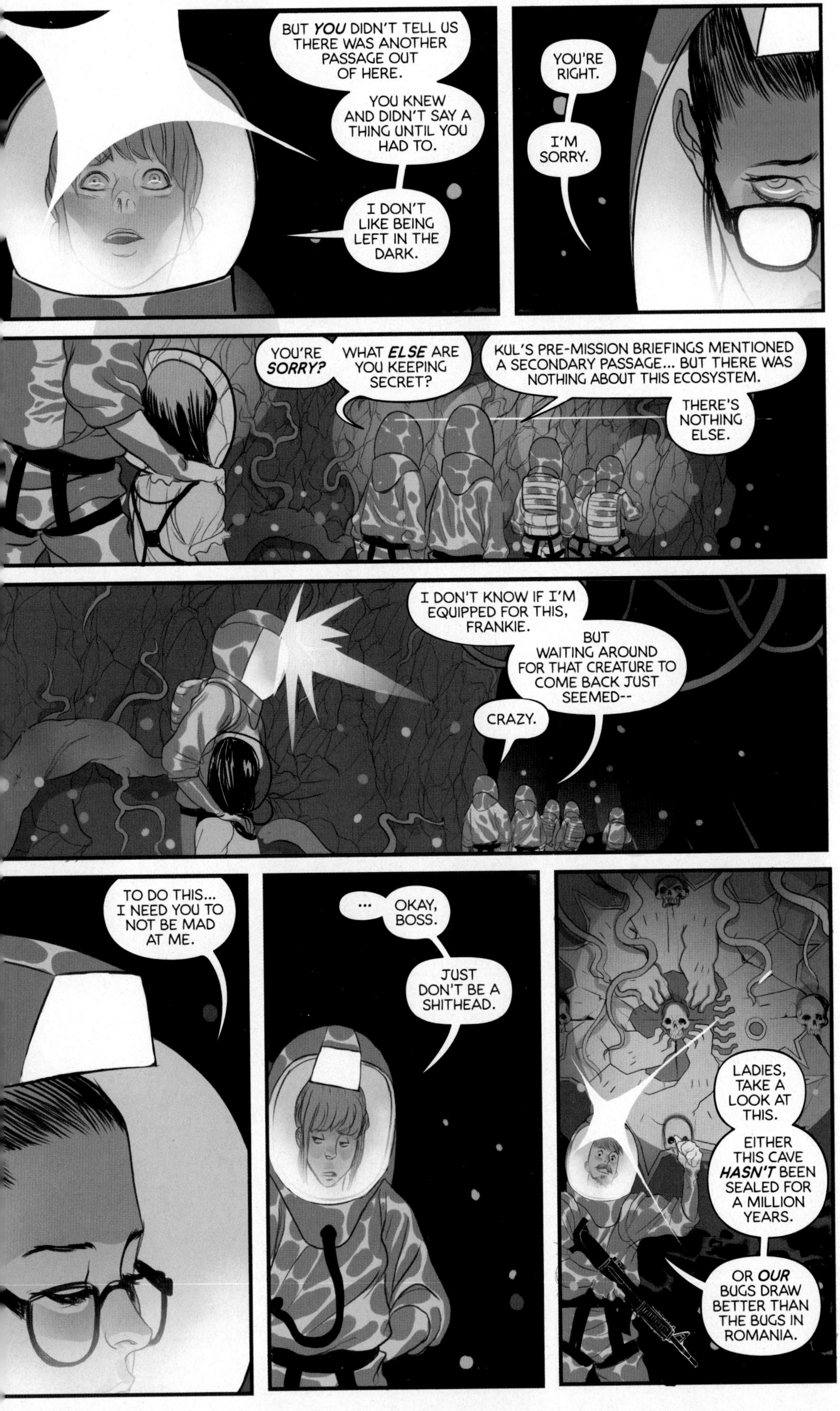
BUT *YOU* DIDN'T TELL US THERE WAS ANOTHER PASSAGE OUT OF HERE.
YOU KNEW AND DIDN'T SAY A THING UNTIL YOU HAD TO.
I DON'T LIKE BEING LEFT IN THE DARK.
YOU'RE RIGHT.
I'M SORRY.
YOU'RE *SORRY?*
WHAT *ELSE* ARE YOU KEEPING SECRET?
KUL'S PRE-MISSION BRIEFINGS MENTIONED A SECONDARY PASSAGE... BUT THERE WAS NOTHING ABOUT THIS ECOSYSTEM.
THERE'S NOTHING ELSE.
I DON'T KNOW IF I'M EQUIPPED FOR THIS, FRANKIE.
BUT WAITING AROUND FOR THAT CREATURE TO COME BACK JUST SEEMED--
CRAZY.
TO DO THIS... I NEED YOU TO NOT BE MAD AT ME.
...
OKAY, BOSS.
JUST DON'T BE A SHITHEAD.
LADIES, TAKE A LOOK AT THIS.
EITHER THIS CAVE *HASN'T* BEEN SEALED FOR A MILLION YEARS.
OR *OUR* BUGS DRAW BETTER THAN THE BUGS IN ROMANIA.

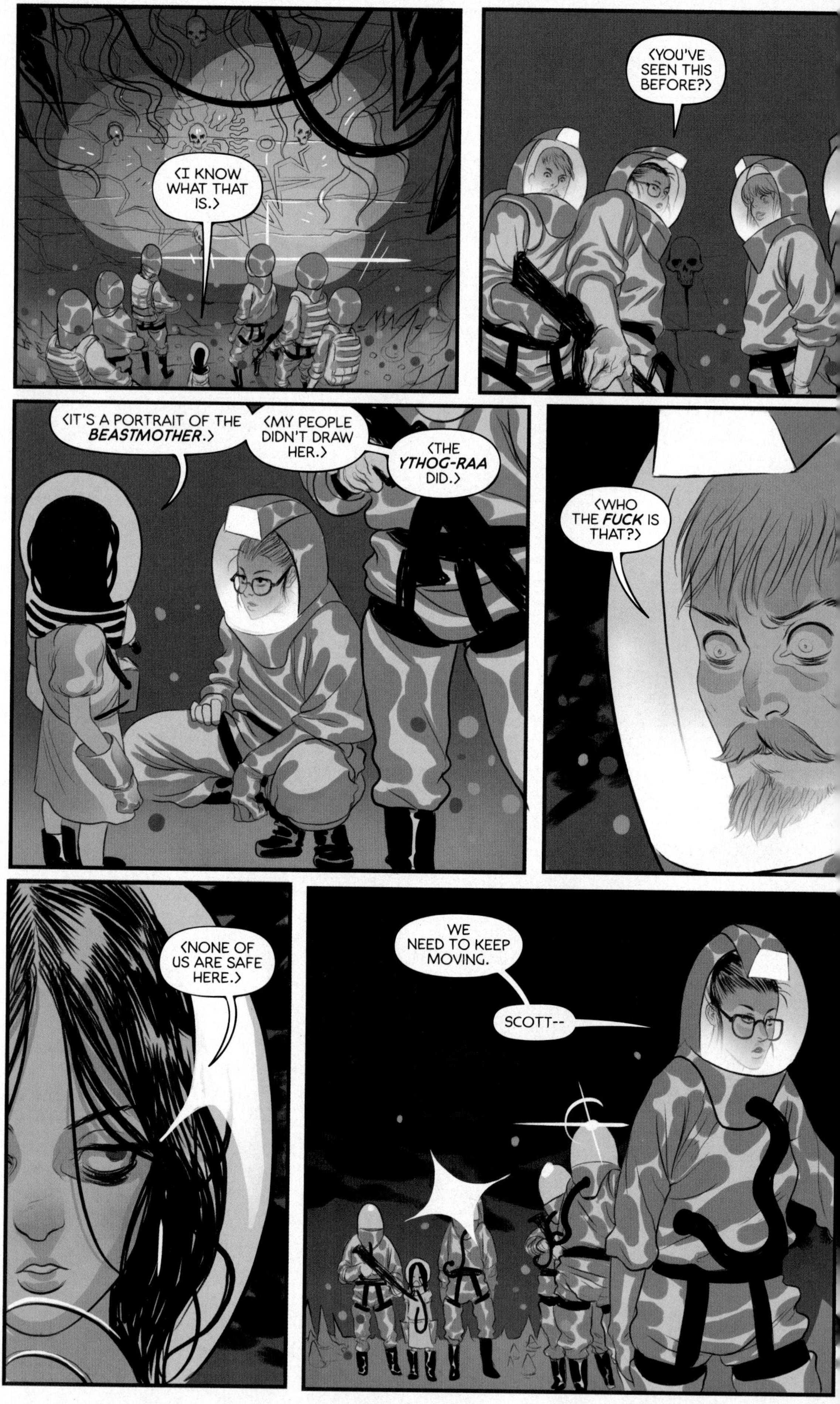

<I KNOW WHAT THAT IS.>
<YOU'VE SEEN THIS BEFORE?>
<IT'S A PORTRAIT OF THE *BEASTMOTHER*.>
<MY PEOPLE DIDN'T DRAW HER.>
<THE *YTHOG-RAA* DID.>
<WHO THE *FUCK* IS THAT?>
<NONE OF US ARE SAFE HERE.>
WE NEED TO KEEP MOVING.
SCOTT--

"--ANY WORD FROM MORRIS'S TEAM?"

WE SHOULD HAVE GONE WITH THEM.

FOR ALL WE KNOW, THIS TUNNEL'S SEALED ALL THE WAY BACK TO THE ENTRANCE.

WE'LL GET THROUGH THIS, NAILS.

STOP WHINING.

KEEP DIGGING.

WHAT DO YOU THINK IS HAPPENING HERE, MORRIS?

WE'RE *TRAPPED*.

AND WE SHOULDN'T HAVE LET REYES... McCOMMICK... THE OTHERS GO OFF BY THEMSELVES.

OUR MISSION IS TO *PROTECT* THEM.

YOUR MISSION IS WHATEVER I *SAY* IT IS.

AND RIGHT NOW, I'M TELLING YOU TO SHUT THE FUCK UP...

...FOLLOW ORDERS...

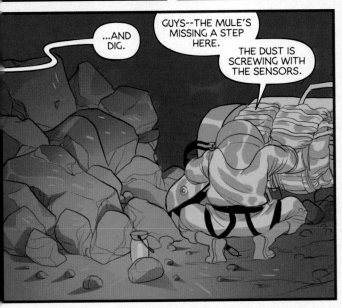

...AND DIG.

GUYS--THE MULE'S MISSING A STEP HERE.

THE DUST IS SCREWING WITH THE SENSORS.

ARE YOU RECEIVING DATA, BUDDY?

DOES ANYONE KNOW...

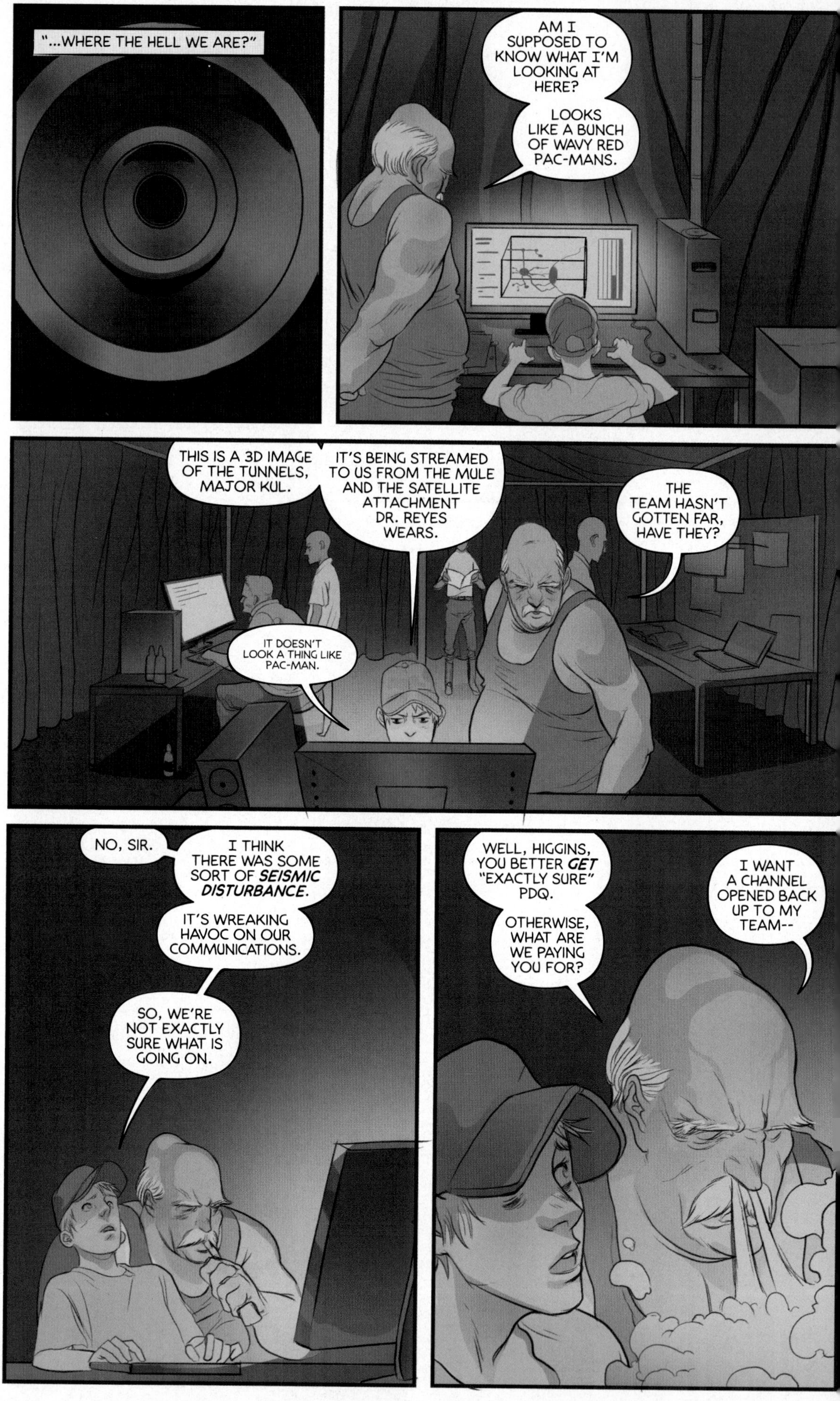
"...WHERE THE HELL WE ARE?"
AM I SUPPOSED TO KNOW WHAT I'M LOOKING AT HERE?
LOOKS LIKE A BUNCH OF WAVY RED PAC-MANS.
THIS IS A 3D IMAGE OF THE TUNNELS, MAJOR KUL.
IT'S BEING STREAMED TO US FROM THE MULE AND THE SATELLITE ATTACHMENT DR. REYES WEARS.
THE TEAM HASN'T GOTTEN FAR, HAVE THEY?
IT DOESN'T LOOK A THING LIKE PAC-MAN.
NO, SIR.
I THINK THERE WAS SOME SORT OF *SEISMIC DISTURBANCE*.
IT'S WREAKING HAVOC ON OUR COMMUNICATIONS.
SO, WE'RE NOT EXACTLY SURE WHAT IS GOING ON.
WELL, HIGGINS, YOU BETTER *GET* "EXACTLY SURE" PDQ.
OTHERWISE, WHAT ARE WE PAYING YOU FOR?
I WANT A CHANNEL OPENED BACK UP TO MY TEAM--

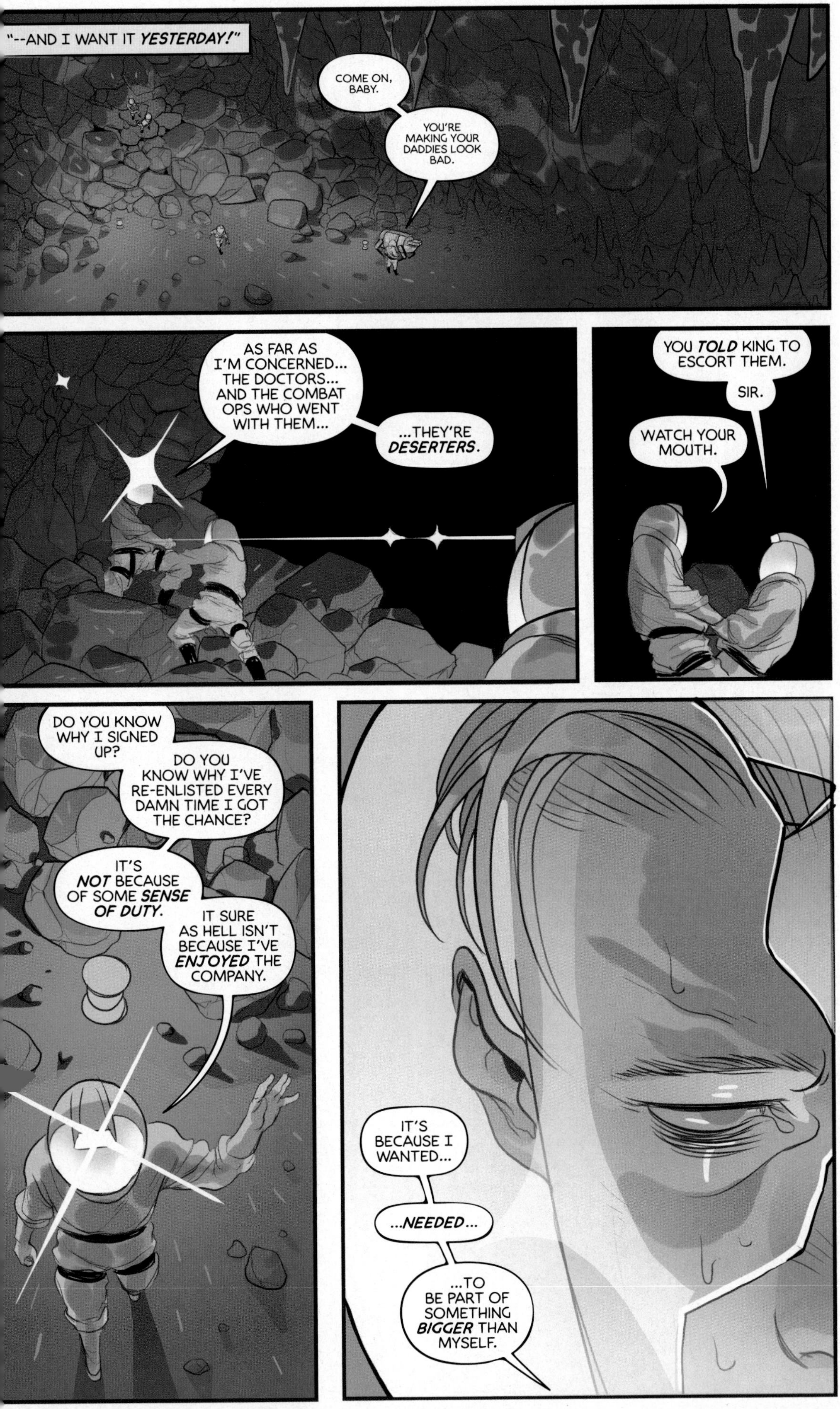
"--AND I WANT IT *YESTERDAY!*"
COME ON, BABY.
YOU'RE MAKING YOUR DADDIES LOOK BAD.
AS FAR AS I'M CONCERNED... THE DOCTORS... AND THE COMBAT OPS WHO WENT WITH THEM...
...THEY'RE *DESERTERS*.
YOU *TOLD* KING TO ESCORT THEM.
SIR.
WATCH YOUR MOUTH.
DO YOU KNOW WHY I SIGNED UP?
DO YOU KNOW WHY I'VE RE-ENLISTED EVERY DAMN TIME I GOT THE CHANCE?
IT'S *NOT* BECAUSE OF SOME *SENSE OF DUTY*.
IT SURE AS HELL ISN'T BECAUSE I'VE *ENJOYED* THE COMPANY.
IT'S BECAUSE I WANTED...
...NEEDED...
...TO BE PART OF SOMETHING *BIGGER* THAN MYSELF.

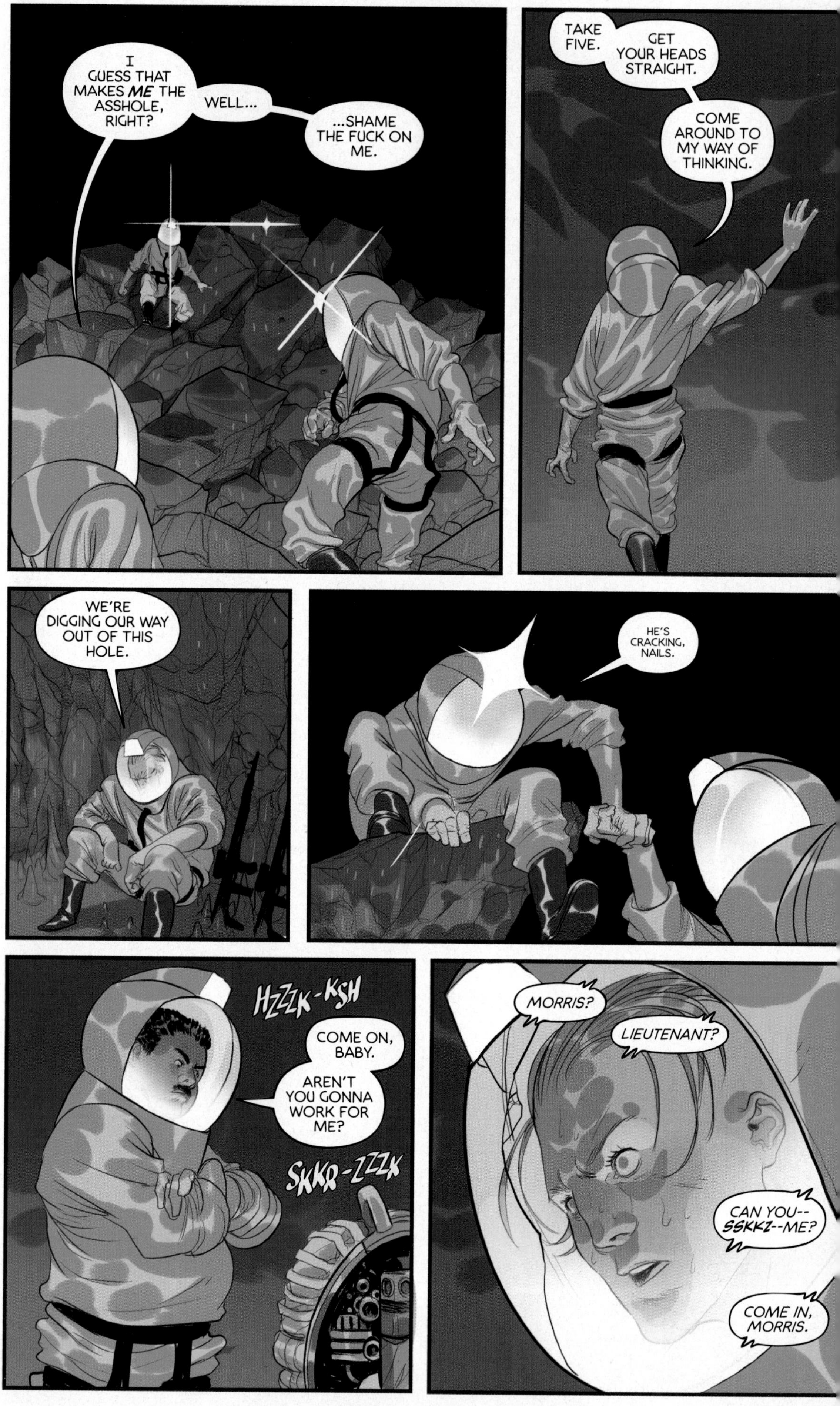
I GUESS THAT MAKES *ME* THE ASSHOLE, RIGHT?
WELL...
...SHAME THE FUCK ON ME.
TAKE FIVE.
GET YOUR HEADS STRAIGHT.
COME AROUND TO MY WAY OF THINKING.
WE'RE DIGGING OUR WAY OUT OF THIS HOLE.
HE'S CRACKING, NAILS.
HZZZK-KSH
COME ON, BABY.
AREN'T YOU GONNA WORK FOR ME?
SKKR-ZZZK
MORRIS?
LIEUTENANT?
CAN YOU-- SSKKZ--ME?
COME IN, MORRIS.

MAJOR KUL!
I HEAR YOU.
YOU'RE COMING IN LOUD AND CLEAR.
WHAT'S GOING ON DOWN THERE?
DID YOU SPLIT YOUR DAMNED TEAM?
I ADVISED AGAINST THAT COURSE OF ACTION, SIR.
THEY WEREN'T LISTENING.
I THINK MAYBE THEY'VE BEEN ***COMPROMISED***.
THEY'RE NOT THINKING CLEARLY.
KUL-- CAN HE HEAR ME?
WHO ARE YOU TALKING TO?
CAN ***WHO*** HEAR YOU?
MORRIS, THE MULE'S NOT PICKING UP ANYTHING BUT SOME SORT OF ***KINETIC ACTIVITY***.
IT MIGHT BE A MINOR TREMOR...
...OR MAYBE...

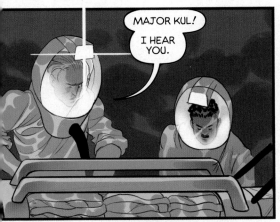

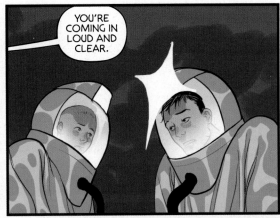

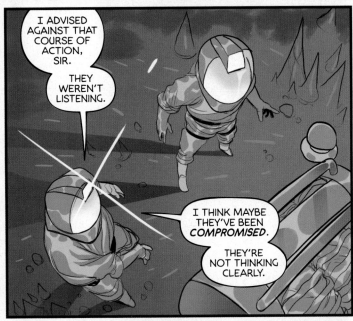

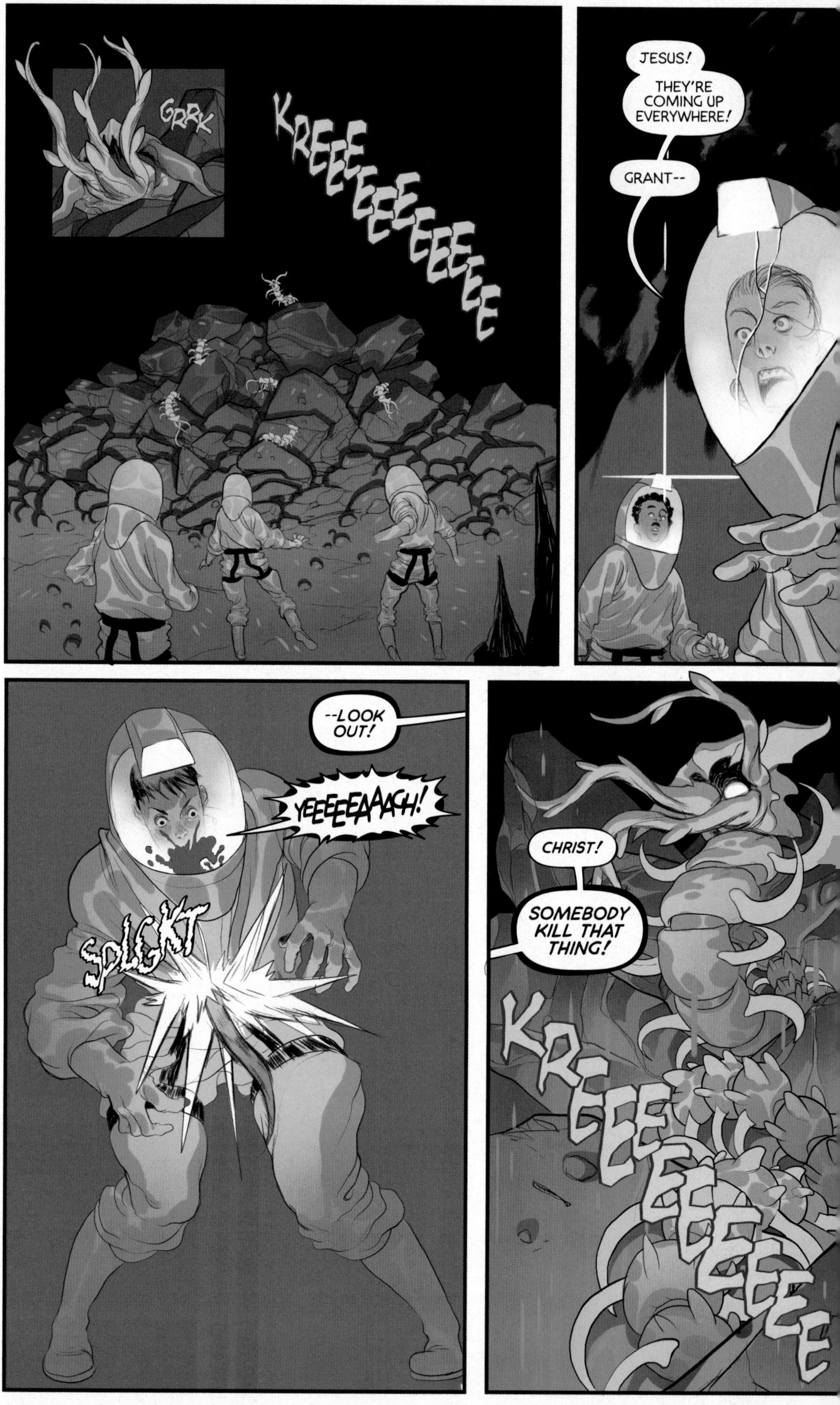
GRRK
KREEEEEEEEEEEEEE
JESUS!
THEY'RE COMING UP EVERYWHERE!
GRANT--
--LOOK OUT!
YEEEEAAACH!
SPLGKT
CHRIST!
SOMEBODY KILL THAT THING!
KR-EEEEEEEEE

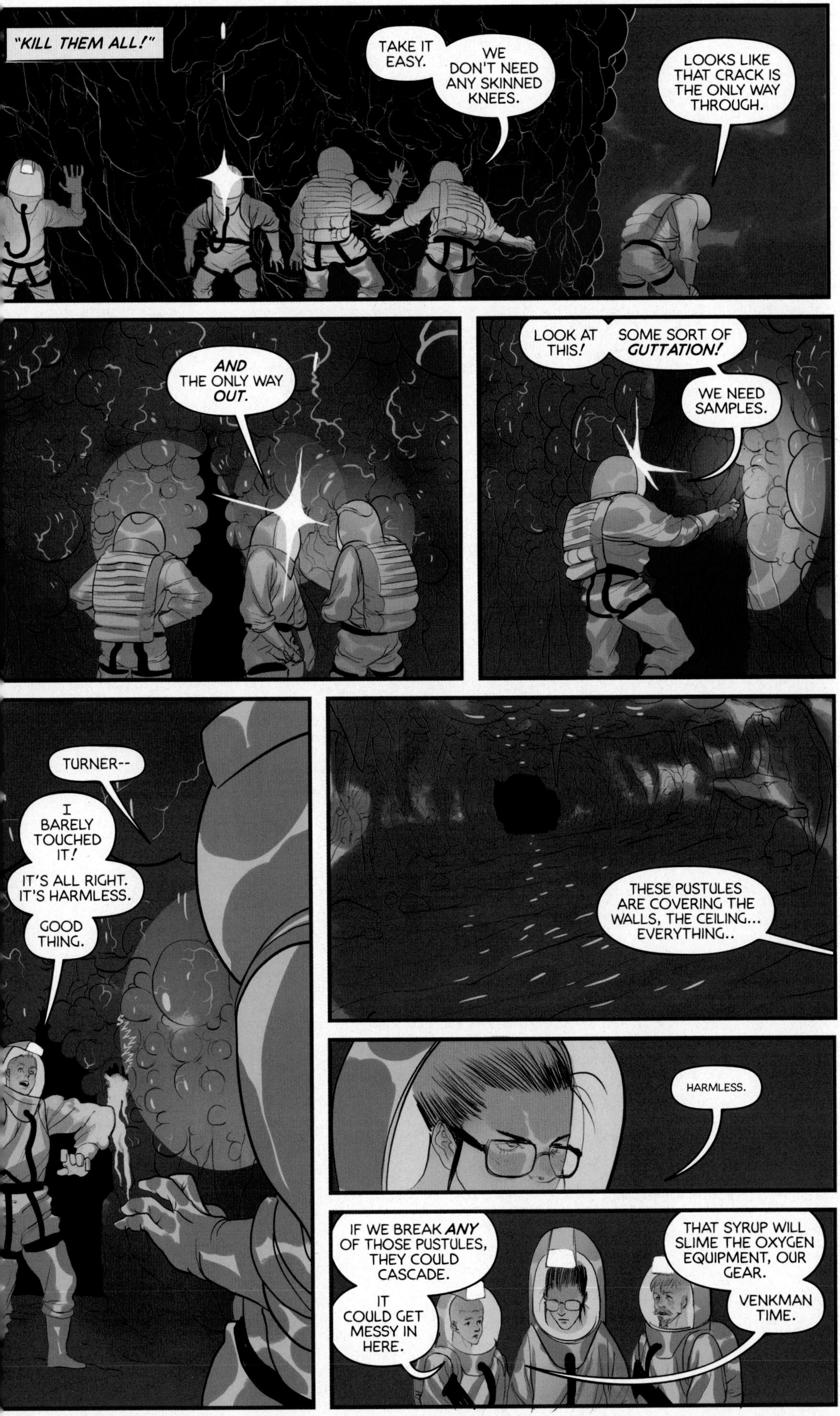
"KILL THEM ALL!"
TAKE IT EASY.
WE DON'T NEED ANY SKINNED KNEES.
LOOKS LIKE THAT CRACK IS THE ONLY WAY THROUGH.
AND THE ONLY WAY OUT.
LOOK AT THIS!
SOME SORT OF GUTTATION!
WE NEED SAMPLES.
TURNER--
I BARELY TOUCHED IT!
IT'S ALL RIGHT. IT'S HARMLESS.
GOOD THING.
THESE PUSTULES ARE COVERING THE WALLS, THE CEILING... EVERYTHING..
HARMLESS.
IF WE BREAK ANY OF THOSE PUSTULES, THEY COULD CASCADE.
IT COULD GET MESSY IN HERE.
THAT SYRUP WILL SLIME THE OXYGEN EQUIPMENT, OUR GEAR.
VENKMAN TIME.

SCOTT, HOW'S THAT RADIO?

WE DON'T *NEED* THE RADIO.

WE CAN FIGURE OUT A WAY THROUGH THIS.

BzzZZTBZZAP AABzzZAABzzA

THE SOUND! TURN IT OFF!

ZZTBZ AABzz

WHAT THE FUCK?

AMELIA-- WE DON'T HEAR *ANYTHING.*

GUYS?

AAARRRRAAAAAACH!

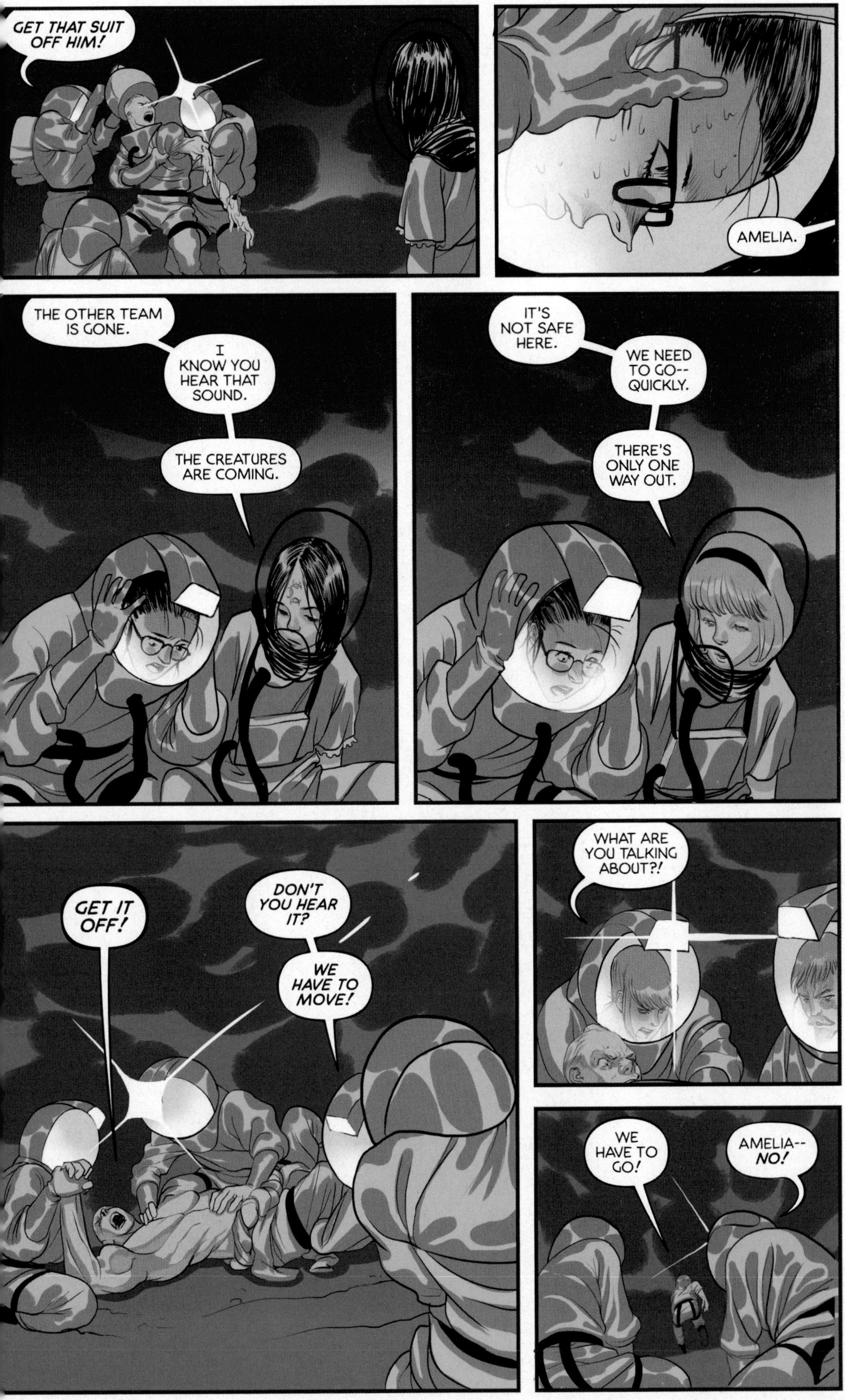
GET THAT SUIT OFF HIM!
AMELIA.
THE OTHER TEAM IS GONE.
I KNOW YOU HEAR THAT SOUND.
THE CREATURES ARE COMING.
IT'S NOT SAFE HERE.
WE NEED TO GO-- QUICKLY.
THERE'S ONLY ONE WAY OUT.
GET IT OFF!
DON'T YOU HEAR IT?
WE HAVE TO MOVE!
WHAT ARE YOU TALKING ABOUT?!
WE HAVE TO GO!
AMELIA-- NO!

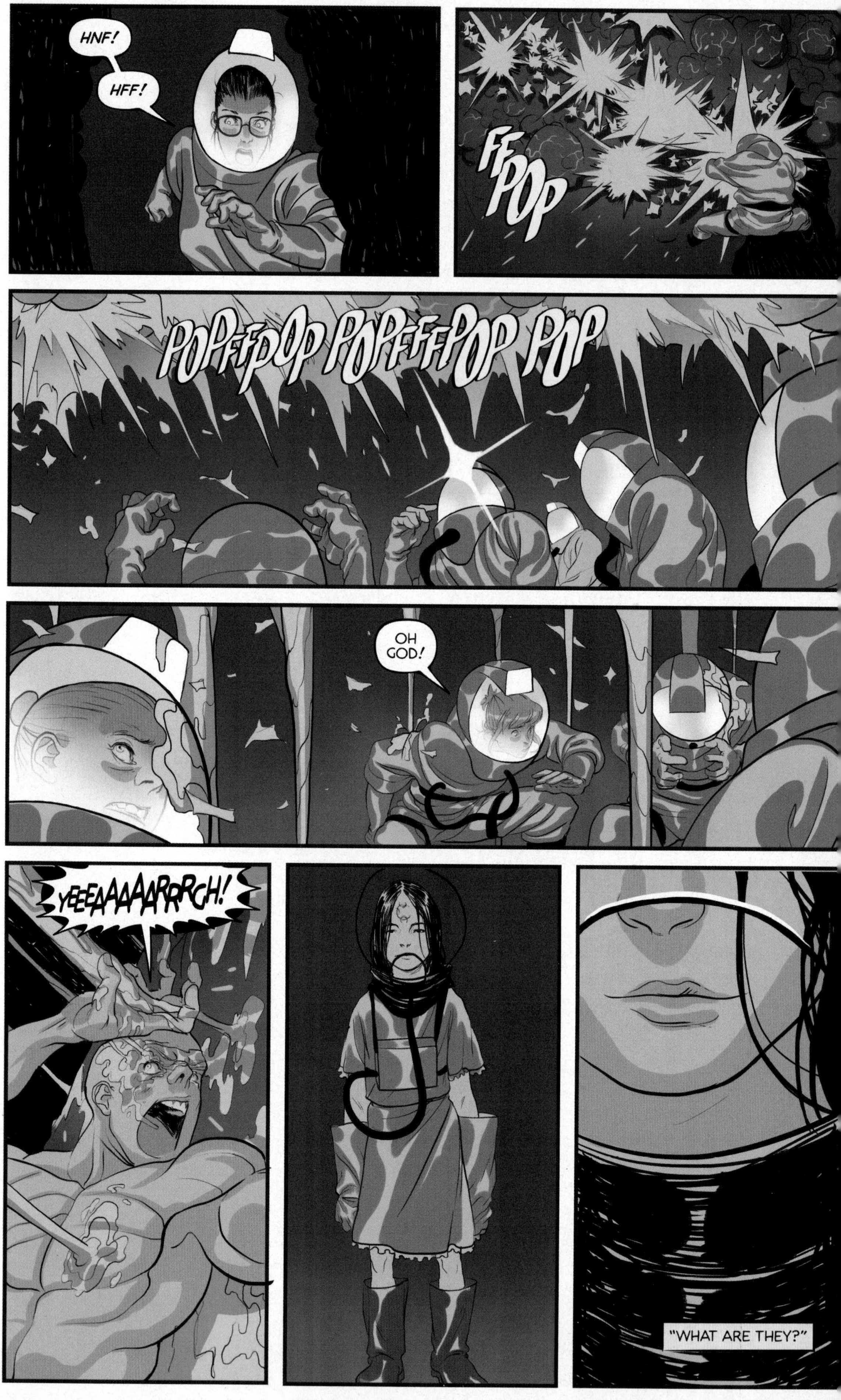
HNF!
HFF!
FFPOP
POPFFPOP POPFFFPOP POP
OH GOD!
YEEEAAAAARRRGH!
"WHAT ARE THEY?"

FUCKING
BUGS!

CENTIPEDES!

THE LIGHT!

THEY'RE
NOT AFRAID
OF IT!

THEY'RE
NOT AFRAID
OF THE LIGHT!

RODRIGUEZ!
SNAP OUT
OF IT!

HELP
ME!

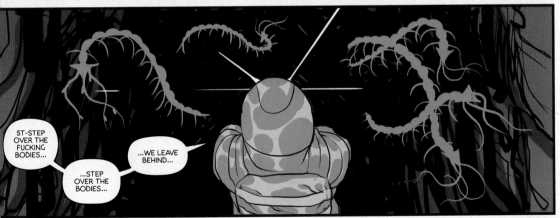

ST-STEP
OVER THE
FUCKING
BODIES...

...STEP
OVER THE
BODIES...

...WE LEAVE
BEHIND...

MORRIS!

SHOOT THE
FUCKERS!

SHOOT
THEM!

MORRIS!

YOU
NEED TO BRING
THEM TO ME,
SON.

ALL OF
THEM.

YOU
DO THAT,
I'LL BUY
YOU--SKZZ--
DINNER.

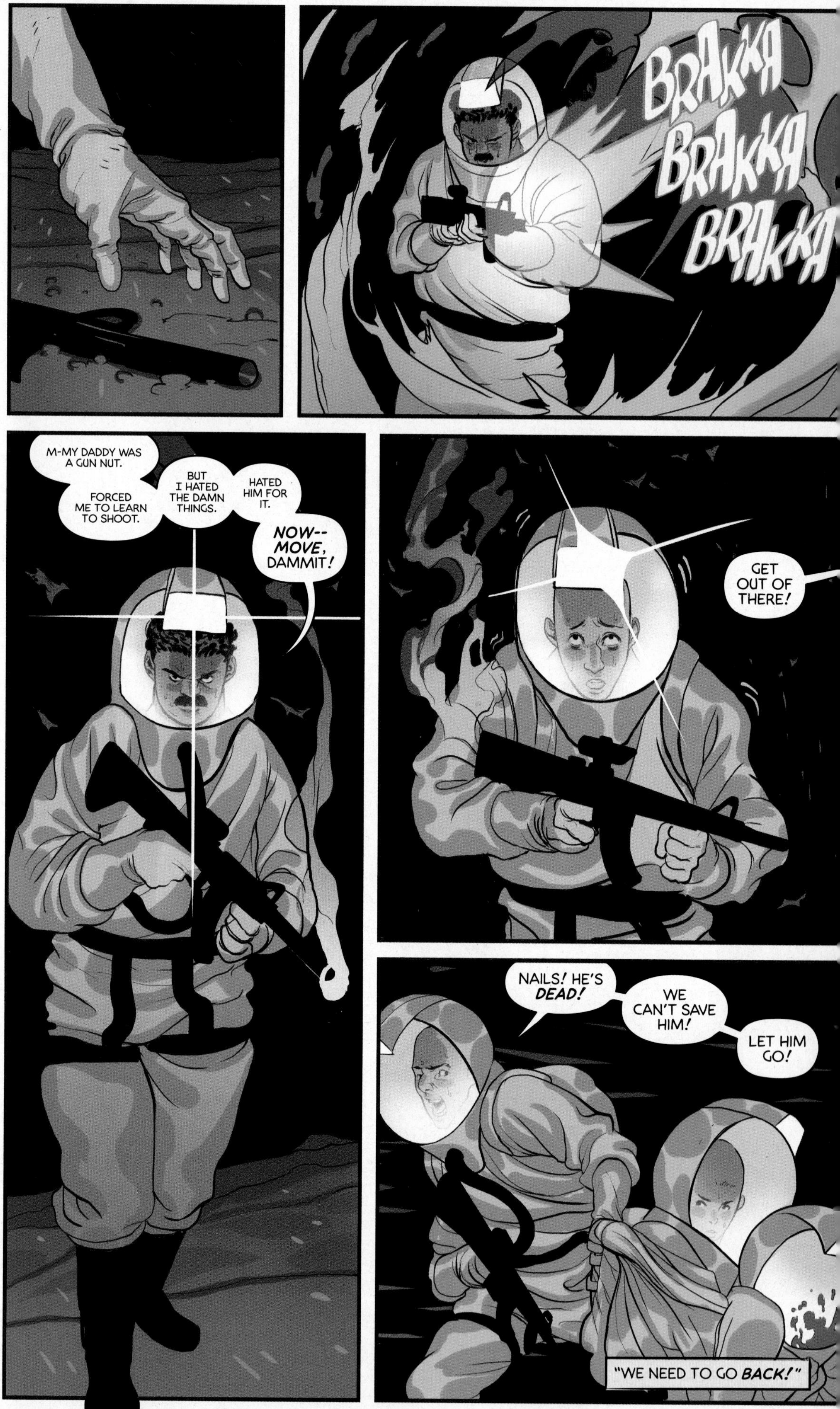

BRAKKA BRAKKA BRAKKA
M-MY DADDY WAS A GUN NUT.
FORCED ME TO LEARN TO SHOOT.
BUT I HATED THE DAMN THINGS.
HATED HIM FOR IT.
NOW-- MOVE, DAMMIT!
GET OUT OF THERE!
NAILS! HE'S DEAD!
WE CAN'T SAVE HIM!
LET HIM GO!
"WE NEED TO GO BACK!"

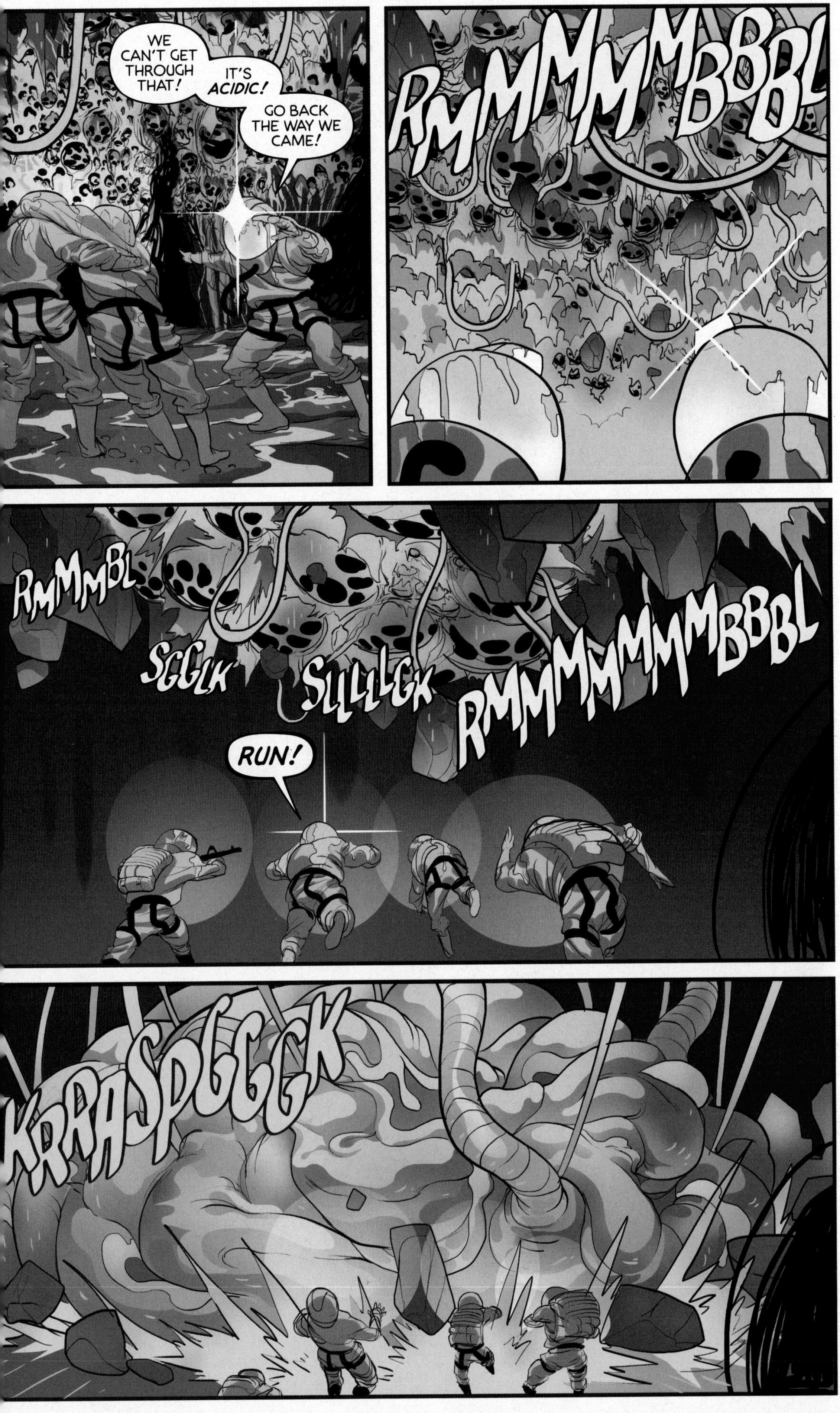
WE CAN'T GET THROUGH THAT!
IT'S ACIDIC!
GO BACK THE WAY WE CAME!
RMMMMMMBBBL
RMMMBL
SGGLK
SLLLLLGK
RMMMMMMMMBBBL
RUN!
KRRASPGGGK

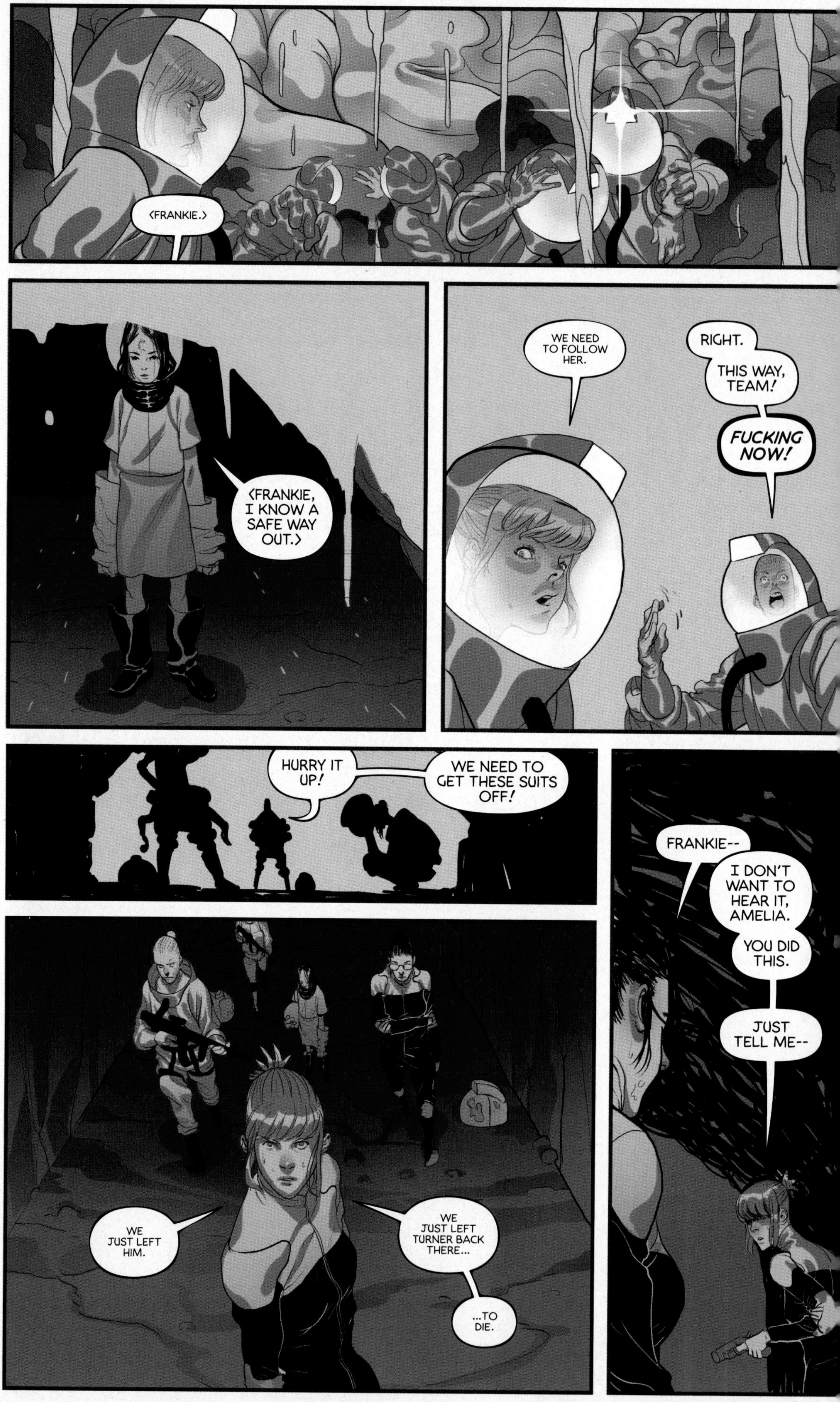
<FRANKIE.>
<FRANKIE, I KNOW A SAFE WAY OUT.>
WE NEED TO FOLLOW HER.
RIGHT.
THIS WAY, TEAM!
FUCKING NOW!
HURRY IT UP!
WE NEED TO GET THESE SUITS OFF!
WE JUST LEFT HIM.
WE JUST LEFT TURNER BACK THERE...
...TO DIE.
FRANKIE--
I DON'T WANT TO HEAR IT, AMELIA.
YOU DID THIS.
JUST TELL ME--

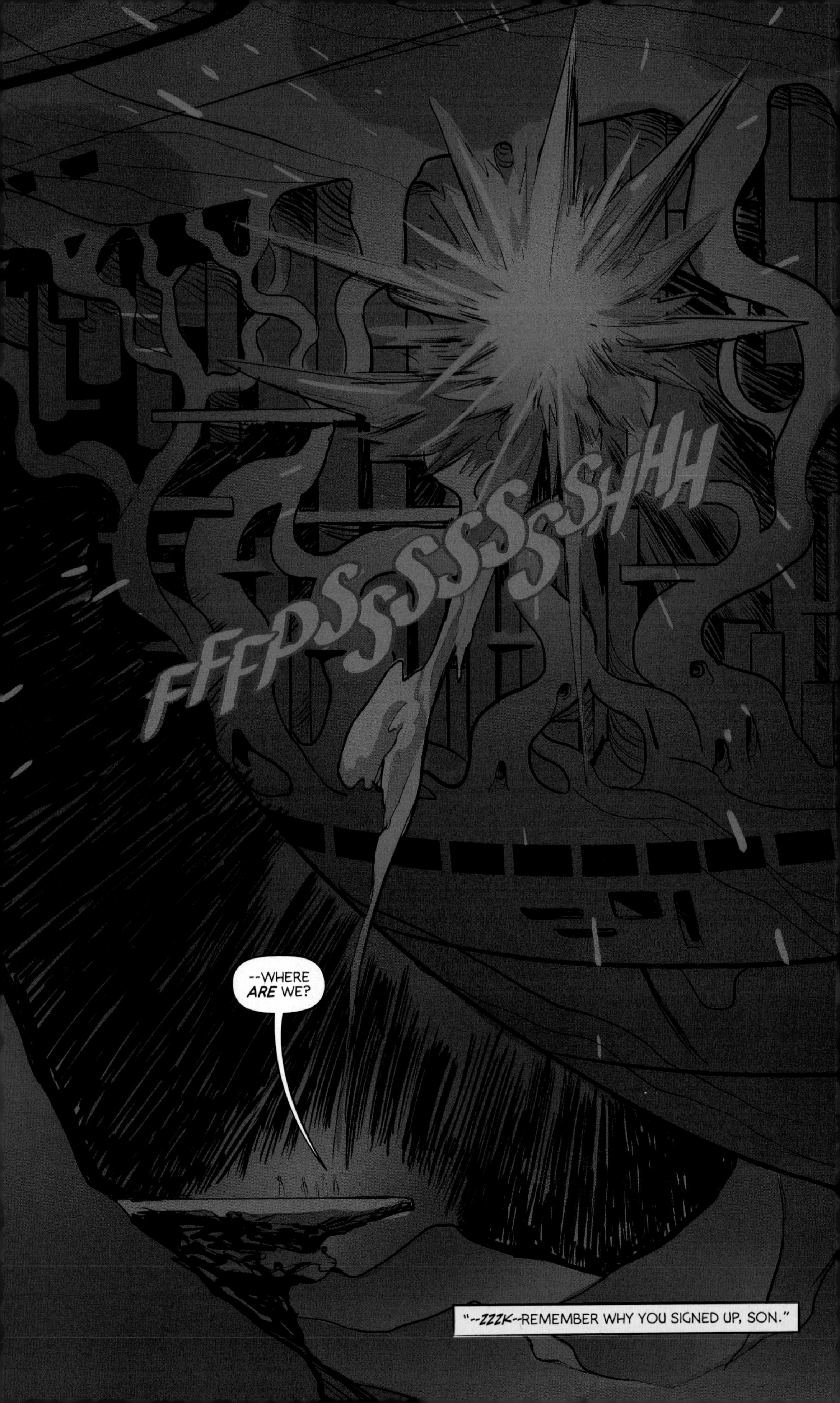

FFFPSSSSSSSSSHHH
--WHERE ARE WE?
"--ZZZK--REMEMBER WHY YOU SIGNED UP, SON."

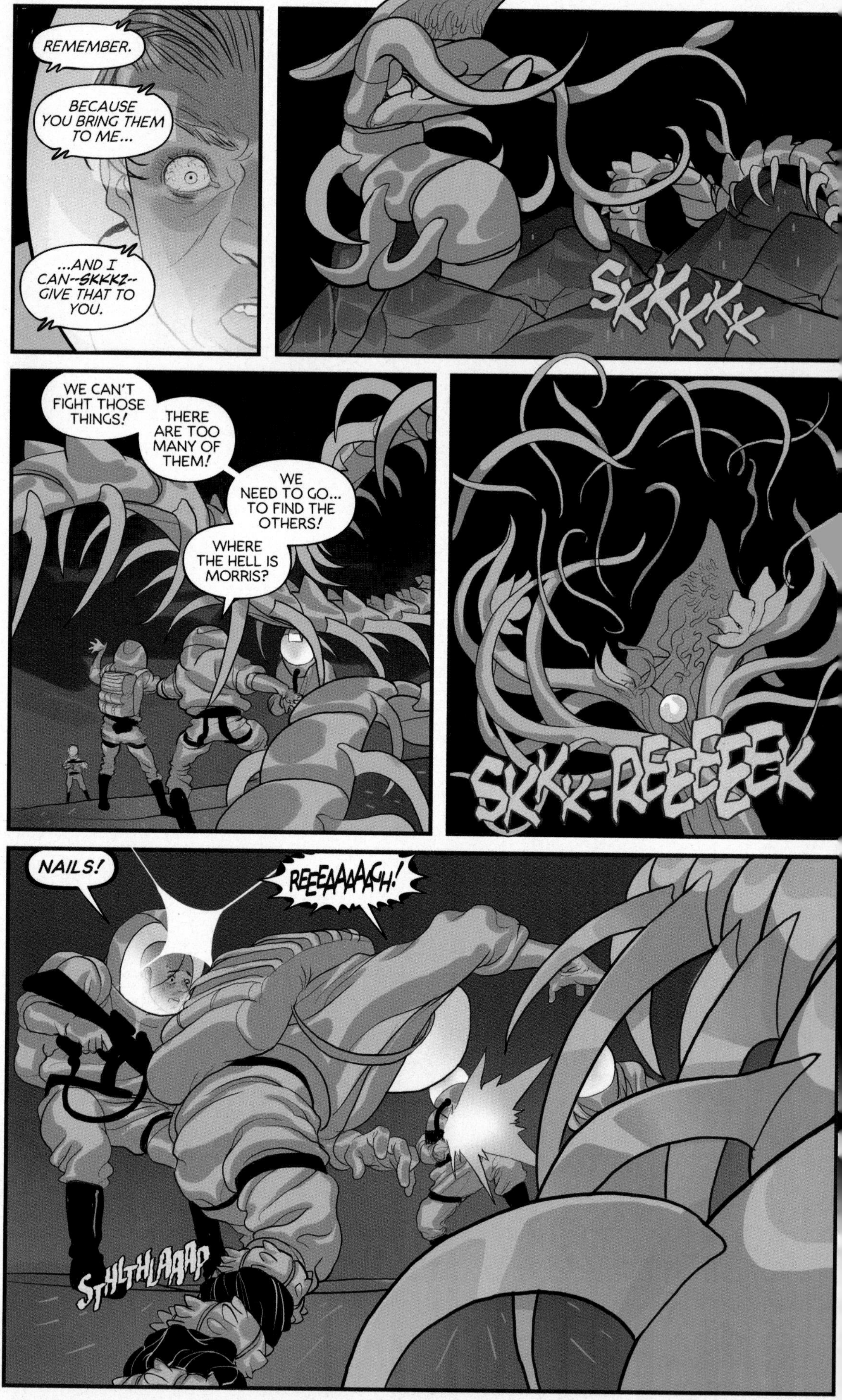
REMEMBER.
BECAUSE YOU BRING THEM TO ME...
...AND I CAN--SKKKZ--GIVE THAT TO YOU.
SKKKKK
WE CAN'T FIGHT THOSE THINGS!
THERE ARE TOO MANY OF THEM!
WE NEED TO GO... TO FIND THE OTHERS!
WHERE THE HELL IS MORRIS?
SKKK-REEEEEEK
NAILS!
REEEAAAAAGH!
STHLTHLAAAP

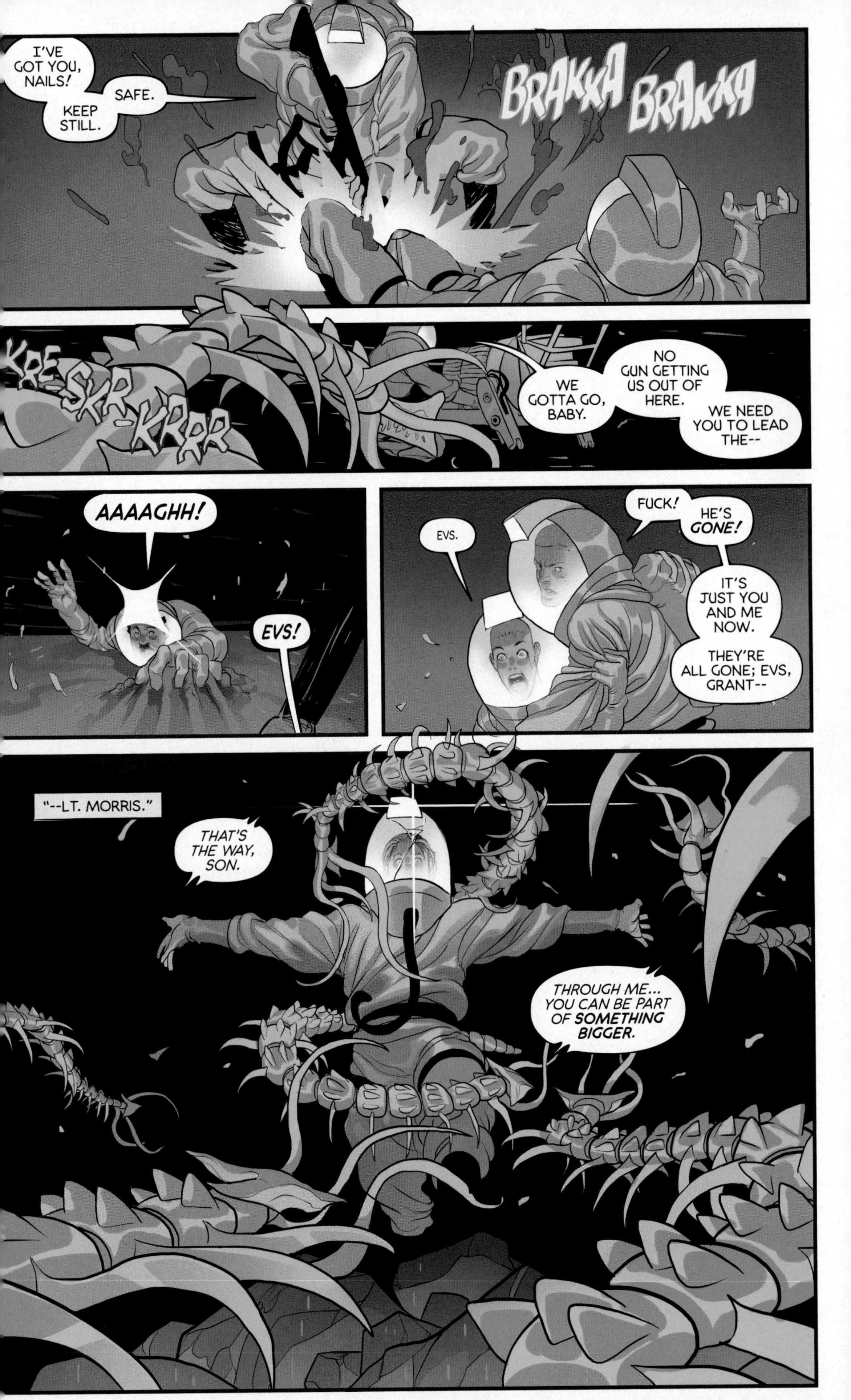
I'VE GOT YOU, NAILS!
SAFE.
KEEP STILL.
BRAKKA BRAKKA
KRE-SKR-KRRR
WE GOTTA GO, BABY.
NO GUN GETTING US OUT OF HERE.
WE NEED YOU TO LEAD THE--
AAAAGHH!
EVS!
EVS.
FUCK!
HE'S GONE!
IT'S JUST YOU AND ME NOW.
THEY'RE ALL GONE; EVS, GRANT--
"--LT. MORRIS."
THAT'S THE WAY, SON.
THROUGH ME... YOU CAN BE PART OF SOMETHING BIGGER.

Ch 03

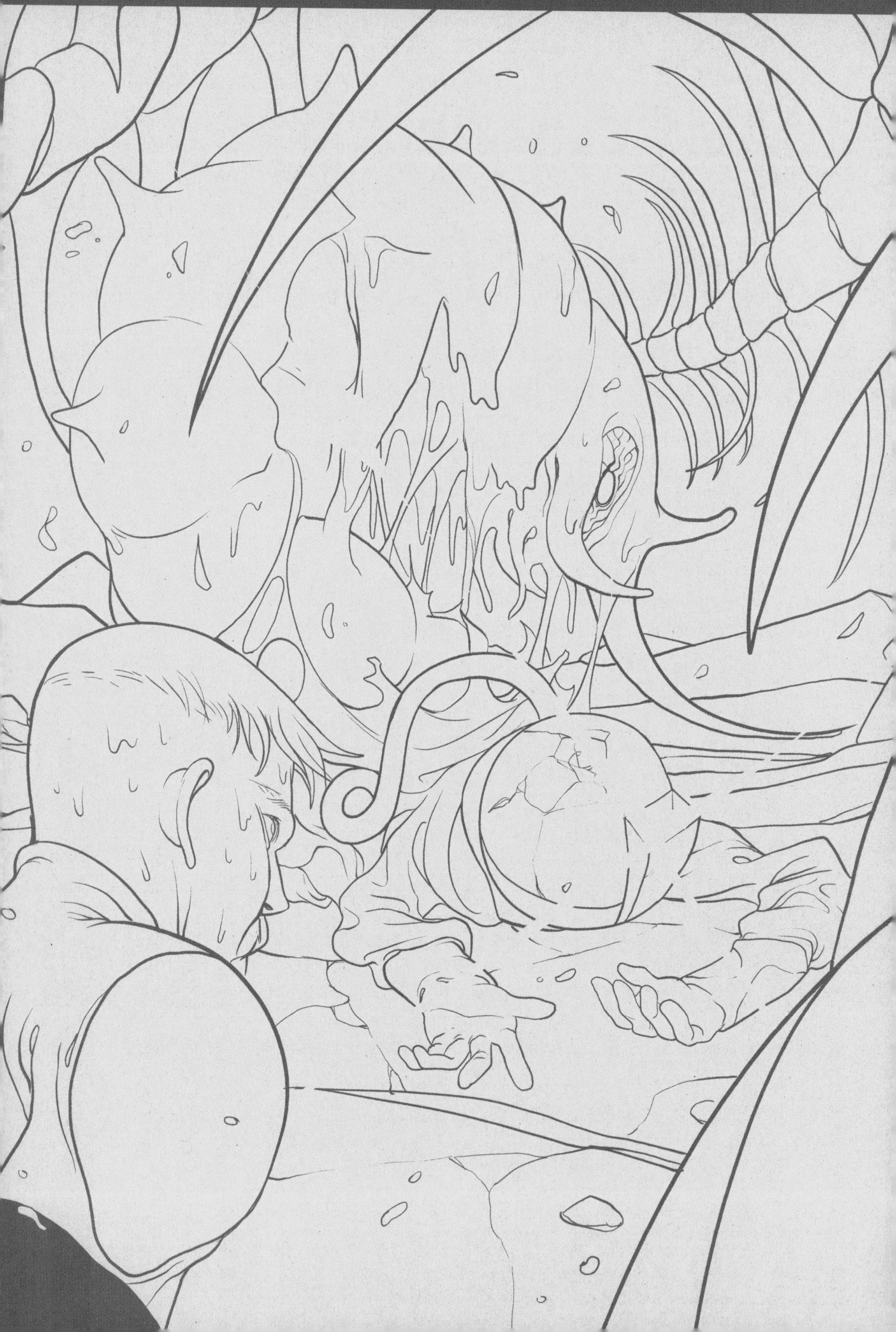

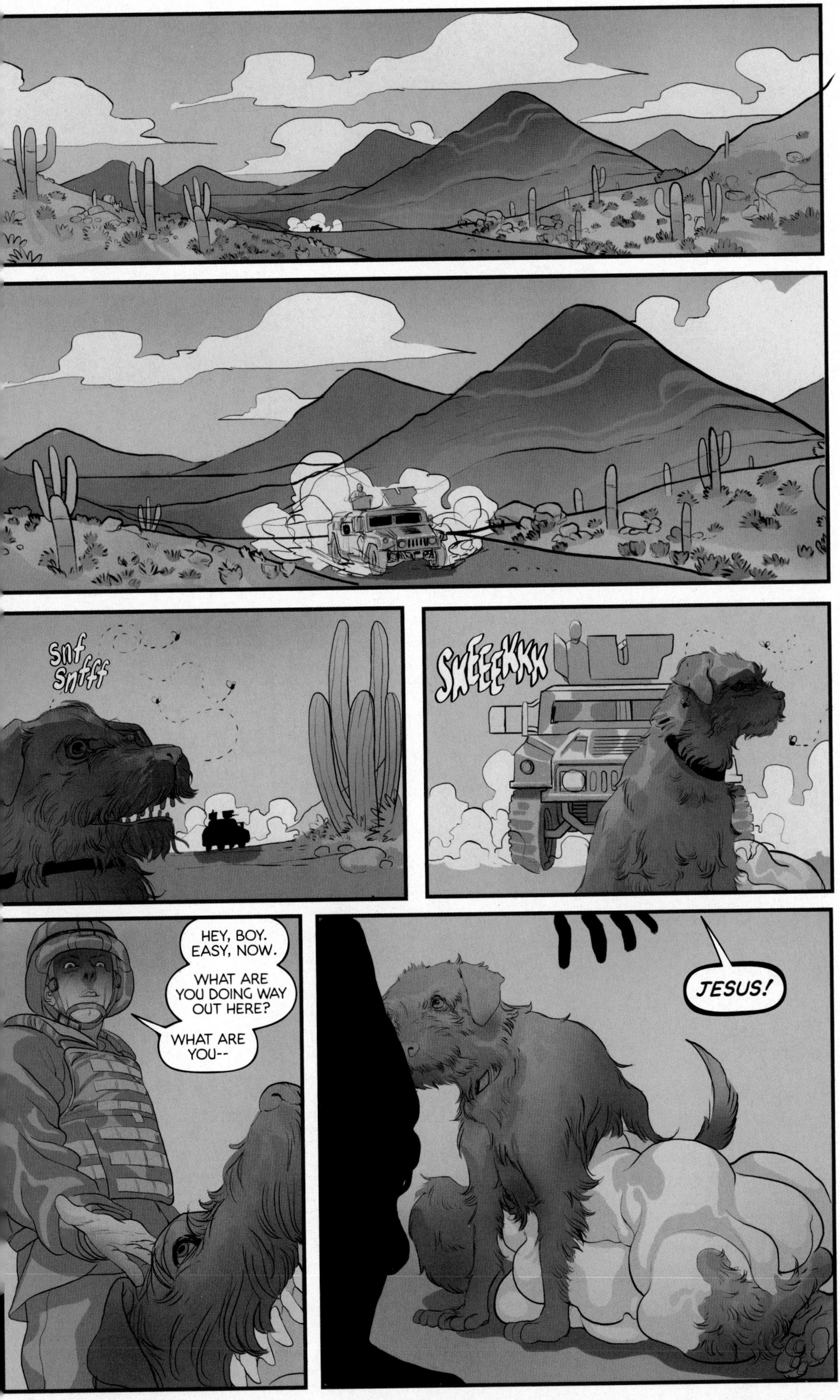
Snf
Snfff
SKEEEKKK
HEY, BOY. EASY, NOW.
WHAT ARE YOU DOING WAY OUT HERE?
WHAT ARE YOU--
JESUS!

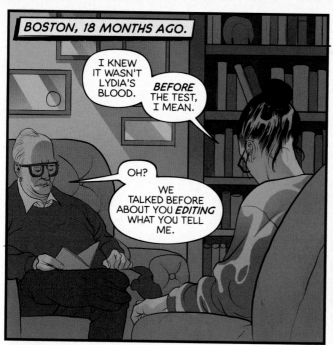

BOSTON, 18 MONTHS AGO.

I KNEW IT WASN'T LYDIA'S BLOOD.

BEFORE THE TEST, I MEAN.

OH?

WE TALKED BEFORE ABOUT YOU *EDITING* WHAT YOU TELL ME.

I LEFT *THAT* OUT.

ALL RIGHT, AMELIA.

LET'S GO THROUGH THE DREAM AGAIN.

I WALK DOWN THE HALL TO HER ROOM.

IT'S A MESS. THE WINDOW IS BROKEN, AND BLOOD...

...IS ON THE SHEETS... ON THE FLOOR.

JUST LIKE THE NIGHT LYDIA... *VANISHED.*

BUT IN THE DREAM, THERE SHE IS, SITTING ON THE BED.

CURLED UP LIKE SOME CREATURE, COVERED IN BLOOD.

AND SHE LOOKS AT ME. SHE *TALKS* TO ME.

WHAT DOES SHE SAY?

SHE SAYS THE BLOOD ISN'T HERS.

AND TODAY THEY TELL ME THE BLOOD SAMPLES DON'T MATCH LYDIA'S.

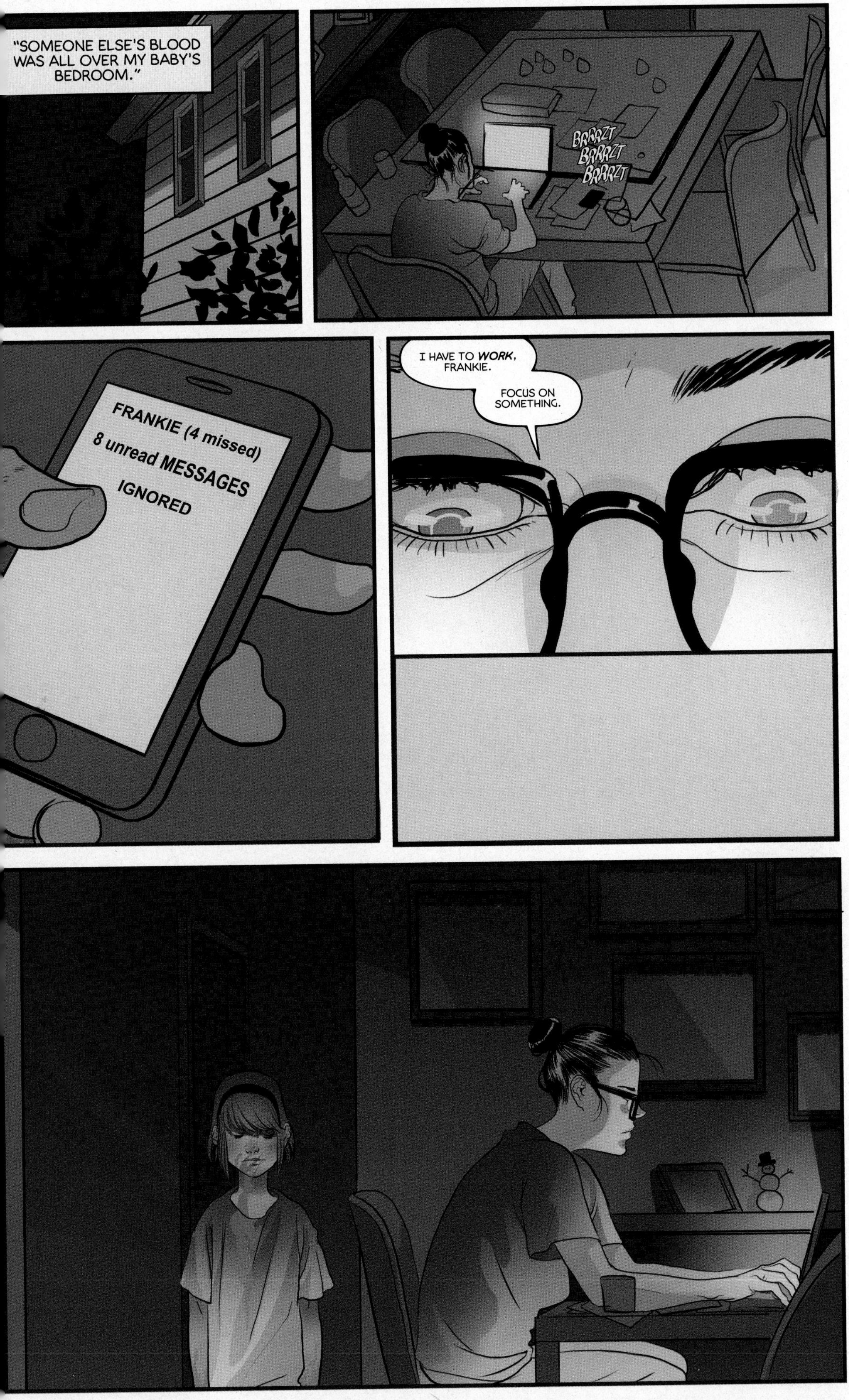
"SOMEONE ELSE'S BLOOD WAS ALL OVER MY BABY'S BEDROOM."
BRRRZT
BRRRZT
BRRRZT
FRANKIE (4 missed)
8 unread MESSAGES
IGNORED
I HAVE TO WORK, FRANKIE.
FOCUS ON SOMETHING.

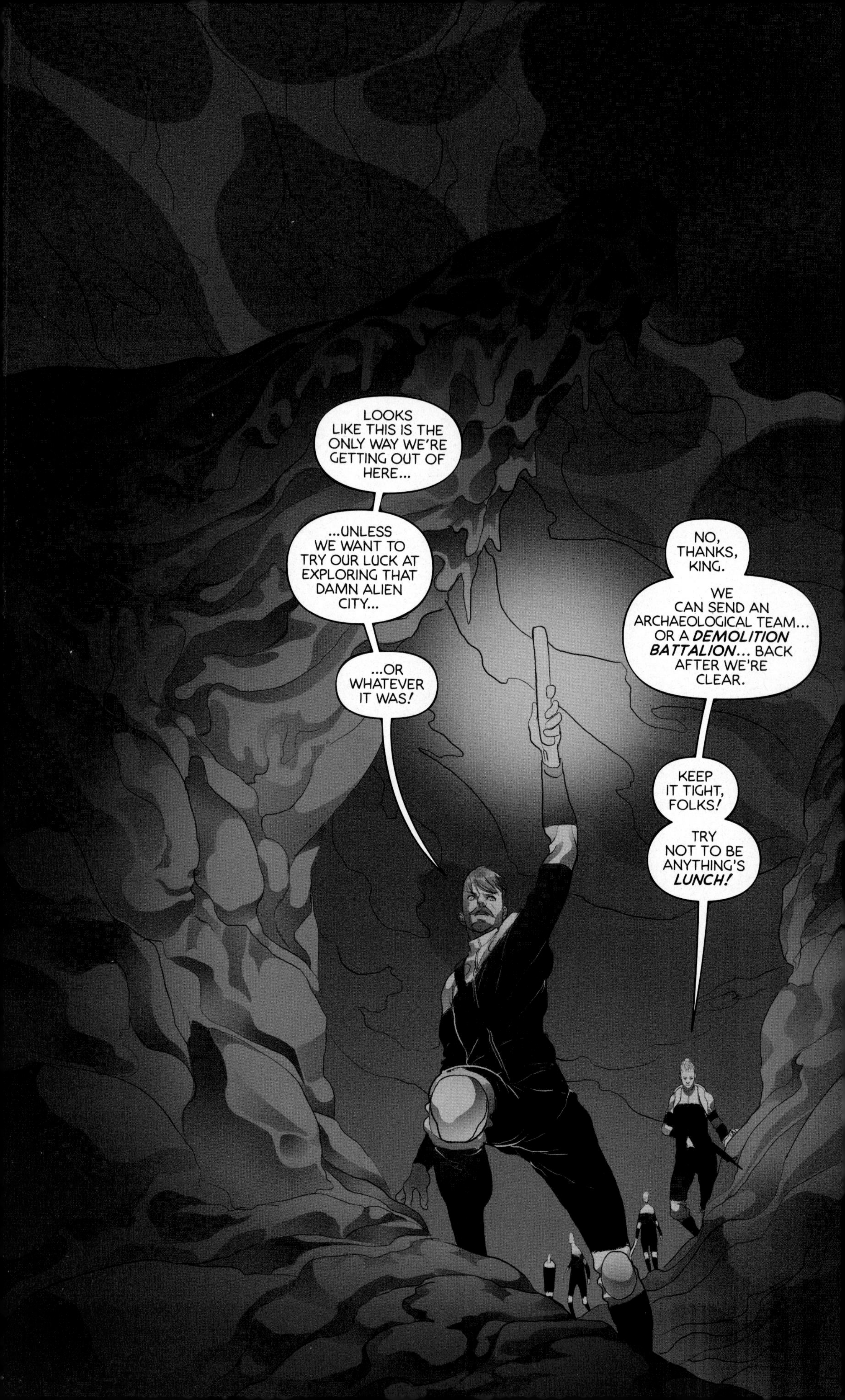

LOOKS LIKE THIS IS THE ONLY WAY WE'RE GETTING OUT OF HERE...
...UNLESS WE WANT TO TRY OUR LUCK AT EXPLORING THAT DAMN ALIEN CITY...
...OR WHATEVER IT WAS!
NO, THANKS, KING.
WE CAN SEND AN ARCHAEOLOGICAL TEAM... OR A ***DEMOLITION BATTALION***... BACK AFTER WE'RE CLEAR.
KEEP IT TIGHT, FOLKS!
TRY NOT TO BE ANYTHING'S ***LUNCH!***

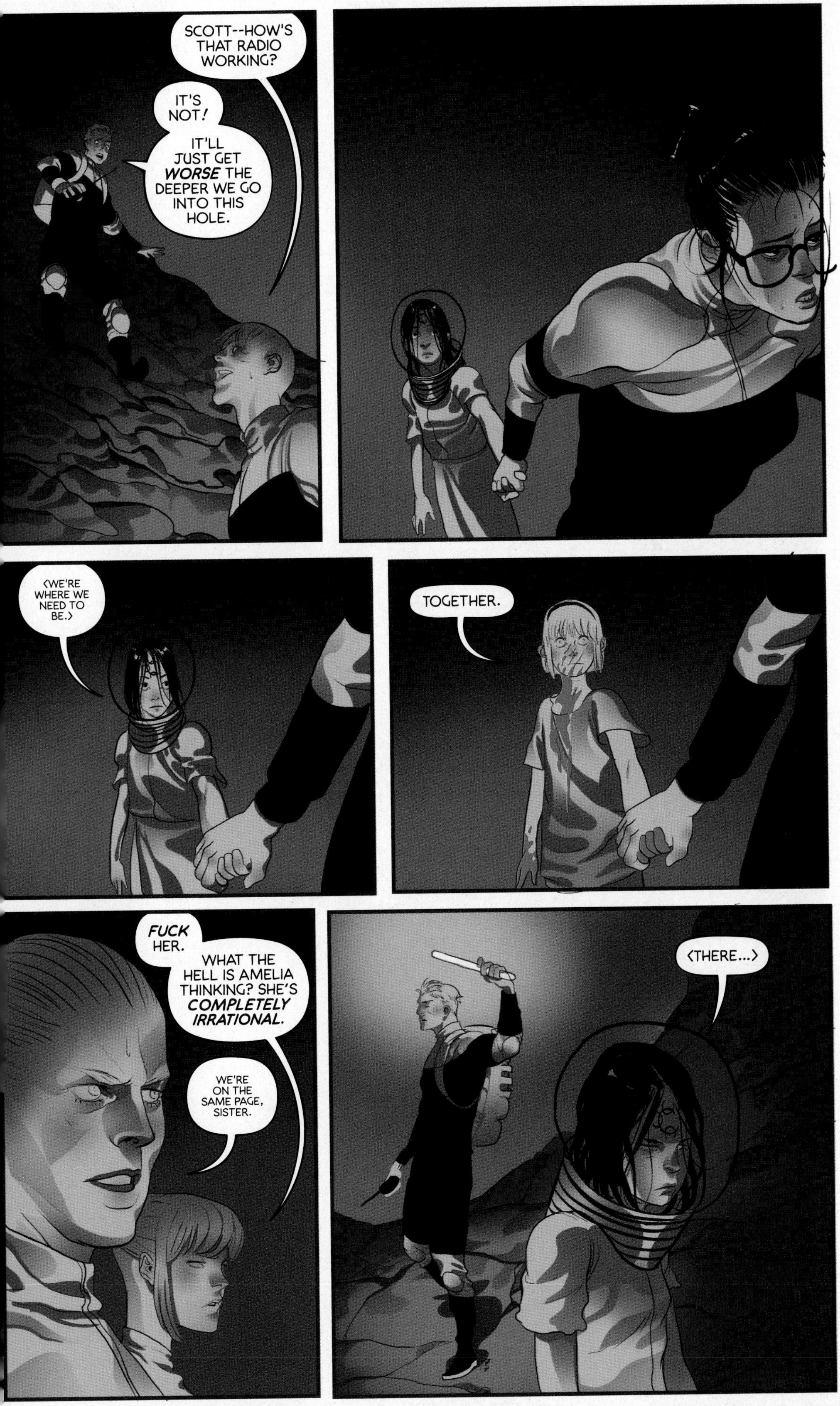
SCOTT--HOW'S THAT RADIO WORKING?
IT'S NOT!
IT'LL JUST GET WORSE THE DEEPER WE GO INTO THIS HOLE.
<WE'RE WHERE WE NEED TO BE.>
TOGETHER.
FUCK HER.
WHAT THE HELL IS AMELIA THINKING? SHE'S COMPLETELY IRRATIONAL.
WE'RE ON THE SAME PAGE, SISTER.
<THERE...>

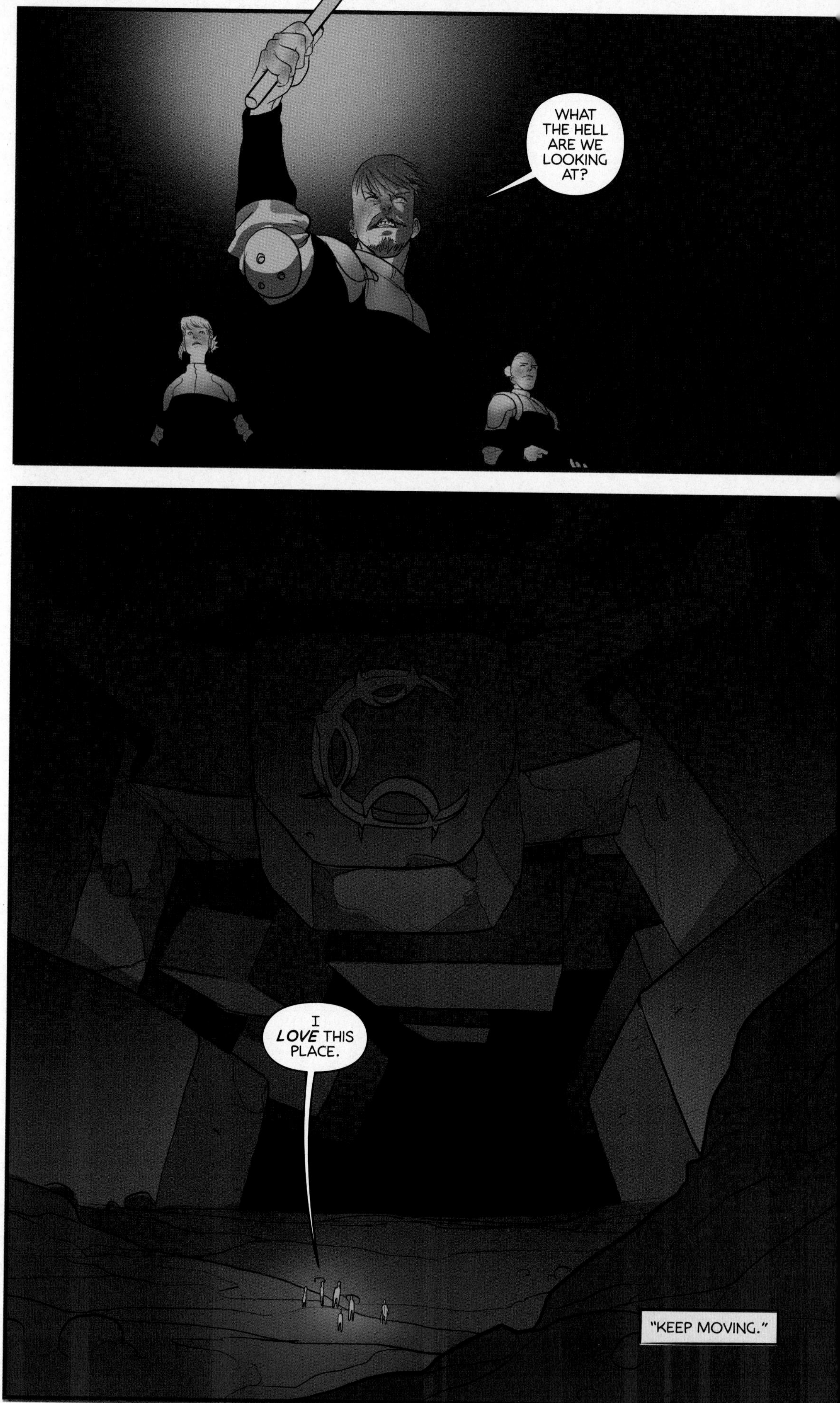
WHAT THE HELL ARE WE LOOKING AT?
I LOVE THIS PLACE.
"KEEP MOVING."

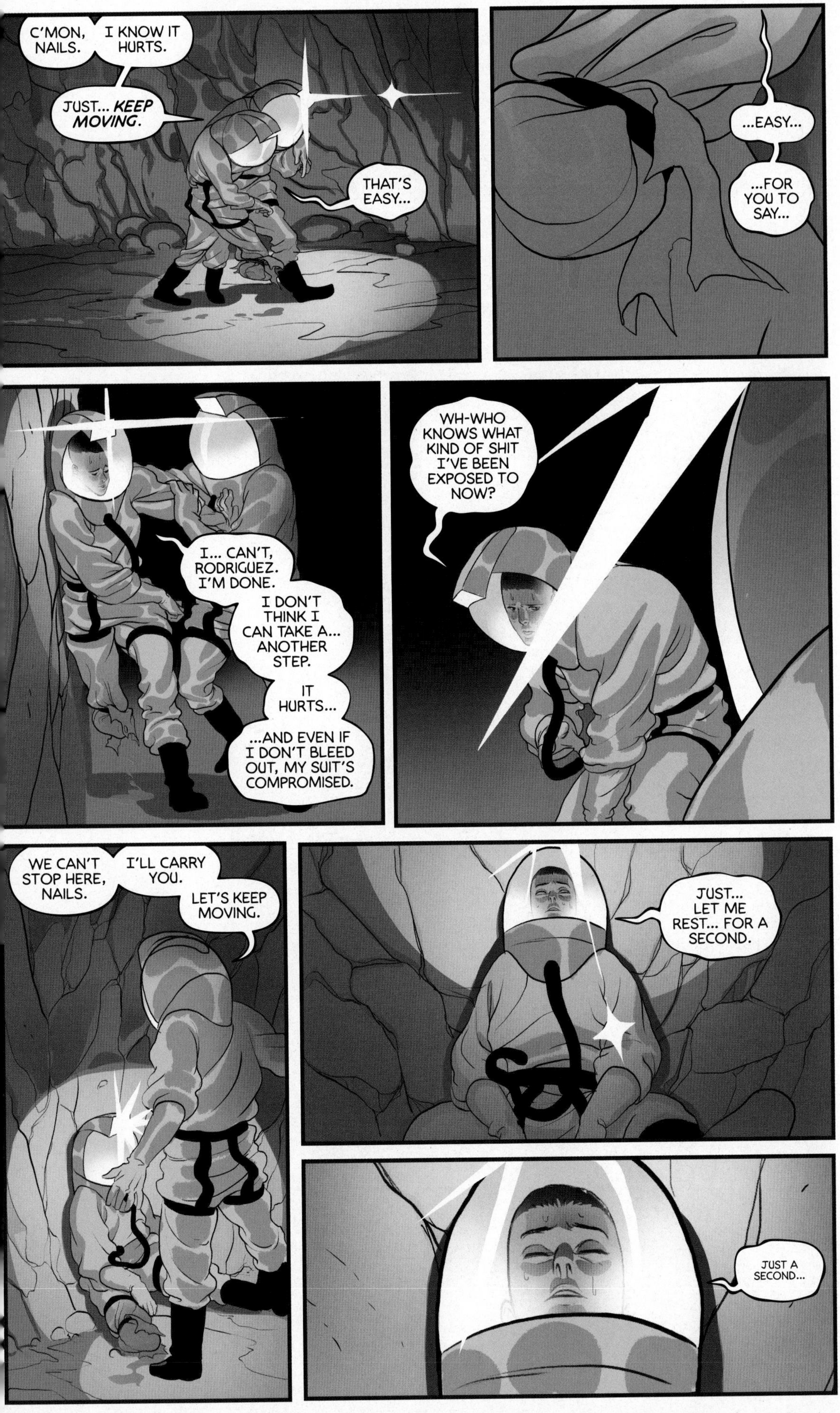
C'MON, NAILS.
I KNOW IT HURTS.
JUST... *KEEP MOVING*.
THAT'S EASY...
...EASY...
...FOR YOU TO SAY...
I... CAN'T, RODRIGUEZ. I'M DONE.
I DON'T THINK I CAN TAKE A... ANOTHER STEP.
IT HURTS...
...AND EVEN IF I DON'T BLEED OUT, MY SUIT'S COMPROMISED.
WH-WHO KNOWS WHAT KIND OF SHIT I'VE BEEN EXPOSED TO NOW?
WE CAN'T STOP HERE, NAILS.
I'LL CARRY YOU.
LET'S KEEP MOVING.
JUST... LET ME REST... FOR A SECOND.
JUST A SECOND...

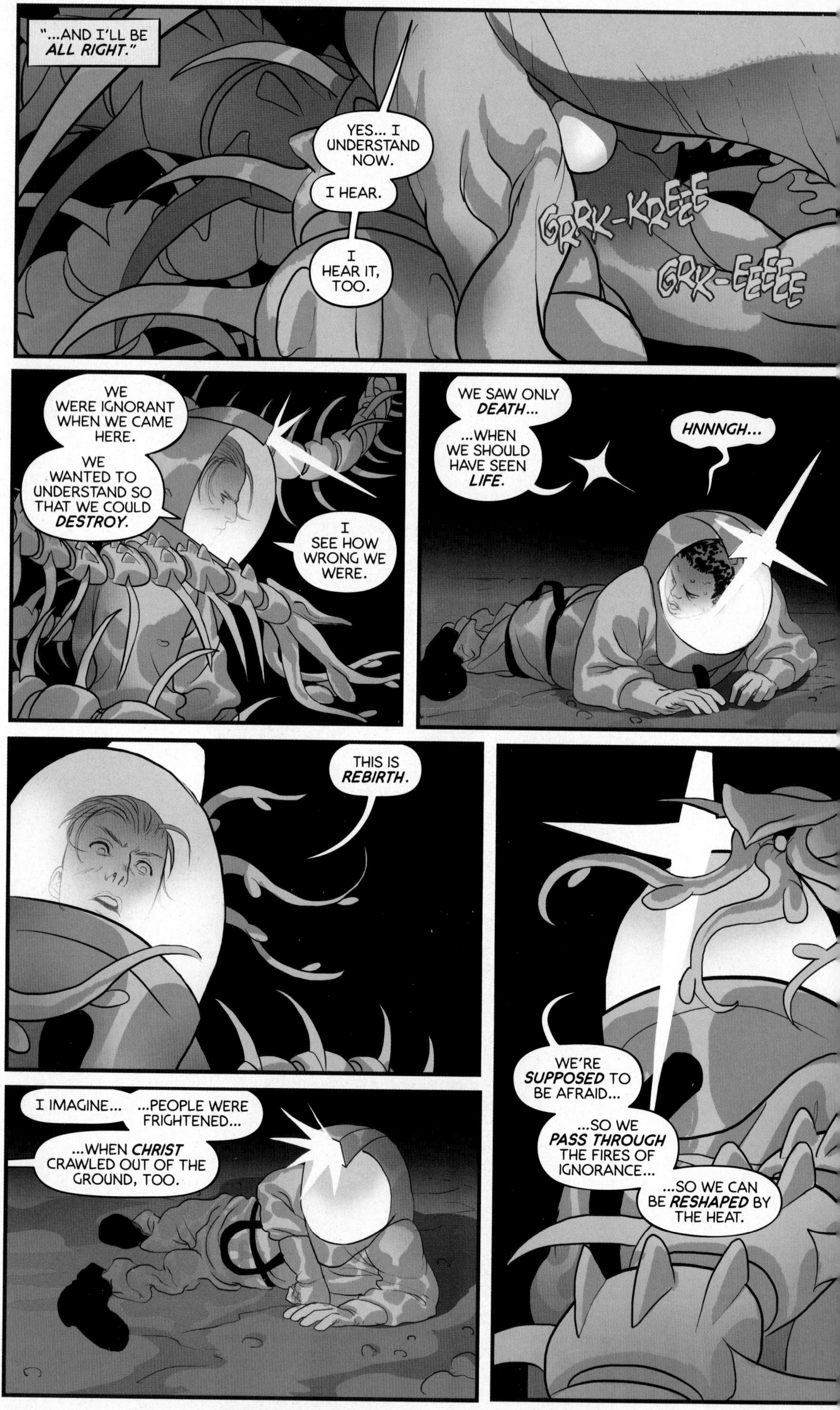
"...AND I'LL BE ALL RIGHT."
YES... I UNDERSTAND NOW.
I HEAR.
I HEAR IT, TOO.
GRRK-KREEEE
GRK-EEEEEE
WE WERE IGNORANT WHEN WE CAME HERE.
WE WANTED TO UNDERSTAND SO THAT WE COULD DESTROY.
I SEE HOW WRONG WE WERE.
WE SAW ONLY DEATH...
...WHEN WE SHOULD HAVE SEEN LIFE.
HNNNGH...
THIS IS REBIRTH.
I IMAGINE... ...PEOPLE WERE FRIGHTENED...
...WHEN CHRIST CRAWLED OUT OF THE GROUND, TOO.
WE'RE SUPPOSED TO BE AFRAID...
...SO WE PASS THROUGH THE FIRES OF IGNORANCE...
...SO WE CAN BE RESHAPED BY THE HEAT.

THIS IS THE *TRUTH* OF WHY WE CAME HERE...

...THOUGH WE DID NOT REALIZE IT...

...TO BE PART OF *SOMETHING BIGGER*...

VRRR

LOST IT...

...LOST YOUR MIND...

...AND NOW YOU'RE CRAZY...

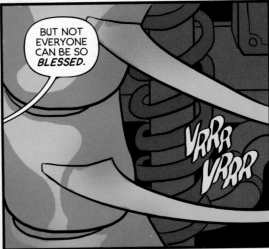

BUT NOT EVERYONE CAN BE SO *BLESSED.*

VRRR VRRR

SOME REFUSE TO *SEE.*

SOME SERVE ONLY AS *SUSTENANCE.*

AS *MEAT.*

VRRR VRRR VRRRRR

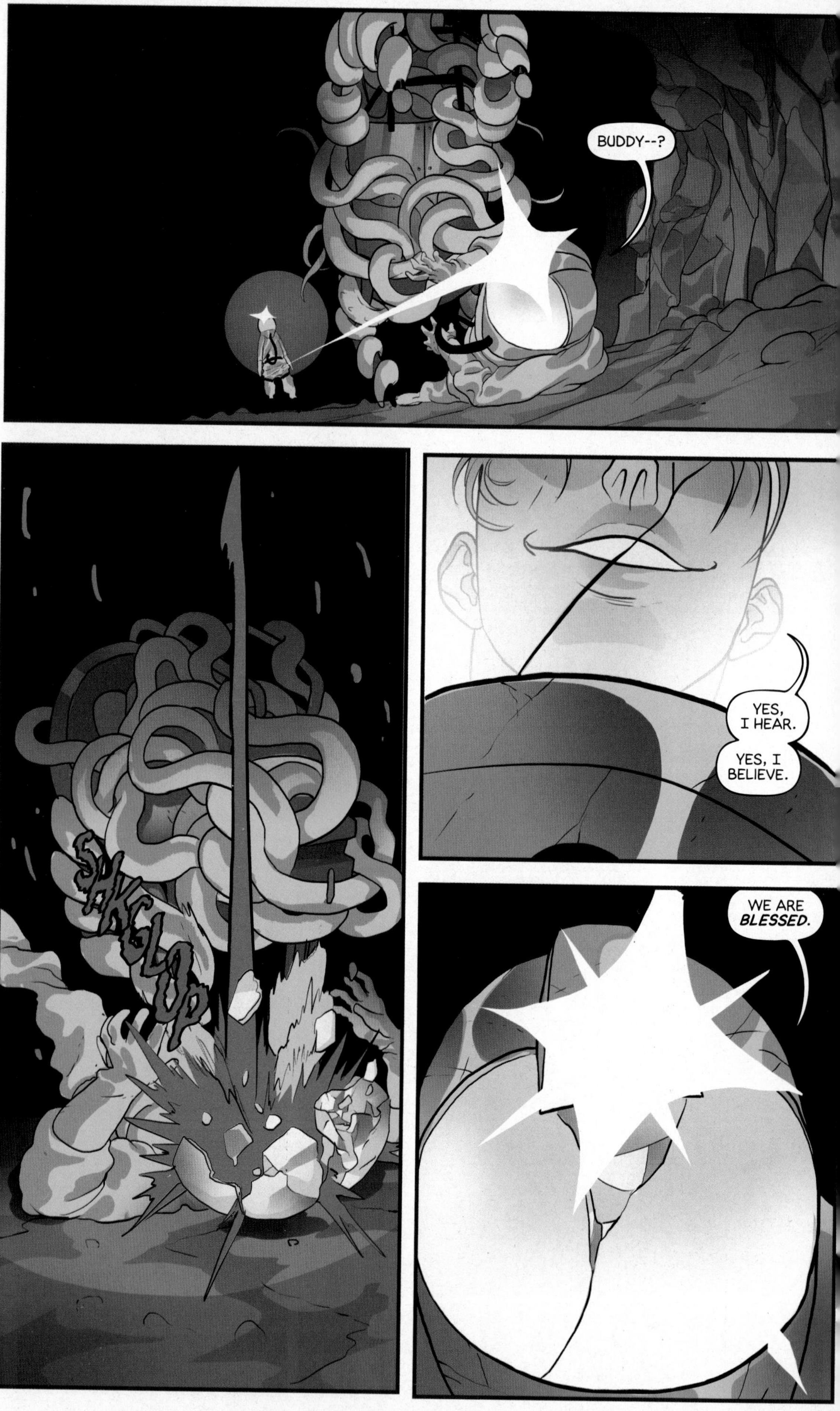
BUDDY--?
SHKGLOP
YES, I HEAR.
YES, I BELIEVE.
WE ARE *BLESSED.*

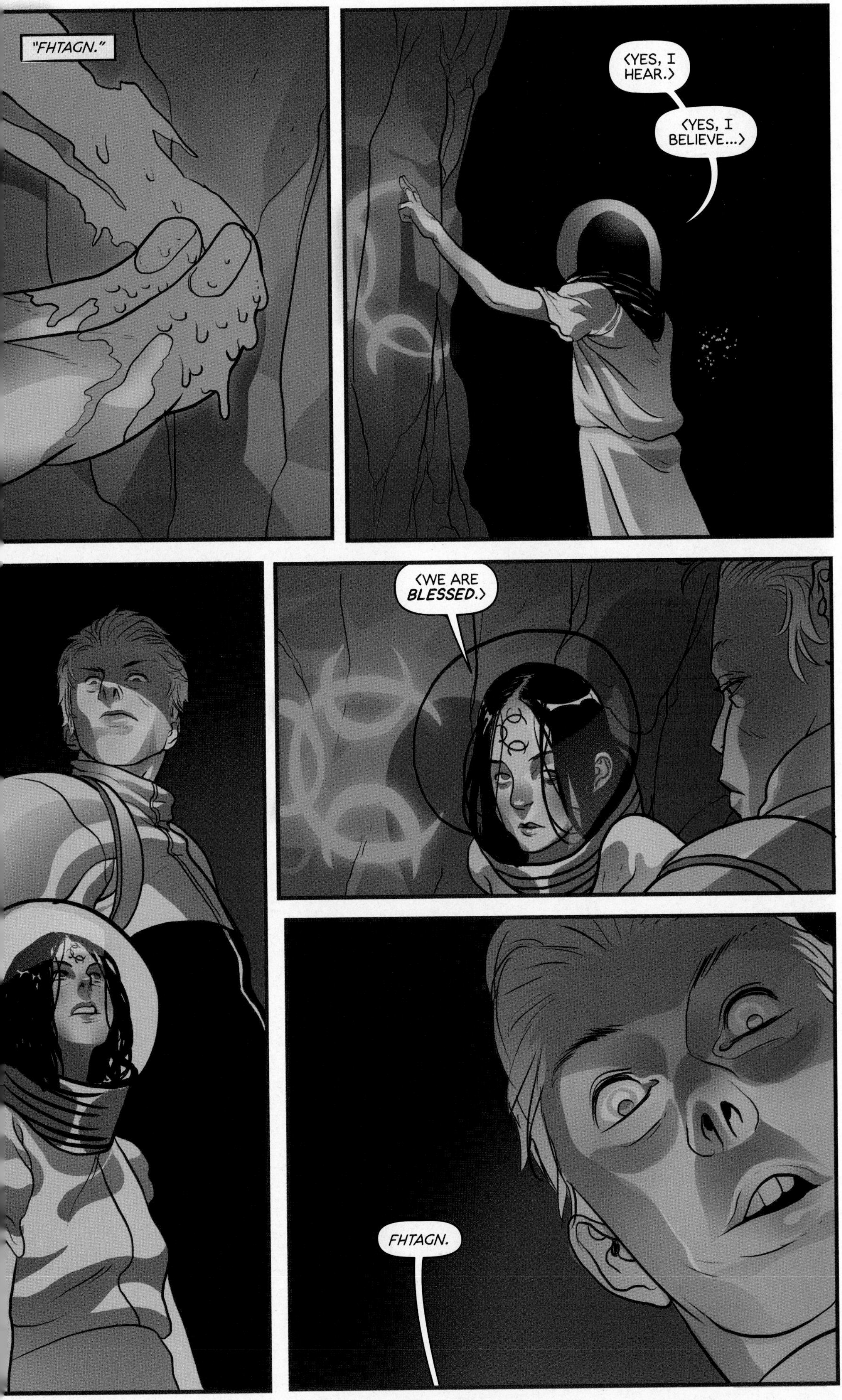
"FHTAGN."
<YES, I HEAR.>
<YES, I BELIEVE...>
<WE ARE BLESSED.>
FHTAGN.

WE ARE... BLESSED.

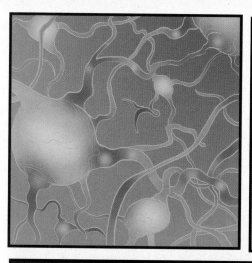

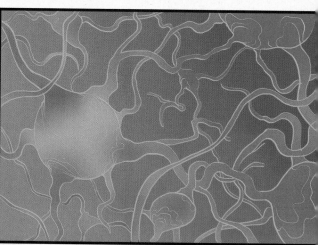

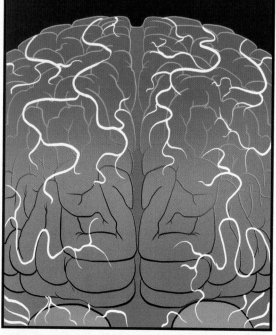

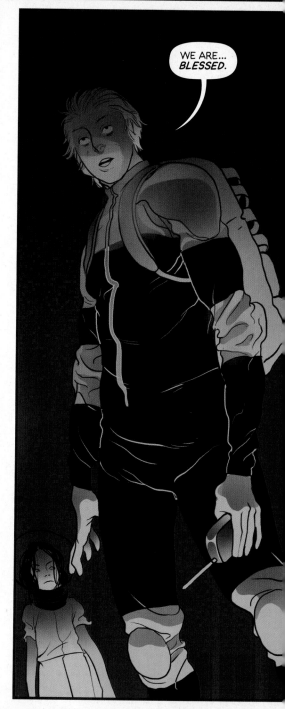

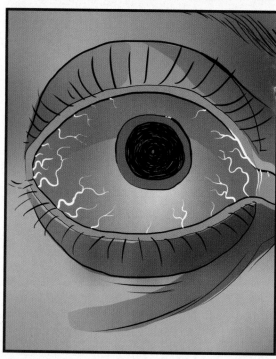

SCOTT-- WHAT'S GOING ON?

WHAT'S WRONG WITH YOU?

SCOTT, WHAT DID SHE SAY TO YOU?

ARE YOU OKAY?

〈WHAT DID YOU DO TO HIM!!〉

DON'T TALK TO HER THAT WAY, FRANKIE!

WHAT IS GOING ON WITH YOU?

THAT GIRL ISN'T LYDIA!

WE DON'T KNOW WHO SHE IS!

YOU'VE BEEN FUCKING US AT EVERY TURN!

TURNER IS DEAD BECAUSE YOU CAN'T THINK OF ANYONE BUT YOURSELF!

YOU ALL NEED TO STAND DOWN.

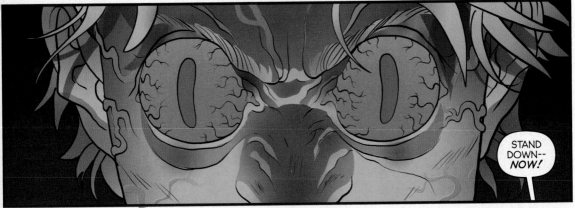

STAND DOWN-- NOW!

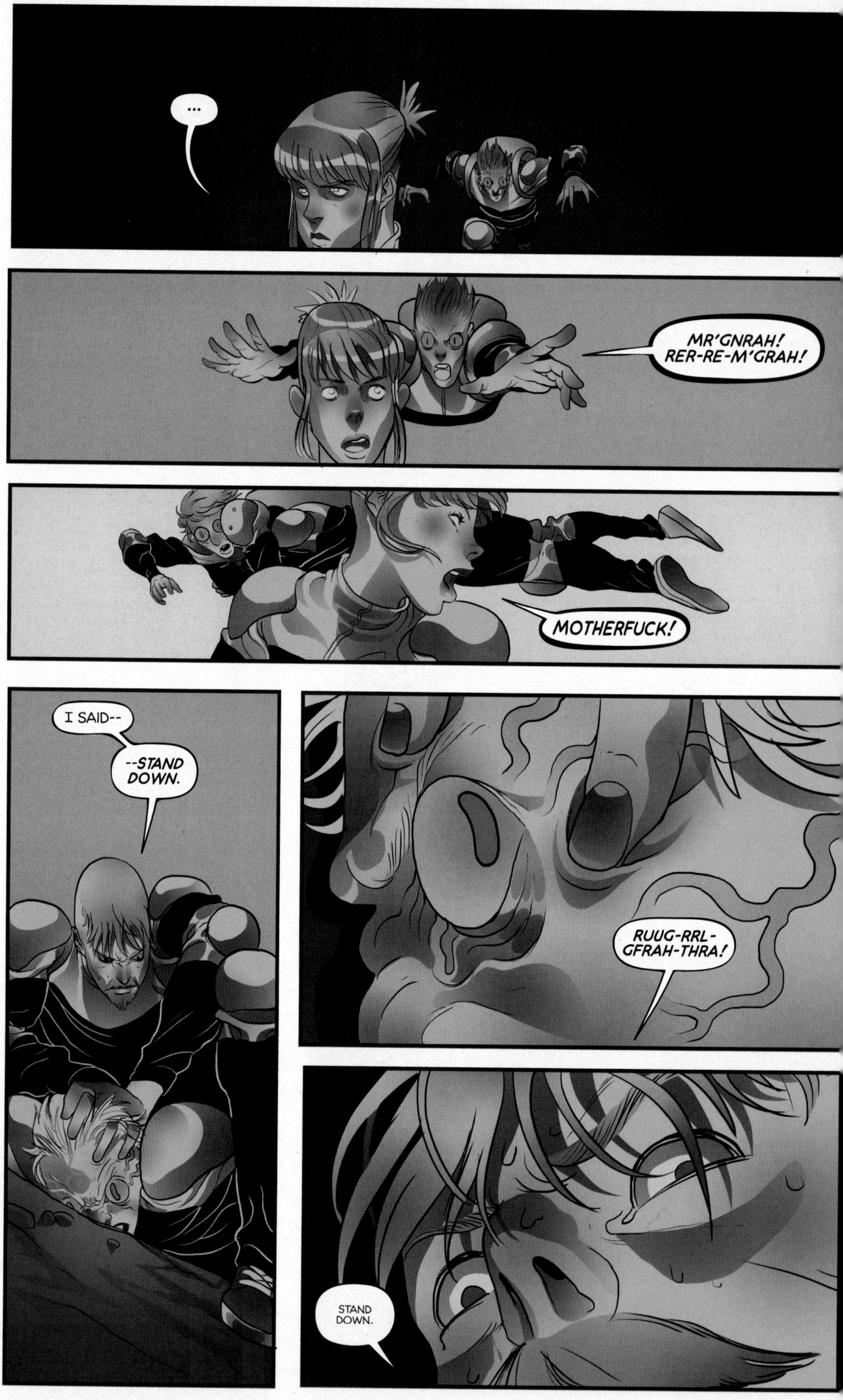
...
MR'GNRAH! RER-RE-M'GRAH!
MOTHERFUCK!
I SAID--
--STAND DOWN.
RUUG-RRL-GFRAH-THRA!
STAND DOWN.

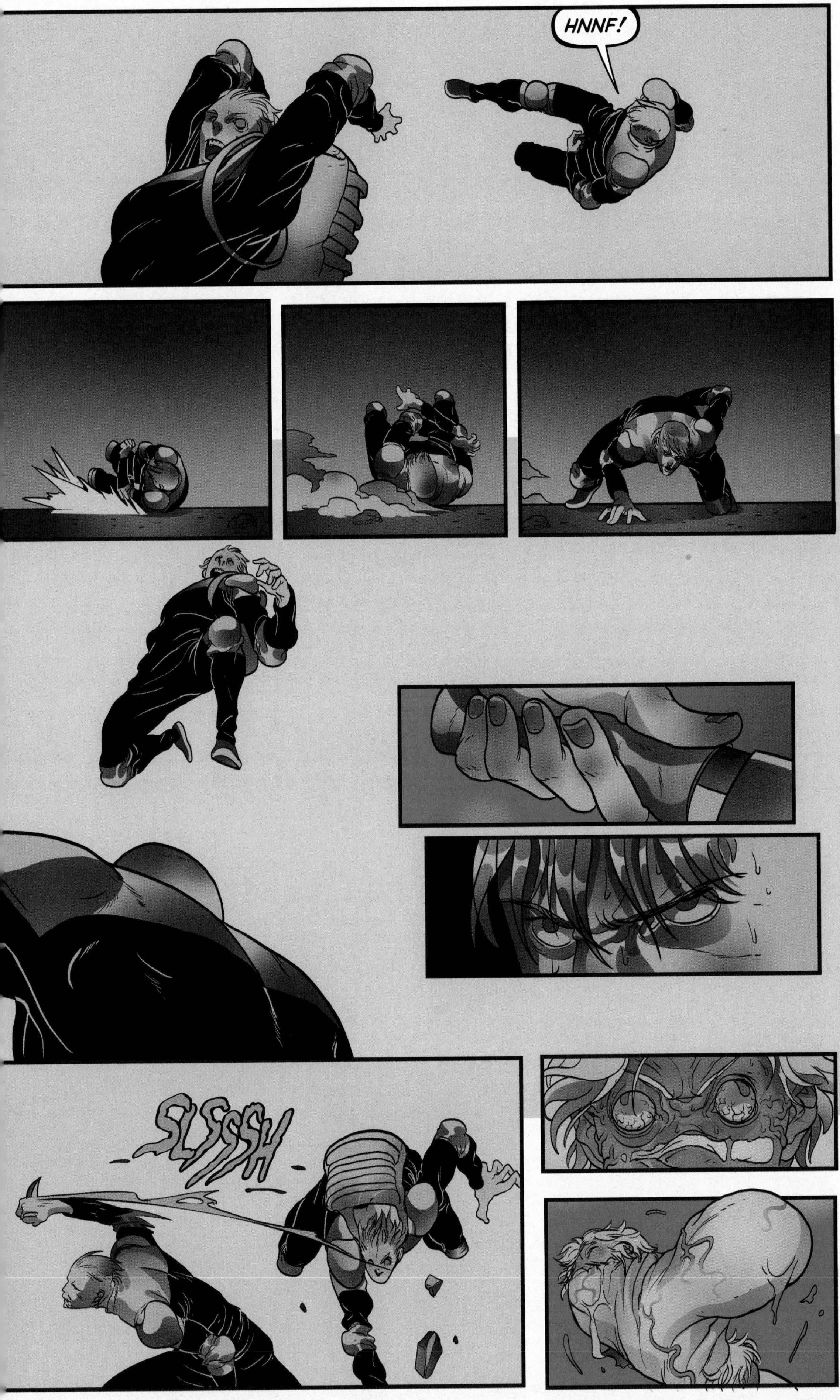
HNNF!
SLSSSH

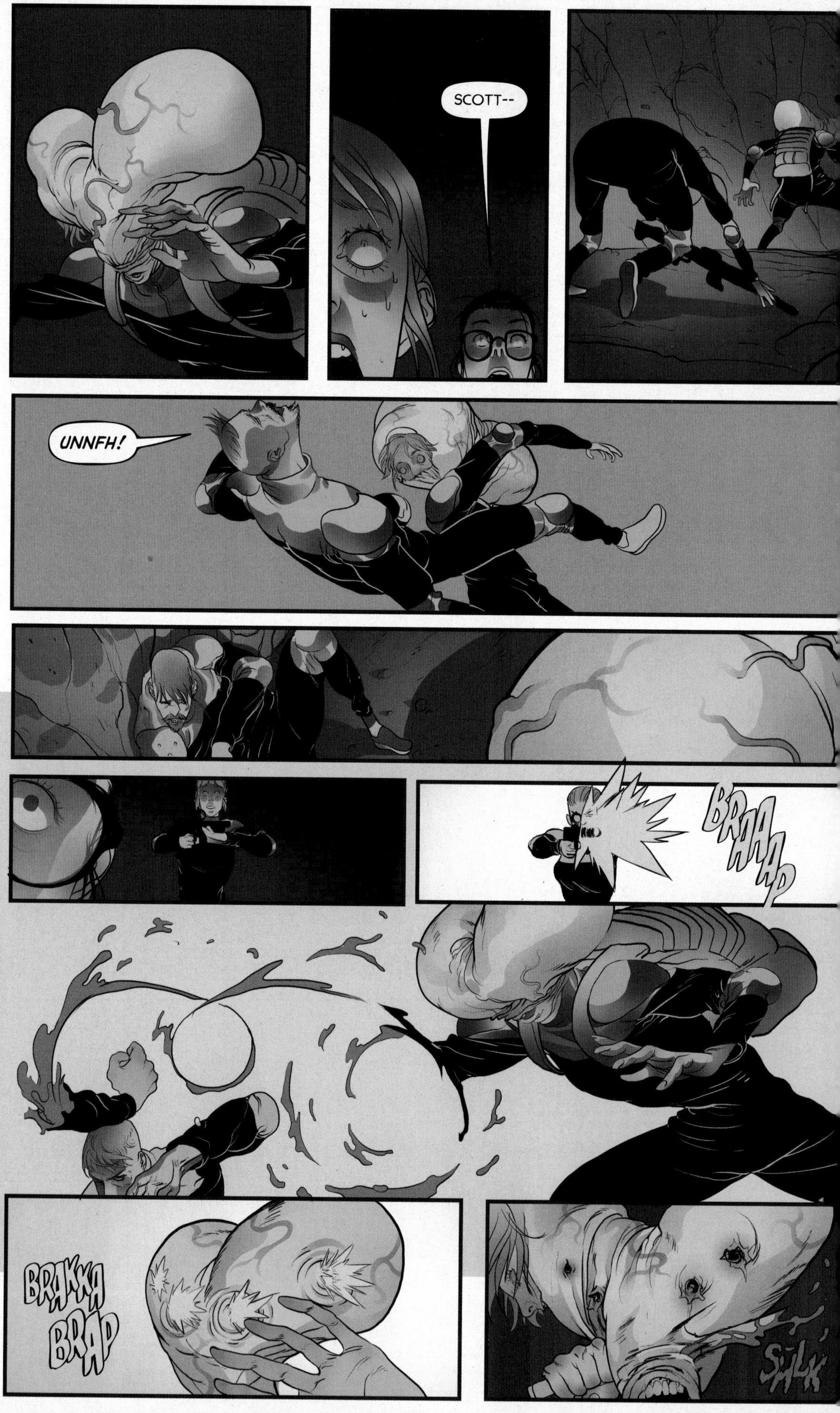
SCOTT--
UNNFH!
BRAAAAP
BRAKKA
BRAP
SHLK

WHAT--?

HIS PHYSIOLOGY HAS COMPLETELY CHANGED.

AND THIS--

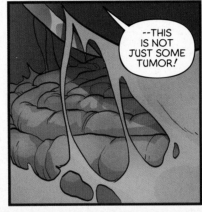

--THIS IS NOT JUST SOME TUMOR!

MAD.

THIS PLACE IS MAD.

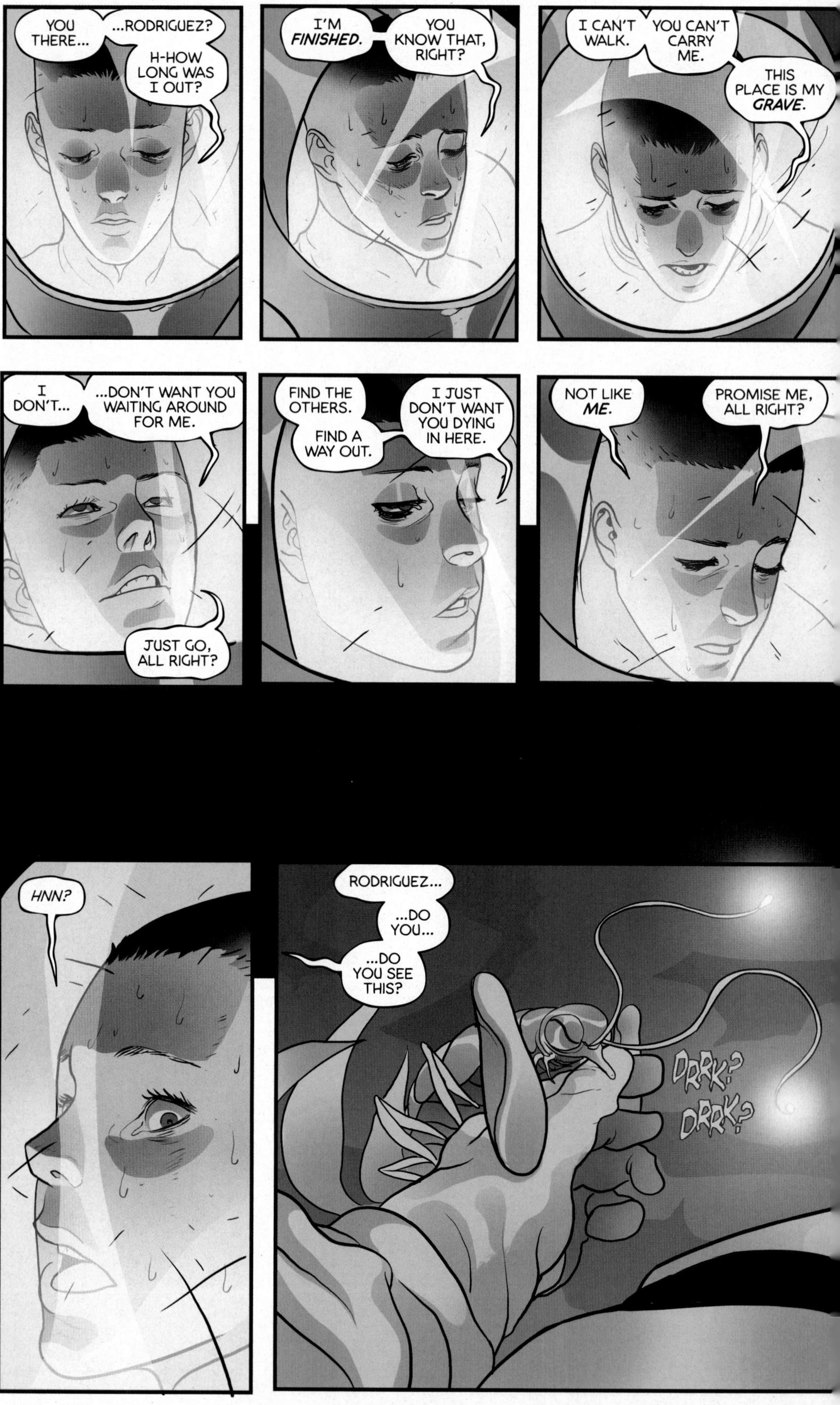
YOU THERE...
...RODRIGUEZ?
H-HOW LONG WAS I OUT?
I'M *FINISHED*.
YOU KNOW THAT, RIGHT?
I CAN'T WALK.
YOU CAN'T CARRY ME.
THIS PLACE IS MY *GRAVE*.
I DON'T...
...DON'T WANT YOU WAITING AROUND FOR ME.
JUST GO, ALL RIGHT?
FIND THE OTHERS.
FIND A WAY OUT.
I JUST DON'T WANT YOU DYING IN HERE.
NOT LIKE *ME*.
PROMISE ME, ALL RIGHT?
HNN?
RODRIGUEZ...
...DO YOU...
...DO YOU SEE THIS?
DRRK?
DRRK?

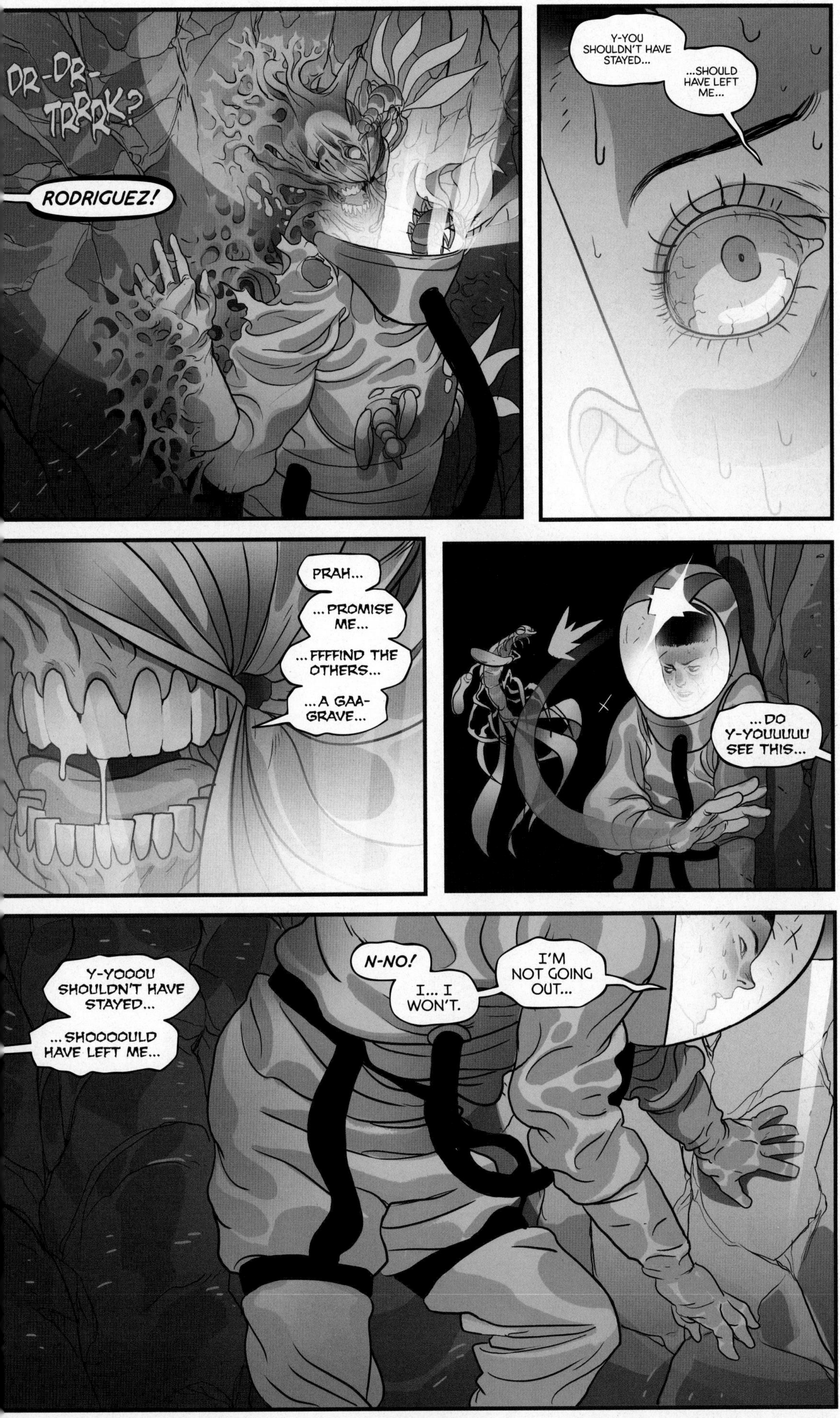
DR-DR-TRRRK?
RODRIGUEZ!
Y-YOU SHOULDN'T HAVE STAYED...
...SHOULD HAVE LEFT ME...
PRAH...
...PROMISE ME...
...FFFFIND THE OTHERS...
...A GAA-GRAVE...
...DO Y-YOUUUUU SEE THIS...
Y-YOOOU SHOULDN'T HAVE STAYED...
...SHOOOOULD HAVE LEFT ME...
N-NO!
I... I WON'T.
I'M NOT GOING OUT...

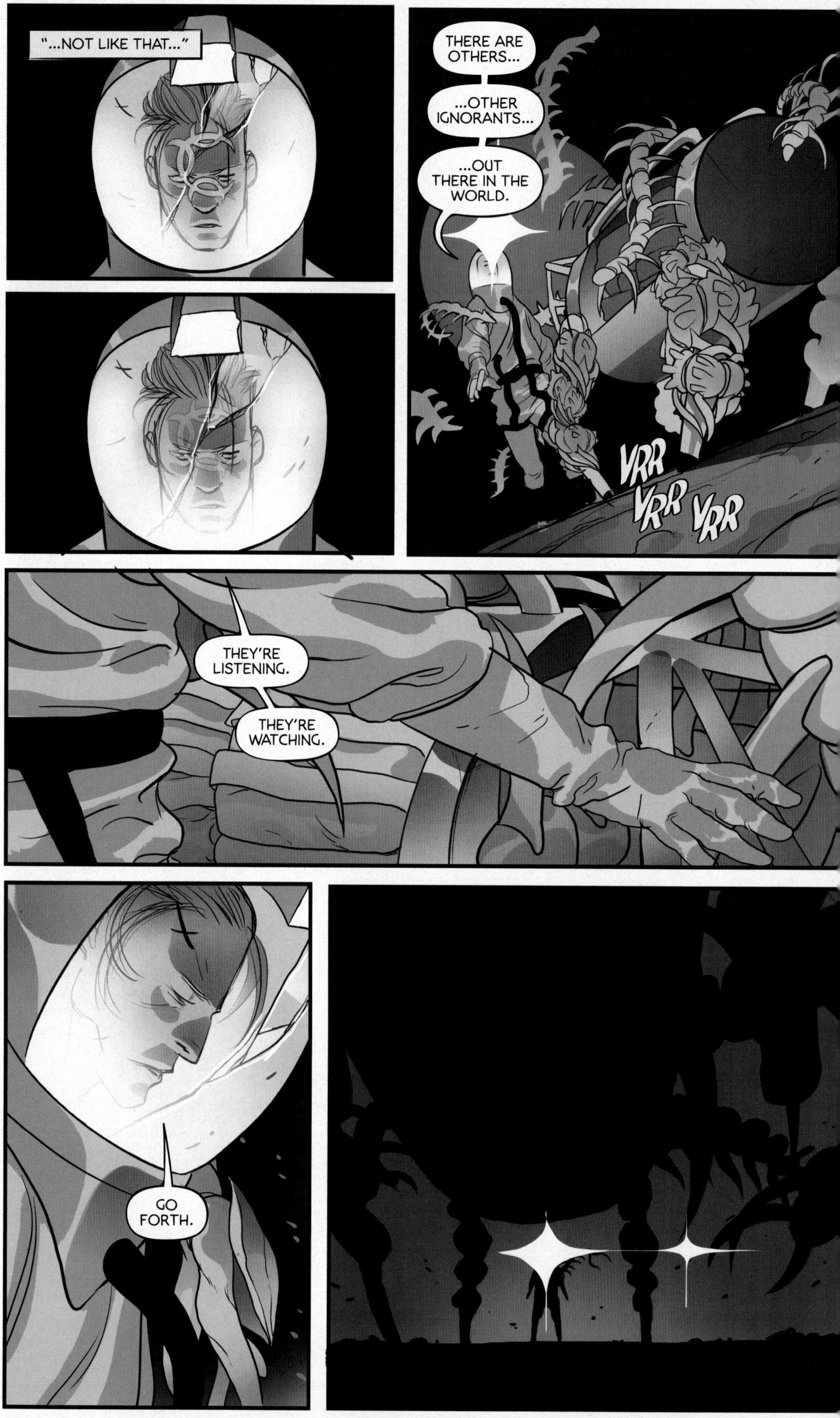
"...NOT LIKE THAT..."
THERE ARE OTHERS...
...OTHER IGNORANTS...
...OUT THERE IN THE WORLD.
VRR
VRR
VRR
THEY'RE LISTENING.
THEY'RE WATCHING.
GO FORTH.

NNNNGH!
YEEEARRRGH!
FHTAGN.
FSSSSSSS
FHTAGN!

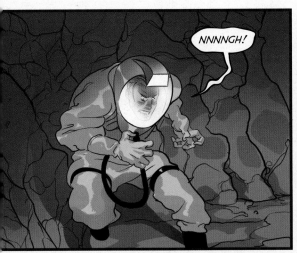

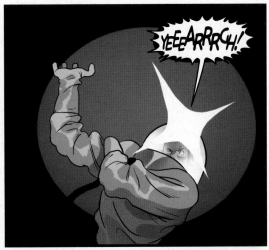

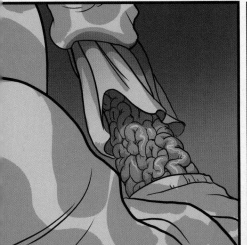

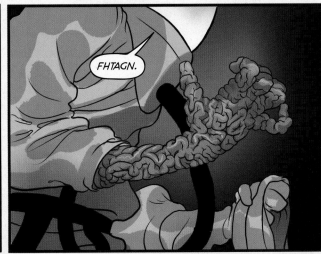

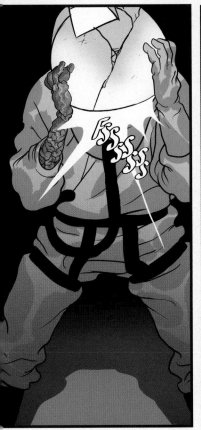

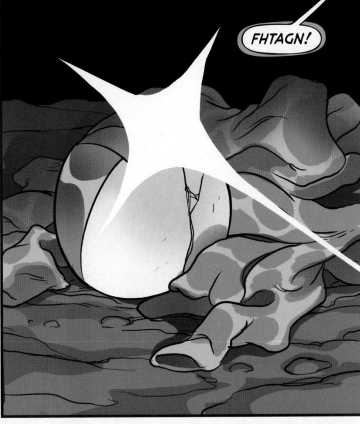

WHO WANTS TO UPDATE ME ON *CURRENT EVENTS?*

THE MULE'S GONE *WILD*, SIR.

IT'S MOVING ERRATICALLY ON AUTO-PILOT.

IT'S REALLY FILLING OUT THE MAP.

WELL *W-T-F*, BOYS.

MAYBE IT'S TRYING TO TELL US SOMETHING.

WRITING OUT A MESSAGE LIKE SOME KIND OF *MULE-PROPHET.*

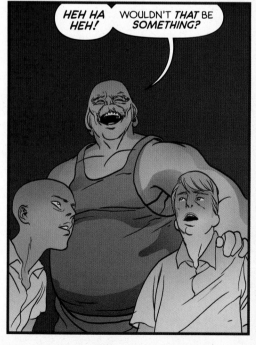

HEH HA HEH!

WOULDN'T *THAT* BE SOMETHING?

TSSHCT

THIS IS SATELLITE UNIT SEVEN TO COMMAND...

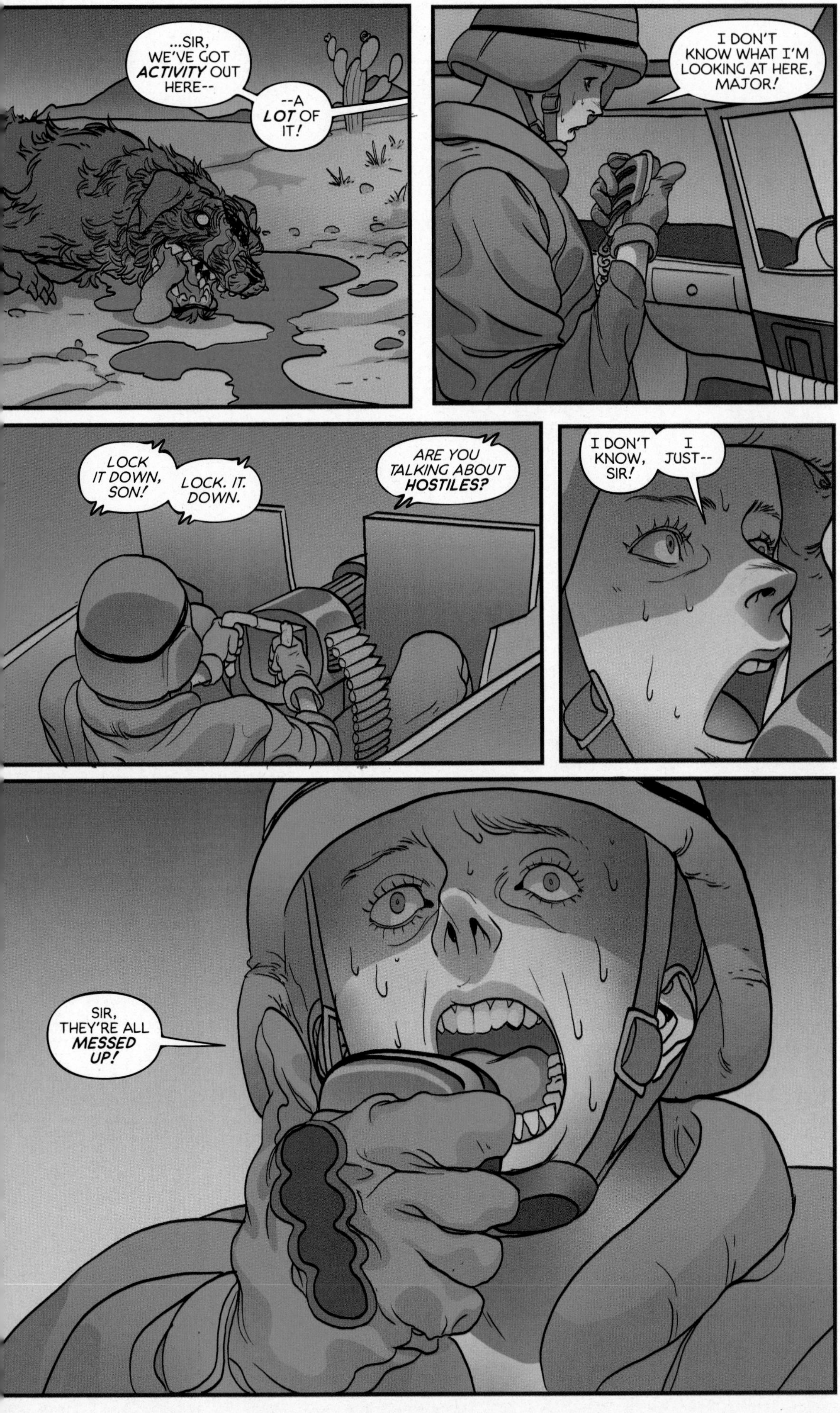
...SIR, WE'VE GOT ACTIVITY OUT HERE--
--A LOT OF IT!
I DON'T KNOW WHAT I'M LOOKING AT HERE, MAJOR!
LOCK IT DOWN, SON!
LOCK. IT. DOWN.
ARE YOU TALKING ABOUT HOSTILES?
I DON'T KNOW, SIR!
I JUST--
SIR, THEY'RE ALL MESSED UP!

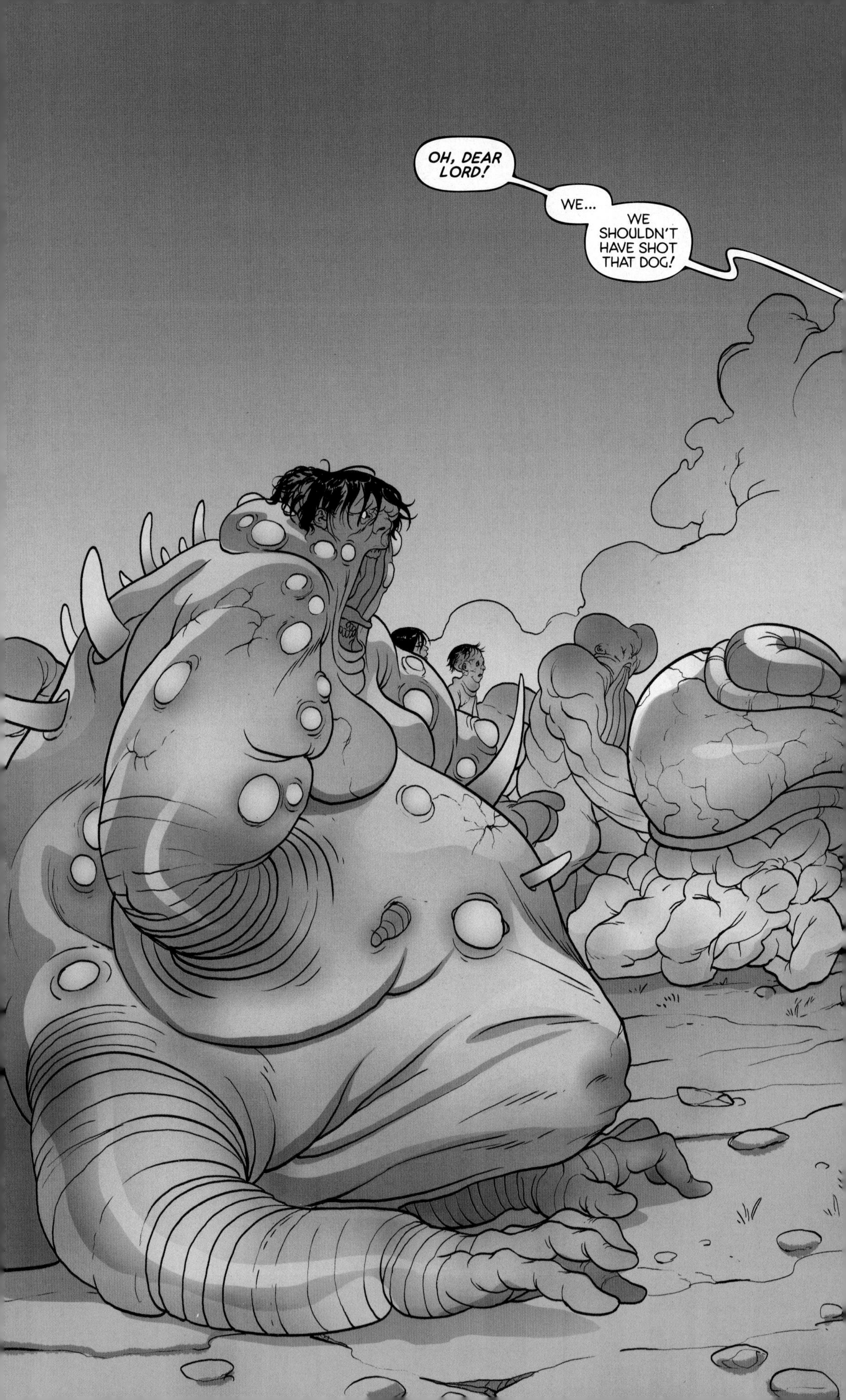
OH, DEAR LORD!
WE...
WE SHOULDN'T HAVE SHOT THAT DOG!

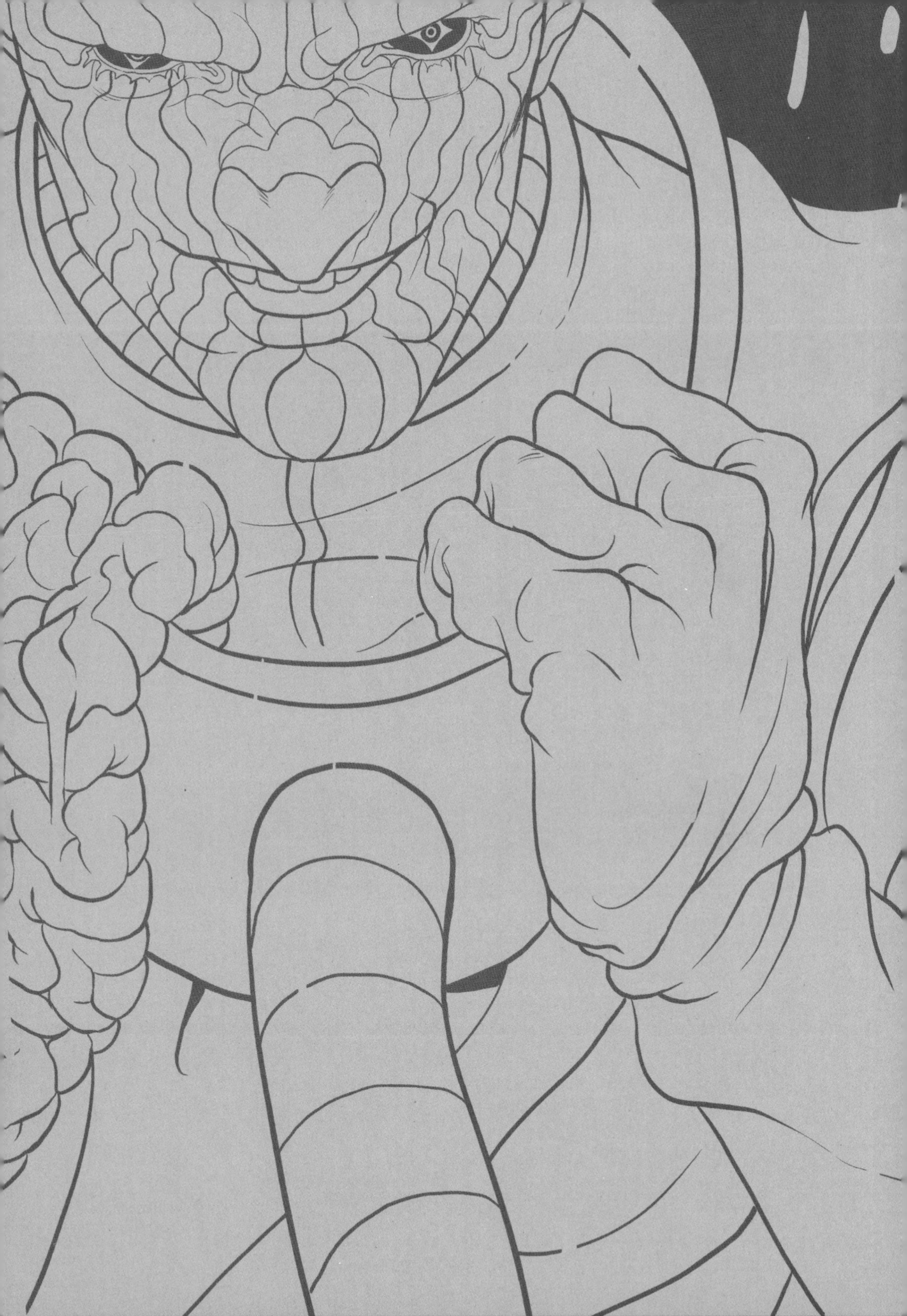

Ch 04

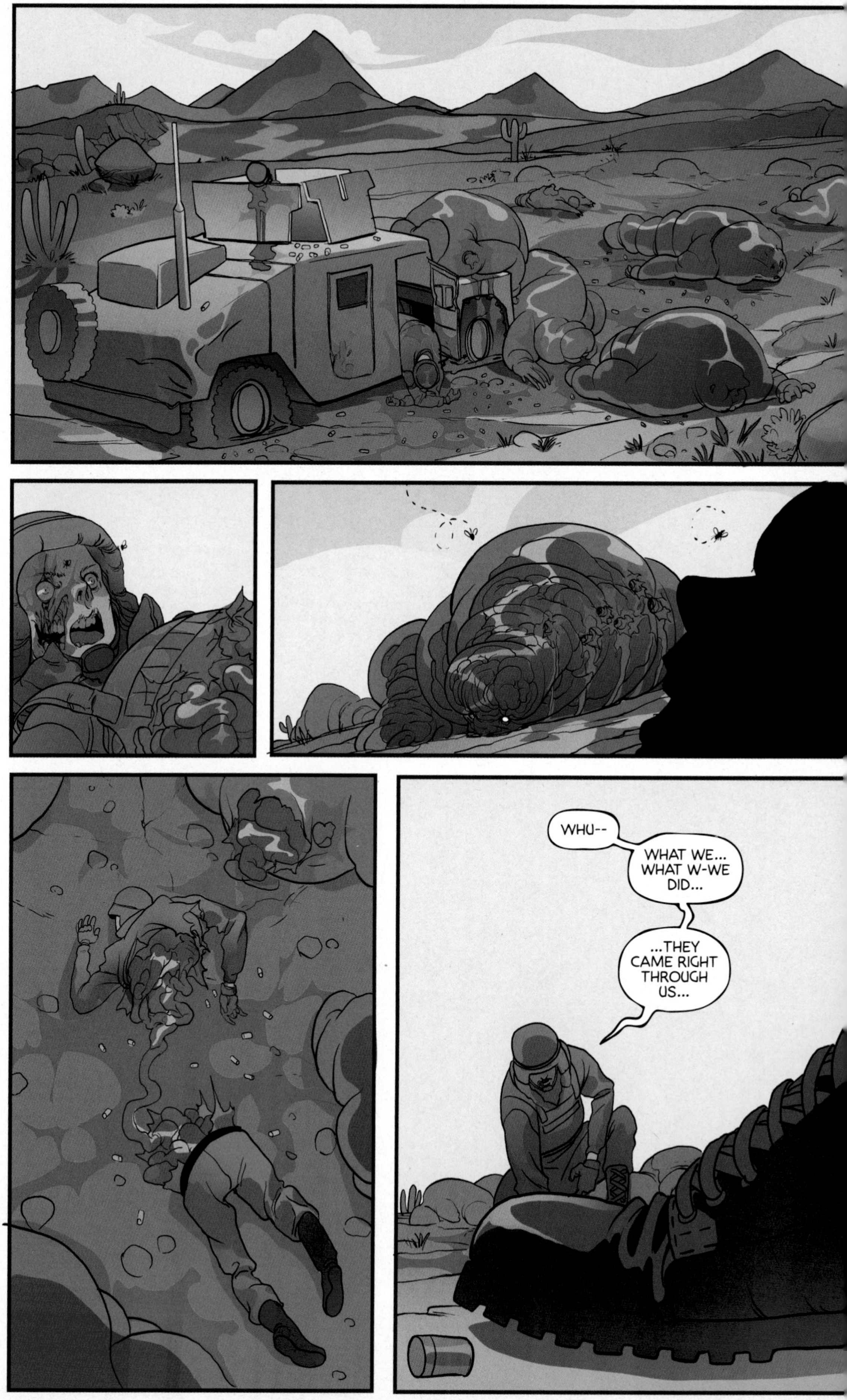
WHU--
WHAT WE... WHAT W-WE DID...
...THEY CAME RIGHT THROUGH US...

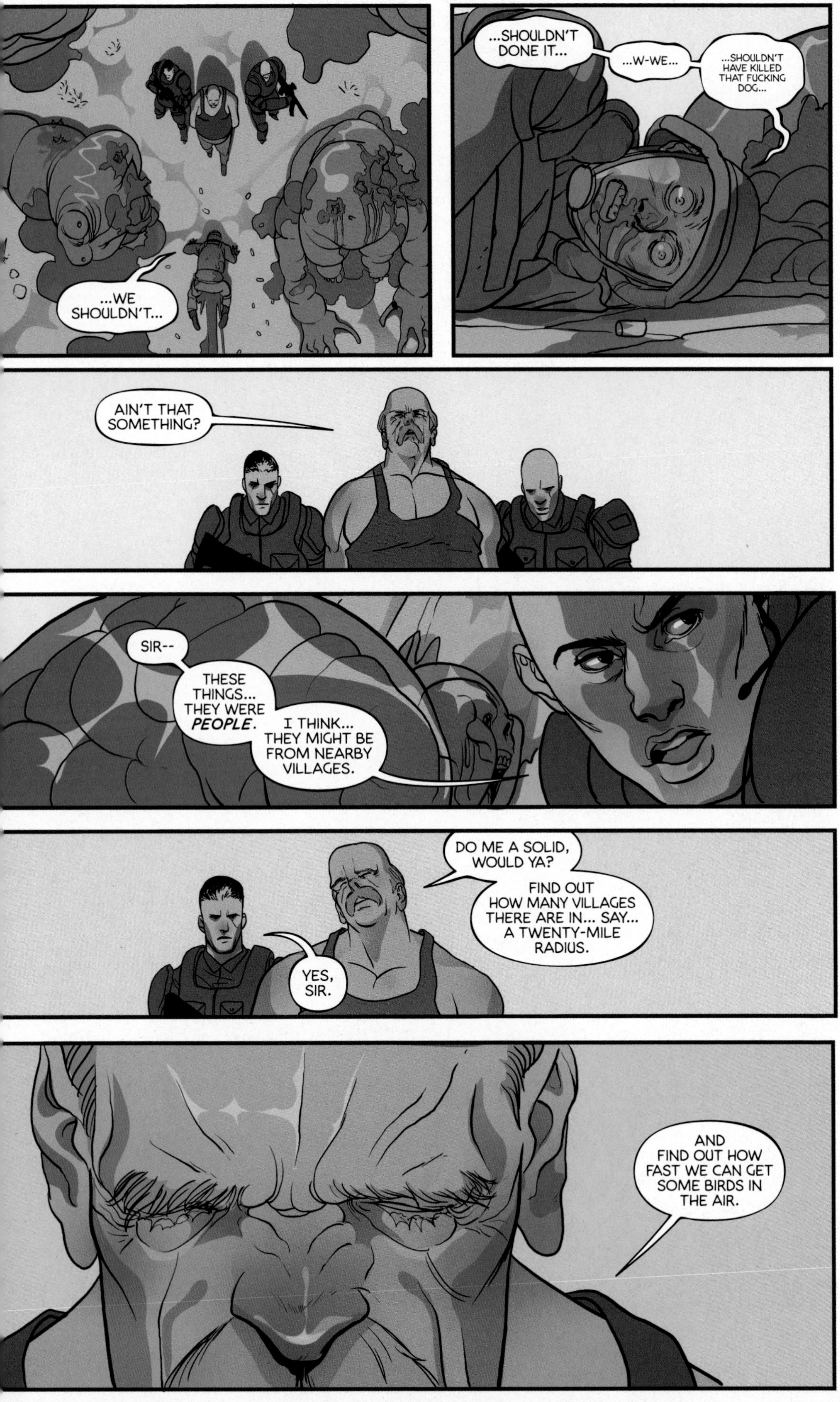
...WE SHOULDN'T...
...SHOULDN'T DONE IT...
...W-WE...
...SHOULDN'T HAVE KILLED THAT FUCKING DOG...
AIN'T THAT SOMETHING?
SIR--
THESE THINGS... THEY WERE *PEOPLE*.
I THINK... THEY MIGHT BE FROM NEARBY VILLAGES.
DO ME A SOLID, WOULD YA?
FIND OUT HOW MANY VILLAGES THERE ARE IN... SAY... A TWENTY-MILE RADIUS.
YES, SIR.
AND FIND OUT HOW FAST WE CAN GET SOME BIRDS IN THE AIR.

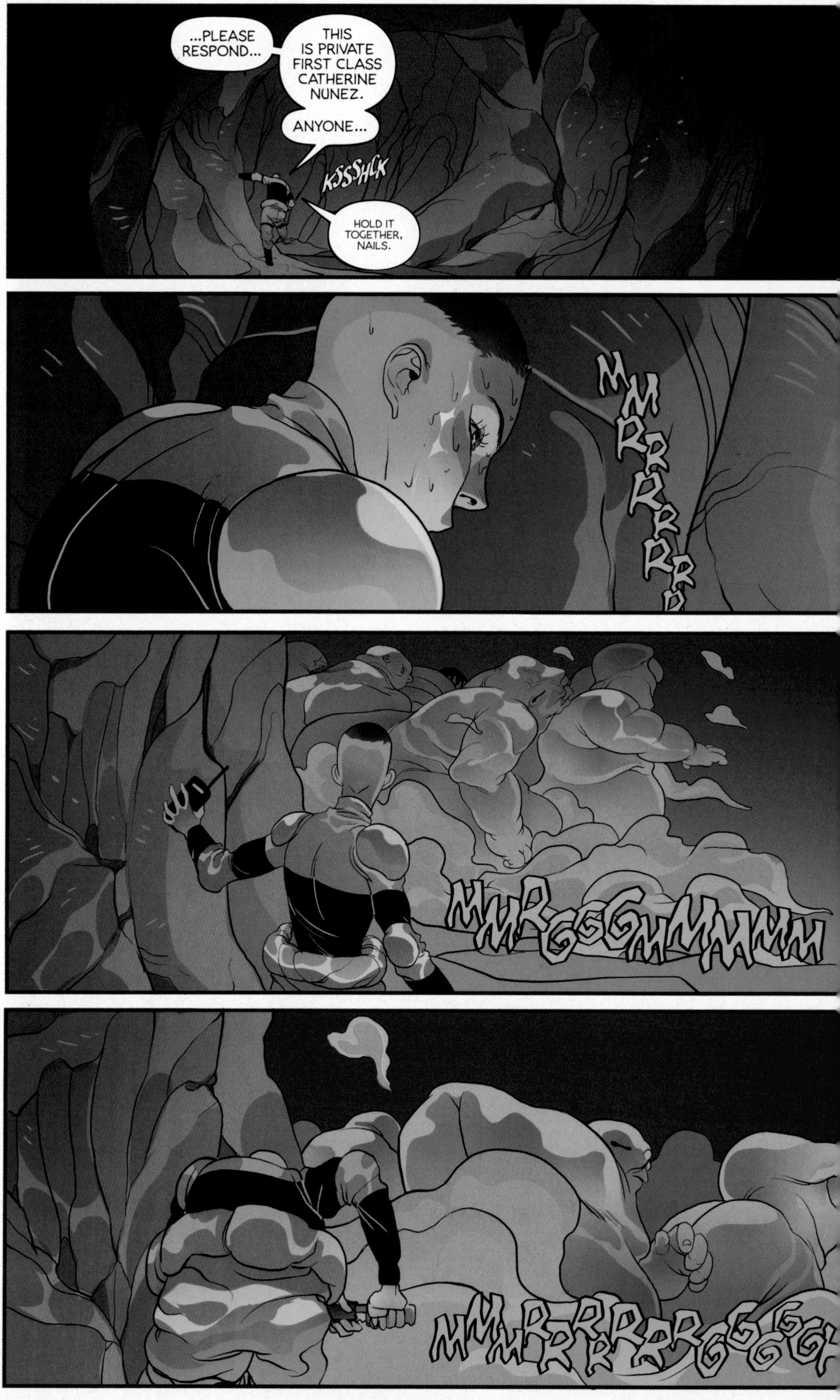
...PLEASE RESPOND...
THIS IS PRIVATE FIRST CLASS CATHERINE NUNEZ.
ANYONE...
KSSSHCK
HOLD IT TOGETHER, NAILS.
MMRRRRR
MMRGGGMMMMMM
MMMRRRRRRRGGGGH

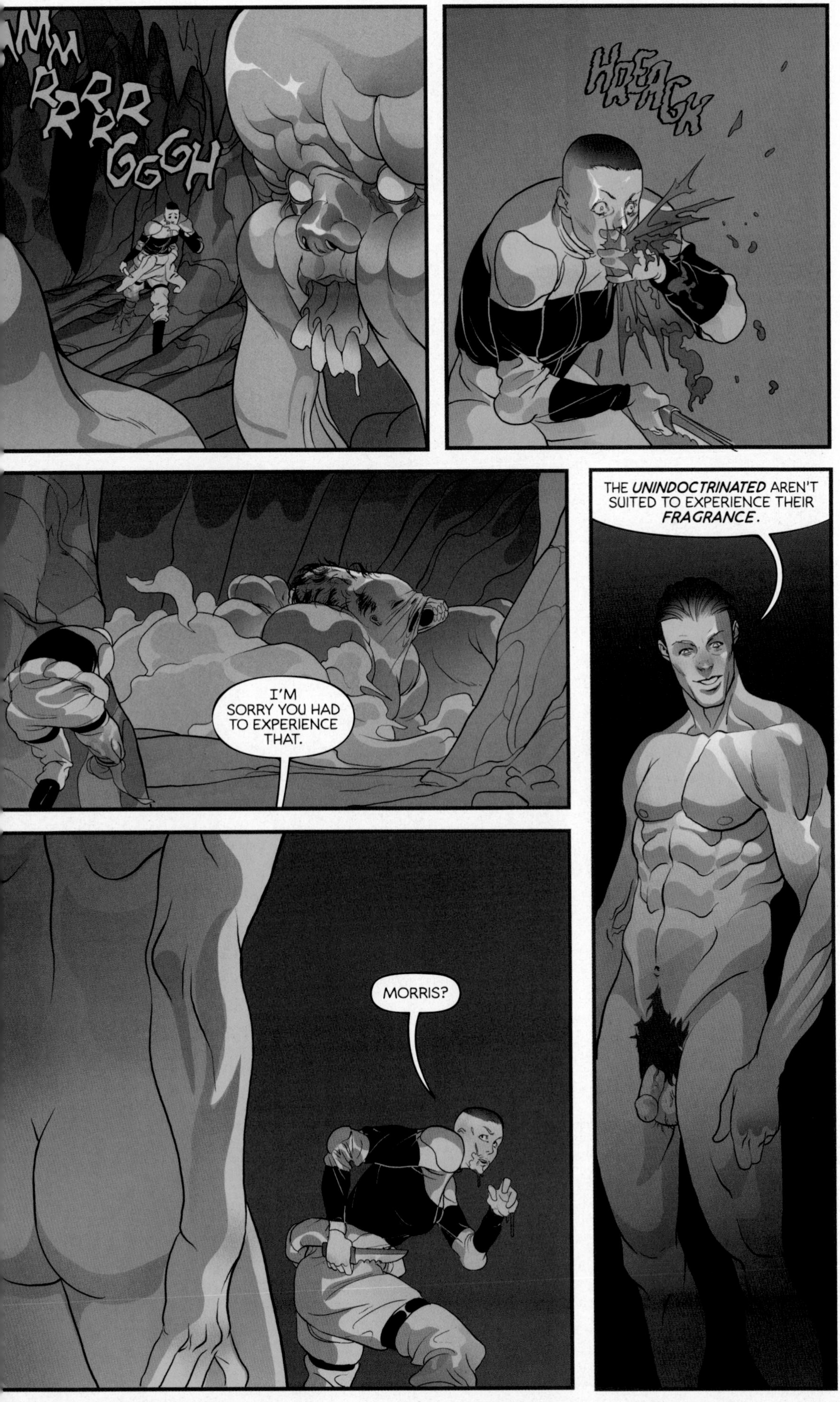
MMMRRRRRRGGGGH
HREACK
I'M SORRY YOU HAD TO EXPERIENCE THAT.
THE *UNINDOCTRINATED* AREN'T SUITED TO EXPERIENCE THEIR *FRAGRANCE*.
MORRIS?

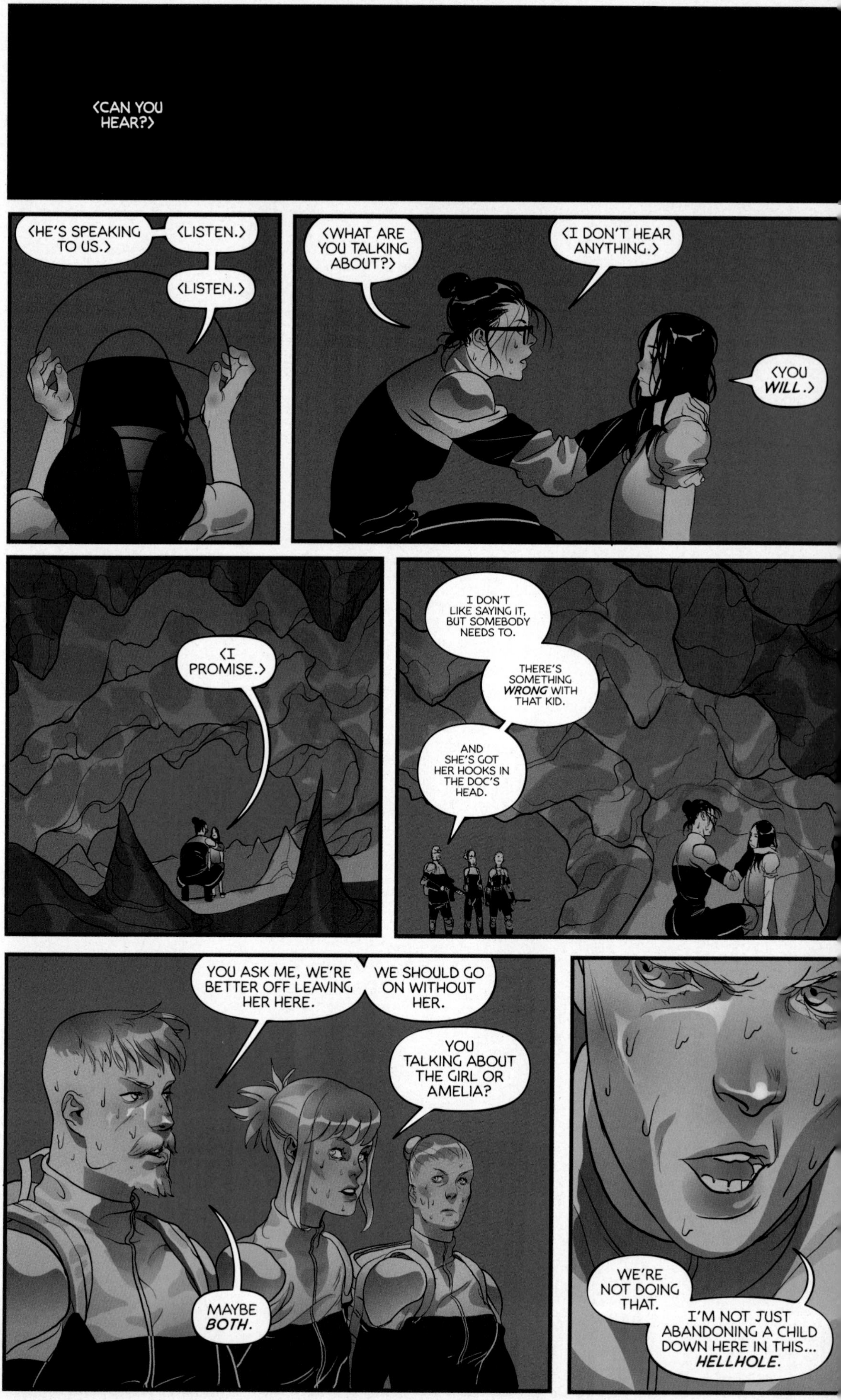

<CAN YOU HEAR?>
<HE'S SPEAKING TO US.>
<LISTEN.>
<LISTEN.>
<WHAT ARE YOU TALKING ABOUT?>
<I DON'T HEAR ANYTHING.>
<YOU *WILL*.>
<I PROMISE.>
I DON'T LIKE SAYING IT, BUT SOMEBODY NEEDS TO.
THERE'S SOMETHING ***WRONG*** WITH THAT KID.
AND SHE'S GOT HER HOOKS IN THE DOC'S HEAD.
YOU ASK ME, WE'RE BETTER OFF LEAVING HER HERE.
WE SHOULD GO ON WITHOUT HER.
YOU TALKING ABOUT THE GIRL OR AMELIA?
MAYBE ***BOTH***.
WE'RE NOT DOING THAT.
I'M NOT JUST ABANDONING A CHILD DOWN HERE IN THIS... ***HELLHOLE***.

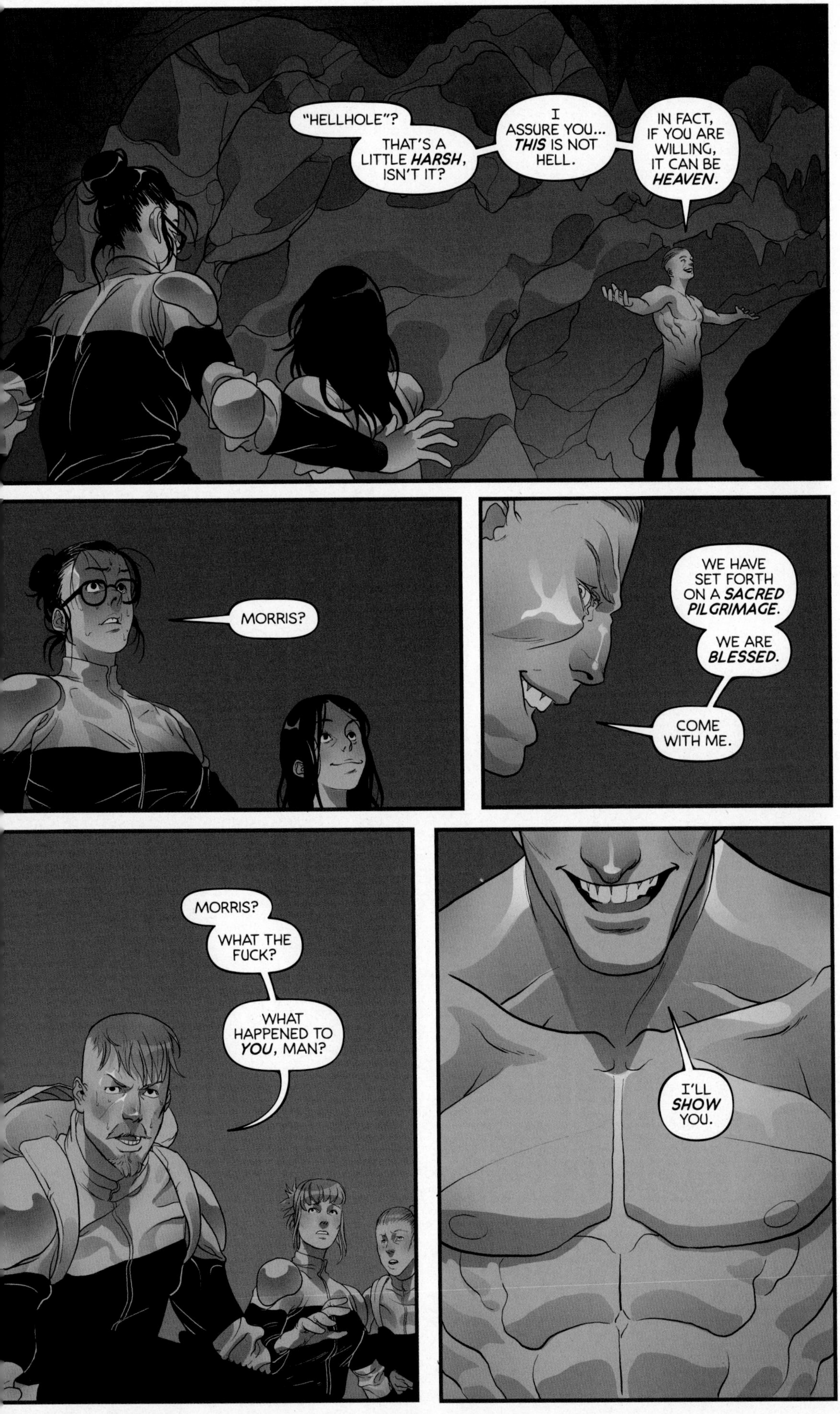
"HELLHOLE"?
THAT'S A LITTLE *HARSH*, ISN'T IT?
I ASSURE YOU... *THIS* IS NOT HELL.
IN FACT, IF YOU ARE WILLING, IT CAN BE *HEAVEN*.
MORRIS?
WE HAVE SET FORTH ON A *SACRED PILGRIMAGE*.
WE ARE *BLESSED*.
COME WITH ME.
MORRIS?
WHAT THE FUCK?
WHAT HAPPENED TO *YOU*, MAN?
I'LL *SHOW* YOU.

MORRIS, I'VE SEEN SOME SHIT TODAY...

...BUT THIS TAKES THE CAKE.

I CAN HELP YOU, NAILS.

YOU'VE LIVED YOUR LIFE *TRAPPED* INSIDE THE *CONFINES* OF HUMAN UNDERSTANDING.

TODAY, YOU GLIMPSED THE WORLD OUTSIDE.

THERE'S MORE... IF YOU COME WITH ME.

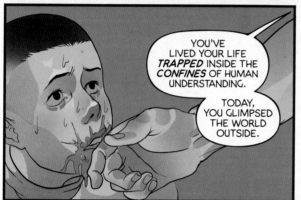

LOOK AT MY LEG, MORRIS!

WHAT THE HELL IS WRONG WITH YOU?!

MORRIS?

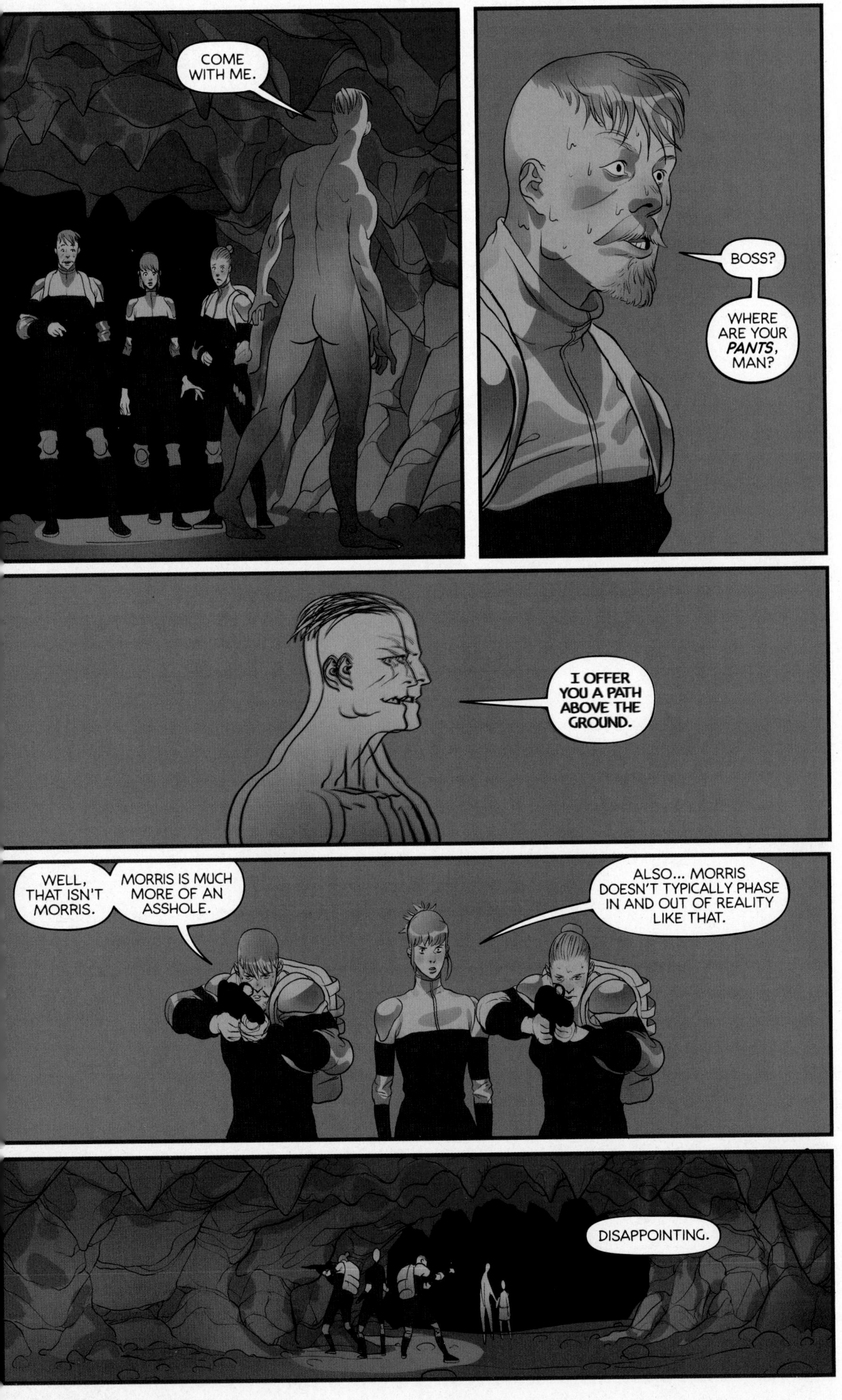
COME WITH ME.
BOSS?
WHERE ARE YOUR *PANTS*, MAN?
I OFFER YOU A PATH ABOVE THE GROUND.
WELL, THAT ISN'T MORRIS.
MORRIS IS MUCH MORE OF AN ASSHOLE.
ALSO... MORRIS DOESN'T TYPICALLY PHASE IN AND OUT OF REALITY LIKE THAT.
DISAPPOINTING.

WHY DO THEY DOUBT?

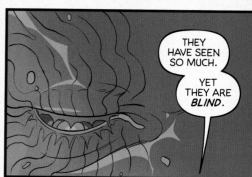

THEY HAVE SEEN SO MUCH.

YET THEY ARE *BLIND*.

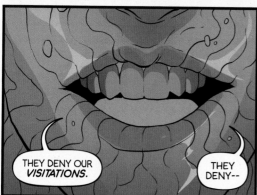

THEY DENY OUR *VISITATIONS*.

THEY DENY--

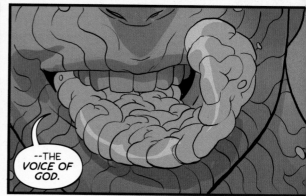

--THE *VOICE OF GOD*.

THE *TOUCH* OF GOD.

BUT THEY WILL COME TO US.

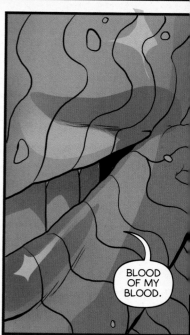

BLOOD OF MY BLOOD.

FLESH OF MY FLESH.

FHTAGN.
YUH...
Y-YES.
I HEAR.
I HEAR AND OBEY.
I WILL SHOW THEM...

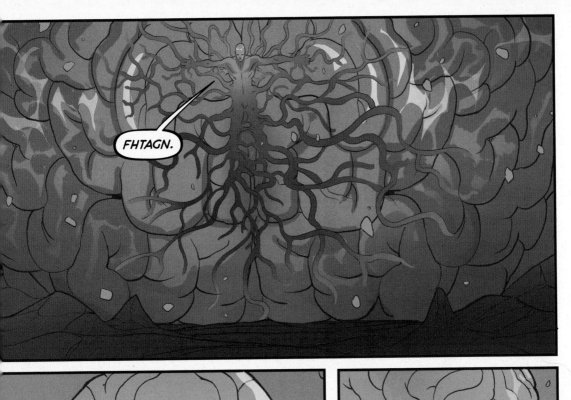

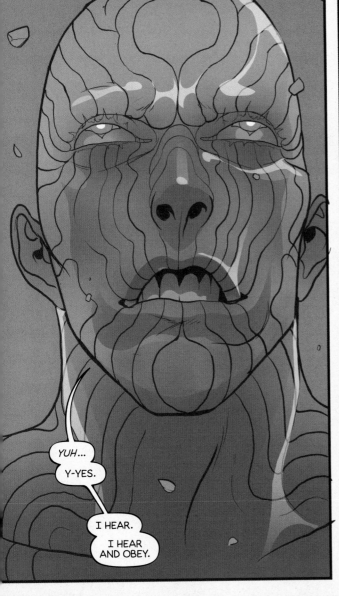

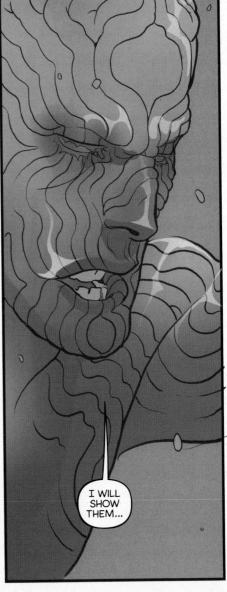

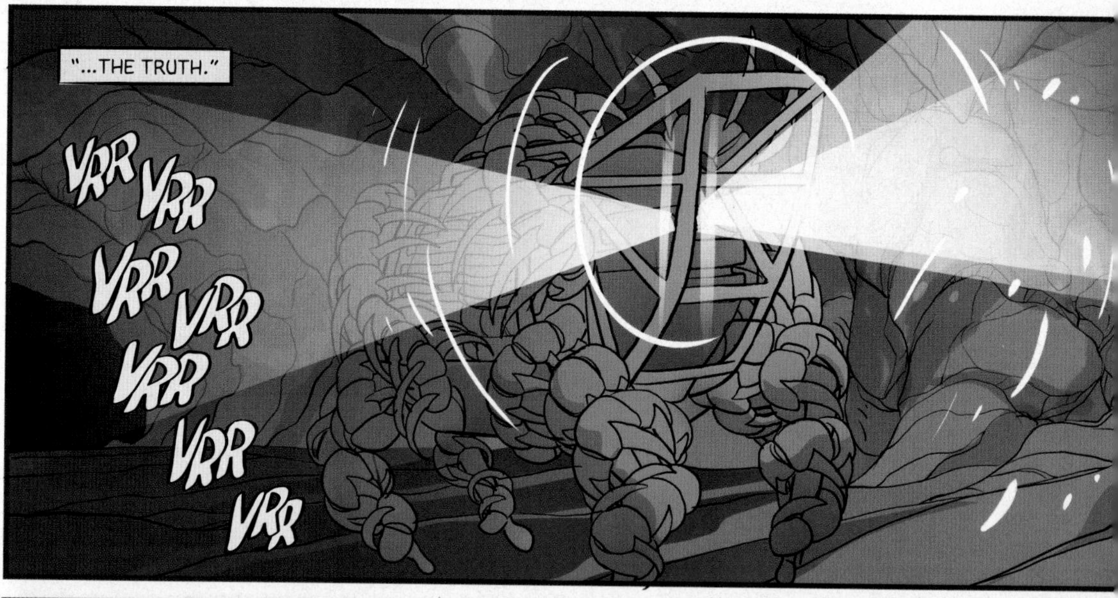
"...THE TRUTH."
VRR VRR
VRR VRR
VRR
VRR
VRR

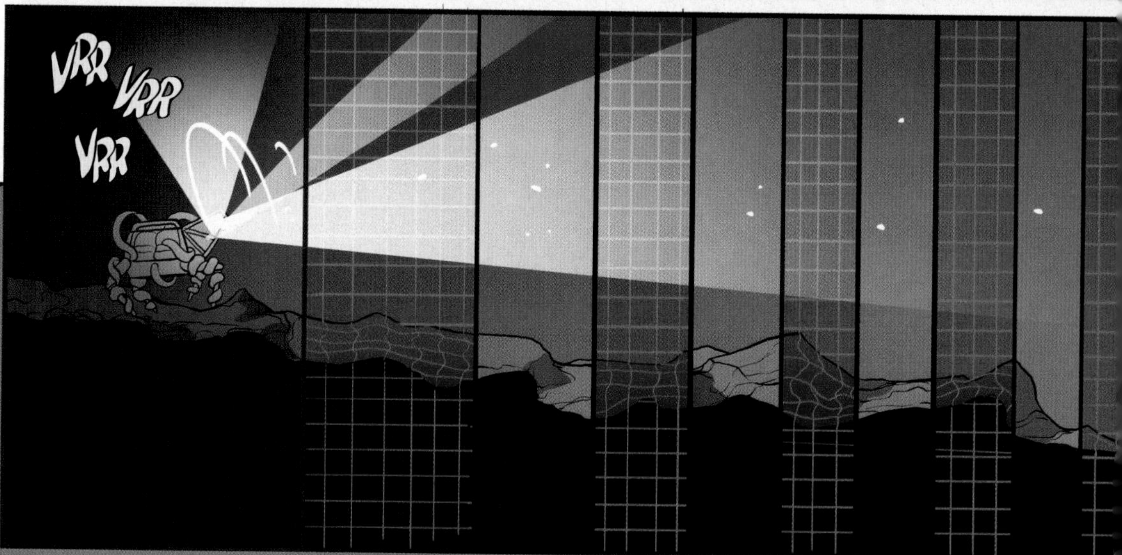
VRR VRR
VRR

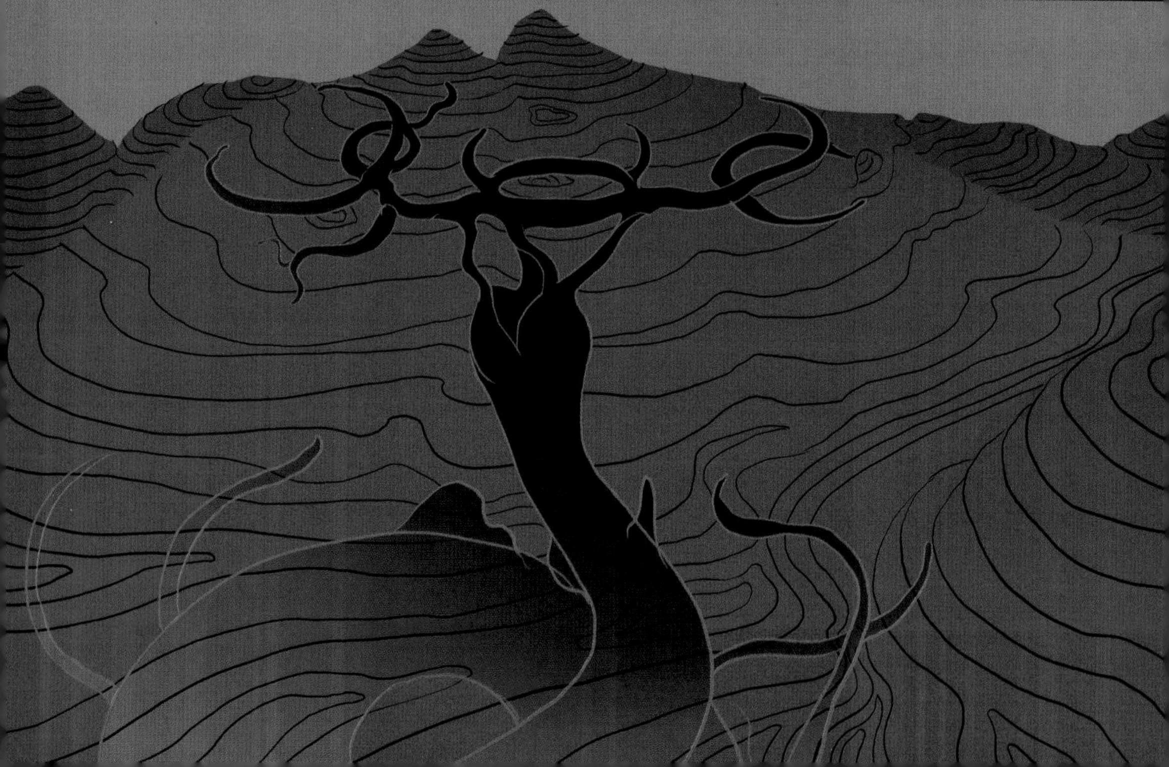

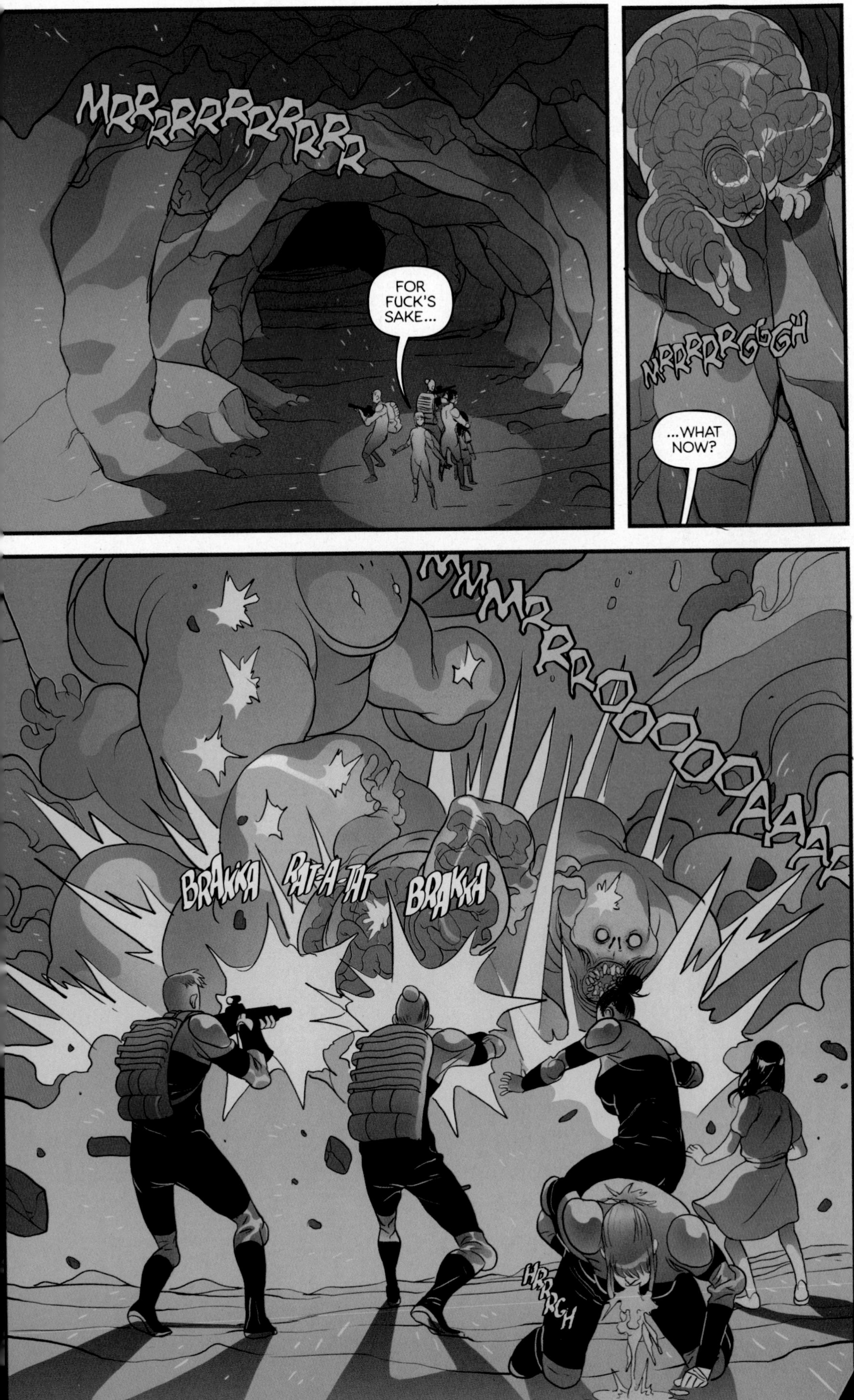
MRRRRRRRRRRRR
FOR FUCK'S SAKE...
MRRRRRGGGH
...WHAT NOW?
MMMRRROOOOOOAAAR
BRAKKA
RAT-A-TAT
BRAKKA
HRRRGH

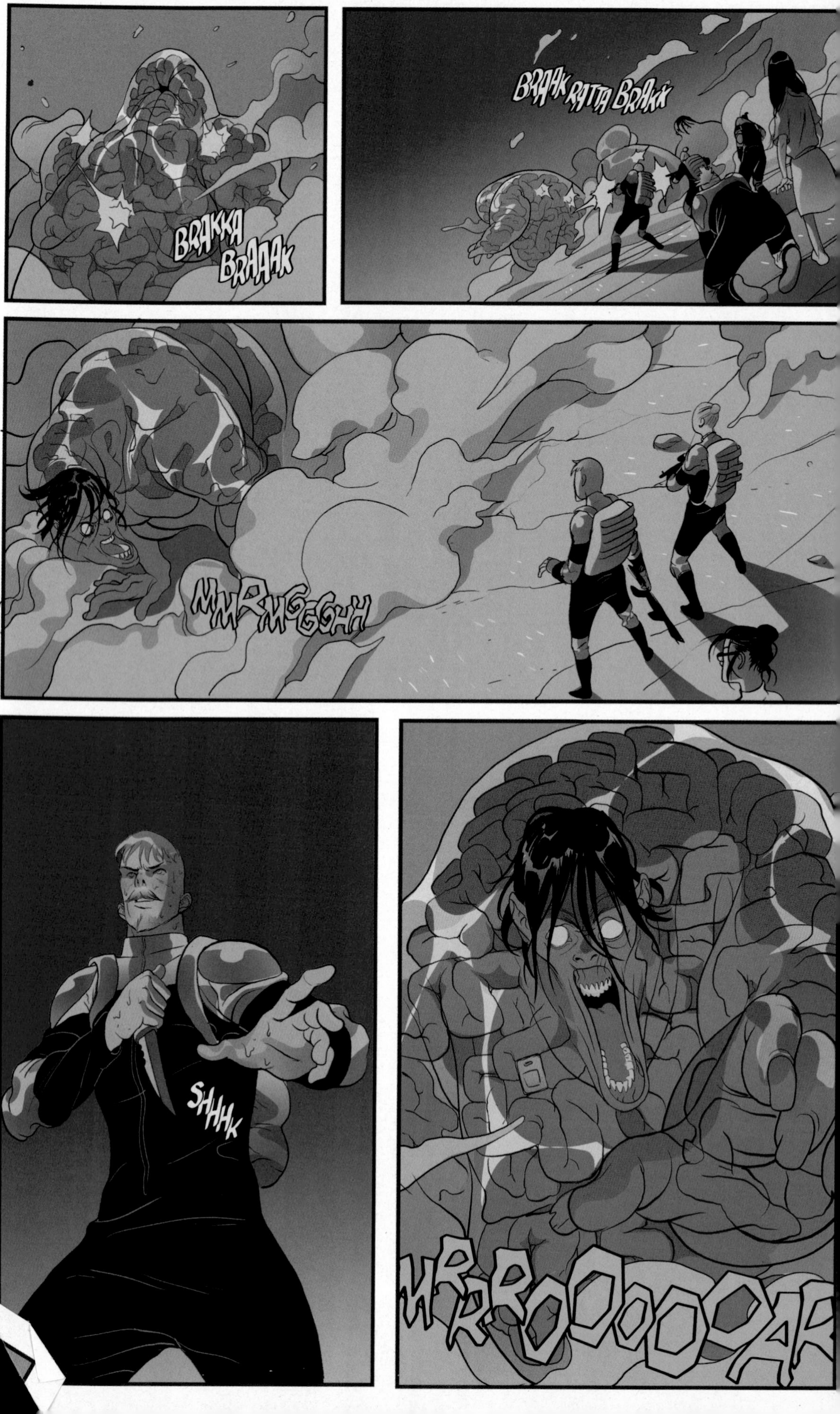
BRAKKA BRAAAK
BRAAK RATTA BRAKK
MMRMGGHH
SHHHK
URRROOOOOOAR

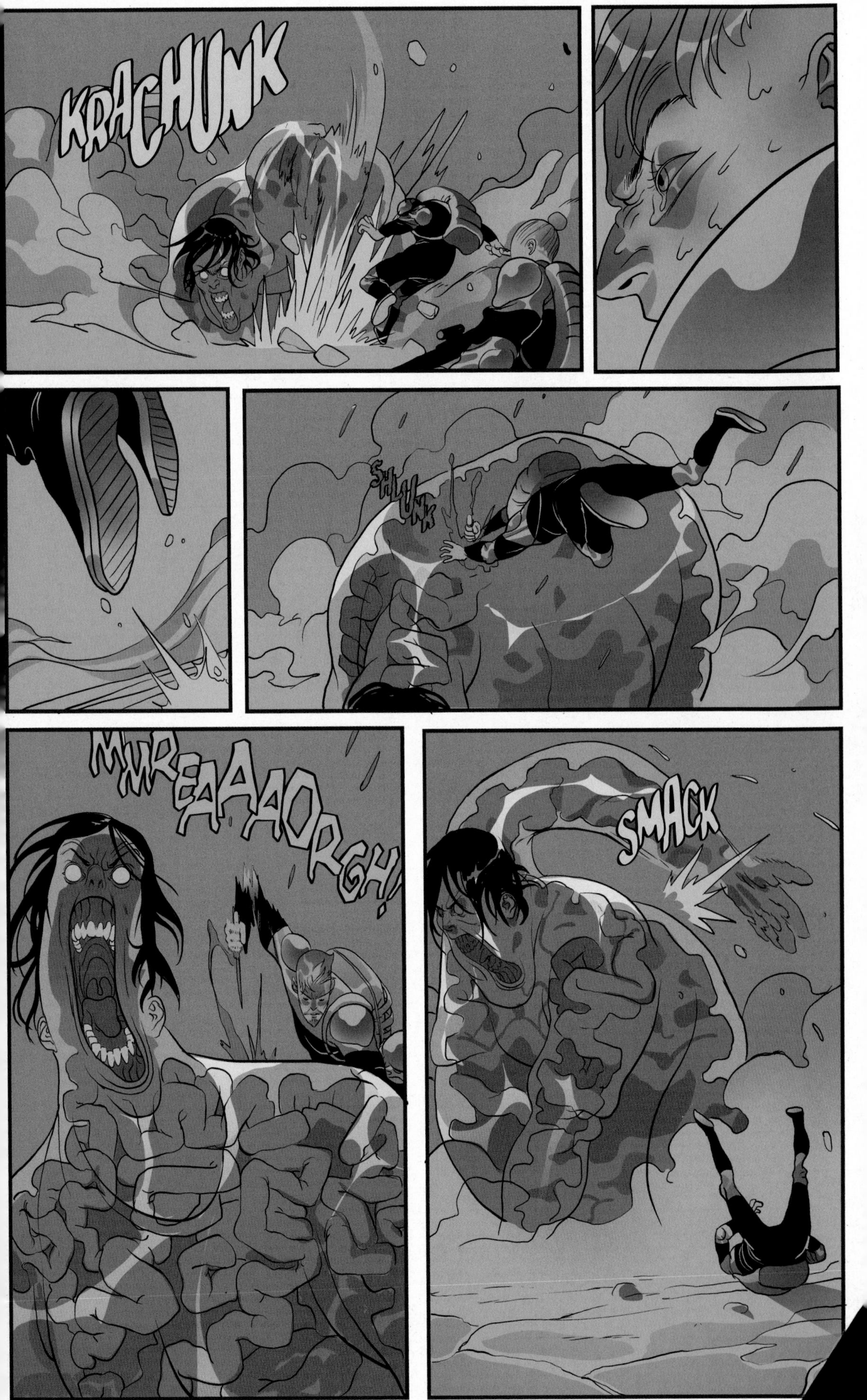
KRACHUNK
SHLUNK
MNREAAAAORGH!
SMACK

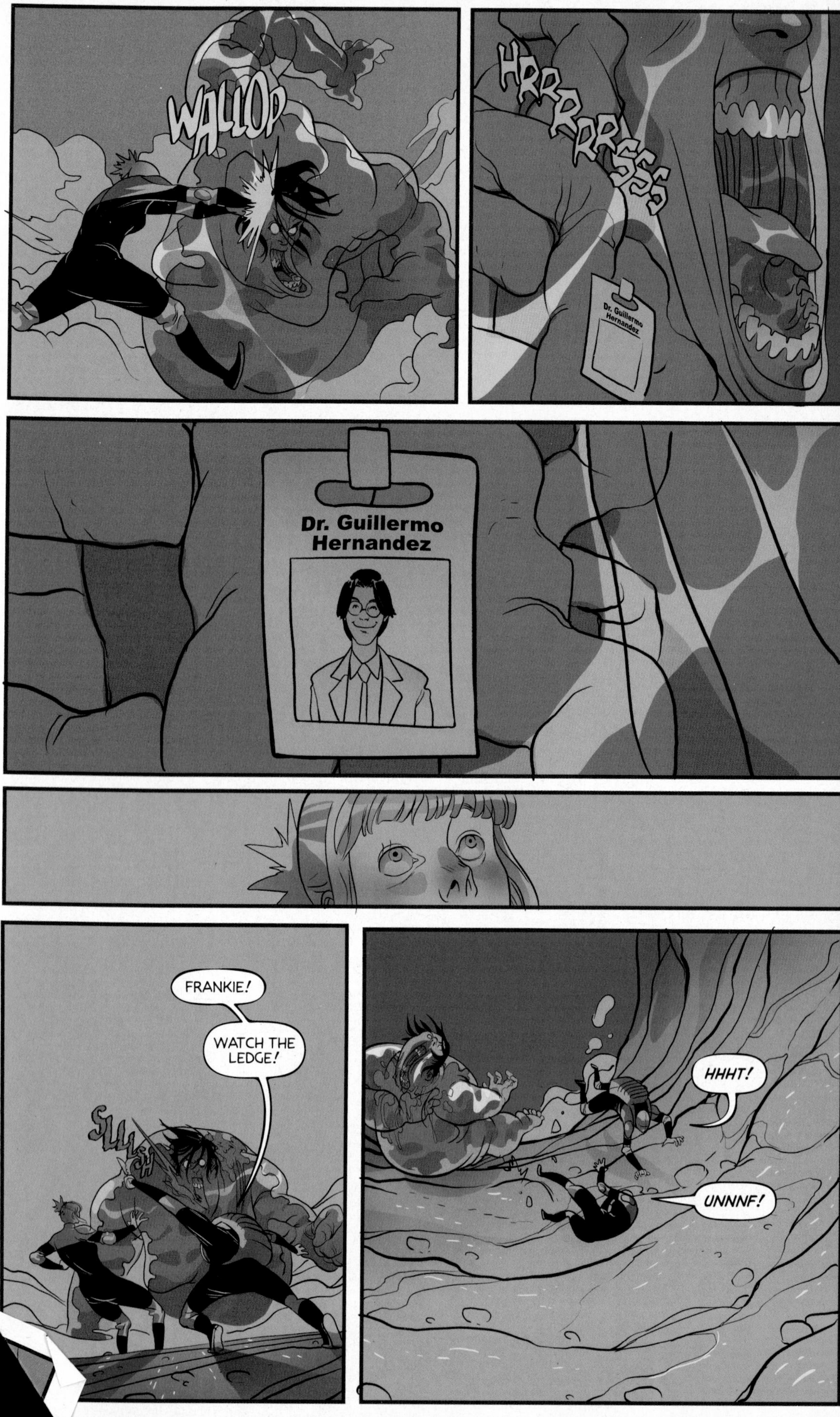
WALLOP
HRRRRRSSS
Dr. Guillermo Hernandez
Dr. Guillermo Hernandez
FRANKIE!
WATCH THE LEDGE!
SLLLSH
HHHT!
UNNNF!

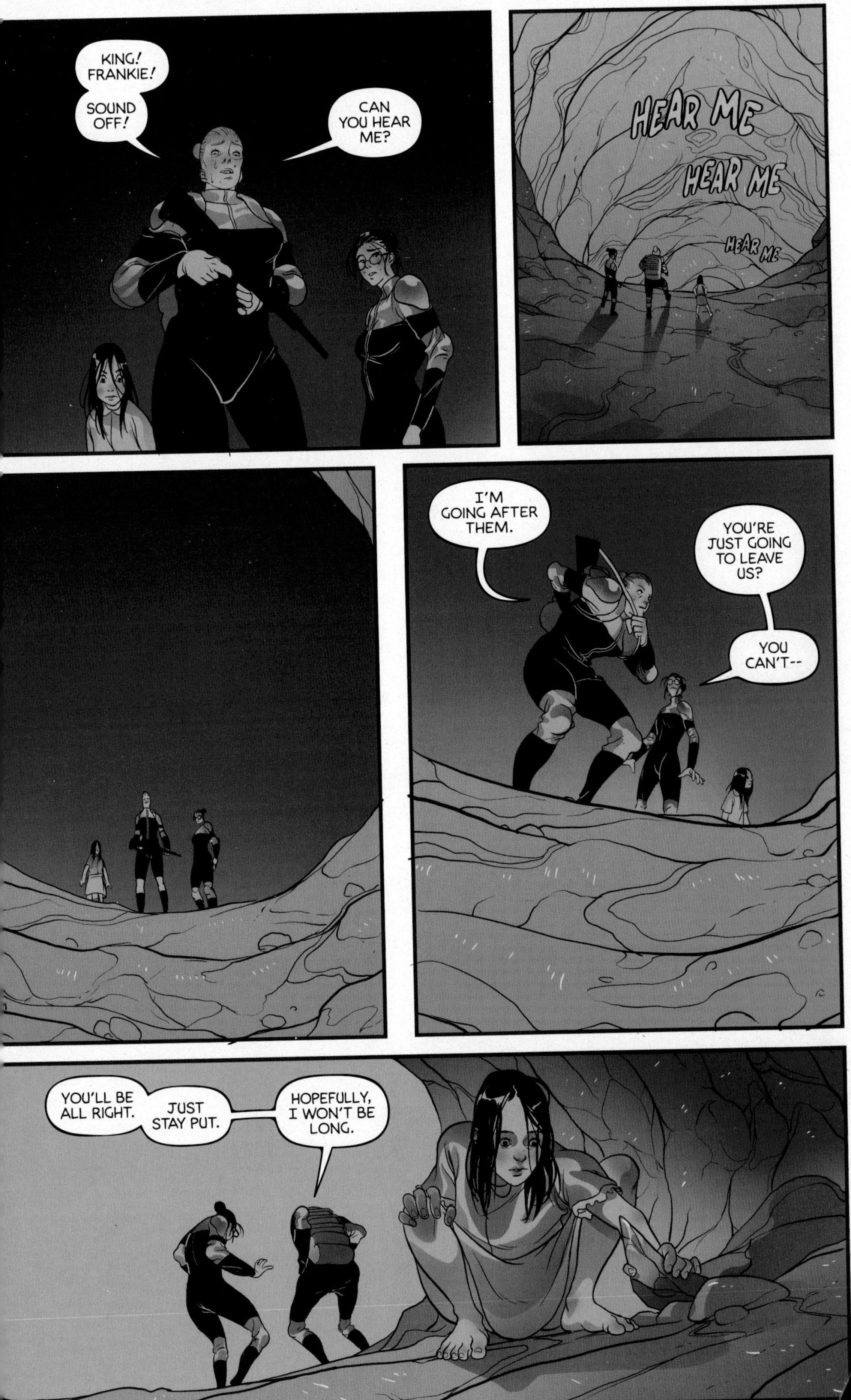
KING! FRANKIE!
SOUND OFF!
CAN YOU HEAR ME?
HEAR ME
HEAR ME
HEAR ME
I'M GOING AFTER THEM.
YOU'RE JUST GOING TO LEAVE US?
YOU CAN'T--
YOU'LL BE ALL RIGHT.
JUST STAY PUT.
HOPEFULLY, I WON'T BE LONG.

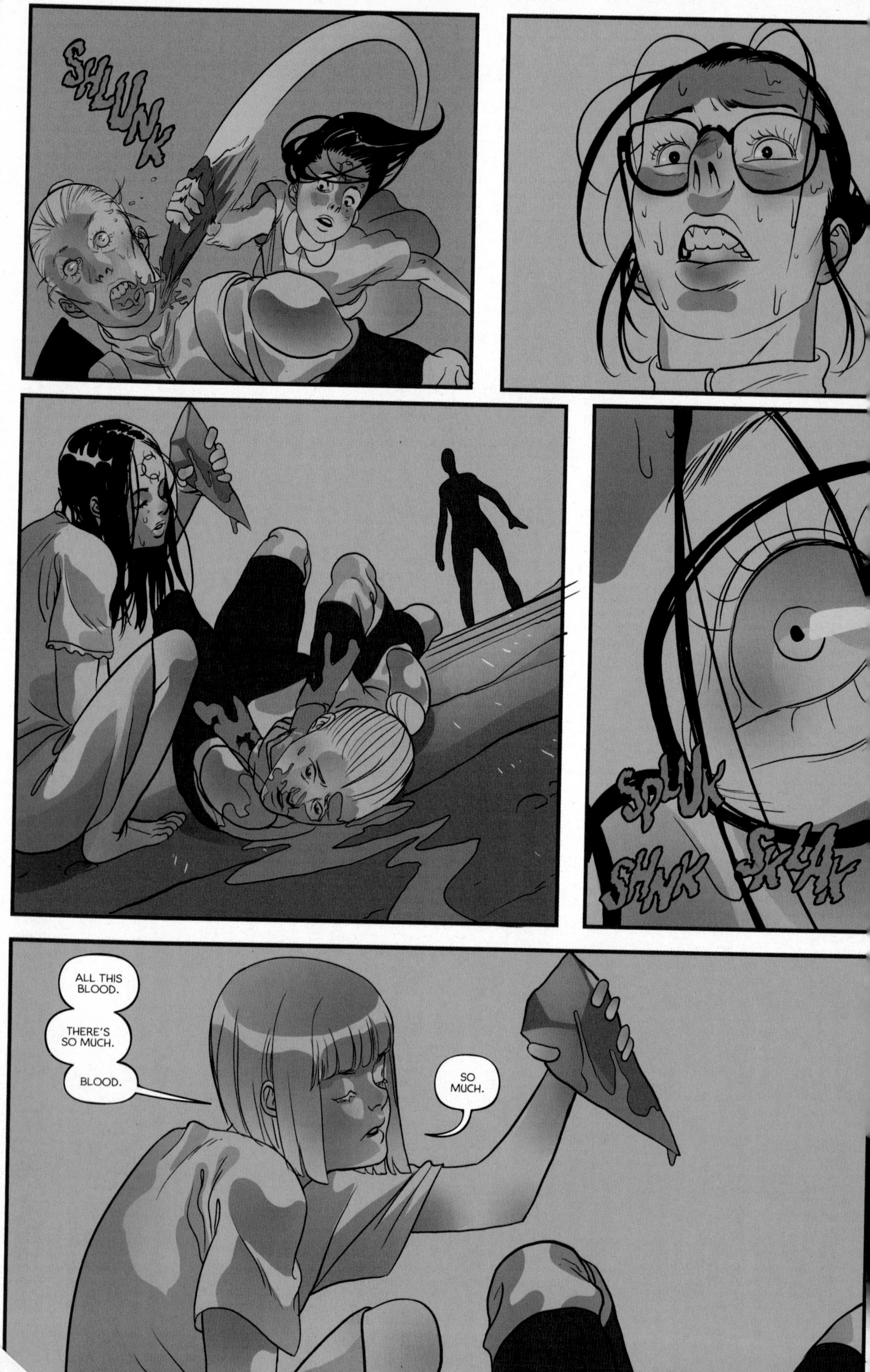
SHLUNK
SPLUK
SHNK
SKLAT
ALL THIS BLOOD.
THERE'S SO MUCH.
BLOOD.
SO MUCH.

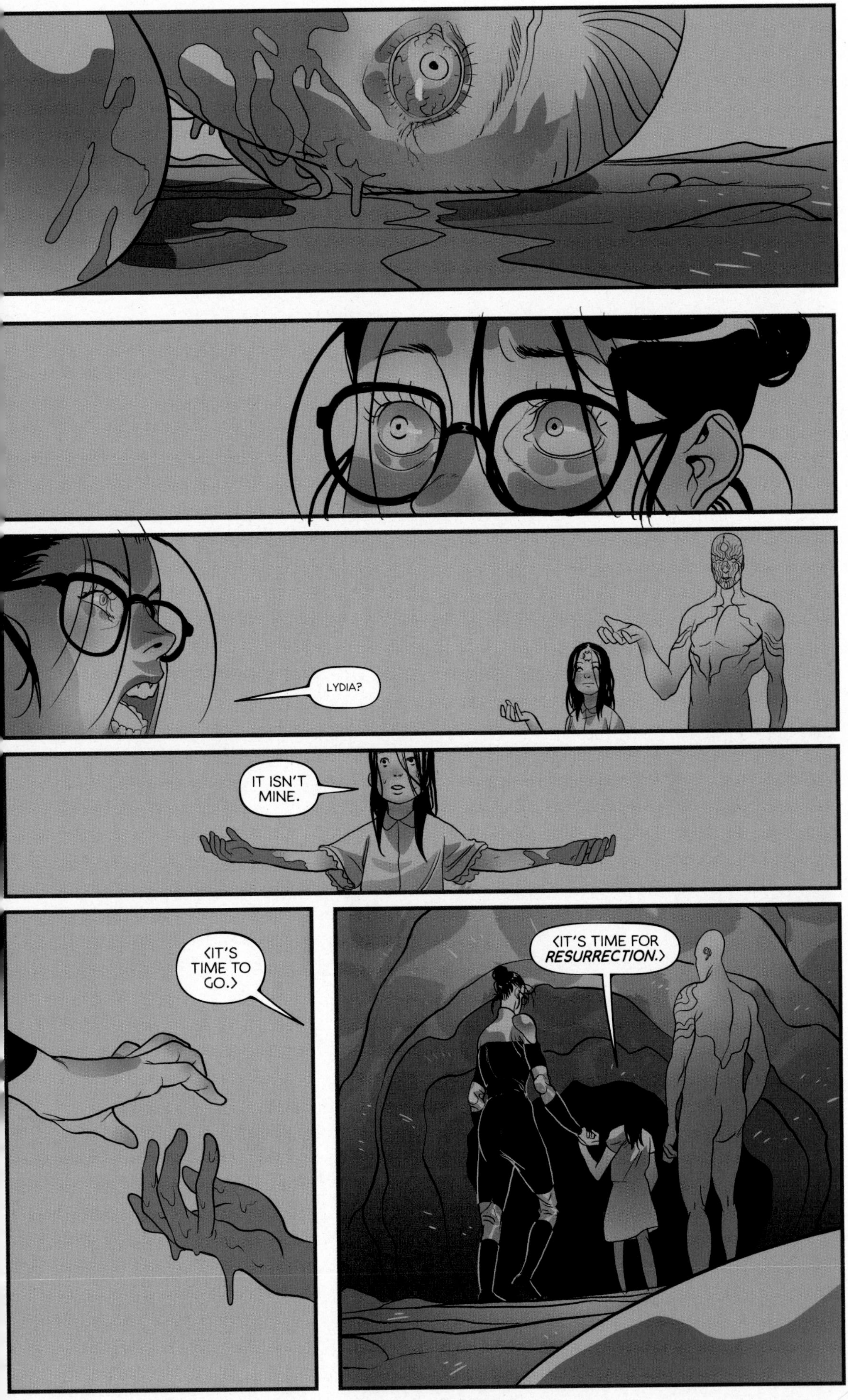
LYDIA?
IT ISN'T MINE.
<IT'S TIME TO GO.>
<IT'S TIME FOR *RESURRECTION.*>

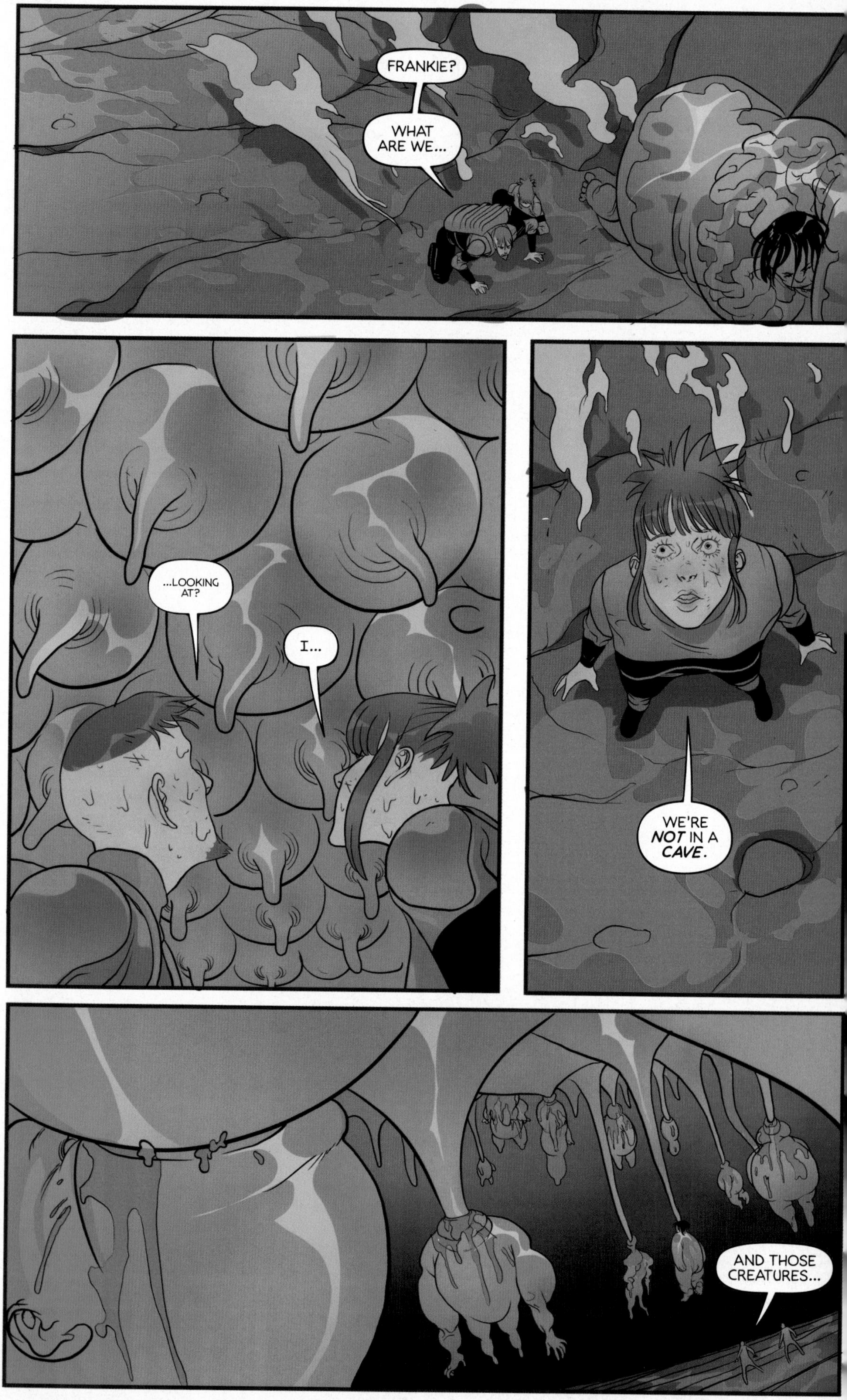
FRANKIE?
WHAT ARE WE...
...LOOKING AT?
I...
WE'RE *NOT* IN A *CAVE*.
AND THOSE CREATURES...

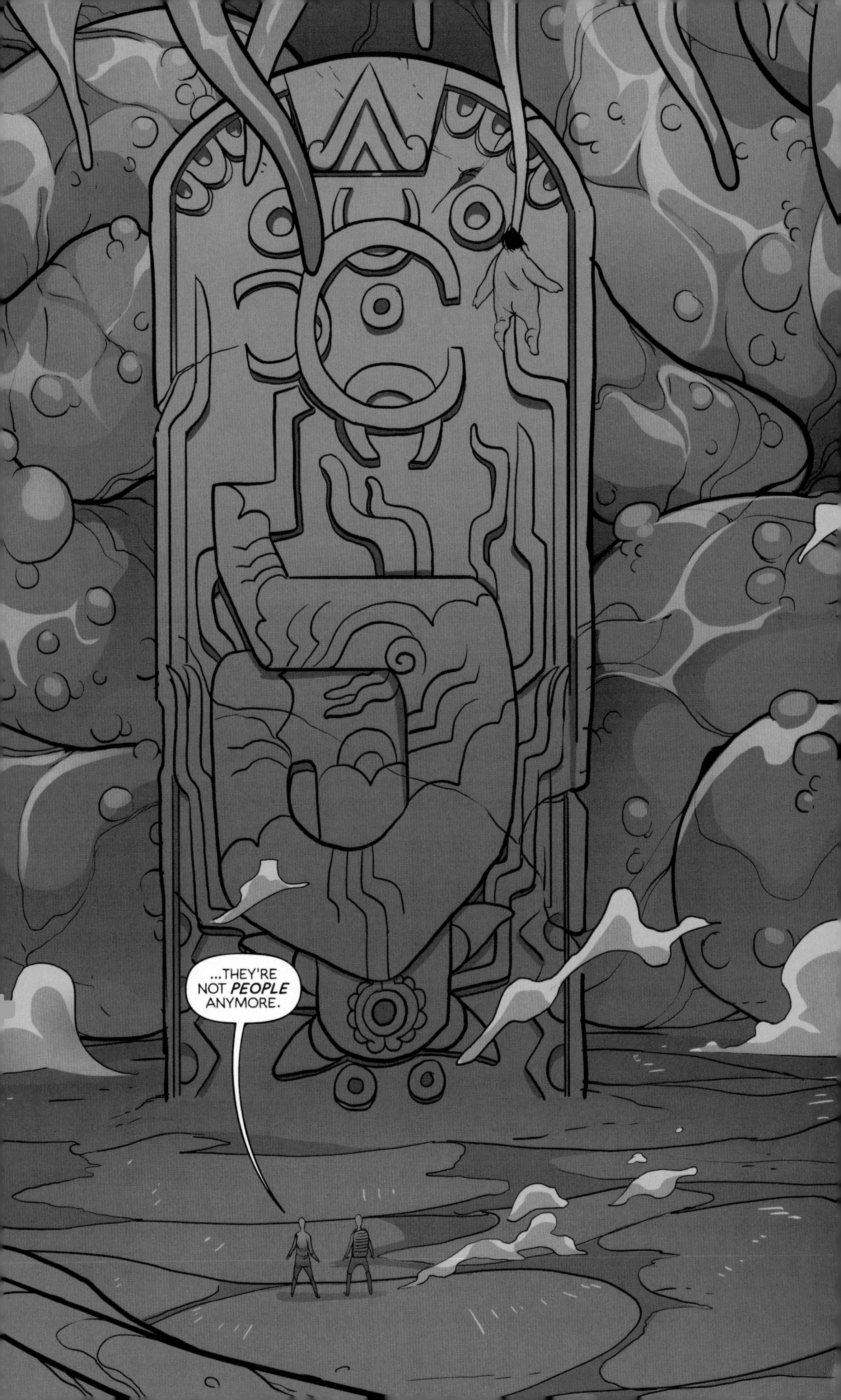
...THEY'RE NOT *PEOPLE* ANYMORE.

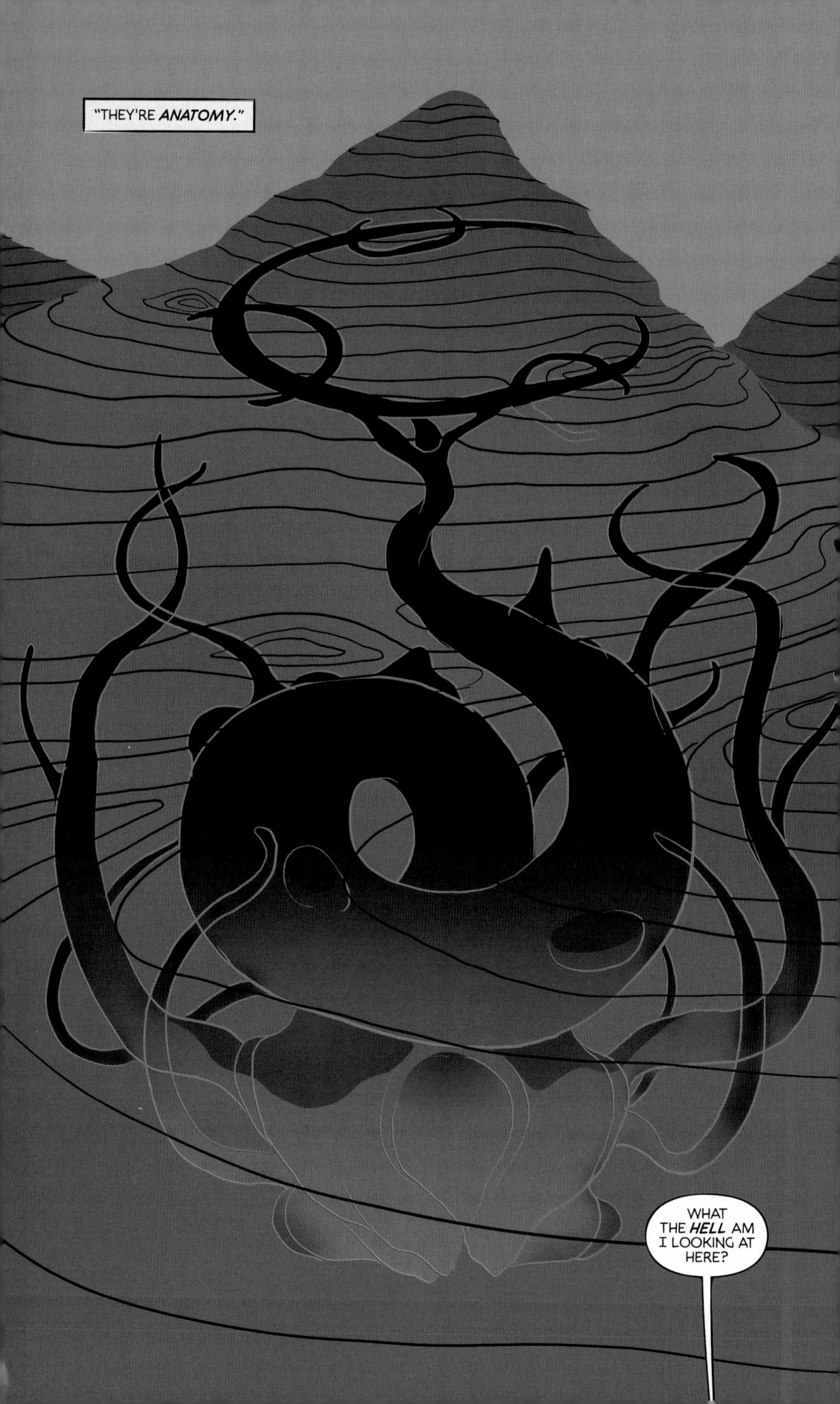
"THEY'RE *ANATOMY*."
WHAT THE ***HELL*** AM I LOOKING AT HERE?

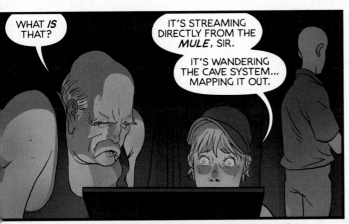

WHAT *IS* THAT?

IT'S STREAMING DIRECTLY FROM THE *MULE*, SIR.

IT'S WANDERING THE CAVE SYSTEM... MAPPING IT OUT.

IT LOOKS LIKE SOME SORT OF--

LIKE SOME SORT OF *LIVING CREATURE*.

HELL, SON.

WHATEVER IT IS, IT *AIN'T* ALIVE.

AND IF IT WAS, IT DAMN SURE DOESN'T WANT TO PLAY A ROUND OF *WHACK-A-MOLE* WITH ME.

NOT RIGHT NOW.

YOU GET A LINE ON THOSE BIRDS?

YES, SIR.

WE'VE GOT A PAIR OF F15s IN THE AREA AND READY FOR YOUR ORDERS.

LIGHT 'EM UP.

Ch 05

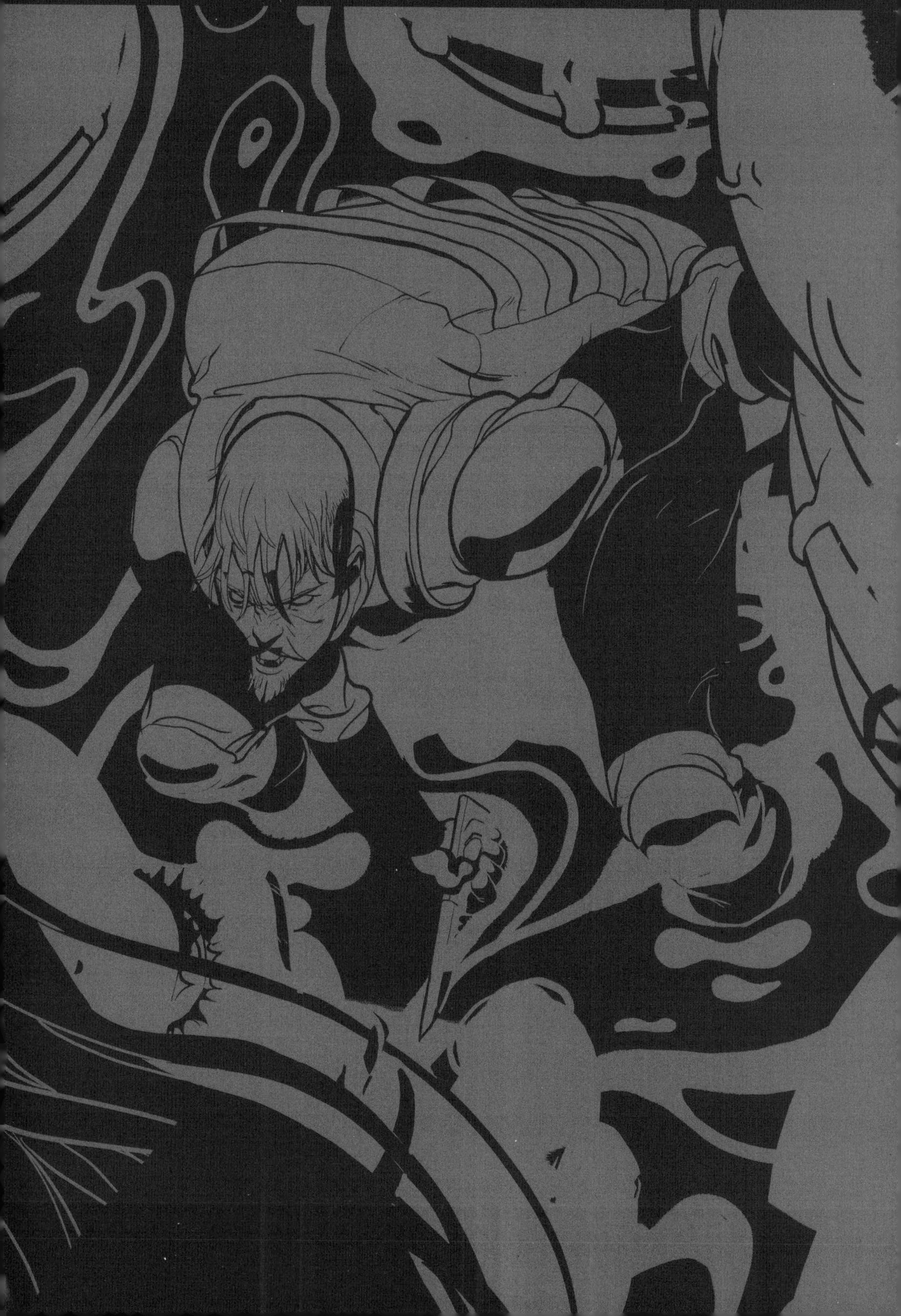

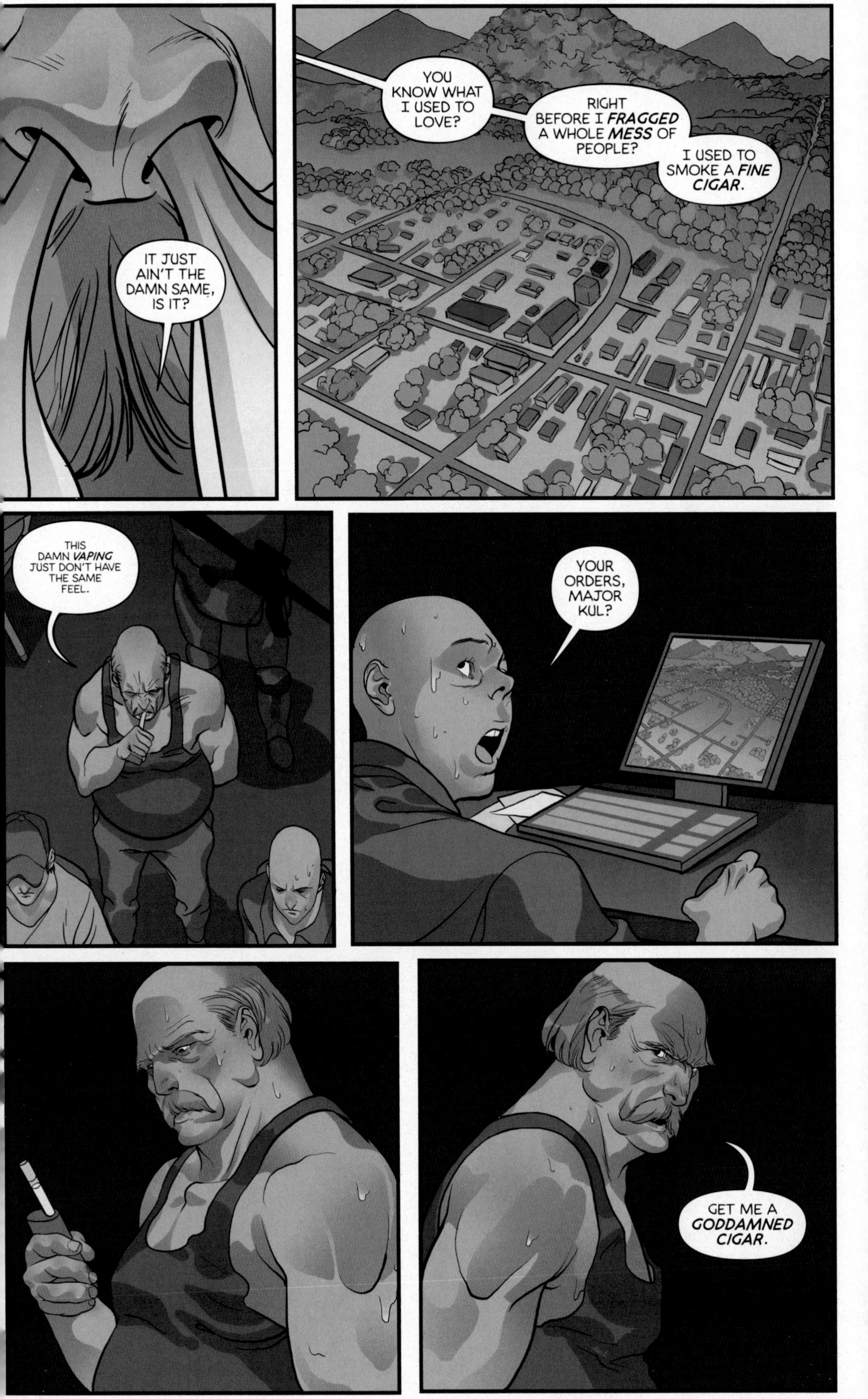
IT JUST AIN'T THE DAMN SAME, IS IT?
YOU KNOW WHAT I USED TO LOVE?
RIGHT BEFORE I *FRAGGED* A WHOLE *MESS* OF PEOPLE?
I USED TO SMOKE A *FINE CIGAR*.
THIS DAMN *VAPING* JUST DON'T HAVE THE SAME FEEL.
YOUR ORDERS, MAJOR KUL?
GET ME A *GODDAMNED CIGAR*.

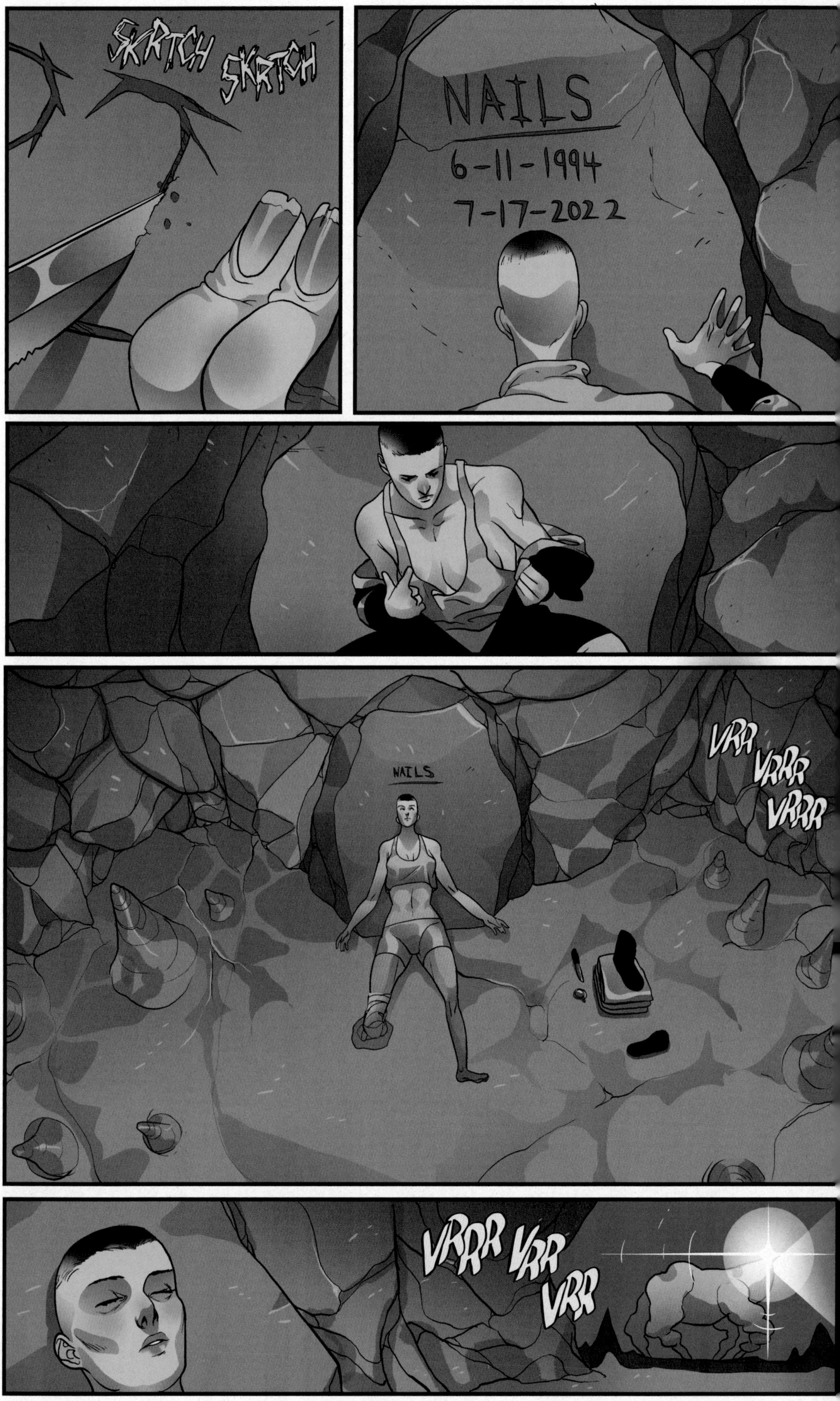
SKRTCH SKRTCH
NAILS
6-11-1994
7-17-2022
NAILS
VRR VRRR VRRR
VRRR VRR VRR

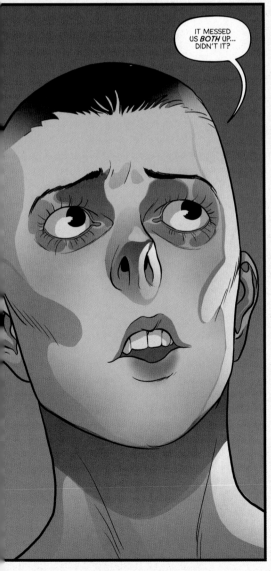

VRR
VRRR
VRR
IT MESSED US *BOTH* UP... DIDN'T IT?
NAILS
6-11-1994
7-17-2022
VRRR
VRR
VRR

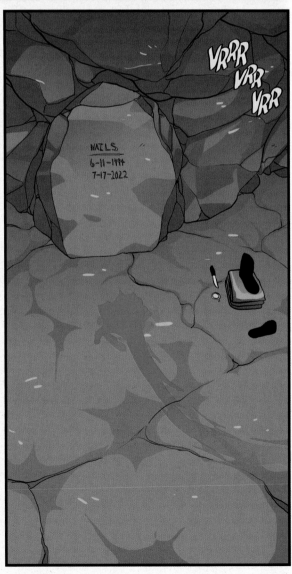

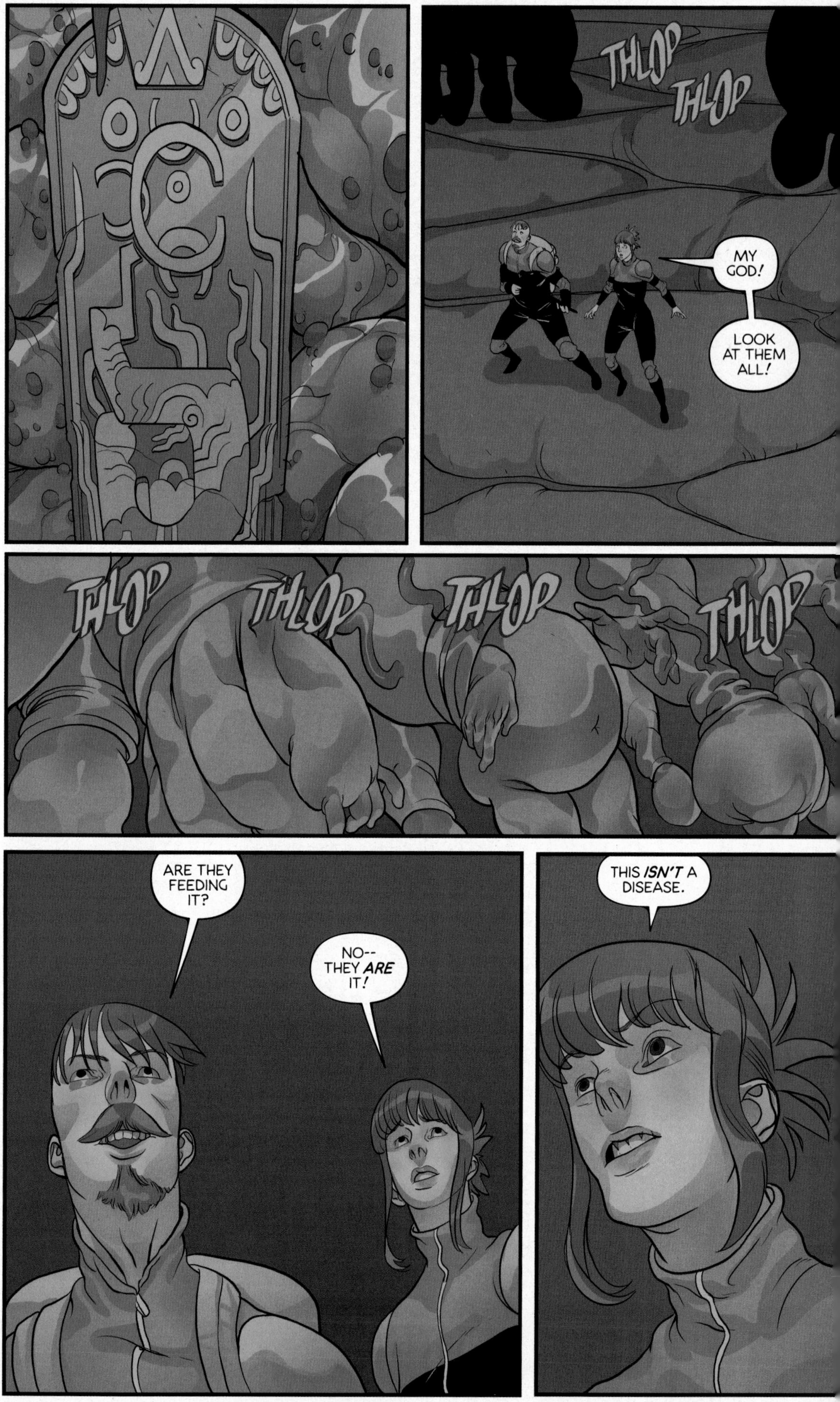
THLOP
THLOP
MY GOD!
LOOK AT THEM ALL!
THLOP
THLOP
THLOP
THLOP
ARE THEY FEEDING IT?
NO-- THEY ARE IT!
THIS ISN'T A DISEASE.

I DON'T CARE WHAT IT IS--

KING--THIS ISN'T RANDOM AT ALL!

WE THOUGHT IT WAS A *CONTAGION.*

WE THOUGHT THIS WAS JUST A CAVE.

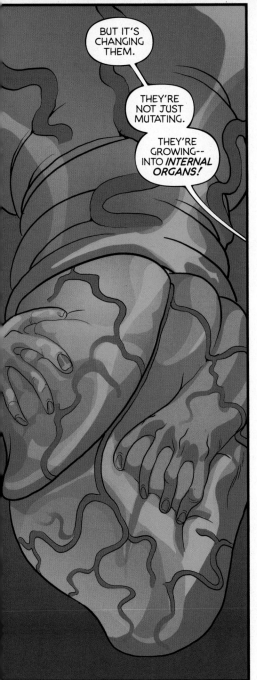

BUT IT'S CHANGING THEM.

THEY'RE NOT JUST MUTATING.

THEY'RE GROWING-- INTO *INTERNAL ORGANS!*

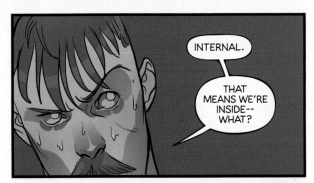

INTERNAL.

THAT MEANS WE'RE INSIDE-- WHAT?

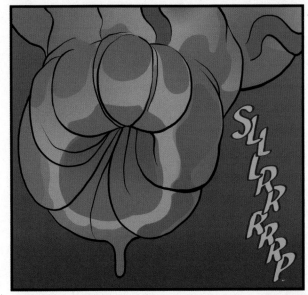

SLLRRRRP

IT'S RESHAPING US...

...IN ITS IMAGE...

...PIECE BY PIECE...

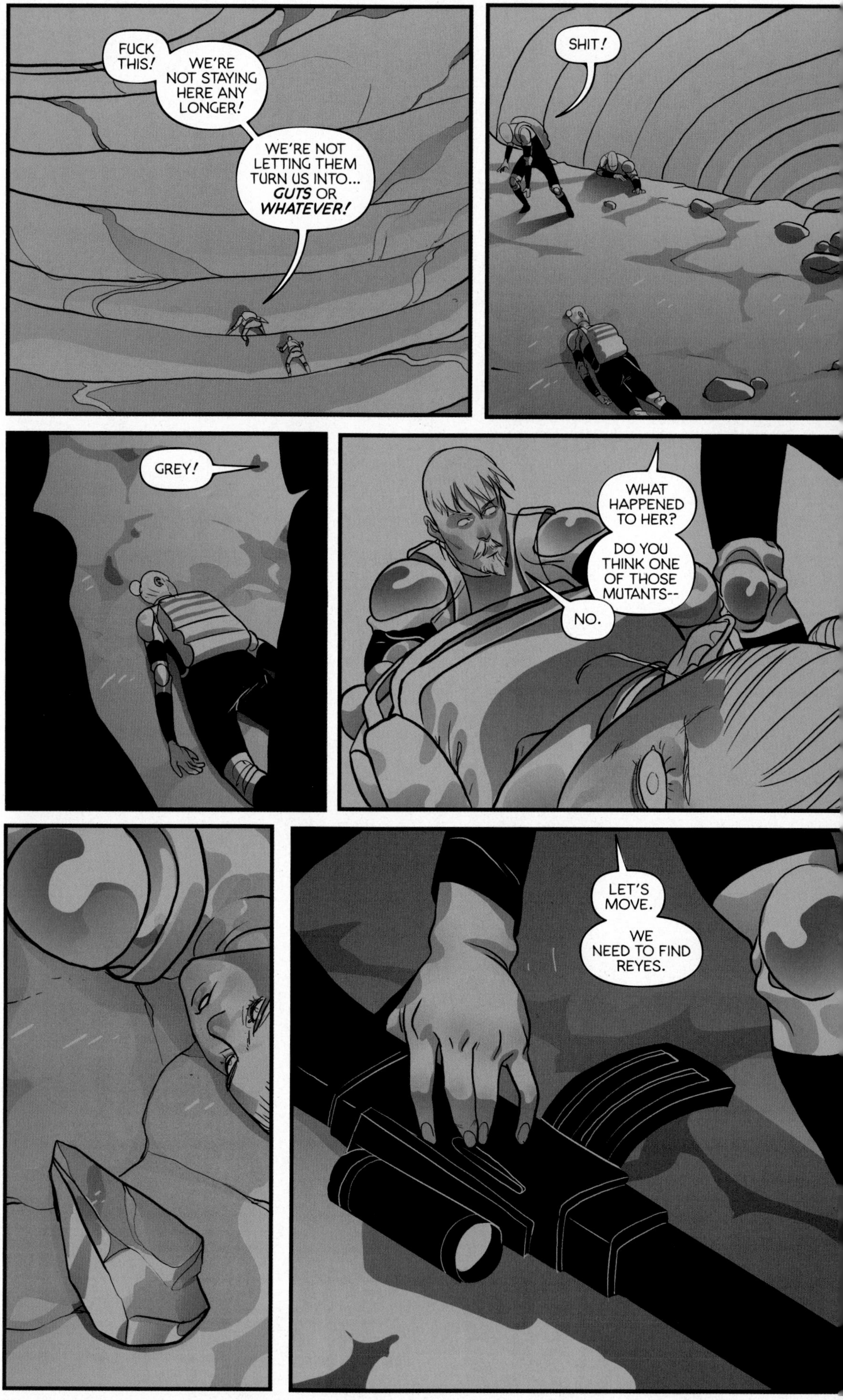
FUCK THIS!
WE'RE NOT STAYING HERE ANY LONGER!
WE'RE NOT LETTING THEM TURN US INTO... ***GUTS*** OR ***WHATEVER!***
SHIT!
GREY!
WHAT HAPPENED TO HER?
DO YOU THINK ONE OF THOSE MUTANTS--
NO.
LET'S MOVE.
WE NEED TO FIND REYES.

I KNOW YOU'RE *RESTLESS*.

YOU'VE BEEN SLEEPING A *LONG* TIME.

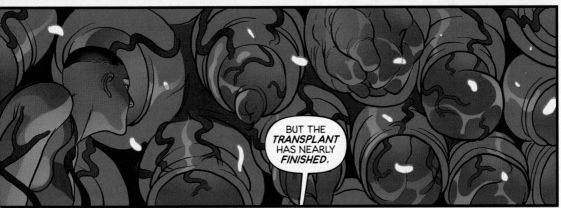

BUT THE *TRANSPLANT* HAS NEARLY *FINISHED*.

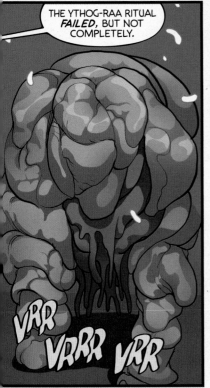

THE YTHOG-RAA RITUAL *FAILED*, BUT NOT COMPLETELY.

VRR VRRR VRR

YOU ARRIVED, BUT MILLENNIA *BEFORE* THOSE WHO SUMMONED YOU WOULD BE CONCEIVED.

SPACE AND *TIME* MEAN *SO LITTLE*.

YOU WERE NOT THEIR *HARBINGER OF CHAOS*...

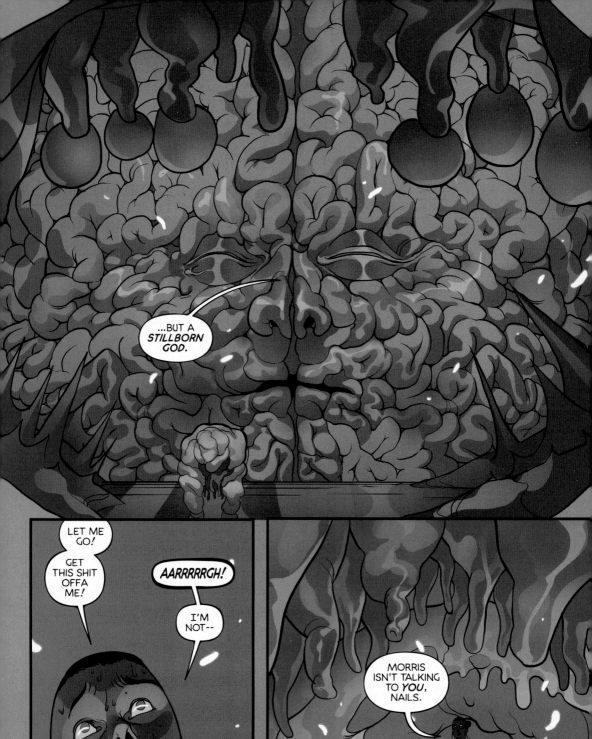

...BUT A *STILLBORN GOD.*

LET ME GO!

GET THIS SHIT OFFA ME!

AARRRRRGH!

I'M NOT--

MORRIS ISN'T TALKING TO *YOU,* NAILS.

DOC--

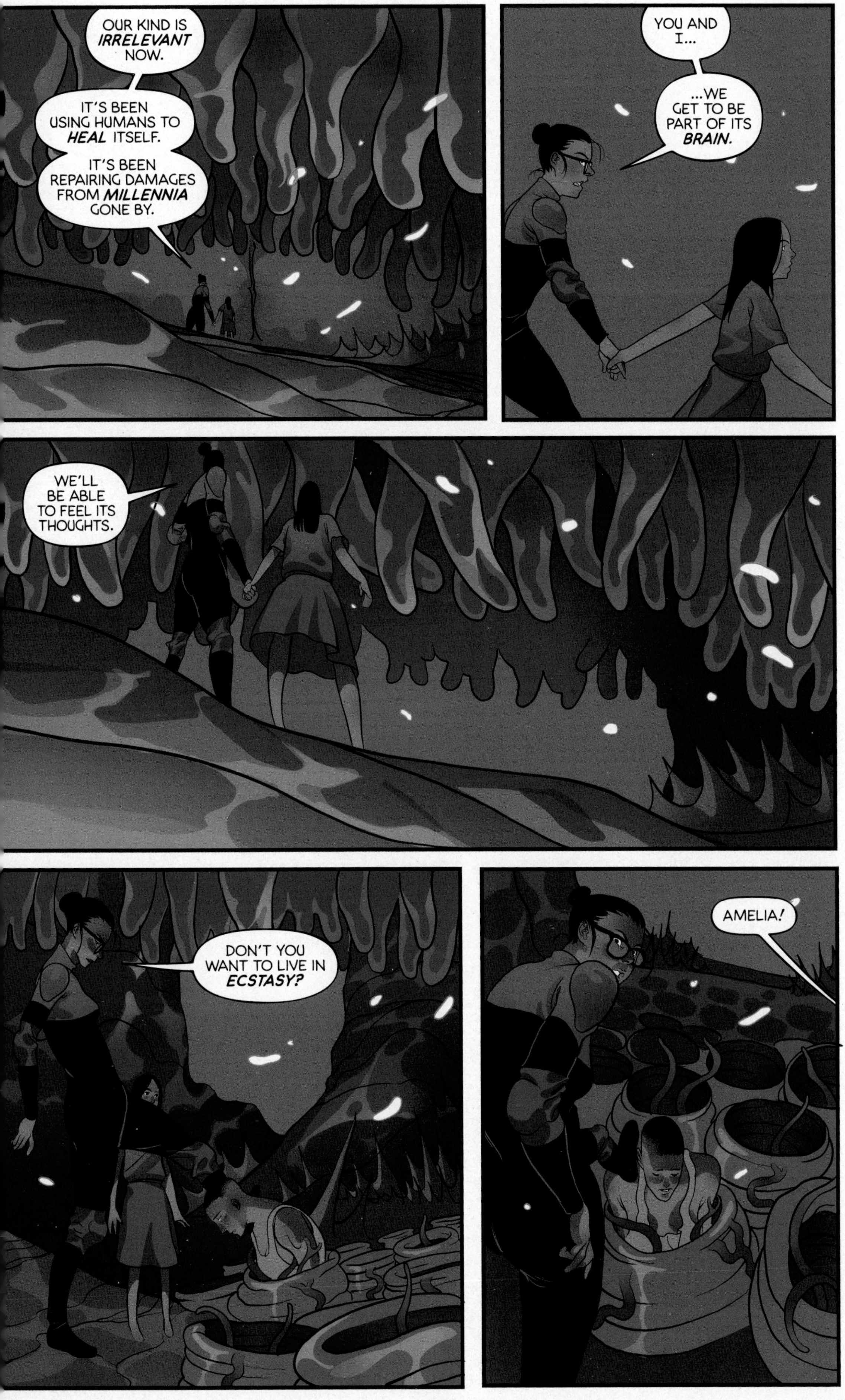
OUR KIND IS IRRELEVANT NOW.
IT'S BEEN USING HUMANS TO HEAL ITSELF.
IT'S BEEN REPAIRING DAMAGES FROM MILLENNIA GONE BY.
YOU AND I...
...WE GET TO BE PART OF ITS BRAIN.
WE'LL BE ABLE TO FEEL ITS THOUGHTS.
DON'T YOU WANT TO LIVE IN ECSTASY?
AMELIA!

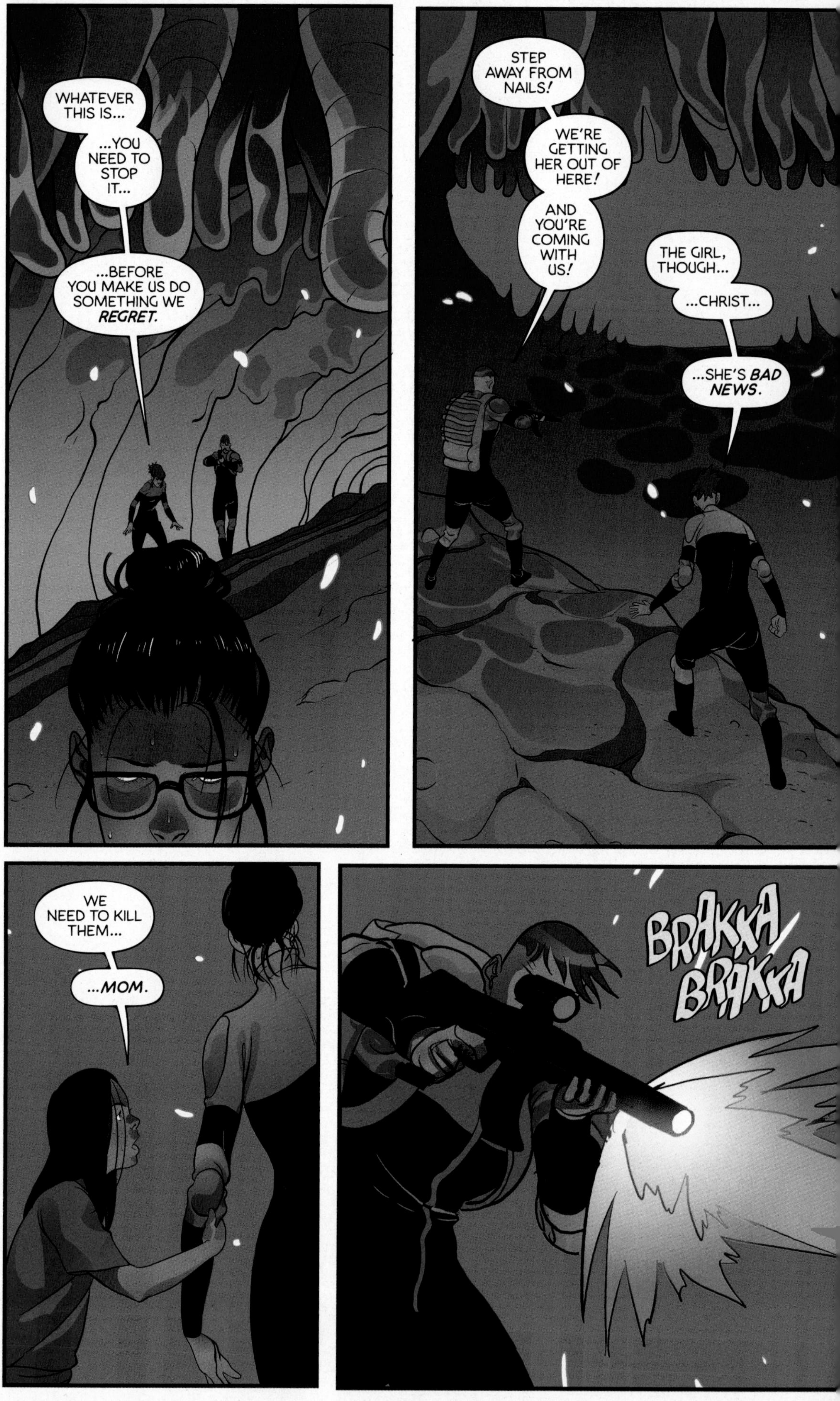
WHATEVER THIS IS...
...YOU NEED TO STOP IT...
...BEFORE YOU MAKE US DO SOMETHING WE *REGRET.*
STEP AWAY FROM NAILS!
WE'RE GETTING HER OUT OF HERE!
AND YOU'RE COMING WITH US!
THE GIRL, THOUGH...
...CHRIST...
...SHE'S *BAD NEWS*.
WE NEED TO KILL THEM...
...*MOM*.
BRAKKA BRAKKA

GOD,
NO!

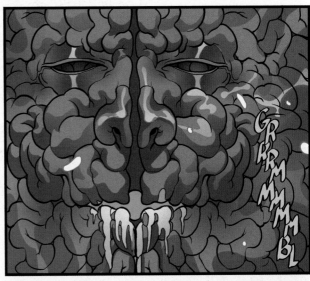

GRRMMMMBL

BLEEORG

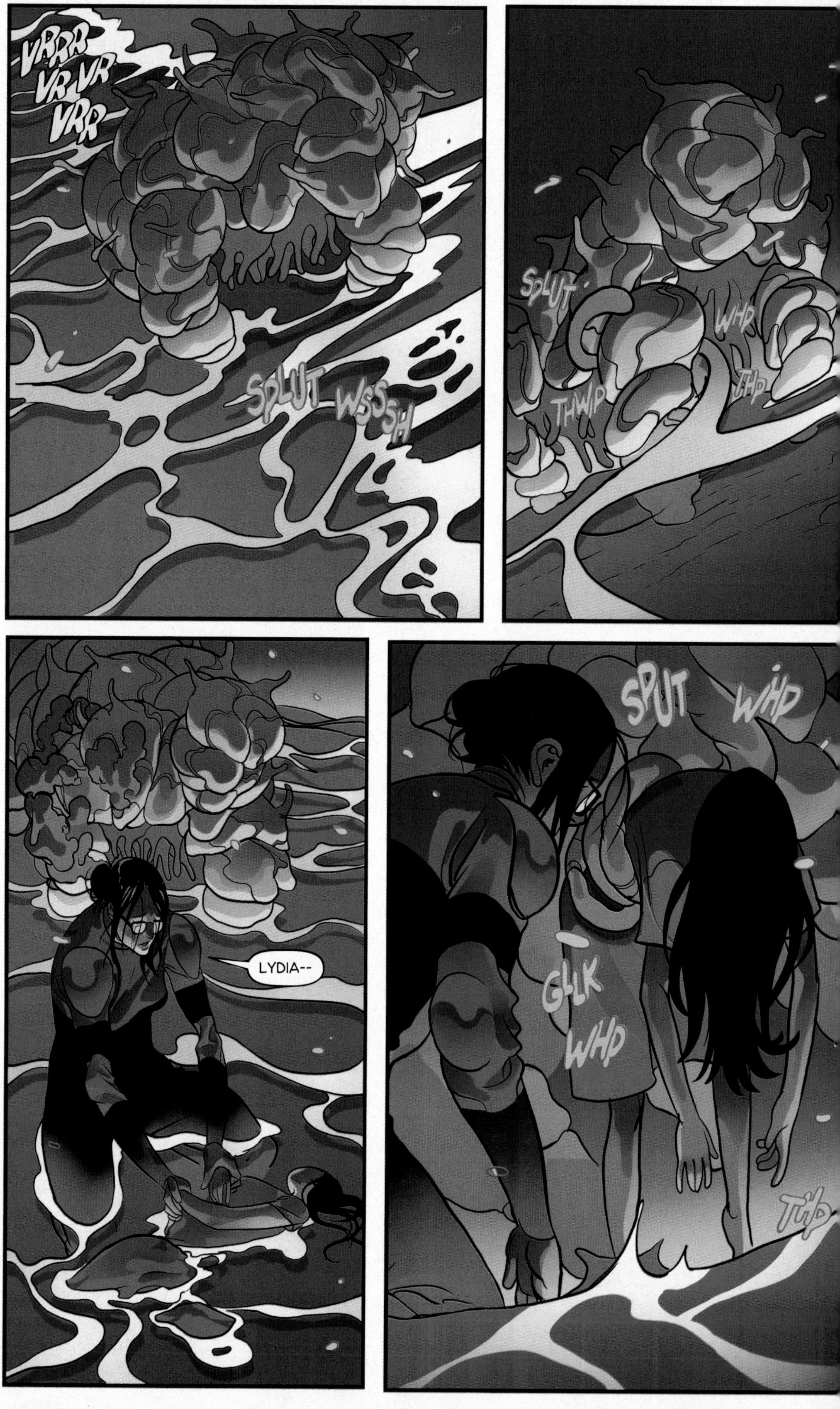
VRRR VR VR VRR
SPLUT WSSSH
SPLUT
WHP
THWIP
THP
LYDIA--
SPUT
WHP
GLLK
WHP
THP

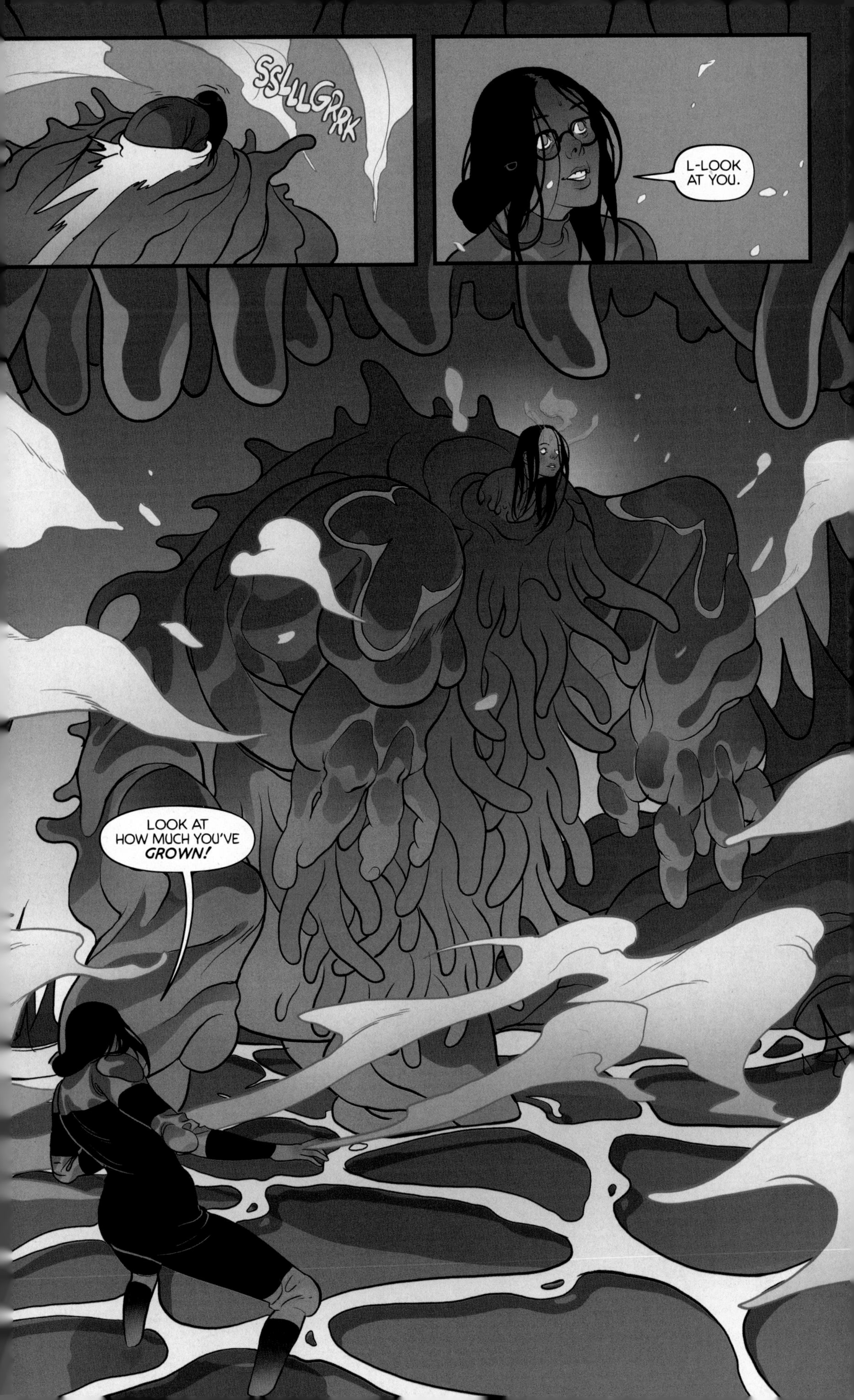
SSLLLGRRK
L-LOOK AT YOU.
LOOK AT HOW MUCH YOU'VE *GROWN!*

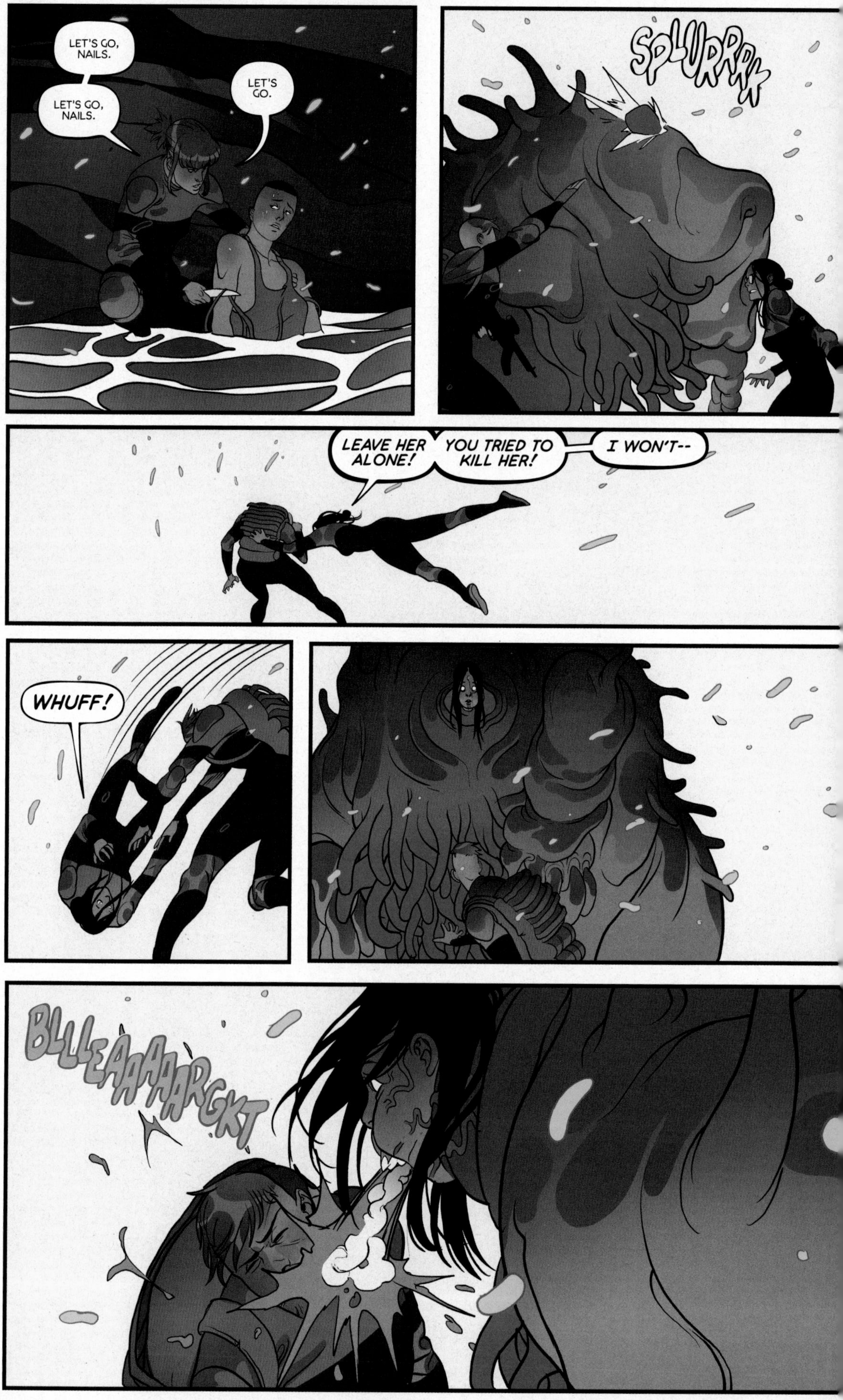
LET'S GO, NAILS.
LET'S GO, NAILS.
LET'S GO.
SPLURRRK
LEAVE HER ALONE!
YOU TRIED TO KILL HER!
I WON'T--
WHUFF!
BLLLEAAAAARGKT

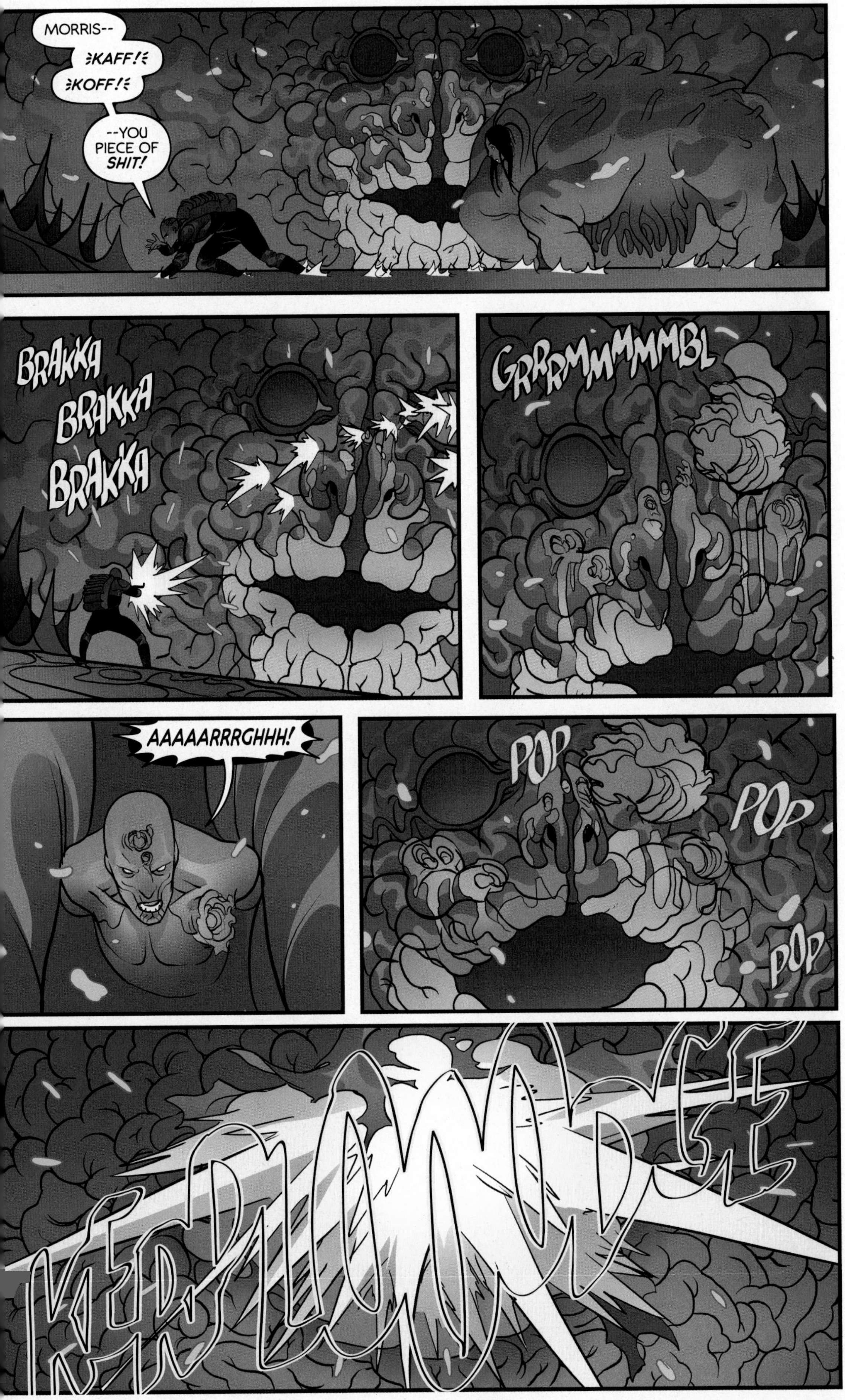
MORRIS--
KAFF!
KOFF!
--YOU PIECE OF SHIT!
BRAKKA
BRAKKA
BRAKKA
GRRRMMMMMBL
AAAAARRRGHHH!
POP
POP
POP
KERBLOOOOOOMMMM

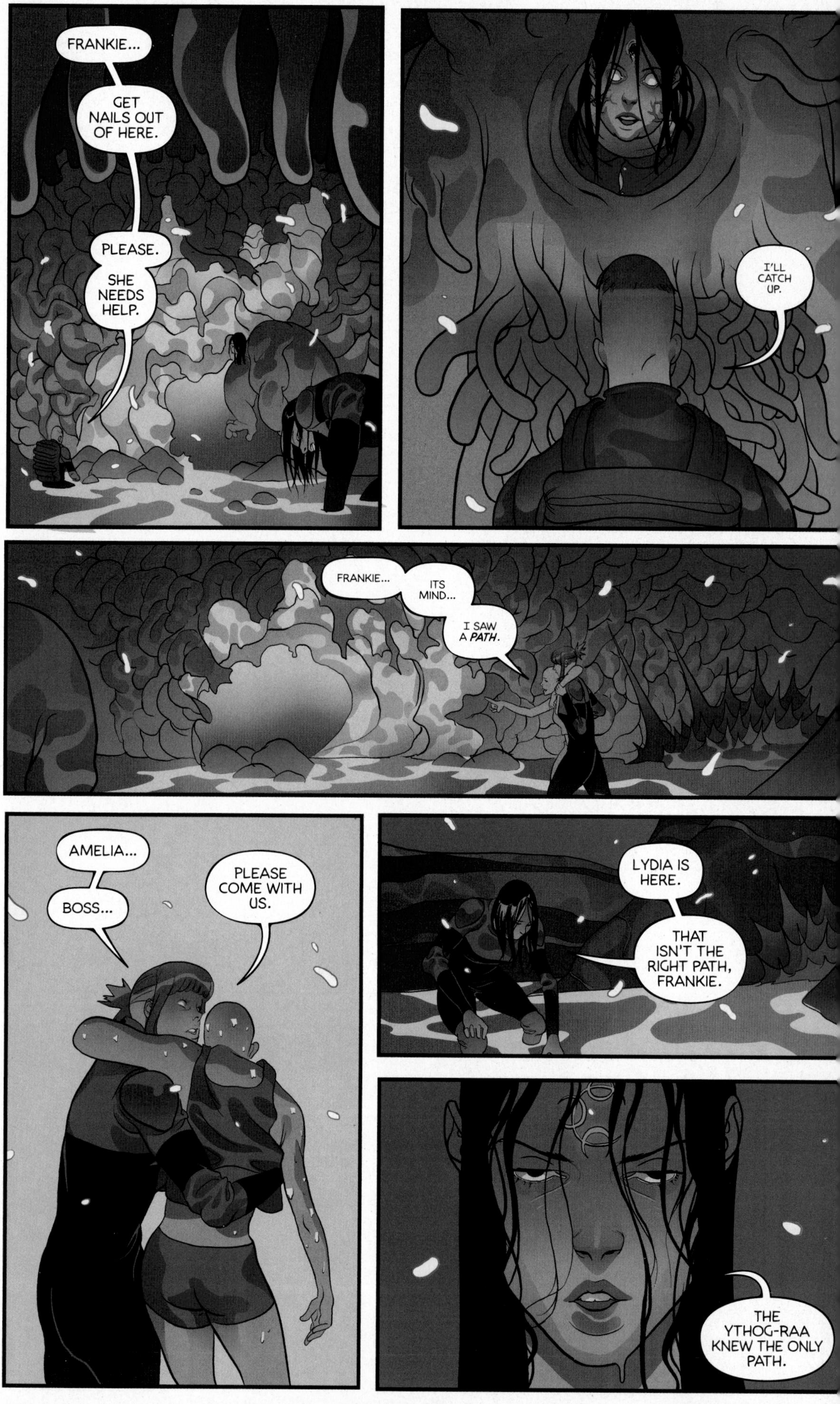
FRANKIE...
GET NAILS OUT OF HERE.
PLEASE.
SHE NEEDS HELP.
I'LL CATCH UP.
FRANKIE...
ITS MIND...
I SAW A *PATH*.
AMELIA...
BOSS...
PLEASE COME WITH US.
LYDIA IS HERE.
THAT ISN'T THE RIGHT PATH, FRANKIE.
THE YTHOG-RAA KNEW THE ONLY PATH.

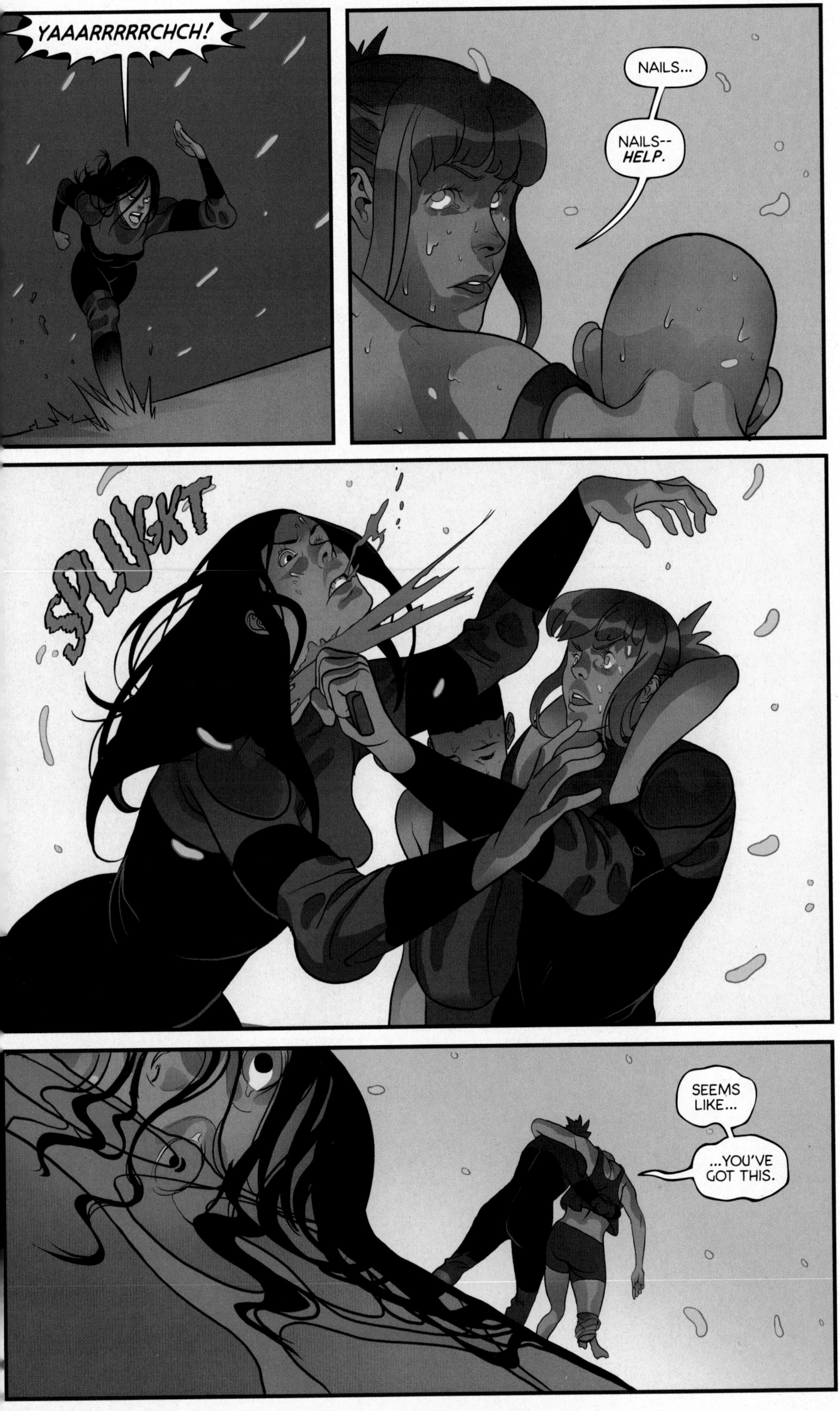
YAAARRRRRCHCH!
NAILS...
NAILS-- *HELP*.
SPLUGKT
SEEMS LIKE...
...YOU'VE GOT THIS.

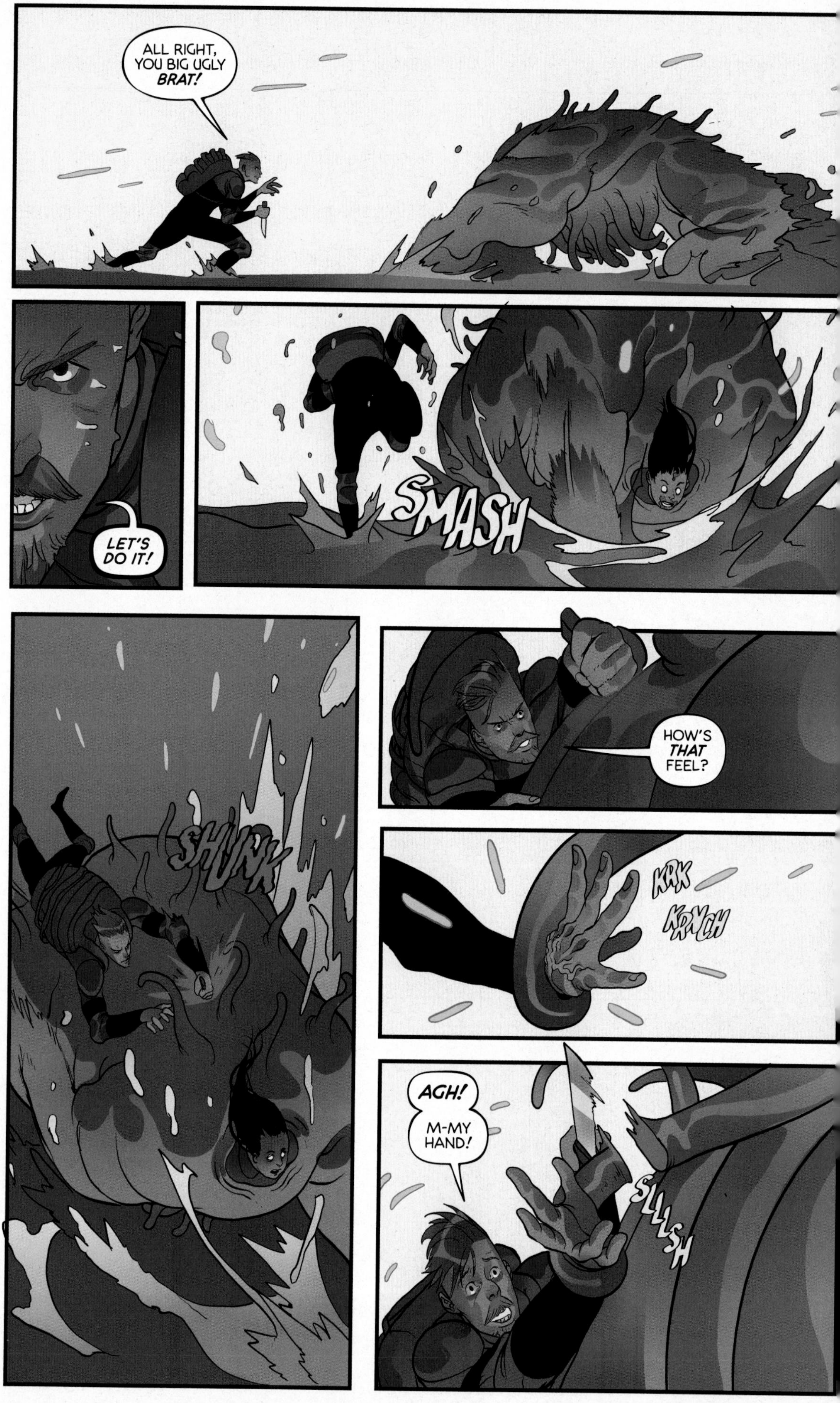
ALL RIGHT, YOU BIG UGLY BRAT!
LET'S DO IT!
SMASH
SHUNK
HOW'S THAT FEEL?
KRAK
KRUNCH
AGH!
M-MY HAND!
SLLLSH

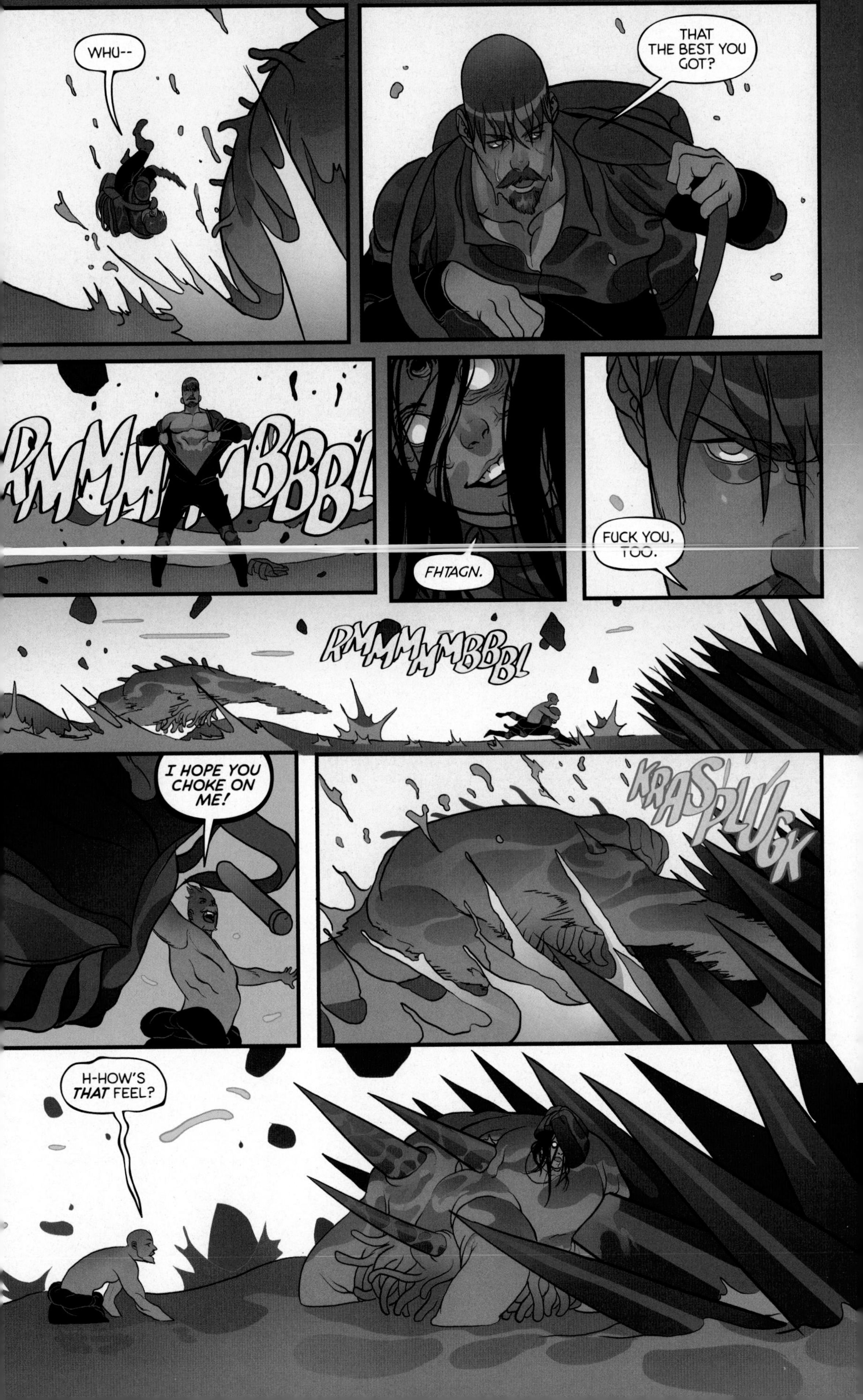
WHU--
THAT THE BEST YOU GOT?
RMMMMMBBBL
FHTAGN.
FUCK YOU, TOO.
RMMMMMBBBL
I HOPE YOU CHOKE ON ME!
KRASPLUGK
H-HOW'S *THAT* FEEL?

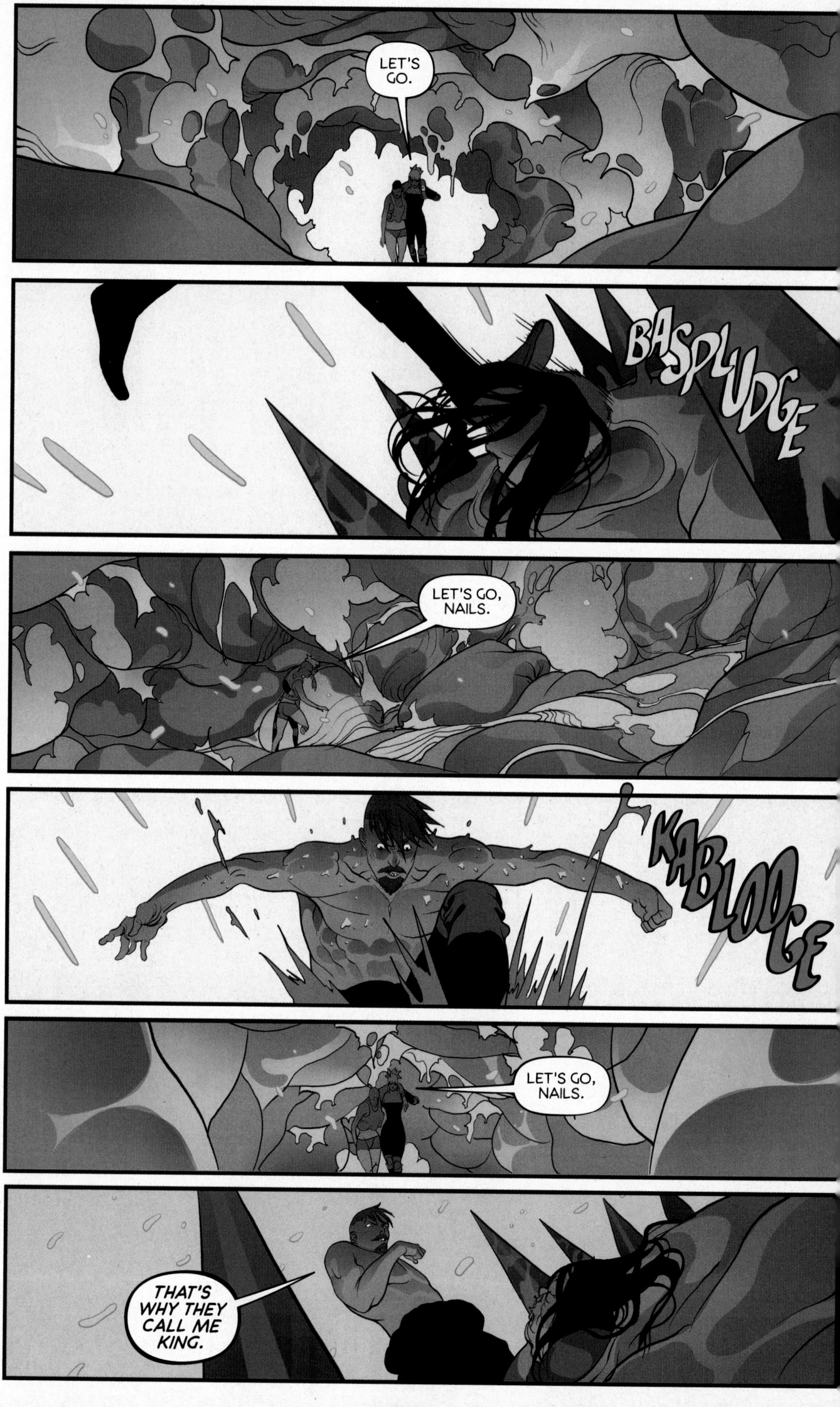
LET'S GO.
BASPLUDGE
LET'S GO, NAILS.
KABLOOGE
LET'S GO, NAILS.
THAT'S WHY THEY CALL ME KING.

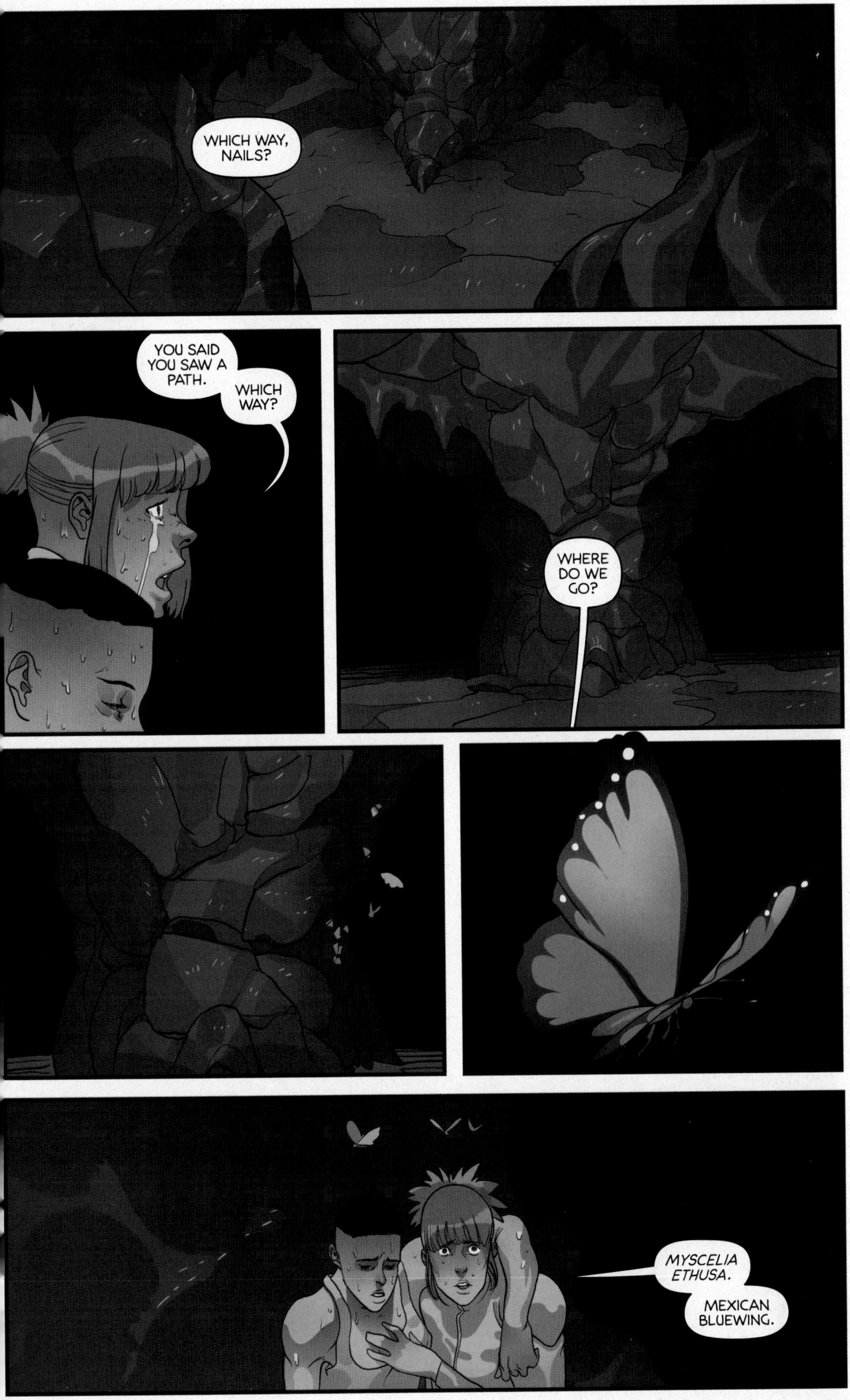
WHICH WAY, NAILS?
YOU SAID YOU SAW A PATH.
WHICH WAY?
WHERE DO WE GO?
MYSCELIA ETHUSA.
MEXICAN BLUEWING.

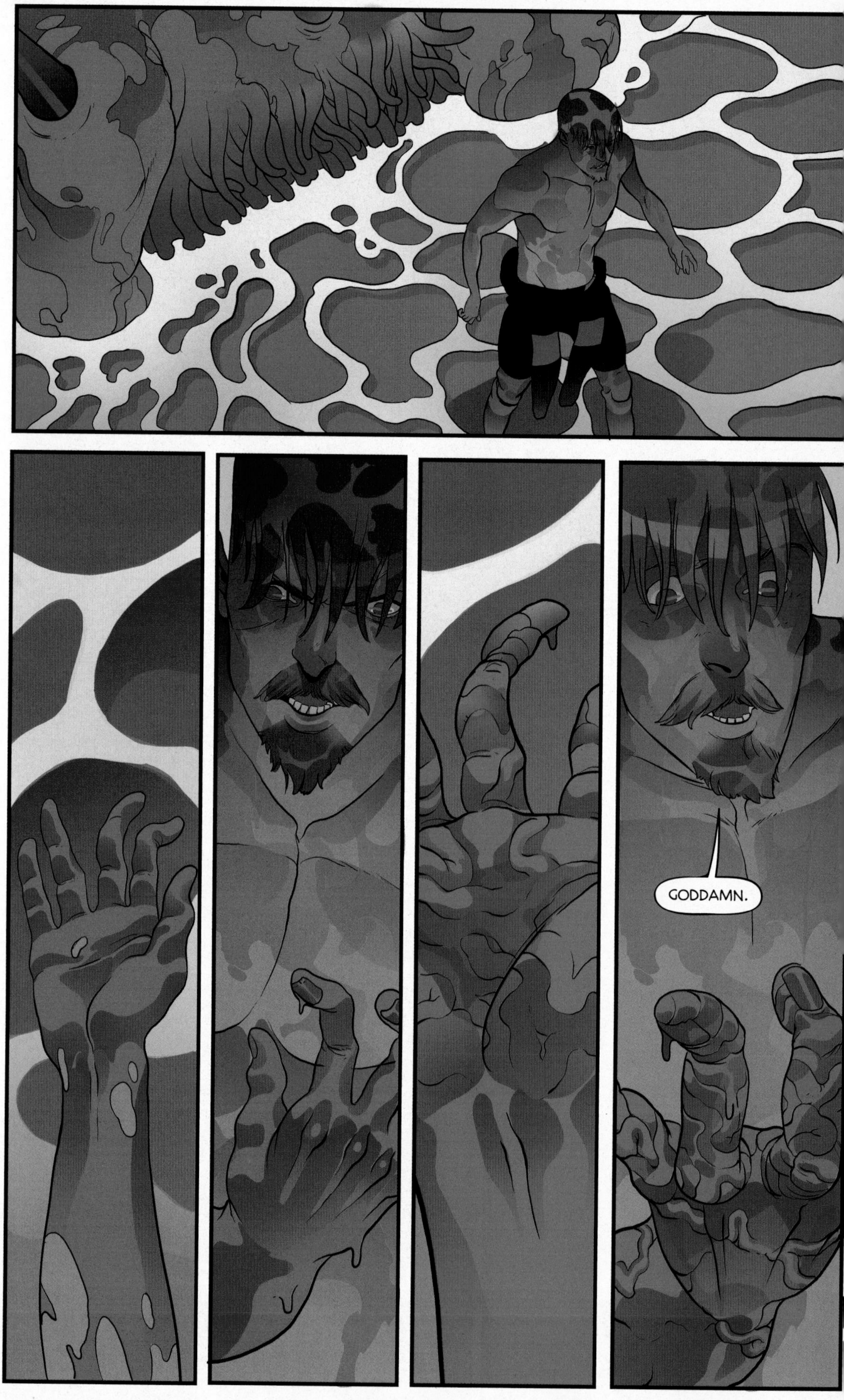
GODDAMN.

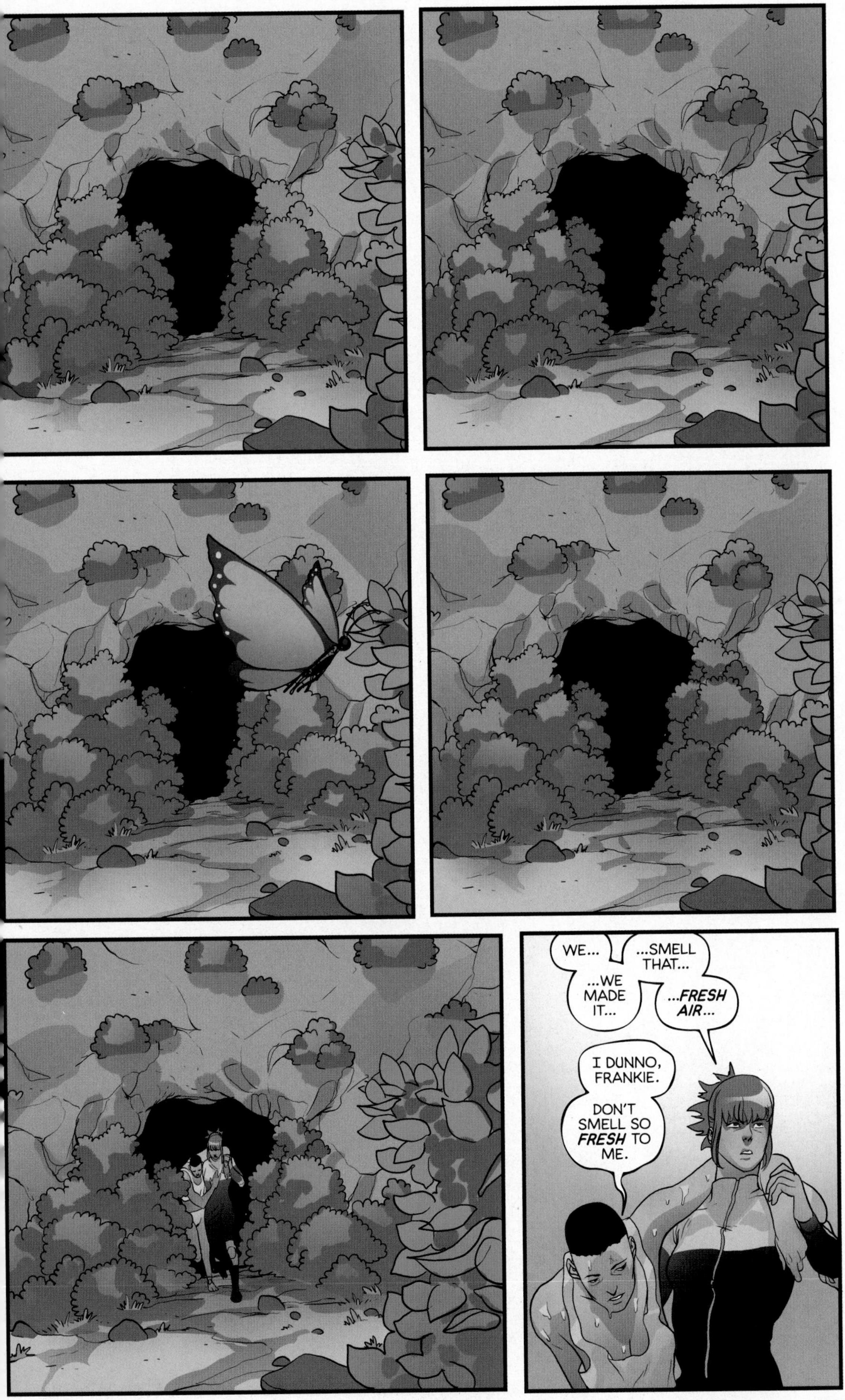
WE...
...SMELL THAT...
...WE MADE IT...
...FRESH AIR...
I DUNNO, FRANKIE.
DON'T SMELL SO FRESH TO ME.

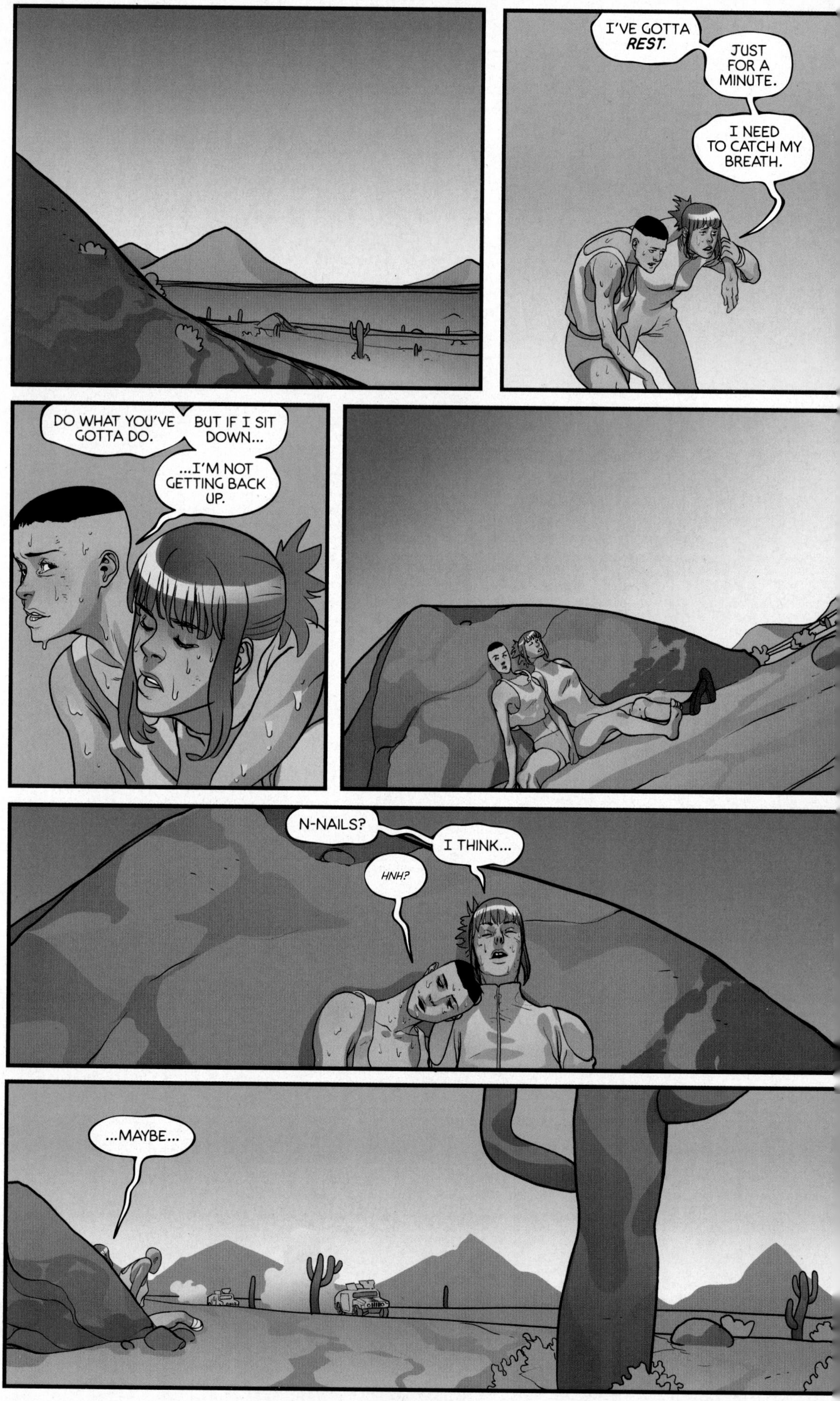

I'VE GOTTA *REST.*
JUST FOR A MINUTE.
I NEED TO CATCH MY BREATH.
DO WHAT YOU'VE GOTTA DO.
BUT IF I SIT DOWN...
...I'M NOT GETTING BACK UP.
N-NAILS?
HNH?
I THINK...
...MAYBE...

"...WE MIGHT BE *SAVED*."

ALL RIGHT, FRANKIE. SAY THAT ONE MORE TIME.

I KNOW IT SOUNDS CRAZY, MAJOR.

BUT IT'S TRUE.

THOSE AREN'T CAVES.

IT'S A *MONSTER*.

AND YOU CRAWLED DOWN ITS THROAT.

AND, IF THAT'S THE CASE, WHAT THE HELL DID YOU CRAWL OUT OF?

HEH.

THIS ORGANISM... IT SEEMS LIKE IT'S BEEN *SLEEPING* BELOW THE SURFACE.

HIBERNATING, NOT *DEAD*.

HEALING.

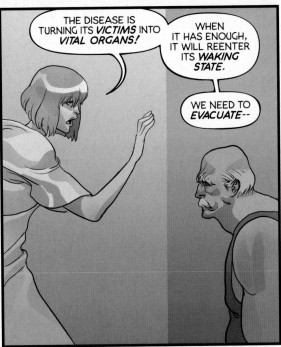

THE DISEASE IS TURNING ITS *VICTIMS* INTO *VITAL ORGANS!*

WHEN IT HAS ENOUGH, IT WILL REENTER ITS *WAKING STATE*.

WE NEED TO *EVACUATE*--

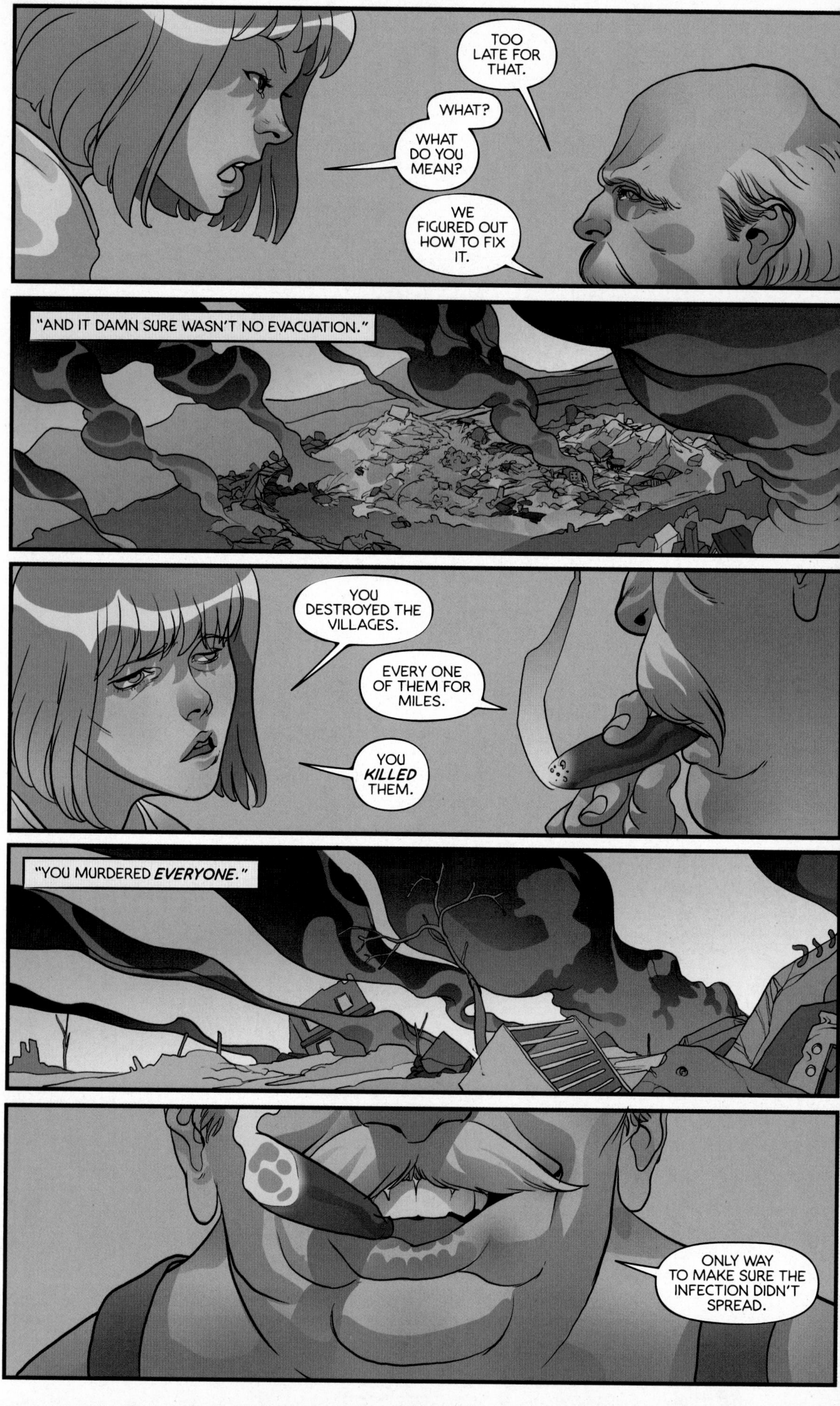
TOO LATE FOR THAT.
WHAT?
WHAT DO YOU MEAN?
WE FIGURED OUT HOW TO FIX IT.
"AND IT DAMN SURE WASN'T NO EVACUATION."
YOU DESTROYED THE VILLAGES.
EVERY ONE OF THEM FOR MILES.
YOU *KILLED* THEM.
"YOU MURDERED *EVERYONE*."
ONLY WAY TO MAKE SURE THE INFECTION DIDN'T SPREAD.

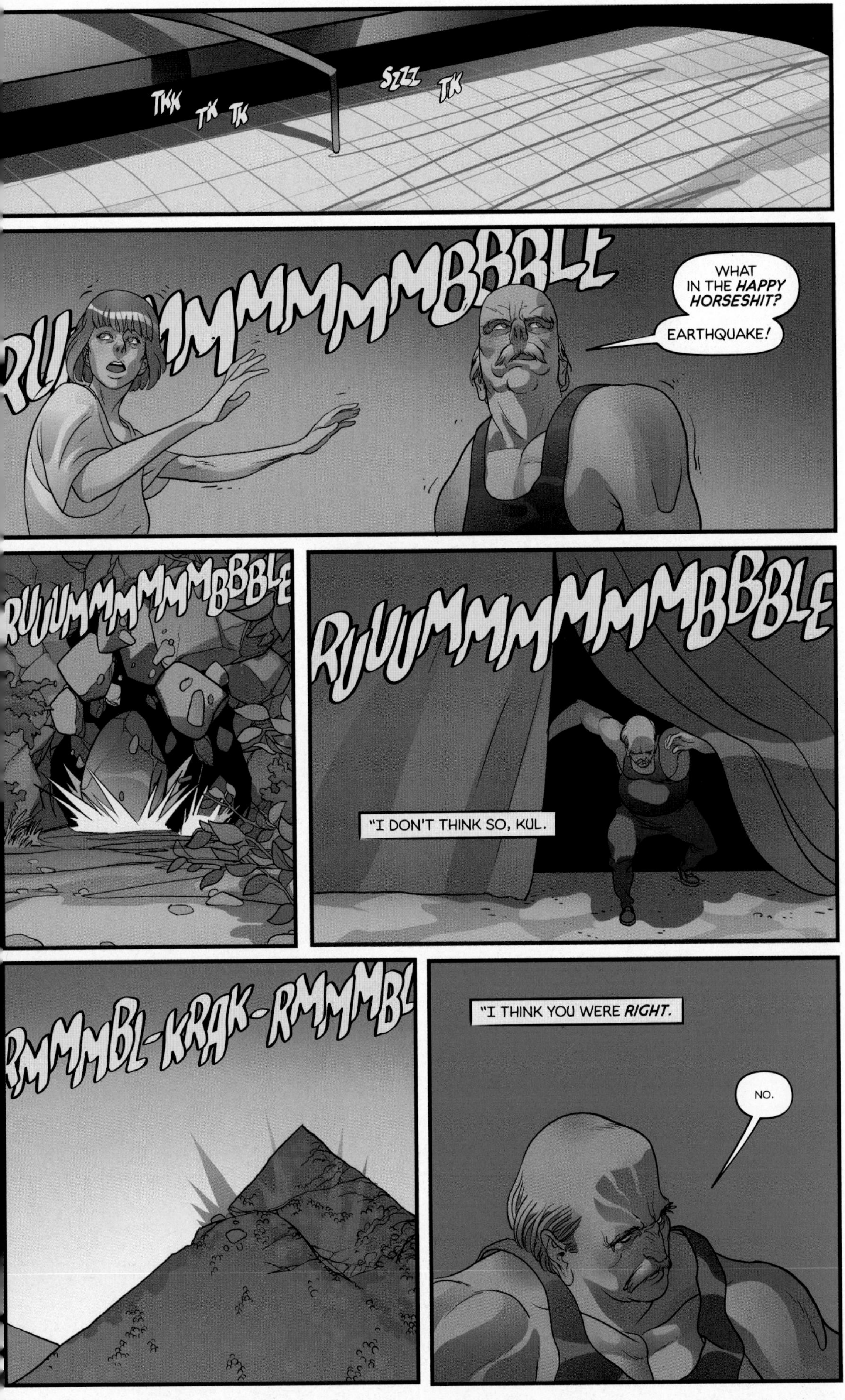
TKK
TK
TK
SZZZ
TK
RUUMMMMMMMBBBLE
WHAT IN THE *HAPPY HORSESHIT?*
EARTHQUAKE!
RUUMMMMMMMBBBLE
RUUMMMMMMMBBBLE
"I DON'T THINK SO, KUL.
RMMMBL-KRAK-RMMMBL
"I THINK YOU WERE *RIGHT.*
NO.

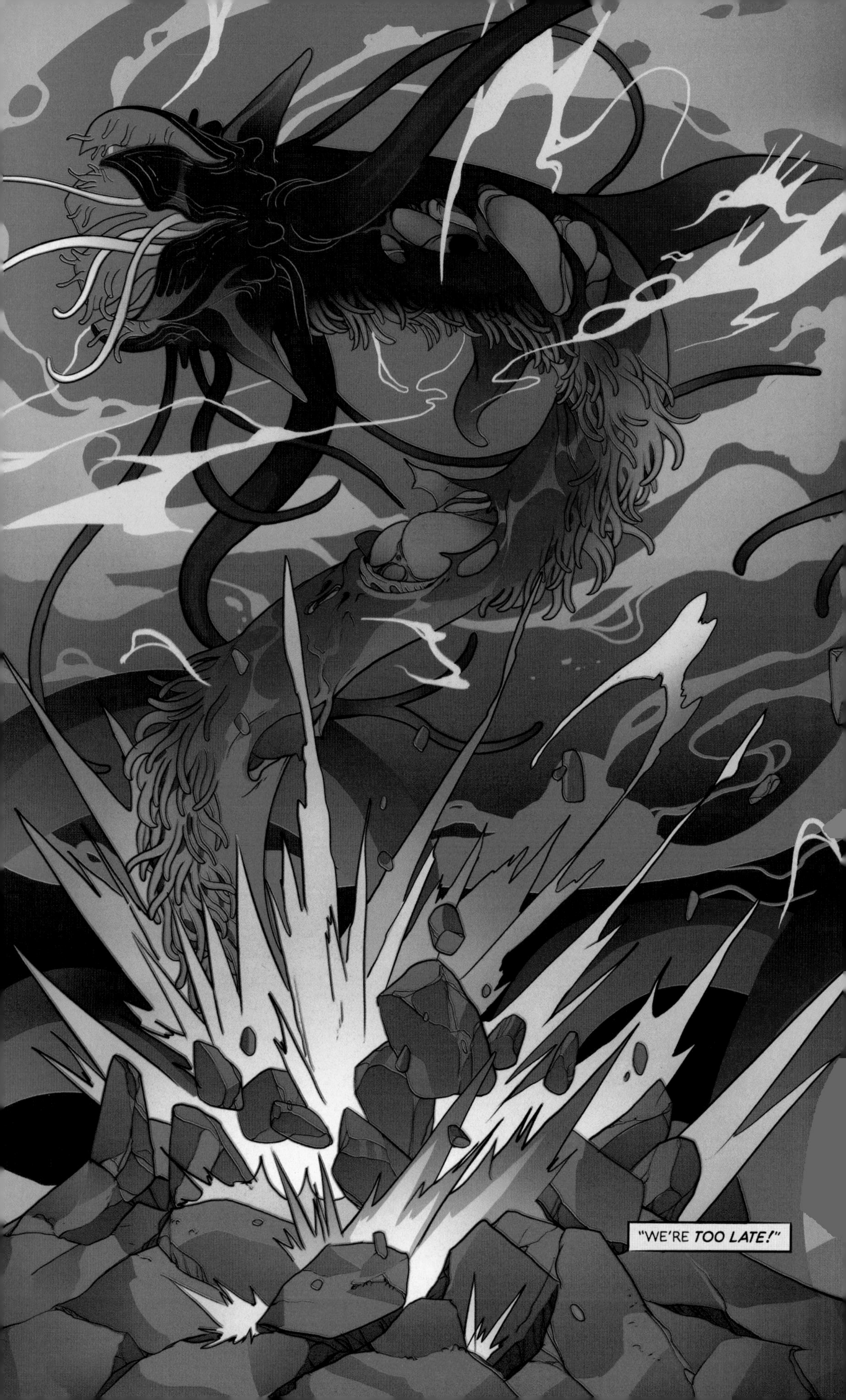
"WE'RE TOO LATE!"

EXTRAS

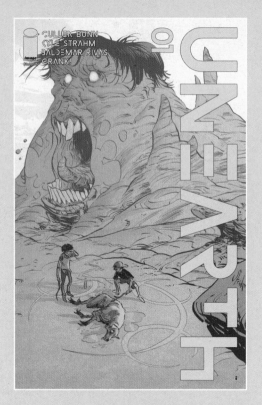

COVERS

UNEARTH
01
CULLEN BUNN
KYLE STRAHM
BALDEMAR RIVAS
CRANK!

#1B BY KYLE STRAHM

UNEARTH
01

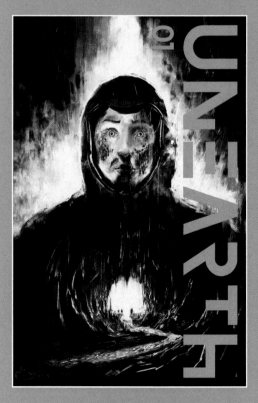

#1C FOR BLACK CAPE COMICS
ART BY ESTEBAN SALINAS

#1 NYCC EXCLUSIVE
ART BY JAMES HARREN

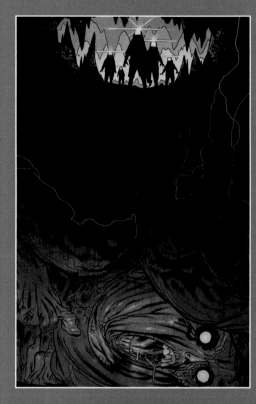

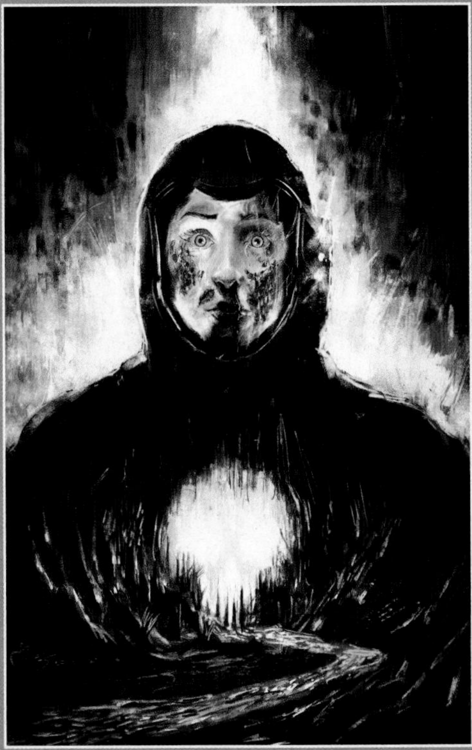

#1D FOR BLACK CAPE COMICS
ART BY ESTEBAN SALINAS

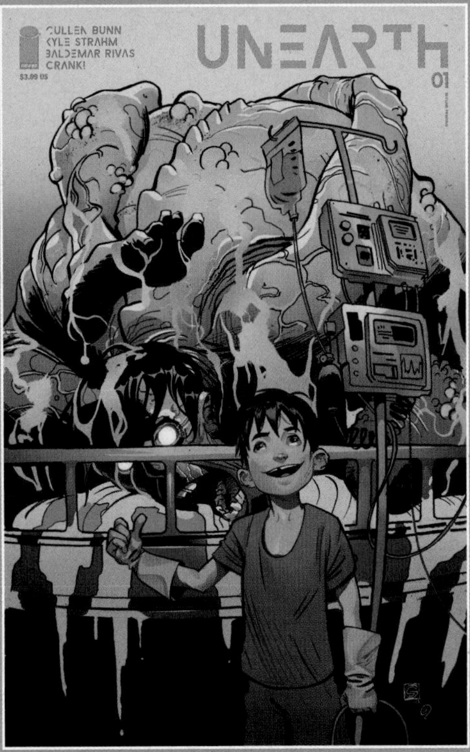

CULLEN BUNN
KYLE STRAHM
BALDEMAR RIVAS
CRANK!
$3.99 US
UNEARTH
01

#1 SECOND PRINTING
ART BY STEPHEN GREEN

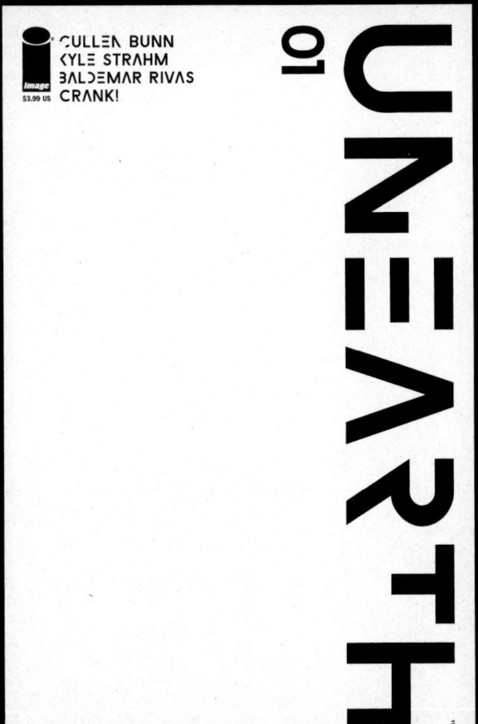

CULLEN BUNN
KYLE STRAHM
BALDEMAR RIVAS
CRANK!
$3.99 US
UNEARTH
01

#1 BLANK SKETCH

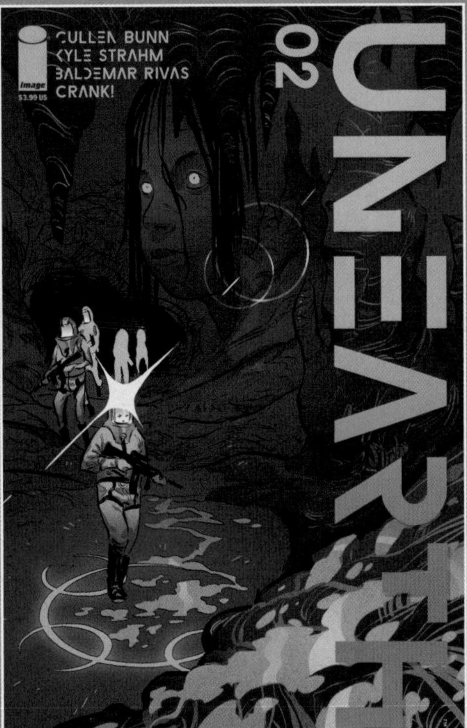

CULLEN BUNN
KYLE STRAHM
BALDEMAR RIVAS
CRANK!
$3.99 US
UNEARTH
02

#2B BY KYLE STRAHM

#3A BY BALDEMAR RIVAS

#4B BY KYLE STRAHM

#5A BY BALDEMAR RIVAS

#5B BY KYLE STRAHM

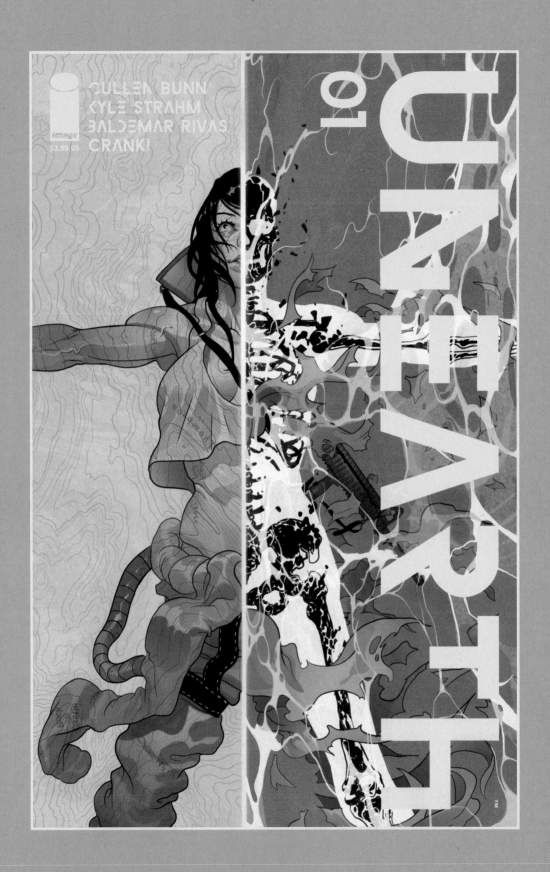

image

CULLEN BUNN
KYLE STRAHM
BALDEMAR RIVAS
CRANK!

$3.99 US

UNEARTH 01

#1A BY BALDEMAR RIVAS

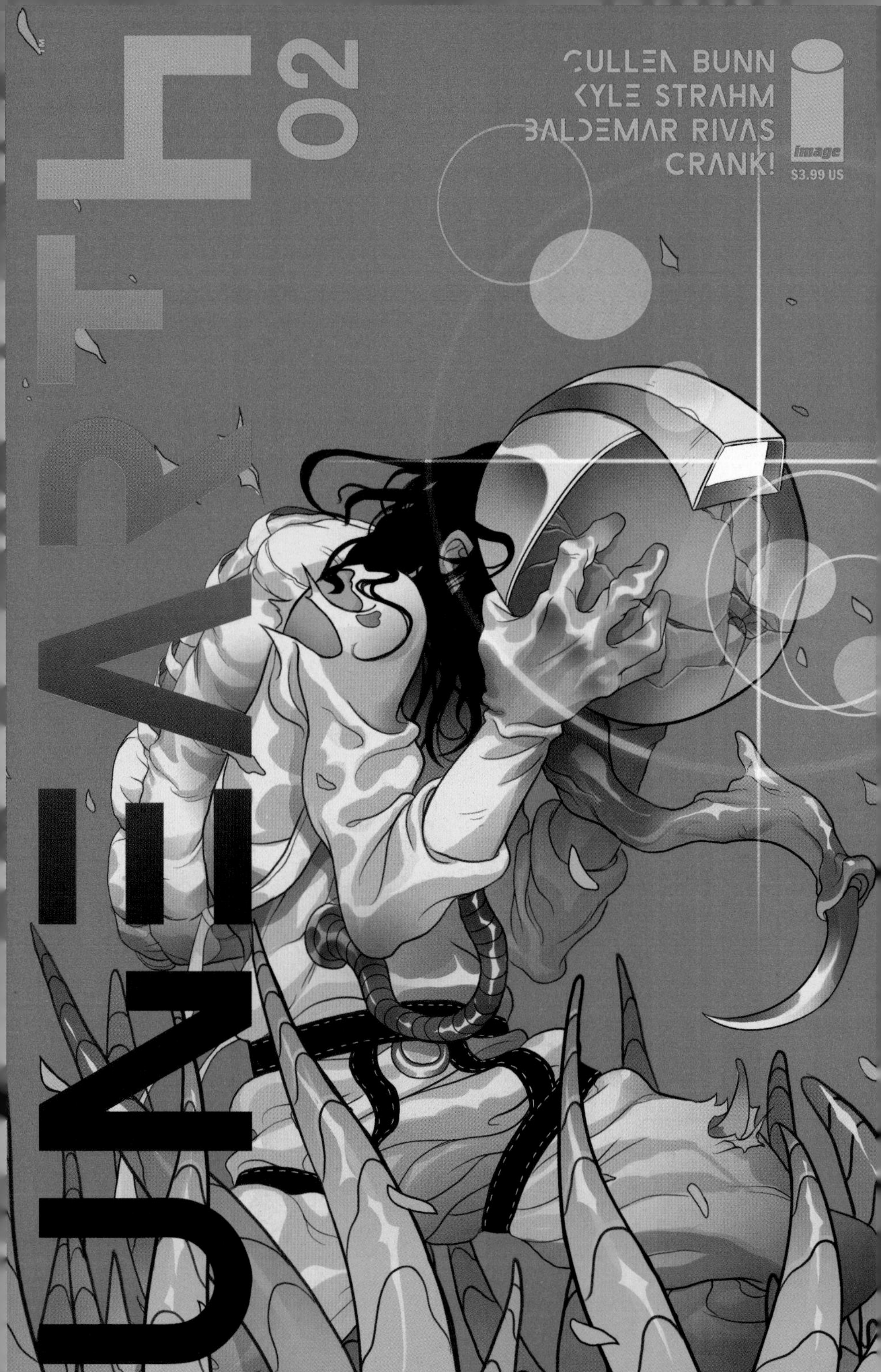
UNEARTH
02
CULLEN BUNN
KYLE STRAHM
BALDEMAR RIVAS
CRANK!
image
$3.99 US

#2A BY BALDEMAR RIVAS

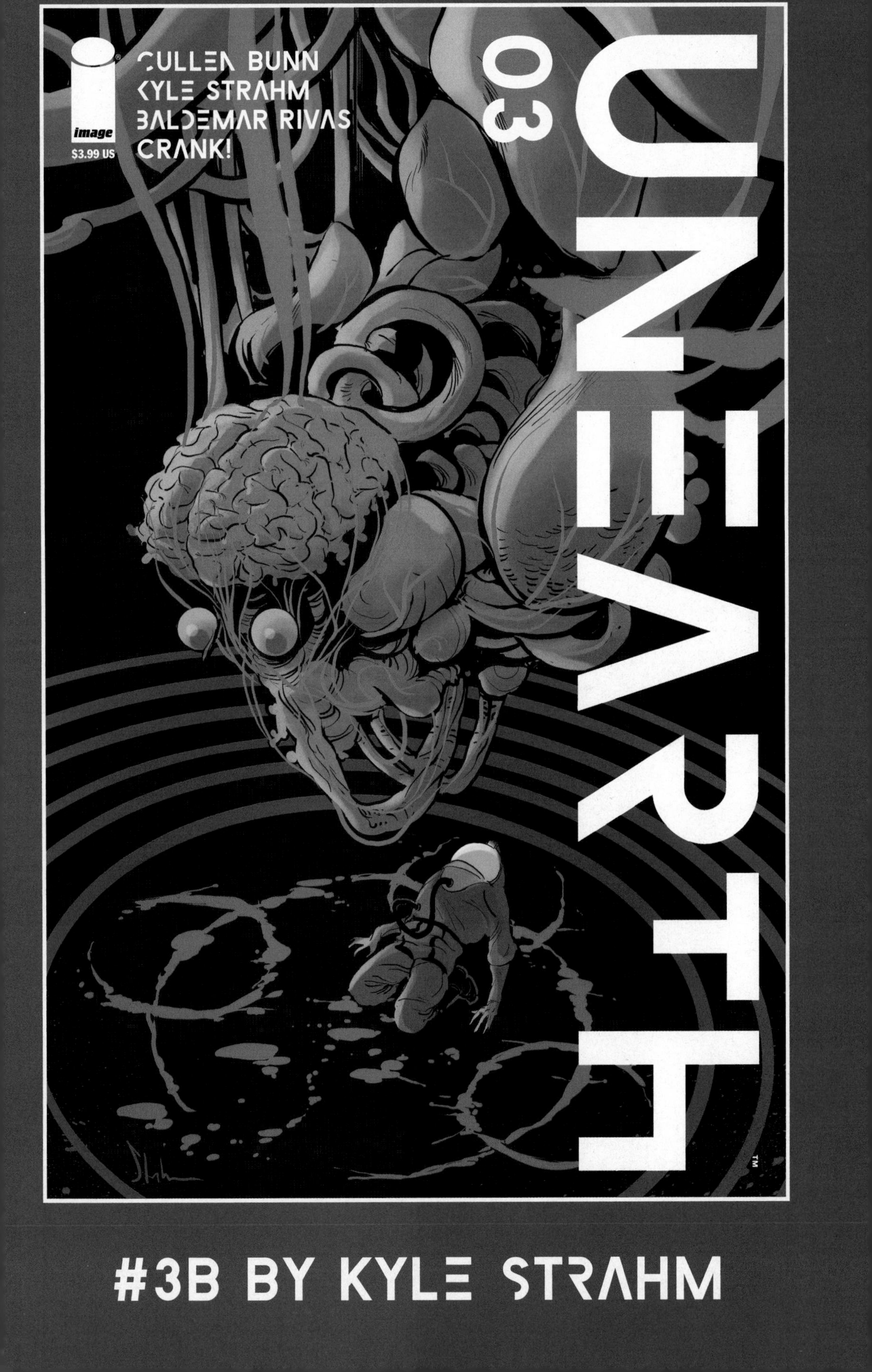

image
$3.99 US
CULLEN BUNN
KYLE STRAHM
BALDEMAR RIVAS
CRANK!
UNEARTH
03
TM

#3B BY KYLE STRAHM

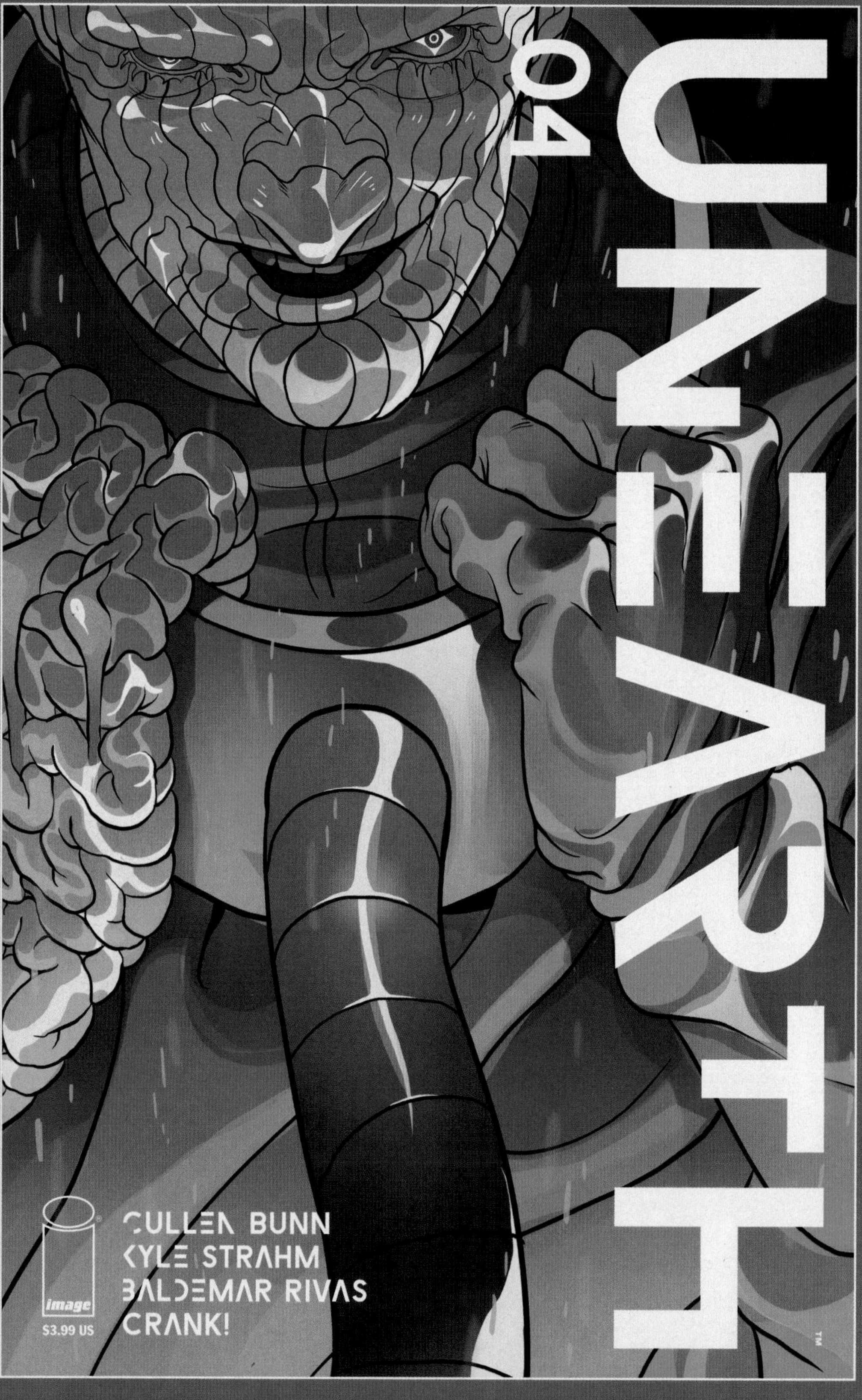
UNEARTH
04
CULLEN BUNN
KYLE STRAHM
BALDEMAR RIVAS
CRANK!
image
$3.99 US
TM

#4A BY BALDEMAR RIVAS

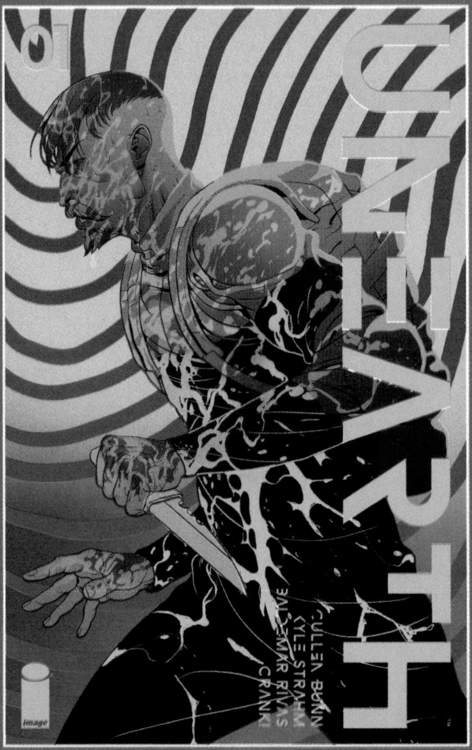
01
UNEARTH
CULLEN BUNN
KYLE STRAHM
BALDEMAR RIVAS
CRANK!
image

#1F BY BALDEMAR RIVAS

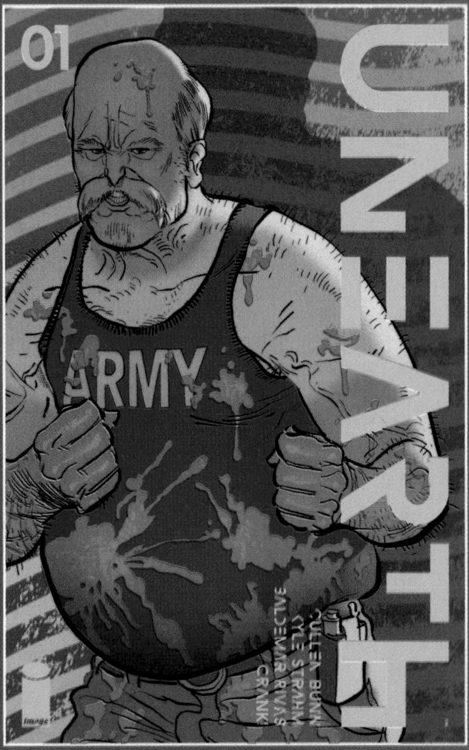
01
UNEARTH
ARMY
CULLEN BUNN
KYLE STRAHM
BALDEMAR RIVAS
CRANK!
image

#1G BY KYLE STRAHM

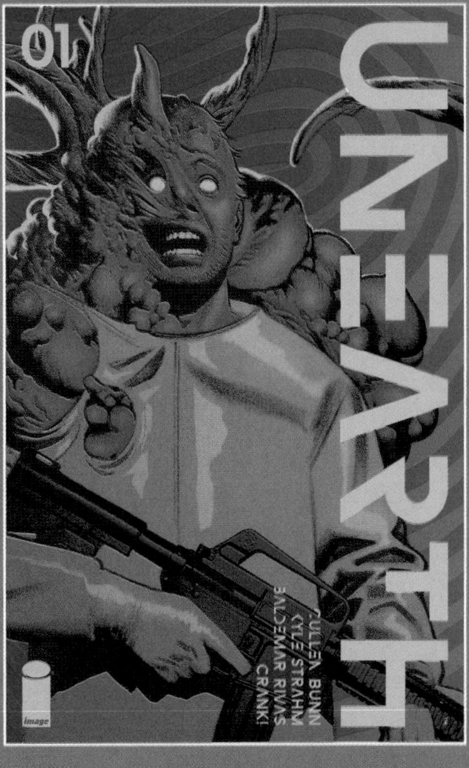
01
UNEARTH
CULLEN BUNN
KYLE STRAHM
BALDEMAR RIVAS
CRANK!
image

#1H BY GREG SMALLWOOD

CREATOR VARIANTS

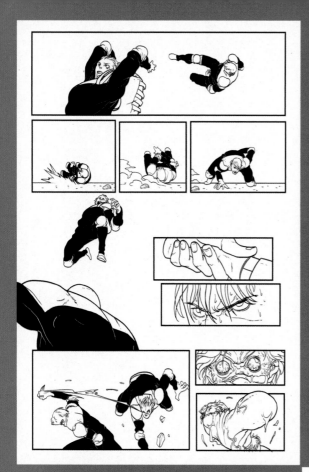

PROCESS: B&W TO COLOR

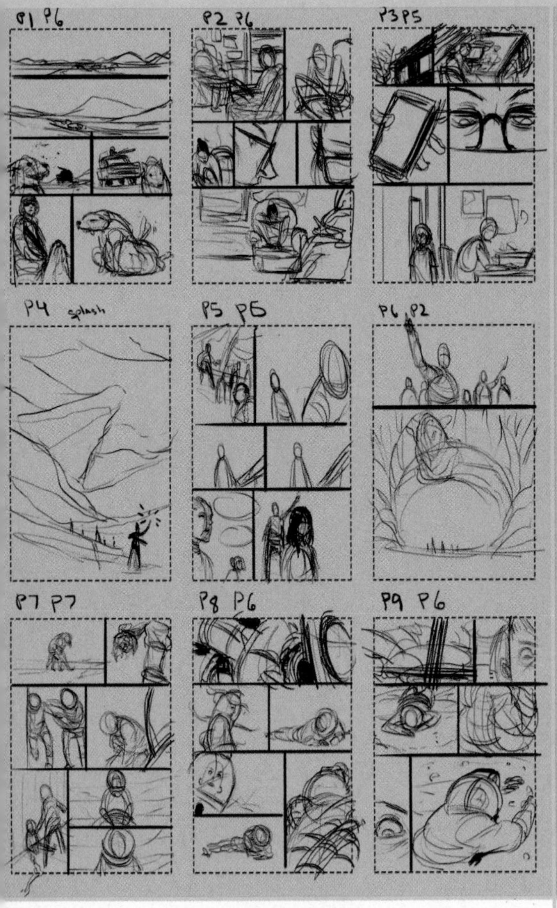
P1 P6
P2 P6
P3 P5
P4 splash
P5 P6
P6 P2
P7 P7
P8 P6
P9 P6

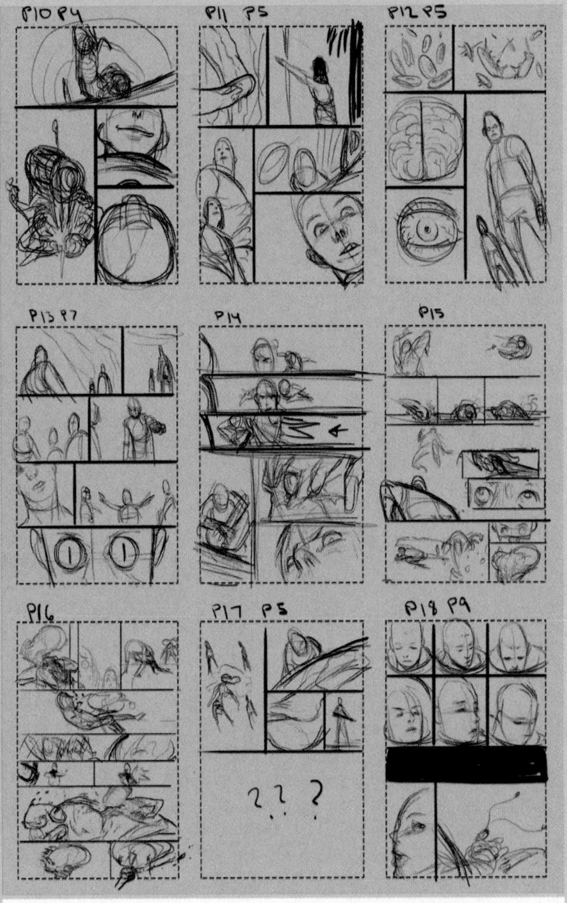
P10 P4
P11 P5
P12 P5
P13 P7
P14
P15
P16
P17 P5
P18 P9
? ? ?

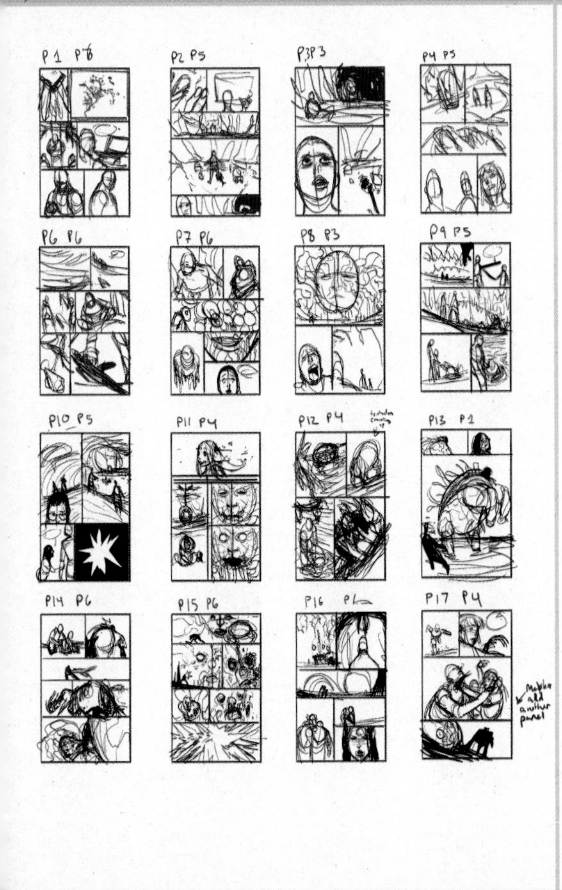
P1 P6
P2 P5
P3 P3
P4 P5
P6 P6
P7 P6
P8 P3
P9 P5
P10 P5
P11 P4
P12 P4
P13 P1
P14 P6
P15 P6
P16 P6
P17 P4
Maybe add another panel

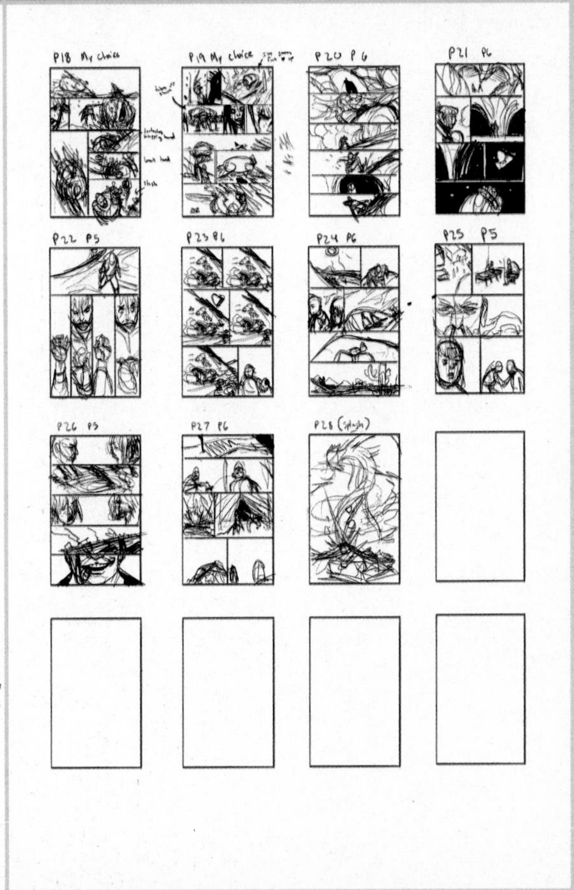
P18 My choice
P19 My choice
P20 P6
P21 P6
P22 P5
P23 P6
P24 P6
P25 P5
P26 P3
P27 P6
P28 (splash)

PROCESS: THUMBS TO TEMPS

CULLEN BUNN is the writer of comics such as REGRESSION, COLD SPOTS, *Harrow County*, and *Manor Black*. He believes in nothing...save for the idea that he is being watched by otherworldly forces.

KYLE STRAHM was spewed from the American Heartland to write and draw dope comics. Before writing UNEARTH, Kyle created and drew the wet horror of SPREAD. He provided covers for *Bebop and Rocksteady Hit the Road*, *Green Lantern: New Guardians*, and countless titles from Image, DC, Valiant, IDW, Aftershock, Lion Forge, and Dynamite. Kyle lives and works in Kansas City, Missouri.

BALDEMAR RIVAS is an artist who has now ventured in the world of sequential storytelling. Born and raised in Visalia California, he was accepted to the Kansas City Art Institute. That is where he met Kyle Strahm and hit it off. He always carries around a sketchbook.

CRANK! Christopher Crank! (crank!) letters a bunch of books put out by Image, Dark Horse, Oni Press, Dynamite, and elsewhere. He also has a podcast with comics artist Mike Norton and members of Four Star Studio in Chicago (crankcast.com) and makes music (sonomorti.bandcamp.com). Catch him on Twitter and Instagram: @ccrank_

CREATOR BIOS